Griffintown

Sisters

J. Émile Turcotte

Back jacket photograph by Wm. Notman & Son, 1896: courtesy of the McCord Stewart Museum
Author's photo by Jan Amell

Library and Archives Canada Cataloguing in Publication
CIP data on file with the National Library and Archives

ISBN (hardcover) 978-1-55483-565-2
ISBN (trade paperback) 978-1-55483-561-4
ISBN (ebook) 978-1-55483-562-1

Follow the author on social media:
X   @jemileturcotte
TikTok   @jemileturcotte

And on his website:
www.jemileturcotte.com

For Kim

Everything that starts ends

Everything that ends is forgotten

Everything forgotten starts again

PART I

Chapter 1

-1-

Montréal, February 1914

Officer Marleau climbed the seven icy steps of the infamous *De Montigny Boarding House* aware that most of the neighbours, snooping under cover of fogged-up window panes, scrutinized his every move. Madame Desjardins—the formerly manicured nail of her left index finger split down to her cuticle, a fillet of blood draining into her palm—had, allegedly, slapped Mrs Dougherty and thrust her pointy Oxford shoe into her shin. "You take care of your business my dear lady and I'll take care of mine," Eugénie Desjardins had warned.

"*S'il vous plaît*, Madame Desjardins, I can't spend all my time here, I can't be coming by every other day," Officer Marleau pleaded, standing on wet soles, his arms wrapped around his chest.

"You think I *want* you here, 'cause I certainly don't," Madame Desjardins said, her bloody finger inches from the *gendarme's* face.

"Be that as it may, I'll have to ask you to—"

"To what? What? I'm not the one causing problems here," the lady added, pointing the finger stump on her right hand where her index finger used to live at the many triplexes lining De Montigny Street. "Everyone in this crazy neighbourhood can believe whatever they want, but they've got to let me run my business," she added, bug-eyed and stomping her heel on the porch's frozen boards.

"You've been warned. Everyone on this street's had a

problem with you, and—"

"And ... and ... I'll tell you something else. My clients happen to be good people," she snapped, eyes drilling into the constable. "Maybe you should jus' go talk to all those thickos round here who've got nothing better to do than interfere with legitimate commerce. I happen to be the proprietor of this business and I'm very proud of it."

Officer Marleau looked up at the misty cloud rising from his mouth. "It's the same lady that complained. She says you hit her. Right here. On this porch. Did you?"

"Did I what?"

"Hit her," said Marleau, lips sucked into his mouth and looking down at Madame Desjardins' smile.

Madame Desjardins nodded and chuckled.

Hands on his hips, Officer Marleau leaned way forward till his forehead nearly brushed the lady's nose. "She says you hit her ... on the head," he whispered, tapping his nightstick on his temple and inadvertently knocking his hat askew.

"Calm down," Madame Desjardins said, stepping back and flashing her palms. "Here's what *you* should do. Leave us be. I told you; this is a legitimate business and I didn't hit nobody, didn't hit no lady," she said, wheeling around while gesturing dramatically. "Look at that sign up there. That's what we do. It's who we are. Jus' go ask any of my boarders, why don't you? Go ask 'em if they're happy living here," she added, bobbing and pointing at the big red letters hanging off the *De Montigny Boarding House's* porch.

"I'll have to report this. The lady registered a complaint. I can't just let this one go."

"Go ahead, make a report. It's nothing but lies, anyway. A big bunch of lies. Do all the reporting you want."

"She's got a big red mark on her forehead. I don't think she's lying. Why would she lie about a thing like that? Besides, why's your finger bleeding?"

"She *is* lying," Madame Desjardins said, a bright smile softening her face as she hid her bleeding hand behind her back.

"It so happens that I hit the side of her head, not her forehead. That bitch's nothing but a lying chippie. "*Maudite chienne*," she said, as if sharing a harmless secret.

"So, you *did* hit her. You admit to hitting her on the side of the head ... to bruising her," Officer Marleau replied, eyes narrowed into slits and pointing at the side of his head–his hat remaining undisturbed.

"Jus' never you mind, my good sir. She's got more bruises on her than a blind, one-armed prizefighter. You wanna find a bruise? She'll show you a bruise. She's got new ones show-ing up every day," she said, slowly poking at the Officer's chest and staring up at his chin, blood still trickling from her fingertip. "And I think yunno why, don'tcha? You know who's responsible for all those bruises," she added under her breath, winking.

Officer Marleau stepped back from the repeated finger jabs, stuck out his butt, and adeptly pinched Madame Des-jardins' wrist between his thumb and index finger, careful to keep her blood from staining his glove. "I'd say you hit her pretty hard by the looks of things," he said, shaking her hand slowly and staring at her bloody red nail; his bushy right brow cocked way up his forehead. The lady's demeanour turned to stone. She abruptly pulled away from his two-fingered grip and, somehow, managed to look down on a man towering eight inches above her. "In any case, I'll have to report this," the Officer said. "This time, I'll have to be—"

"Arrest her! She's right in front of you, she assaulted me. Why don't you arrest that awful woman?" Mrs Dougherty yelled from across the street, her bruised head sticking out from her kitchen window, blood dripping from her gouged temple pooling on the fabric of her dress; panicked at the thought that Madame Desjardins would, yet again, get off with nothing more than a warning.

"Jus' look at that hysterical woman disturbing the peace with her crazy accusations," Eugénie Desjardins said, stand-ing at the edge of the porch while leaking a bloody stain onto her emerald green dress. "You were trespassing, lady. It's *me* you threatened. You're lucky you didn't get worse than you did, is all I'll say … *crisse de vieille folle*," she added, Officer Marleau behind her, arms out, his frozen whistle pinched between his blue lips.

"Don't let this be, Officer. This can't go on," Mrs Dougherty pleaded. "Look at my face, look at this. I was assaulted in broad daylight. She … she—"

"She what? Defended herself from a discombobulated woman who came banging on her door, is what *she* did, yeah, that's all I did," Madame Desjardins answered, defiantly walking down a few steps before Officer Marleau held out his big stick in front of her.

"Okay ladies, I've heard enough. Get back inside, both of you. Inside!"

"You can't be serious, Officer," Mrs Dougherty frowned, slapping the window sill. "Don't you see what she's doing here? What that is? She's running a whorehouse on our street and you do nothing about it."

"That's a new one. A whore accusing me of running a whorehouse. Daaah! Nobody's gonna ruin your business, deary. Everybody knows that."

"Business? I *have* no business. My business is about living in a peaceful neighbourhood without strange men, drunken men coming and going at all times of day and night."

"I told you before deary, there's plenty to go around, stop pestering and leave us be," Madame Desjardins screamed, the tint of her face matching her pink, wind-seared ears.

Rose, who had watched from the foyer, stepped out and wrapped a shawl over Madame Desjardins' shoulders while several young ladies, gawking and snickering, had gathered in the parlour.

"And there's another one of her strumpets" Mrs Dougherty yelled, pointing at the young woman on the Boarding House's porch.

"Shut up and get back inside, you whore … *vieille putain*,"

Rose yelled back.

"That's it, either all of you get back inside or you're all coming with me to the station," Officer Marleau warned, coiling and recoiling back and forth, his black eyes pointed like pistols.

Mrs Dougherty, chin up and lips pursed, stared long and hard at the Officer. Meanwhile, a few girls spilled out and joined Madame Desjardins, all of them expecting the usual fireworks to erupt. Resigned, but intent on displaying one final gesture of outrage, Mrs Dougherty snapped her head back dramatically and yelled at Officer Marleau, "You're nothing but a useless dick." In doing so, fuelled by a river of molten anger, she smashed her skull on the bottom edge of the open window sash. The impact shot her dentures from her gaping mouth; both plates landing in her front yard. But, worst of all, her *dick* insult came out sounding as if she had said 'duck'.

Dazed, she pushed the window shut, closed the drapes and disappeared for a while. Minutes passed before she emerged from her front door. She stood there, smoothing the apron hanging below her waist, fixated on Officer Marleau who, out of pity, looked away. She cleared her throat, ran her fingers through her greying hair and fished the three parts of her irreparably damaged choppers from the frozen ground.

Madame Desjardins, unaware she had walked down to the sidewalk, stared across at her neighbour while the girls behind her on the porch quacked at the woman. *Quack, quack,* they chanted, thumbs stuck in their armpits, bent at the waist and elbows flapping. The street buzzed with laughter while the lady picked bits of ice and debris from her damaged teeth before carefully storing all three pieces into the right pocket of her flowery apron.

"Get back inside. All of you. I've had enough. We've all wasted enough time for today," Madame Desjardins said, waving at her girls, frozen blood stuck to her wrist.

Seizing on Madame Desjardins's loss of appetite for the

fight, Officer Marleau herded the women off the porch. Mrs Dougherty, who had remained on her stoop, looked back at the woman who had struck her, taking in the scene and feeding her hatred for that lady, that Madam who seemed to float above the law.

-2-

Kneeling on the long Chesterfield, face parting the parlour's lace curtains, Arthur had watched, mesmerized by the nastiness of the latest standoff. Certainly, he knew his Aunt Eugénie (he was the last person remaining allowed to use her Christian name) was a tough lady. Everyone whirling near her orbit was keenly aware of her legendary grit. But for young Arthur, the idea of a woman barely taller than he was with courage enough to stand toe to toe with a Montreal cop—part of a corps reputed for its liberal use of chokeholds, batons, and brass knuckles—was something to behold.

Rose, still chuckling at the *duck* thing, stroked Arthur's thin, blond hair and watched the people that had gathered just beyond the porch. Boisterous, angry neighbours had encircled the policeman. Drawn by the anonymity of the growing crowd, a man stepped up and punched the Officer's chest as he brought his whistle up to his lips.

Though only ten years old, the boy had grown used to confrontations and wild scenes; that time when someone had thrown over-ripened produce at the door, or when horse manure was smeared all over the steps (he's the one that had been ordered to wash it off). But this time, the look of anger plastered on those many faces tightened Arthur's belly. "*Qu'est-ce qui se passe?* What'd they want? What're they gonna do to us?" Arthur asked, running into the foyer where his aunt stood, a long Panatela scissored between her finger and stump.

"They won't do squat, boy. They never do. Don't be such

— 14 —

a nervous wreck. You get that from that no-good-father of yours," Madame Desjardins said, looking through holes in the embroidered curtains covering red sidelights on either side of the door. "Jus' a bunch of benjos out there having a bit of fun at our expense is all they're doing," she added, the light passing through the curtains casting tiny round shadows on her face as she assessed the residuum of the morning's tussle.

"But they're still there. They're not going away," the boy said, perched on tiptoes, looking through the curtains on the other side of the door, hands on his backside ensuring the flap of his long johns remained closed.

"Yeah, yeah, I know," said Madame Desjardins, her breath fogging the glass. "Don't worry, that cop's gonna get rid of 'em. You'll see."

"But what'll they do once he's gone? No one can stop 'em from coming in. What'll we do then?"

Madame Desjardins looked at her nephew, her pinky finger hooked on the curtains and one eye closed while taking a long drag from her Panatela. She inhaled deeply, then whispered through a veil of smoke, "But *I'll* be here, boy. Nobody's coming through this door unless they pay the current rate. You'll see, everybody's gonna leave, and this'll blow over. It always does." A column of white smoke rose slowly from the corners of her lips as she spoke, skimming along the contours of her prominent cheekbones before pooling in her dark hair. Arthur, his little face scrunched up and looking like an old man's, pressed his forehead on the sidelight.

"But what'll we do if they don't?" He asked, his voice quivering.

By now, girls that hadn't yet come down for breakfast had gathered along the second-floor's palladium window. Downstairs, a half-dozen more had assembled in the parlour, some fretting, others giggling at the small crowd that seemed to grow.

"That's it, boy, go put something on and get ready for

work. All the girls are up," Madame Desjardins ordered, pushing away from the door, her blood-stained dress twirled by the momentum of her swift motion. "Sooner or later you're jus' gonna have to learn that you don't take guff from nobody … or else *you're* the nobody," she instructed, squeezing Arthur's shoulder and steering him toward the cellar door.

"But, Monsieur Lafleur's still not back from his walk, it's just us and a bunch of girls. What if—"

"Listen to me," she said, Arthur's chin pinched between her thumb and stump. "I've had enough of this second-guessing. Stop being a meater. *Pour l'amour de Dieu*, you can't spend your life being a coward. Be a man," she said, bent over and wrapping her knuckles on his forehead. "You've got to be courageous, like your mother was," she added, clearing her throat. "I'm sure that part of her's in you, somewhere in there, in your blood. So don't be afraid all the time."

Arthur ran off, gliding along the shiny oak flooring, riding atop his thick, woollen socks along the way to the cellar's door. He looked back at his aunt and flinched at the sound of her clap beckoning the girls into the kitchen. Two-inch-thick treads led him below ground; each step covered by a layer of coal dust that made them slippery and difficult to manoeuvre. Arthur, having tumbled down before, straddled the handrail and glissaded all the way to the cement floor, his stocking feet kicking up a small cloud of black dust upon landing in the darkness. There, at the foot of the stairs, a string dangled off a bare ceiling joist barely low enough for Arthur, stilted at the very top of his toes, to grab and yank at; the light from the bulb transforming obscurity into mere dimness.

Amidst the half-dozen clotheslines strung along the ceiling stood a colossal cast iron furnace, six feet tall and looking like a massive black turret plunked out of a medieval fortress. It sat perched on two layers of brick mortared to the floor barely fifteen feet from Arthur's room. The behemoth kept watch over Arthur through a grid of sooty windows, offering, in turn, a view to its orange flames and undigested embers.

Long, corroded pipes hissed and puffed, steel arms rising on either side of its round body waiting to snatch up young boys. "Did you load the furnace?" Aunt Eugénie's voice seeped down through the ceiling.

"Got it," Arthur bellowed back, his words aimed at the stairs.

Like he did several times a day, from early October and sometimes up until mid-May, Arthur unhooked the poker dangling from the brick chimney, inserted the business end of it into the furnace's door latch and pulled it open. The high-pitched squeal of rusted hinges scraping at hot iron echoed through the dimness and gave the ancient incinerator its sinister voice. Cold air rushing into the belly of the creature set the remaining embers alight to the sound of a low-pitched whoooosh—the malevolent heater forever intent on sucking children into its glowing belly. Shovel in hand, the boy tossed coal lumps into the guts of the thing till the chamber turned black. Then, standing back as far as he could, he stabbed a shovel at the iron hatch till it slammed shut; a puff of black smoke rising to the joists signalling the mission was complete.

Job done, Arthur sat on the moist cement and watched, knees pulled tightly to his chest, observing as the blackness inside ignited; pipes creaking, the spectacle of the routine never failing to light a shiver up his spine.

-3-

The walls of Arthur's room, clad with asbestos-laced cardboard sheets nailed to a grid of rough, oxidized two-by-four spruce studs, reminded him of Jonah and his three days spent inside a whale. Faint recollections of his third-grade teacher (he would never graduate to the fourth grade) reading him this fantastical story somehow helped to uncoil his mind and set him adrift away from this cellar; the lightbulb dangling from the centre of this lifeless ribcage casting evil shadow lines that reached every corner of the space; intermingling odours of mould, coal dust and smoke ensuring his nose-bleeds and piercing headaches would persist.

For this space—his cellar cellule formally reserved for clients who preferred the rough stuff—Madame Desjardins supplied a small dresser, a free-standing ashtray that she brought upstairs whenever she organized a fancy soirée for her better clients, a baby blue arrowback chair and a pinkish Chesterfield she couldn't bring herself to get rid of. Arthur often slept on that Chesterfield, shoulders dug into the heavily padded backrest, especially on those nights when shadows bent into ominous shapes, or when the furnace's vocalizations morphed into words.

Arthur reached into one of the dresser's drawers and pulled out his clothes. His coat, oversized and heavy, dangled off the doorknob. Looking back, he stared at the door as if able to see through it, waiting for the fiery beast's lamentations to begin. Slowly, he cracked the door open, a single eye looking at the iron fiend. Watching. Listening. He walked backwards toward his dresser, pulled the bottom drawer and took out his Eaton's catalogue. Sprawled on the Chesterfield, he flipped through the pages till they parted where he had left the photograph. Two girls, side-by-side; a grainy image of his Aunt Eugénie and his mother.

He brought the small tintype close to his nose, eyes crossed, scanning the blurry details while, beyond his door, the colicky furnace came to life, grumbling and spitting. He focused on his mother's image, looking for clues, trying to see in that girl the courage his aunt talked about. *Part of her's in you*, she always said. But, the boom of his heart lit sparks in the back of his eyes, the littlest hairs on the nape of his neck stiffening as shivers climbed from his itchy socks. The monster had awakened and Arthur had forgotten all about getting ready for the workday. Trembling, he gazed deeper into the photograph. *Hisss, grumff, hisss*, the racket from the cyclops burst into his tiny, dark room. His face buried into the couch's plush (mouldy) upholstery. He held the photograph tightly to his chest in the hopes that courage would seep into him.

Soon enough, the boy's pliable imagination came to the rescue, sweeping him away from the dank cellar to drift along on a happy ride; Arthur, his Aunt Eugénie and his mother, side-by-side in a *cliché*, all of them together in the old tintype. The soothing reverie eased Arthur's mind and drew him into a deep sleep, one that lasted but mere seconds.

Sounds, jarring and unfamiliar—the source of which seemed to originate from nowhere and everywhere at the same time—left him paralyzed, motionless on the Chesterfield. Sucking in deep breaths, he finally managed to clutch at the needlepoint cushion, eyes darting through the dimness, and reached down to retrieve the photograph that had fallen to the cement floor. The commotion paused just long enough for him to stand and holler at the ceiling, "Hey! Who's making all that racket?"

Loud, crunching, crackling sounds crashed through the walls of his room. Bright lights, flickering and beaming from all around the contours of his closed door illuminated the dimness. "There's something wrong here. Something's going on down here," Arthur yelled till his throat hurt. "Hey, hey ... anybody up there? There's a problem down here," he yelled again. The door's hinges, noisy and rusted, creaked and squealed as brilliant light and moist heat slowly pushed and worked their way throughout the room.

The heat radiating from the door melted the paint off in long, dirty strips that stuck to Arthur's hands when he tried to push against its momentum. His palms sizzled; the smell of scorched flesh burned his nostrils. "Help!" He howled, gagging and retching. A bank of steam rose a few inches above the wet cement and he slipped to the floor. He felt his face being sucked into his skull; his eyes roasted and withered. A scintillating, yellow light flooded the room just before the door blew off its frame.

"Fire! Fire! Help! Somebody up there … help! Fire!" He yelled into the void, panicked, tears dripping off his chin vaporizing before they hit the floor. A thunderous *bang*, then a powerful gust of scorching air blew in and knocked Arthur back onto his bed. Flames flowed like waves of goo oozing from the walls and dripping from the ceiling. Fiery droplets sounding like tiny, fluttering buzz bombs rained down on the Chesterfield. "Fire!" Arthur screamed again and again; his broiling lungs struggling to draw breath.

The furnace, perched on its pile of bricks, the fire no longer contained within it, feasted beyond its womb and reached for whatever it could torch.

Arthur covered his eyes, and his burned palms fused to his melting face. Tons of stored coal was now alight, vaporizing remnants of moisture seeping from the hundred-year-old ceiling joists. Panes of glass from the tiny widows shattered as smoke elbowed its way out; cold air whistling in to feed the flames. He'd soon be with that woman in the photo, he thought. He would meet his mother. He was ready to disappear.

The main beam let go and the ceiling fell amidst a loud *boom. Boom, boom* ... "Come on boy, it's time for breakfast," Aunt Eugénie yelled, stomping at the floor while mixing dough for her crumpets. "And you better be dressed for work. Dress up good; it's cold outside, and you know it'll be windy at the wharf," she added, abandoning her flamenco jabs into the floor.

Arthur, face down on the Chesterfield, needlepoint pillow clutched to his chest, opened his eyes and instinctively answered. "Coming!" His voice not sounding like his own. "Be right there," he added a second later, hoping to buy himself some time.

This wasn't the first time he'd survived *the dream*. That's what he called it. *The dream* could show up whenever he fell asleep. Happy times, sad times, angry, bored, it never mattered. He had never told anyone about it; not even Rose. Certainly not his Aunt Eugénie. He looked down, cheek covered in drool, and reached for the tintype on the floor. He slipped the photo back into the catalogue, page 285, the section where women in corsets twirled fancy umbrellas, and put it away in the dresser. Hair drenched, beads of sweat dripping down his breastbone, he swallowed hard and rinsed the bitter taste from his mouth. "Coming!" He yelled again, layering on sweaters and lacing his boots. He opened the narrow door and hugged the wall, keeping as far away from the furnace as he could and ran up the thick oak treads.

"What's wrong with you, boy? You've been down there fifteen minutes. How long does it take to get dressed? You know I need you to help with breakfast before you leave. We all have to do our jobs here or else it's all gonna go to hell, don't you know that? Jus' tell me you'll take over here and finish in the kitchen while I go do other things. Can you do that?"

"Yes Ma'am," Arthur replied, snapping his suspenders over his sweater-padded shoulders.

"I need to know I can trust you is all I'm saying," Madame Desjardins said, looking down at Arthur. "Well, can I?" She probed, handing over her big, wooden spoon.

"Yes, Aunt Eugénie," Arthur responded as he took control of the stove and the frying crumpets, watching as the girls, ignoring him, ate and chatted about the latest hullaballoo outside. Arthur, staring at the pan, replayed the nightmare that had revisited him. Assaulted him.

"And make sure you bring along plenty of cards this time; no use to be out there if you run out of cards again," his aunt said as she climbed the stairs.

Chapter 2

-1-

June 1894

Eugénie's feet hovered above the kneeler, leaning forward to look at her father; tears sliding into her ear as she turned and faced the man's casual demeanour. Saraphine, her arm locked around her sister's, couldn't stop her jaw from trembling though she had been warned to *act like a grownup*. Eugénie had assumed her father would have remained stoic during her mother's funeral but to see him, legs crossed, elbow perched on the pew's back–like an employee on break—scared her. His long fingers laced together, he'd look back at the assembly once in a while and even winked at one of his buddies during the homily.

When time came to lower the pine casket into the ground, Maurice just stood there next to one of the men holding on to the ropes, hat in hand and wiping his forehead with his handkerchief. "You must have developed strong shoulders doing a job like this," he leaned over and told the pallbearer who, puzzled, stared back at him.

Later, during the brief reception in the church basement that Blanche, his sister, had arranged, the tall man avoided eye contact despite friends and relatives queuing up to shake his hand; some of the men squeezing his elbow as they said what people say on such occasions.

"Annette was a beautiful woman," Jean told his brother, hand clasped around Maurice's forearm.

"Yeah ... oh, yeah," Maurice said, looking over Jean's shoulder.

"Blanche told me that she'd help you out. Marc too. I'd

love to help but, you know, I'll be leaving in three days. I'm sure Annette told you, going to the States, Winooski."

"Yeah, the US," he replied, limps pinched and nodding. "Well ... anyway."

Jean nodded back at his brother and slipped away to join the group that had assembled around one of the long tables where mourners ate some of the food that Blanche had prepared.

Every once in a while, he'd look down at his girls and shake his head, just a bit of a bob, but enough for Saraphine and Eugénie to notice. Saraphine, the youngest, had just turned ten. Eugénie was thirteen, or fourteen, he could never remember. Probably old enough to quit school and start working, he thought.

Having dutifully acknowledged and participated in the day's sombre rituals, Maurice walked back home, hands stored in his pants pockets and staring at his shoes. The girls, arm in arm, trotted and sobbed, trying to keep up with their father's long strides, looking at the backside of a man with whom they shared nothing but flesh and blood.

By the time Maurice had climbed the first flight of winding stairs leading to the apartment, he knew he had to make changes. Pulling the keys from his pocket, he realized he had to stop drinking. This time for good. Later, while reading the paper, his destiny flashed before his eyes.

-2-

Saraphine sat on a bench waiting for her sister's classes to finish. A set of long, black, silk ribbons pinned to her blazer's lapel—the nuns had insisted they wear the symbol for two weeks out of respect for her mother and mourning father—felt like an unnecessary reminder that her heart had been pulverized; that her mother had vanished. Her school clothes weren't as crisp or as clean as they used to be; her loosely woven dark brown braids left her feeling ashamed and self-conscious about ... feeling ashamed. At a time like this, how could such feelings intrude upon her grief?

The bell rang to release the older girls from their desks. Saraphine watched as hundreds of uniformed young ladies walked out, two by two, marching to the rhythm of Sister Claudette's prickly voice. Hélène, Eugénie's usual partner in line, was alone. Saraphine, who had never walked home from school without her sister, felt her brain ignite as panic took hold and shortened her breaths. She bounced to her feet, eyes darting in all directions. She was about to call her sister's name when Eugénie appeared from the side door, Sister Jeannine by her side. Saraphine ran to her. "No, no, young ladies do not run," Sister Jeannine warned, waving her wooden clapper at Saraphine. Usually obedient, Saraphine ignored the casually ferocious, shrouded lady and raced to embrace her sister. "That's quite enough," Sister Jeannine said. "You two will have to learn that without a mother, the discipline you learn from us will become even more important for your upbringing."

"Thank you, Sister," Eugénie said, robotically.

"So, go on. Be on your way. Don't delay. Don't make your father worry about you two. I'm sure he has enough on his mind these days, *n'est-ce pas*? You'll have to do your part and take care of your father."

The sisters walked back home along the usual route; arms linked as usual, seagulls flying high overhead, as usual.

"What did Sister Jeannine want?" Saraphine asked.

"Told me what she told you. You know, that we should be taking care of our father."

"What does that mean?"

"Well, I think it jus' means things like cooking and cleaning, I suppose. Not making him mad or anything."

"Can you cook anything?"

"Sure, you've seen me cook. I've prepared all sorts of things."

"No, I mean can you cook supper? Meat, vegetables?

Things we eat for supper."

"Certainly. I watched mom do it for my whole life. I can do it."

Saraphine had never seen her big sister prepare supper, and Eugénie knew she hadn't convinced Saraphine she could. So far, since their mother had passed, the girls had eaten whatever had been left over from the funeral reception and some hard cheese, canned beans, and the dried beef that had been the last thing their mother had prepared for the family. But now, except for some condiments, pickles, and a few potatoes their father had bought from a man selling vegetables door-to-door, the pantry was bare and the icebox was warm and empty, its water pan full.

Walking home along Dufresne Street—sisters in lockstep, mourning ribbons pinned for all to see—Eugénie looked at her feet hoping to avoid the pitying stares of ladies sweeping porches or sitting on balconies on the sunny side of the street.

"You girls all right? Let me know if you need anything … anything at all," Madame Faucher called down from her third-floor window, elbows parked on a small cushion while puffing away at a cigarette.

"How's your dad doing? Got enough food?" Madame Archambault asked, shaking dust bunnies off her dry mop by banging it on the edge of the railing.

Eugénie and Saraphine, heads down, moved forward, offering the occasional smile or wave, mortified at the thought of having become objects of pity … *those poor girls who lost their mother*. Having reached the base of the long, winding, exterior staircase leading up to their home, Madame Laplante, the upstairs neighbour, flung her door open upon hearing footsteps rattling the iron.

"*Allô les filles*. D'you forget something?" The gossipy lady asked, looking down at them, a twinkle in her eye at the thought of prying some juicy tidbit from the girls.

"Forget? Forget what, Madame Laplante?" Eugénie asked.

"Everything. Anything. Didn't your dad pick you up? He

said he was taking you to his sister's place."

"Aunt Blanche? To go to Aunt Blanche. Is that what you mean?"

"That's what he said. Aren't you going over there?"

". . . Yes ... yes. Of course," Eugénie replied, clueless.

"We're going in now. Thanks, Madame Laplante," Eugénie said, turning the key to the rotary doorbell, expecting the usual clank of her father yanking at the cord that ran along the staircase wall and unlocked the door.

Pointing up at the Desjardins' apartment, Madame Laplante said, "I don't think he's there, darling ... left right after lunch ... everything all packed up. A bunch of bags, a big suitcase, a really big one ... brown with straps around it. Told me that he brought everything to your aunt's house. Pretty sure that's what he said."

"Do we go in?" Saraphine whispered to her sister, eyes wide and watery.

Eugénie turned the knob, the door was unlocked. A breath of cool air rushed up the long staircase and through the upstairs door. "Father?" Eugénie called, poking her nose inside the hallway. "Father?" She called again, looking at the lifeless furniture in the front parlour. Everything seemed the same. The kitchen table and chairs remained; the living room was intact. The lace and velvet curtains were drawn and sheet music sat on the piano bench. Looking into the bedroom she shared with Saraphine, Eugénie was relieved to see their dresser hadn't been touched. From her parent's bedroom, Saraphine called to her sister.

"He took everything out of his drawers. Everything's gone, all his things."

"All of mom's things are here, the drawers aren't even opened," Eugénie said, standing in the doorway. Saraphine rushed to the closet and flung the small door open.

"He took his suit, too. Only mom's things are here," Saraphine said, looking up at the wooden rod.

They looked at each other, expressionless, hoping the other

could explain the scene. "Did he leave any food?" Saraphine asked.

Eugénie took her sister's arm and dragged her to the kitchen. They froze at the sight of a folded piece of paper sitting on the dinner table, a few coins stacked on it. "You think that maybe that's for us?" Saraphine asked under her breath. Eugénie looked back at her sister, walked toward the table, picked up the note, and read it aloud.

Dear Daughters,

I've left for the West Coast, a place called Cayoosh Creek. There is a lot of gold there and I'm going to be a miner for a while. We'll have a lot of money one day. Don't worry, you won't be on your own. Go to your Aunt Blanche's house and she'll take care of you until I send for the both of you to join me here.

Tell your aunt to take whatever they want from the apartment. Make sure to help out and be good girls.

Your Father

-3-

Saraphine pulled a chair, plunked her elbows on the table and scrutinized Eugénie's face, hoping to gauge her older sister's understanding of what they had just learned.

"Where's the West Coast?" Saraphine asked, her words dripping slowly from her lips.

Eugénie reread the note, twice, three times, looking for words hidden somewhere in the text, turning the paper over and over.

"Where's Ca... Cay... Yoosh?"

"Cayoosh. It says Cayoosh Creek," Eugénie replied, fixated on the note.

"Are we going to that place, to Cayoosh?"

"Dunno. I think we're supposed to go to Aunt Blanche's house."

"Now?" Saraphine asked, lurching towards her sister and latching onto her forearm.

Eugénie looked out the kitchen window and watched as a woman broomed her balcony.

"What are we gonna do? Saraphine asked, shaking her sister's arm.

"Maybe we can find a bag or something to put some of our things in. We'll come back and get the rest of our stuff later," Eugénie said, her mind plunged in a dungeon of chaos.

"You know how to get to Aunt Blanche's house?"

"We've been there before. It's next to the abattoirs on Wilson Street. Remember? Remember how it always stinks there."

Saraphine's face finally crumpled and tears dripped from her long lashes. "But they're the ones who came here, we never went there. I don't even know how to get to their house," she said.

Eugénie picked up the note, folded it along its original creases, took hold of her sister's shoulders and said, "It's us now. Jus' us. We're going to be all right. We'll go to Aunt Blanche's place and she'll explain the whole thing. You'll see, everything's gonna be fine."

"Is she going to take us in … let us live with her?"

"You heard what the note said. It's only for a little while. He's going to send for us. We'll be going to the West Coast, too."

"When?" Saraphine asked, wiping the snot from her nose. "When are we going to the West Coast?"

"We're going to Aunt Blanche's now, that's all I know."

Saraphine hitched herself to the back of her sister's dress while Eugénie foraged through the kitchen's corner hutch and pulled out a couple of burlap bags. Randomly plucking items from their dresser drawers: a box of handkerchiefs, ribbons their mother used to weave into their long ponytails, mittens made from old socks, a hairbrush, pantaloons, they moved as if their actions could—would—negate the gravity of their situation. "I've got to bring Adina," Saraphine said, grabbing her doll off the dresser. Her cracked, wooden noggin dangling off limp shoulders, the blue cotton dress she wore identical to ones her mother had made for her daughters.

"You'll have to hold on to her, we've got to save space for more important things," Eugénie answered. Noticing a small tintype of their mother left behind in their father's drawer, Eugénie looked at it, smiled, and dropped it atop the mish-mash piled in the burlap sack.

Arms hooked under the bags, Eugénie drew her lips together and nodded at Madame Laplante as they descended the staircase. Saraphine, Adina held to her chest, looked away.

"So, you two … you'll be living at your aunt's now, right?" Madame Laplante asked, moving down a few steps.

"Yes, Madame Laplante. We're going to my Aunt Blanche's house. I dunno, but I think that's where we'll be living for a while," Eugénie replied, not looking back.

"Well, uh, say hello to your father when you get there."

Children, friends, playing along the sidewalk stopped to watch the girls-whose-mother-died walk past. On their own. Burlap sacks and doll in hand.

-4-

The sun dipped below Forsyth Street's tall triplexes and a cool breeze rolled off Mount Royal, whooshing away the stench of manure. Neither of the sisters knew Aunt Blanche's address but they hoped one of them would recognize the look of the place once they saw it. By now, they had travelled eight city blocks all the way to the corner of Préfontaine, scrutinizing each door as they wandered, hoping one of them would, eventually, look familiar.

Blanche and her husband, Marc Albert, were having supper when Eugénie spun the doorbell's key. Marc wiped his mouth, tilted his chair back to look down the hallway and saw two tiny faces peeking in through the bottom of the front door's window. No longer able to contain the day's stress, Saraphine erupted into tears and blew mucus all over the door. Eugénie, used to her sister's emotions, stood quietly on the porch, looking in, arms shaking under the weight of the bags.

"Where's your father?" Marc asked as he opened the door, crouching down, wrapping his left arm around Saraphine, his hand on Eugénie's shoulder.

"He left for the West Coast," Eugénie answered.

"The West Coast," Saraphine repeated, her words drowned in heaps of snot and spit. "Blanche, it's your nieces," Marc yelled and coughed. "Blanche, Eugénie, and Saraphine are here," he repeated, taking the bags from Eugénie's arms while herding the girls inside.

"Good Lord, what's going on? Where's your father?" Blanche asked, walking down the hallway and wiping her palms on her flowery apron.

"I asked, he's not with them," Marc said, his tone implying some discussions on the subject had previously taken place. "West Coast? What'd you mean, girls?" Marc, hands on his knees, asked.

Eugénie pulled her father's note from her jacket's pocket and pointed it at her aunt.

"Euge-Euge-Saf-Saraphine," Eugénie heard the voice coming from the kitchen and ran to her cousin.

"How are you, Ephrem?" She asked, hugging him, his foot kicking the bottom of the table as he tried to stand. Ephrem's round face beamed and nothing but gurgling sounds came from his opened mouth.

"Sa-Sa-Saraf," the boy struggled to say, reaching out to his other cousin. Saraphine's smile beamed despite her wet face, and all three of them were soon locked in an embrace. "Sar-fine. Eunie-Euge," the boy repeated, remnants on his chin summarizing the evening's menu.

"Sit girls. Sit, sit. You two had supper yet? Tell us what's going on," Blanche asked, hurriedly sliding chairs around the small dining table. "So, where exactly *is* your father?"

Eugénie, no longer able to maintain her stolid demeanour, broke down while trying to describe the unexpected turn of events.

"But your father never mentioned any of this to me. This comes as a complete surprise," Blanche said, long after the girls had cried out the details of the situation. Marc took the note from Eugénie and read it aloud.

"That's so strange. I can't believe my brother's gone … to the West Coast. He never mentioned anything about leaving … anything about the West Coast. Cayoosh Creek?"

"He's obviously gone, Blanche. Nobody else wrote this note. There's no misunderstanding here," Marc said, looking sideways at his wife, hand running along the crown of his re-maining hair.

"He never told you anything about this? About coming here?" Blanche asked her nieces, wiping their cheeks with her apron, her pink, freckled face reddening.

"No. Madame Laplante's the one who told us to come here," Eugénie said, shoulders bobbing while sucking in big gulps of air.

"Who's she … Madame Laplante?" Marc asked, squinting through his pipe's smoke, hacking, trying to expel the frog that had long taken residence deep in his throat.

"She lives next door. She saw us arrive, and she's the one who told us about my father being gone," Saraphine said.

"All right, all right, we'll talk some more about this later. Let's get some food in you two," Blanche said, and marched towards the cupboard.

Later that evening—the sisters asleep—Blanche and Marc discussed how they could possibly cope with having to feed two additional children and find a place to shoehorn a couple of girls into such a tiny apartment. "You sure my brother never gave you any clues that he'd be leaving? Did he say anything to you at the funeral? Did he ever—"

"No, no, of course he didn't. I would've told you if he did. I'm just as shocked as you are about all this," Marc said, his words whistling through his pipe, ashes floating up into a smoky cumulus. "The West Coast? Good God, what's he gonna be? A miner? What in God's name was he thinking? He's lived in the city his whole life. Now he's a miner? What the hell does he know about finding gold? He can hardly speak English for God's sake. *Y'a pas d'Canadien la ...* they're all English over there, you know," Marc added, wiping his forehead with the crook of his elbow and shaking his head, his face drifting in and out of the smoke that gushed from his mouth and nose. "And what now? Is he gone for good? Is this a temporary thing? Are we supposed to go clean out his apartment?"

"He's always been hard to read, my brother . . ." Blanche said, rubbing her hands along her hips. "I don't know what to do. I don't know where he is. I don't know what to tell you. I'm so sorry. I know this isn't the first time he's—"

"So, do we go get his stuff out of his apartment? We'll need to get the girls' clothes and things. Did you see what they had packed in their sacks? They'll need more than a hairbrush and mittens, you know. We'll have to get everything out of there or else we're likely to be the ones who're gonna have to pay the rent for that place. We'll have to—"

"Look, let's agree that the girls are here now and that we don't know much about the story. Let's give it a couple of days and see what happens. Who knows, this *might be* a big misunderstanding. Maybe Maurice'll be back tomorrow,"

Blanche said, joining her husband inside his smoke cloud and wrapping her arms around his shoulders.

Blanche finished cleaning up the kitchen, and Marc read his paper; each of them privately pondering the next move. Marc reloaded his pipe, scratched a match along the sole of his shoe and, as he leaned in to set the wad of tobacco alight, said, "Ephrem really loves those two. They always seem so happy together, like they're branches of the same tree. It's like … *Ayoye*! Ouch! *Maudite marde*!" He yelled and hacked, shaking his hand and dropping the match that had burnt his fingers. Blanche laughed.

"Watch it old man or you might set that tree on fire," she said, putting away the plate she had dried.

-6-

By summer, the girls felt at home tucked away in what used to be Ephrem's room; their clothes neatly folded in the old six-drawer dresser they had always shared. The whole place looked different now that Marc had replaced a lot of their own furniture with what they had retrieved from Maurice's apartment; including the piano that seven men had wrestled down the steep staircase and hauled down the street in the butcher shop's wagon that Marc had borrowed from Monsieur Charpentier.

It took a while for Marc and Blanche—Marc especially— to get used to the boy's bed being just a few feet away from theirs. They had grown familiar with the boy's nocturnal monologues; ramblings mostly, and the occasional scream that smashed through the night. But now, with Ephrem being so close, those nightly verbalizations sounded more as if someone was shouting in their ears. "Strange," Marc often said as Blanche rubbed his neck trying to get him to fall back asleep, "how the boy doesn't stutter when he's talking in his sleep."

Leaves from the tall ash tree had turned the sidewalk

golden and brittle. The girls had switched schools and resumed their piano lessons with Sister Marie-Angeline. By Christmas time, Eugénie had started helping out at the butchery after school, her meagre earnings contributing to the purchase of winter coats for herself and Saraphine. Their father's vanishing act was never brought up, but the crater left by their mother's death soured their every reminiscence. The little tintype, the one Eugénie had retrieved from her mother's room—a sepia tone picture of a young woman wearing a fluffy, white dress and an oversized hat, umbrella held over her shoulder in front of a Niagara Falls' background—had found a hallowed place atop the dresser. But, despite the few mementos, the flow of each passing day dissolved the crispness of her memory and slowly flattened the memory of her voice. Lying in bed, Marc and Blanche sometimes heard the girls whispering; little ones trying hard to replenish their dwindling store of remembrances as they fell asleep.

By early spring, workers had begun work on Forsyth Street. For nearly five years, city officials had promised to replace the street's macadam top with new cobblestone paving. "This was all supposed to be done by now!" Marc yelled at the workers on his way to work, walking along the finished portions of the street, lunchbox in hand, his taunts ignored. Ephrem, delighted by the activity taking place right in front of his porch, sat and watched all day as the street slowly crawled forward. Used to spending his days alone with his mother, Ephrem liked to keep his nose buried in books, most of them meant for younger children. From time to time, clamming up whenever someone walked by, he'd read aloud for his mother, Blanche forever encouraging him as he stumbled along.

"You're getting better every day. Soon you'll be able to go to school with other boys your age. You'll see." His mother had been promising for years, somehow unaware that the thought of being with others—boys that went out of their way to walk in front of his porch to mock and ridicule—terrified him.

The wall behind where Ephrem slept was covered by pictures drawn on large sheets of brown paper, artwork made possible by the grease pencils and supplies Marc *brought* home courtesy of the butcher shop. On days when he lacked inspiration, he stacked his wooden blocks or rode a small wagon his father had built for him. But, despite whatever he was doing, he'd never fail to move to the parlour or go sit on the porch by three o'clock, waiting for his cousins to appear.

As spring drew people out on porches, Blanche installed a small folding table where Ephrem could make his drawings and check out the flow of people and horses gliding along the new cobblestones. He'd greet passersby, even the few he didn't recognize, with a perfectly enunciated *bonjour*. To those he was familiar with, he always made certain to add: *Madame* or *Monsieur* to his greeting. When his cousins came into view, he'd jump out of his chair and smile a smile that transformed his face into a canvas of pure joy.

-7-

It had taken some time before Blanche let her nieces participate in the rituals of supper; to allow them to meddle in what had been her privileged territory. But now, all three had evolved a highly choreographed meal preparation routine. Blanche did the prep and actual cooking, Eugénie washed pots and utensils while Saraphine set the table. The strict division of labour allowed for plenty of time for talking, gossip and mirth. Ephrem, on his bench next to the icebox, contributed to the discussion as best he could.

"Something smells good," Marc said, shaking his match to death.

"Uncle Marc's paper's in the way. I can't set the table," Saraphine, hands on her hips, complained. Marc, his *La Presse* newspaper sprawled in front of him, smiled and winked, his yellow teeth clenching at his pipe's stem, smoke oozing from his nose and mouth.

"Oh, he'll move away all right, don't you worry 'cause you know he wants his dinner on time. Isn't that right, Marc?" Blanche asked.

"Yeah, okay, I'll get out of your way," he coughed, winking at Ephrem. "C'mon Ephrem, the men will retire to the parlour," he said, reaching for the boy's hand. "But I guess that means I won't be able to give you the good news. Anyway, I 'spose you shooing me away suggests you're not that interested," he added, walking down the short hallway and coyly looking back over his shoulder.

"What good news?" Eugénie had taken the bait, looking back at her uncle while scraping burnt remains off the bottom of a pot.

"No, it's okay. I guess it can wait," Marc said, puffing away.

"Okay old man, out with it, enough games. You've got something to say?" Blanche said, wiping her hands on her apron.

"All right then, since you've put it that way, here's the thing. Monsieur Charpentier is going ahead with the other shop. He says it's going to be ready in a couple of months … by the fall for sure."

"OK, but why's that so good for you?" Blanche asked, still rubbing her apron.

"That's not all," Marc added, pointing with his pipe. "It just so happens that he's decided to keep me at the main shop. So, that means I can stay put … I won't have to go all the way to his new place."

"OK. So, nothing's gonna change."

"Oh yeah, I almost forgot," he added, keenly aware that Eugénie had been expecting news. "So, with all the extra work that's expected this summer and fall, Monsieur Charpentier has decided to hire you, full-time during the summer," Marc, nodding and smiling, told Eugénie.

"I'm so happy, Uncle Marc," Eugénie said, hopping and clapping.

"You'll be full-time at the counter and, you know, help in the back when it's quiet, the same as you're doing now on Saturday mornings."

"That's so wonderful," Eugénie said, beaming, arms around her uncle while Ephrem pulled at her dress.

"Oh, and uh … I thought you might find it interesting to know that Monsieur Charpentier's boy is also gonna be working this summer. Just more good news for you, I guess," Marc added, having caught Orance glancing at his niece on several occasions, and having caught Eugénie glancing back … from time to time. Discreetly.

"Yes, I do suppose that's good news. Good news for him, I'd say. At least he has a job," she replied, dryly, her tone indicating she had not appreciated her uncle's innuendo.

Marc leaned back a bit and smiled. Aware of the boy's intentions vis-à-vis his niece—he had just recently allowed the boy to court her—he figured they were a good match.

"Imagine, my niece and the boss's son. I couldn't ask for more. Right?" Marc said, turning to Ephrem and winking at the boy.

"O-Orance? His n-n-na-name is O-Orance?" Ephrem asked, head cocked to the side.

"In any case, you're starting on Monday, so enjoy the weekend 'cause you'll be busy all of next week," Marc concluded, punctuating his sentence by clearing the phlegm from his throat and hitting the spittoon with the precision of a sniper … this time.

-8-

Orance was flipping over the *Sorry We're Closed* sign when he saw Eugénie tiptoeing her way along Hochelaga Street, sidestepping manure bombs on her way to her first day as a full-time employee at the *Boucherie Salaison Charpentier*.

Dressed in her best business casual outfit, she wore a black, bell-shaped, floor-length skirt gored to fit neatly over her hips. She had borrowed her aunt's white blouse—spending much of her Sunday afternoon pressing and starching the garment—with the nice vertical puff at the shoulders and a row of delicate black buttons. She wrapped a short, silver, silk cravat scarf around her collar, neatly synched in a black ring. Her grey, serge bodice with gigot sleeves stayed on till everyone had noticed it, but it would have to come off before the early morning sun splashed through the shop's window and turned the still breathable air into smelly, meaty liquid. Following Monsieur Charpentier's orders, she had spent much of the morning forcing her hair into submission, all of it pulled back into a bun laced with a matching grey ribbon. "I don't want customers to chew on employee's hair," he had told her the very first day when she used to be part-time, worried patrons would find long, thick, chestnut strands comingling with their chops or minced pork.

Orance held the door open, wiping his nose with his elbow and watching as Eugénie stepped onto the sidewalk. "Close the door you idiot, bugs'll come in," his father warned, finger pointed at his son like a sword. "People don't want to buy meat from a place that's full of flies. Why aren't you in the back, anyway?"

Startled, Orance let go of the door and scooted to the back. Eugénie, looking in, tapped on the glass, lips pinched together in a tight line. Orance turned and stared at her as if waking from a trance. "Oh, sorry," he apologised, jogging back to open the door.

"Thanks," she said, rolling her eyes as she walked by.

"*Bon matin*," Orance said over the fading sound of the little bell suspended above the door. "So ... hum, I hear you'll be working here pretty much full-time. Right?" He added.

Eugénie, concealed a smile as she nestled herself behind the register. "Yes. I'll be at the register and will do some work in the back when it's not so busy out here," she answered, content with the cool demeanour she had presented. So far. Confident that she alone was aware of the butterflies that had settled in.

"Well, I suppose I'll see you in the back, then … if things aren't busy out here, that is," the young man replied, bobbing and scratching at his chin, his unease on full display.

All week, Orance arrived early to open the door for Eugénie. He'd cluck nervously around the girl, speaking yet saying nothing, finding reasons to come out front: checking inside the counters, replacing sawdust on the shop's floor, asking Eugénie if she had enough change in the register. Marc, who spent most days out front serving customers and preparing orders, watched dejectedly as the boy fluttered all around Eugénie's space.

At the end of each day, Orance, in a constant state of readiness, watched and prepared to snake his way near the front door in order to wish Eugénie a good evening before she left. "*Bonne soirée, et à demain ma chère*," he'd say and look directly at the bridge of her nose. Aware of the boy's finagling and disappointed by his lack of aplomb, Eugénie sometimes liked to play along by stalling, observing him as he tried to look busy and finding excuses to stay out front, to be there at the moment of her departure.

Marc, who for weeks had been a witness to the boy's ineptitude, decided it was time to nudge destiny forward.

"Hey, Orance," Marc addressed his boss's son as the lad lugged a large container of ground beef destined for the counter. "I read this morning in *La Presse* that there's gonna be a concert at the grandstand in Sohmer park this Sunday. I bet that'd make for a nice outing."

"I suppose so. Sounds nice," Orance said, transferring meat into trays inside the counter.

Marc pursed his lips, exhaled, put his arm around the young man's shoulders and pulled him out from inside the counter.

"You understand that maybe you're not the only young

man who finds my niece attractive? That someday, you know, you might regret not having been more assertive. You understand what I'm saying? About not taking a chance?" Marc said, trying to be delicate yet clear. "Besides, take it from me, I'm sure she's not going to say no."

"Well, maybe you could ask her if she's—"

"No. I'm not asking my niece if she wants to be courted by you. You're the one who's gonna have to cross that bridge. Let me tell you about an ol' saying my dad used to recite all the time. 'Take time to deliberate; but when the time for action arrives, stop thinking and go in'... you know who said that? Napoleon. You know? Bonaparte." Marc said, nodding, eyes wide and bright. "Pretty smart man, right? So, think about that, you know, when you're having trouble finding your courage."

"Thanks, Monsieur Albert," he said, his chin lifting up a smidge.

The next day, Marc kept an eye on Orance who wandered around the shop wiping counters, repositioning price markers and sliding the toe of his shoe along the sawdust to gauge the floor's cleanliness. Marc shook his head and grabbed the boy's elbow as he walked by. "Do me a favour and stay at the counter for a while. There's something I've got to do in the back," he told Orance who stared back at him dully, lips parted.

Marc peeked through the door's round window hoping Orance would grow a backbone and approach his niece, but the boy stood frozen behind the counter, fidgeting and watching customers milling around. He bent down low and grabbed pans of sausages and blood pudding, sliding them back and forth inside the counter. "These've gotta be sitting on ice or else it's all gonna go bad in a hurry, you know," Orance said, straightening up and wiping his hands on his bloody, white apron.

"Well, of course," Eugénie said. "My uncle always makes sure about that. I see him do that all day long."

"Oh yeah, I'm sure about that. For certain he does. I just wanted to make sure, you know, that everything was okay in the counter. Looks like we need more sawdust on the floor, though. It's really getting soaked."

"I'm not sure we need more. It looks pretty much the way it usually does. I think it's fine, but you're the butcher. You should know," she said, standing at attention behind the register, hands on the drawer.

"Yeah, I guess you're right. You know what your father's needing back there?"

"I don't. He goes in the back all the time. Could be gone all morning. He's not my father, by the way. He's my uncle. My father's gone to the West Coast. A place called Cayoosh Creek. He's a miner ... gold miner."

"Oh," Orance said, looking at his fingers tapping on the counter. "Hey, I found out something earlier from your fa ... uh, I mean, your uncle. He said there's a concert this Sunday at Sohmer Park, you know, at the grandstand. He said that it sounded like it was going to be a pretty good thing."

"I'm sure it will."

"I think I'm gonna go, you know, unless it rains. If it rains, I'm not gonna go, you know, because of the rain. Who wants to get all wet ... right?"

"Yes. I wouldn't go if it rained, either. It just makes sense."

"Yeah. But would you go if it didn't rain?"

"Maybe. Probably."

"Then, maybe it would make sense if we went together, you know, on Sunday. If it doesn't rain."

"I'd like to go. I enjoy music. I play the piano, you know. But, this Sunday, I can't. I promised my Aunt Blanche that I'd help in the kitchen on Sunday. Now that I work all week I don't have time to help as much at home, and she needs me to help her this Sunday."

Orance ran his sleeve over his mouth, looked away and said, "Oh sure, I understand. Well, maybe I'll see you there if you don't have to work, or if you finish early ... maybe. I wonder where your fa … your uncle is. I've got lots of work to do back there."

They stood, statue-like on either side of the counter. Eugénie, hands on the register's drawer, peeked sideways at Orance who had coiled back to look through the door's round window. "Monsieur Albert, you coming back soon?" He yelled at the door, aware that Eugénie was looking sideways at him. The white door flapped back and forth after Marc burst through it; rubbing his hands and coughing through a wide smile. "I'm good Orance, thanks for the help out here," he said, winking at the boy whose face, he noticed, seemed surprisingly placid for someone who had plans to escort a lovely young woman to Sohmer Park.

"So? You and the boy going to the concert? Did he ask you?" Marc, leaning forward and pointing his pipe at the back, asked as soon as Orance had bolted through the still-swinging door.

"He asked. But, no … I'm not going."

Marc frowned. "No? You said no?"

"That's right."

"Why?"

"I've got work to do on Sunday … help out in the kitchen … there's lots to do. I won't be around much this summer and I want to make sure I do my part at home."

"No, it's all right. Your aunt won't mind. She knows you've got a lot of work now and that you can't help out as much as you used to. Besides, it's up to Saraphine to help out more at the house, now. It's up to all of us to take our turn, that's how things work."

"I'd rather not go," she said, staring straight ahead and smoothing the non-existent wrinkles along the sleeves of her blouse.

"But I already told Orance that you'd—"

The bell sitting atop the front door chimed and a customer walked in.

"*Bonjour Madame Champlain,*" Marc greeted. "*Que puis-*

je faire pour vous aujourd'hui?" He enquired, responding automatically to the sound of the bell, eyes locked on his niece who made sure not to look back at her uncle.

"I'll need a roast for this weekend, and I'm—"

Eugénie grunted and slapped the swinging door open as if wanting to punish it. She stood there, alone, and noticed the large door leading to the back alley was partially opened. "Did you see Orance?" She asked, walking out onto the loading dock. Seamus—a half-burned cigarette tucked in the corner of his mouth and feet dangling off the loading dock—was dropping pieces of fat and gristle for dogs gathered below. Without turning back, one eye closed as smoke rose up along his cheek, he answered, "He's in the cellar," and brushed away ashes that had fallen from his jiggling cigarette.

"Could you please ask him to come see me at the register when he gets back?"

"Sure."

"Tell him … tell him I need to speak with him."

"Yeah, yeah," Seamus repeated, hoisting his right cheek up to close his eye. "Don't know that I need to remind him about that, though. Haven't you noticed that he's always finding excuses to go out front?"

Orance, unaware he had been summoned to the front, burst ass-first through the swinging door, large buckets filled with ice hanging from his arms.

"You got my message? Good," Eugénie said.

"Message? What message?" Orance asked, face creased and puzzled.

"I had a discussion with my uncle, and he convinced me to go to Sohmer Park on Sunday … if it doesn't rain."

"OK, that's good. Really good. It'll be a fun day. Thanks for coming … well, uh, for coming with me," he said, loading chunks of ice under the counter's many trays.

"I was just a bit concerned that you didn't think enough of me to ask earlier. Jus' seemed like you weren't really sure you wanted to be my escort on Sunday. That's all."

"No … oh no … that's not it. I … I just wanted to make sure, is all. It'll be top-notch," Orance said on his way back, his empty buckets hitting the swinging door as he walked through. "I was worried that … that it would rain, you know, that the day'd be ruined."

Eugénie, chin up, stood at her post behind the register, stiff as a plank, hands on the drawer like a pianist waiting for the conductor's instructions. From behind the table where Marc stacked a small mountain of pigs' heads and feet, he saw what he believed might have been her lips forming the outline of a faint smile. And, why not? After all, she was being courted by a young man who would soon be responsible for managing his own butchery. A young man who stood to inherit a small chain of shops.

-9-

Growling, thumping thunder shook the house on its foundations. Ephrem bawled and howled, stomping in all directions down the hallway. "S-s-stop da-dat," he cried. The toilet, recently installed in what used to be the entrance closet, backed up and belched malignant odours throughout the apartment as small waves of rainwater flowed along Forsyth street's new pavers; flooding drains and reversing the flow. Blanche tried to reassure Ephrem while mopping up the brown sludge spewing up and out from the open sewer that had become their small WC.

"It won't stop coming up," Blanche yelled at Marc as she wiped the soaked floor on her hands and knees; Ephrem tugging at her hip. "Put newspapers on the toilet," she ordered, pointing at the kitchen with her noxious cloth. Marc ran to the back, his leather soles squishing as brown water leached out from them, and grabbed a few copies of his *La Presse* newspaper from the pile he kept next to the stove and shoved them between the erupting ceramic bowl and wooden seat.

Eugénie and Saraphine, kneeling on the sofa, elbows resting on the back, stared out the window and watched the rain flowing off the second-floor balcony. "It seems to be clearing up out there," Eugénie whispered from time to time, eyes turned upwards and trying hard to convince herself the storm would clear by Sunday.

"I think I see a small patch of blue, over there … look, above the house across the street," Saraphine said, pointing at the sky and looking at her sister, nodding and smiling. "It really is," she added when no one from the cleaning crew agreed.

"Don't worry, it can't rain like this forever. It's coming down so hard I don't think anything's gonna be left up there," Blanche replied, wringing her rag into a roasting pan already overflowing with brown water.

"I'm sure it's gonna be nice. Anyway, this much rain can only be good for the grass," Eugénie said.

"I suppose so," Marc said, careful not to splash onto the walls while dropping sheets of newspaper onto the muck and hoping the thin paper would sop up much of the mess. "What're you worried about, anyway? You won't have to sit on the grass. The grandstand's been open since June. You'll be sitting on a bench, not on the grass. Anyway, it's still gonna be soaked tomorrow so you better leave early to make sure you get a spot in the stands. Otherwise, you'll be standing all afternoon."

A smoky mist rose off Forsyth Street by late afternoon; diagonal beams from a vermillion sunset burning moisture out from the cobbles. All evening, Eugénie pondered her accoutrement for the concert; a wheel of mix-and-match options spinning in her mind. Saraphine, looking down at the contents of her own three drawers, pulled out all she had and lay it out on her rose chenille bedspread.

"None of that'll fit me. Not even your hat, you've got a tiny head," Eugénie told her sister, raising her voice for her aunt to hear.

"What about an umbrella? Were you planning on carrying an umbrella?" Blanche asked, scrubbing away at the sink.

"Not tomorrow, don't think so. The sun was bright red when it went down tonight," Eugénie replied, her tone suggesting she didn't appreciate the mention of rain.

"It's not about rain," Blanche added, drying her hands in her armpits on her way to the girls' room. "It's not about rain," she repeated, standing in the doorway, smiling, weaving long strands of greying hair back inside her coiffe. "You want an umbrella to protect yourself from the sun."

"But you've already said that I could wear your hat. It's plenty big enough to cover my whole face."

"That's not the point," Blanche said, disappearing to her room before returning with her umbrella in hand. "Take my white umbrella."

Eugénie took the umbrella and started strutting—carefully jabbing the fancy accessory at the floor.

"It's your uncle who bought it for me," Blanche said, still trying to wrestle her hair into place. "We were just courting when I saw it in the window at *Dupuis Frères* on St Catherine. I said something about how much I liked it and, a few days later, Marc showed up one day and gave it to me as a gift. My mother thought it was so nice of him," Blanche said, eyes out of focus, unaware she was caressing her cheek with the back of her fingers, her mind far away. "Marc, remember when you gave me the umbrella?" She said, arched back to look into the kitchen.

"What? Gave you what?" Marc asked, his voice groggy and wet.

"Anyway," Blanche went on, "it's the kind of accessory fancy ladies carry with them. Not to mention that it'll keep you from sweating if it gets hot. You don't want that beautiful complexion of yours burned by the sun. You'll see, you'll look very elegant. Refined," she added, nodding and smiling, eyebrows creasing her forehead.

"Like a real lady," Saraphine added.

"Should I open it even if it's not hot?" Eugénie asked.

"Just look at what the other ladies do. But make sure not to open it if you're sitting in the grandstand, though."

"You know, an umbrella for the sun is called a parasol," Marc, who had crept near, said while nodding smartly.

Chapter 3

September 1895

The uninterrupted flow of Urbin Charpentier's life had included all a man could possibly fancy. A dedicated wife, five children—three of the male persuasion—and a job he considered his vocation. Born to be a butcher, he had apprenticed under his father, expertly slicing pork bellies into thin strips by the time he was five.

He'd spend most of his evenings upstairs, in the apartment above his father's shop delighting in the rhythm of his usual post-supper choreography. Sitting, back leaning on the wainscoted kitchen wall while spearing at recalcitrant morsels of meat wedged between his teeth with a toothpick, Urbin watched his wife and daughters clear the table. This was his time to breathe. Uriette, his wife, would have said, '*His time to belch.*' His boys, twitchy and energetic, never lingered. They'd push away from the table, mouths full, and rush downstairs to join other teens from the neighbourhood to do what boys do.

He'd listen for a while as the women, left to wash dishes—water brought to a boil over the woodstove dissolving the greasy mess—discussed the pleasant hither and thither of the day. He mostly enjoyed the gossiping, contributing from time to time whenever the slandered individual *du-jour* was of some interest. As usual, he would quickly lose track of who had done what to whom and drop the front legs of his chair to the floor; the sound of his feet slapping at the oilcloth setting in motion a much-evolved routine. Dahlia, his youngest girl, would reach into the cupboard's drawer, pull out the square of waxed canvas and place it on the table; Urbin, elbows to his side, watching as she smoothed it out for him. Florie, just eleven months older than her sister, would skip down the hallway, fetch the tobacco pouch from her father's little table next to his chair in the front parlour and place it on said waxed canvas.

Fully equipped, the smell of freshly chopped tobacco mingling with the persistent aroma of whatever cut of meat had just been fried, broiled or roasted, Urbin corralled a mess of tobacco with the sides of his hands into a neat, little pile. The next day's allotment ready to be prepared, he'd meticulously roll forty, tightly packed cigarettes that he'd stash, soldier row style, in his worn leather wallet. Before sliding his bulging case into his shirt pocket, he'd light the last cig he'd assembled, run his hand across his long forehead all the way around to the nape of his neck, and say, "There's a few things I've got left to do downstairs." Then, as always, his wife would respond, as she always did: "don't stay down there too late, dear."

Urbin, fingernails raking his increasingly visible scalp, would sidle away from the dinner table and skitter back downstairs to the oak counters oozing tangy, intermingling smells of blood, fat, and flesh. The man had grown up in this place and every part of it fanned his passion. The dainty ding of the bell acknowledging each customer, the way December's orange sunbeams peeked in under the awning late in the afternoon, the heavy scale on the counter that the Montreal Meat Distributors had awarded his father back when he was still just a kid. But, most of all, Urbin loved the large poster pinned to the wall—up there, above the new sausage rack—a colourful illustration of a cow and pig, the geography of their bodies mapped out identifying the various cuts they would yield.

Alone, downstairs in the shop, he ensured meat platters sat on freshly chipped ice, swept up bloody sawdust, and prepared checks to pay for the next day's deliveries. In the back, knife edges were honed, saws and cleavers cleaned, and soiled aprons dropped into the wash bin. Taking care of his father's business was *his* business. Soon, he would inherit it all. One day. Too soon, he feared. Then, the plan had always been, he'd continue to grow the business and, in turn, leave it all to his son, his firstborn, Siméon. One day.

Lately, though Urbin still found his way downstairs after supper, the satisfaction of wandering alone through the shop had dissolved. Life had taken a turn, mangled by destiny's other plans.

-2-

Urbin grabbed a chair that customers—those too old to stand at the counter—used whenever the shop was crowded or when hot summer days caused the air inside to nauseate even the sturdiest of carnivores. That's where he spent many of his evenings now, slumped on that chair, arms crossed over his thighs, looking up at his father's photograph hanging on the nail where the calendar used to be. The old man was gone along with his two grandsons, all of them victims of the St. Lawrence River. That picture, displayed out of reverence for the founder of the *Boucherie Salaison Charpentier*, was a shroud over the business, a daily reminder that a slow parade of yesterdays had passed and that his future had been obliterated.

Time—almost five years since that awful event—hadn't lightened Urbin's bleakness, or done anything to lessen the burden of the calamity. Orance, his youngest and only surviving son, had never displayed the type of passion his brothers felt for the business - had never fully appreciated the privilege of what it meant to be a butcher. Still, Urbin moved forward, methodically. Responsibly. Ensuring his wife and children were taken care of, though the fire that had once burned inside him had been doused. These days, when Urbin escaped downstairs, he mostly looked forward to the Black

Horse Lager he drank while reading the paper, draping himself over the tin-topped meat wrapping counter in the back, away from his father's gaze. That old sepia tone face staring down. Watching. Judging.

-3-

Montreal, March 1891

Wintertime Sundays were special to the Charpentier men. From December till late March, Urbin, his father Josime, and all three of his sons—Siméon, Charles and Orance—walked on water. Together, in their windowless shanty, tin roof tiles letting the West wind whistle its way in, they'd feed the little potbelly stove 'till the pipe turned red. Stomping their feet, blowing warmth through their fingers, they watched Urbin bore five new holes letting some of the St. Lawrence splash in as the auger spun through.

They arrived on the ice long before the Montreal lights had turned off and didn't return till well after they had lit up the city's shore. Some years, when the North wind blew in the freeze sooner than expected, the season could start as early as mid-December and last all the way till the big ice flows cracked and heaved along the Victoria Bridge piers in April. Generations of Charpentier men had staked out their space on the river. The best spot in the basin, right off Britannia Street, inside the protective jetty across from Griffintown. Regulars, some of whom spent time on the ice every day, called this area *The Flats*, the term used by most to refer to the area's stability and absence of large fissures. Each trip to the river required a heaping load of firewood and a jug full of Urbin's homemade Caribou to fuel their spirits.

The winter had been ferocious and the boys had pulled some impressive specimens from beneath the thirty inches of ice. The cold never let up that year extending through the season until late into spring, drawing huge crowds of anglers on the river. But this would be the last Sunday of the season, and

like every season's end, Urbin's father had planned to cel-
ebrate winter's death by doing a bit of fishing, a lot of shack
dismantling and a copious amount of drinking.

"That's it, boys, that's all the ice there is between us and
the St. Lawrence," Urbin said pulling the auger from the
water on what looked to become a sunny day.

"That can't be more than six inches thick, pops," Siméon
replied, looking down into the hole and taking the auger away
from his father.

The shack still kept the boys sheltered from the wind but
did little to keep them warm since the stove had been hauled
away two Sundays before. Soon after sunup, neighbours from
The Flats had been dropping by, saying their goodbyes for
the season and sharing spirits from their respective jugs.
Some offered gin, some had rum, but most offered swigs
from their personal supply of homemade apple cider. The
Charpentier boys always returned the kindness, travelling
from shack to shanty, swapping fishing stories and some of
their famous Caribou.

Orance, still too young for the drink—at least too young
to get drunk—restless from the absence of fishing and an
overabundance of chatting, took off in search of like-minded
friends. Soon after lunch, the Charpentier men were scattered
all over *The Flats,* helping others dismantle their huts, drinking, and making merry.

The sun's arc had travelled well beyond Nuns Island by
the time Siméon returned to the shanty, drunkenly singing an
aria from *Les Troyens* as he started to dismantle it. Charles
and his grandfather, Josime, soon joined him and, before
long, much of what used to be their shelter was nothing more
than old boards and corrugated steel piled high on a sled.

"Whoa, where's the boy?" Josime asked, referring to
Orance, his youngest grandson.

"With his friends, I guess ... still fishing," his father said,
returning from his many social calls. "You know he's always
the last one to leave, anyway. You'll see, he'll show up when

he sees the shack's gone."

"*Saint Sacrifice*, the boy should be here, with us, helping. He's twice the size you were at his age. A big boy like that should be doing his part. He's too old to be playing around all the time," Josime said, though no one listened.

Urbin, knee pressed on sheets of corrugated steel, pulled a knot and locked the pile of stuff that used to be their shanty onto the sled. Arm outstretched, shielding his eyes against the waning light as if pushing away the western sun, he turned to his father.

"It *is* getting late, though. Any of you see him?" He asked, looking at each of them in turn.

"The boy shoo … should be here … shoo be helping out. We've been here all day," Josime replied, his unfocussed eyes seeming to float in oil.

"Go look for your brother," Urbin told Siméon and Charles while pulling the ropes, further strangling the boards and tin. The boys, trying hard to camouflage the effects of the liquor they had binged, set off, each in different directions, yelling Orance's name, their long shadows sliding along the snow behind them. Josime and his son, piling whatever else was left onto the sled, watched squinting as the boys disappeared into the brightness.

"I might as well go look for him, too. You stay here," Urbin said, handing off a length of rope to his father. "Just finish tying this up so we're ready to go when we get back," he added, placing his hand on his father's shoulder and leaning forward to look closely into his red and yellow eyes.

-4-

Everyone along the *Flats* knew to never venture beyond the pier guard. The currents there were treacherous; strong enough to cause huge ice packs to conglomerate and churn against the jetty's large stones. The idea that anyone, let alone a boy like Orance, would consider climbing the pier was ridiculous to the point that no one even considered glancing in that direction.

Josime sat on the weathered boards, legs astride a neatly entwined mound of what used to be his shelter. Slurring, he entertained himself by humming a ditty old man Seguin planted in his brain during his visit earlier that day, trying as best he could to stay alert and finish tightening the last few knots that held everything together. *Come on man, you can do this*, he thought. *Just one rope left to tie* and yanked at the braided hemp with both hands. Overly confident, he lost his grip when his frozen leather mitts slipped while pulling the cord. Too weak (sloshed) to resist the push from his legs, he fell backwards and cracked his head on the ice.

His pickled brain abruptly shut down. Lying on the snow, face turned into the hood of his parka, he dozed till afternoon rays dissolved into starlight. Eyes closed, mumbling, the chord of his son and grandsons calling out Orance's name eventually seeped into his mind. But those voices, distant and syncopated, soon lost their meaning and morphed into a long, beautiful tone. In time, the voices faded into nothing. Josime was alone, unconscious.

The growl and quake of ice sheets colliding and fracturing in a distance popped in and out of Josime's awareness and provided the soundtrack to his inebriated dreams. Snow, surfing along the glacial veneer, collected along his cheek and filled the back of his hood. Then, faint and distant, somewhat familiar, as if propelled along with the multitude of crystals skating along the ice, another sound caught his attention. High pitched. Barely noticeable, but real. A voice. A familiar voice.

-5-

Josime forced his frozen eyelids open and stared at the inside of his hood. A rivulet of frozen drool that had clung to his whiskers cracked and peeled off when he swallowed the melted snow that had collected in his mouth. The old man, his insides marinated in Caribou and cider, rolled over and faced the black sky. Propped up on his elbows, he listened for the sound to come again, his head winding into the wind. He scoped the landscape, eyes creased into tiny slivers. "Urbin," he instinctively said his son's name then called for his grandsons. "Help!" He yelped. "Urbin … Urbin." He cried into the howl of drifting snow. Had the voice been a sonic mirage, he wondered? He pushed himself off the snow, his head swivelling like a snowy owl. *Had the voice been real?* He turned to face south, his back to the city, his face sticking out from his hood, and looked at where the voice had seemed to come from. Out there, beyond the jetty.

He leaned into the wind, pushed the hood off his head, and removed his wool tuque. His ears instantly turned red. Swaying in the wind, the blowing snow sticking to his face, he struggled to remain conscious. "Orance!" He yelled; his scruffy voice unable to push through the dense wind. His knees buckled. He sat on the heels of his boots, trying to stay awake long enough to hear the voice again but dropped to his side. There, his bare head lying on the snow and ice, the voice broke through. The boy *had* gone to the other side of the jetty.

A surge of adrenaline galloped through Josime's veins from his toes to his brain, clearing his mind and energizing his boozed-up body. He took a few steps south, stopped and hollered, hands cupped on either side of his mouth, "Orance... Orance," before stumbling (he thought he was running) toward the stone jetty, his feet sinking into the snow.

-6-

There had always been an argument amongst the Charpentier boys as to where the ideal spot was to set up their ice fishing shack. Should they return to their ancestral spot or, was it best to establish their site close to the jetty where some fish liked to peck and pick at the stones? Maybe the best idea was to stay in the middle somewhere between the pier guard and the shore where the river ran deep and large fish roamed the depths. For some reason, from a remote corner of Josime's mind—lungs on fire, leg muscles melting like hot wax—he conjured this thought. This reminiscence. Why? Why now? He couldn't fathom.

"Urbin!" He yelled, his voice barely disturbing the snowflakes colliding with his breath. Alone, the old man started to climb the large granite boulders stacked and piled along the northern edge of the jetty's road, large stones twinkling in the moonlight. Exhausted, moaning and coughing, he crawled and gripped the searing cold rocks, the leather patches sewed to the knees of his trousers providing barely enough grip to keep him from sliding off. He reached the pier's crest, stood, and felt his eyeballs beating to the pulse of his racing heartbeat. He tilted his head back, took in a deep breath, and as the sound of his grandson's name passed his lips, a torrent of whatever liquor remained in his stomach spewed out. Bent over, he scanned boulders along the south side and screamed Orance's name at breaking waves heaving large chunks of ice amongst a constant tumult of slushy, black water."Dad," Josime heard his son's faint voice. "Dad … we're coming," Urbin, said.

I can't find Orance, can't find the boy, the grandfather, lungs aflame, muttered to himself.

"Heeeey," the high-pitched sound of Orance's voice broke through the wind and thunder of waves slapping at the ragged shore.

"Orance! Where are you?" Josime asked, repeating his grandson's name while heading closer to the shore down along the glazed rocks. Looking out into darkness, he placed his foot on the downslope of a large ice chunk jammed amongst boulders and slipped. The thud of his hip as it smashed on a pointy slab reminded him of the sound pigs' legs made when pulled out of their sockets before he sliced them off. The pain numbed his leg all the way to his foot. He continued toward the river, sliding on his hands and butt, eyes darting along the shoreline. Having nearly reached the water, he paused and listened, hoping his grandson's voice would cut through again.

"Aaaaaaah," he heard, the sound clear but faint.

"Orance," Josime answered, facing in the direction of the voice. "Where are you?" The old man sat, hands cupped on either side of his head like ear trumpets, his blue lips quivering.

Seconds passed with nothing but slushy water answering his call. Josime felt the air petrify his lungs; hope had drained from his body, the void leaving just the space for a thought to plant itself in his mind. Soon, as the waves lapped at his heels, his son, Urbin, would come running down the north side of the jetty and he'd have to explain how he failed at finding his grandson in the water.

-7-

Urbin dashed in all directions, spit flying as he bellowed his son's name at the skysill; Siméon and Charles tracing awkward orbits around him in the snow. Looking south past the jetty's shadow, he imagined—thought he could feel—ice water filling his youngest son's lungs and pinning him to the river's bottom. He stomped about, shook his head and called his boy's name but the ugly vision overwhelmed his mind. The thought of Orance trying to beat away the water—his clothing imbibed and heavy, the weight dragging his nostrils below the surface—fuelled his panic and filled his shoes with lead.

He heard Charles calling Orance's name, and, just then, an old story—a happy story—about a girl who had fallen through the ice during the spring thaw percolated through his despair. Kate was her name. She had spent nearly thirty minutes under before being revived after a man squeezed the water out from inside her ribcage. Then, just like that, another reminiscence suddenly burst through his glumness. "The Irish Setter," Urbin whispered to himself. *Why not, this could be like the Irish Setter*, he thought, that old dog that had gone missing on *The Flats* a couple of years ago before being found, hours later, clinging to the edge of a fishing hole, fat paws scraping and clinging to the ice. Hope had found a way into Urbin's soul. That's when he heard his father's voice coming from the jetty.

The old man had seen Orance. The boy had gone where he shouldn't have, beyond the rocks to the south side of the pier guard. "Your grandpa's found him. Follow me, he's at the jetty," Urbin hollered at Siméon and Charles. The three of them headed in the direction of Josime's voice; Siméon and Charles blowing by their father. Siméon was first to cross over the jetty.

"See him?" Charles asked, seconds before joining his brother.

"Not sure if this is where dad saw grandpa," Siméon said. "Is this where grandpa was when you saw him?" He asked, as his father joined his sons atop a pile of rocks and gritty lumps of ice.

"Pretty sure," Urbin said, his teeth sore from the gulps of cold air he was sucking in. "Dad! Where are you, dad?" Urbin called; his words aimed at the shore.

"Quiet for a second. Listen," Urbin ordered, waving his left arm and pushing at his sons' chests. They stood silently, looking down at the shore, at the stones, at the waves.

"Hep," the sound, faint and weak, barely reached them.

"D'you hear that? Did you?" Charles asked, all three heads aimed at the voice that came from below.

"Orance!" The brothers yelled.

"Orance! Dad!" Urbin joined in.

"Hep." The voice had come through clearly.

"There. There he is," Siméon screamed as he pointed to his left while all three men hopped and bounced from rock to rock down to the water's edge.

The boy was amongst the rocks, lying on his side, his legs in the water, his right cheek grinding on a slab of ice. His body trembled as if charged by an electrical current. His wool coat and cotton corduroy pants were drenched, the boot and sock covering his left foot, gone. The skin on his face and hands was nearly translucent; the path of each vein under his forehead and temple ghosting sinuous blue lines under the moonlight. Seeing his youngest son inches from death, his pale face gleaming against the blackness of the rocks, black eyes opened wide and fixed, reminded Urbin of the walleye he had pulled from the water just a few hours earlier. "Take your coats off," he told his sons as he hastily removed his. "Son," he said, clutching Orance's shoulders while Charles stuffed his dad's balled up coat under his brother's head. "You'll be all right, son," he tried to reassure Orance, the words sounding insincere to his own ears. "This is no good. He can't just lie here. Take his clothes off, he's going to freeze to death," Urbin ordered.

"Where's grandpa?" Siméon asked, arms wrapped around Orance in a bear hug while Charles tried to peel his brother's pants off, his long legs dangling like ropes. "Grandpa! Grandpa!" Charles yelled, wrestling Orance's pant leg over his one remaining boot.

"Unlace it, just take it off," Siméon told his brother who was struggling to hold Orance against himself, shifting the weight of his limp body as it slid down his chest.

"I'm doing my best here. I can't even feel my dratted fingers."

"Pull, pull it off his foot."

Charles yanked at Orance's boot, one hand behind the heel, his other braced against his calf but the tightly knotted leather lace, bound and frozen, kept it firmly in place.

"Pull. Come on, pull harder... get it off," Siméon shouted

over and over.

Charles, crying and groaning, pulled till the corduroy tore into strips. The sudden release caused Siméon to lose his grip and for Orance to fall on his back. A stream of blood, dark against his cheek, trickled off Orance's face and pooled onto the ice. Urbin, who had been running along the river's edge in search of his father, returned and saw his youngest boy, unconscious, lying on the rocks, remnants of his pants down to his ankles.

"What in blazes are you doing? Never mind his darned boot, just take off his coat and shirt and we'll wrap'em in ours. Quick! Quick!" Urbin's raspy voice trembled. "You two take care of him and I'll keep looking for your grandpa," he added, heading off along the edge of the waves, sloshing granular swells of liquid ice along the rocks. "Dad," Urbin yelled at the river, each call blasting a thick cloud of mist from his lips. Peering into the nothingness, eyes creased like tiny gashes, he looked for a reflection, a white face, a hand … something amidst the mass of sugary ice floes. "Dad. Can you hear me, dad?" His voice cracking, jumping from rock to rock eastward along the current, shivering, wind boring through his ears.

"Over here! Quick! Grandpa's over here," Siméon yelled, pointing at the body floating fifteen to twenty feet offshore.

-9-

Dark images inside Josime's stewed brain nearly convinced him he wouldn't find his grandson; that he had failed at saving the boy's life. Sitting on the edge of the jetty—slow-moving waves rhythmically heaving a coarse batter of wet snow at his boots—Josime's thoughts were as black as the horizon. "Orance," he called, unconvincingly, his voice held back by the force of a stiff northern wind.

"Haaaaalp," the noise, dim and distant, seemed to have materialized itself directly between Josime's ears.

"Boy. Where are you, boy?" Josime cried, lifting himself off the rocks, his left knee flexing to the sound of pops and creaks. "Where are you?" He repeated, burning off the last vestiges of adrenaline left in his bloodstream. He stood. Quiet. Concentrated. Focused. Hands braced along the small of his back. A brief reflection bouncing off Orance's face found Josime's eye. There he was, nearly thirty feet from shore, his chin hooked over the edge of a frozen plate, arm cradling the ice and feebly motioning for help with the other.

"I see you, boy," Josime tried to yell, the sonic strength of his voice barely making it past the white puff of breath that had risen over his face. Without removing his boots or coat, he stepped off the rocks and into the river, trying to maintain his footing while probing underfoot— fully expecting to sink down to his waist before heading into the deep. He sank. His feet hit bottom, weighed down by his soaked clothes. He coiled his legs and thrust himself to the surface, taking a deep breath as soon as his mouth peaked above water. Lungs inflated, he frantically removed his coat, floating, his face submerged. He thrashed around, elbows and shoulders banging into lumps of ice bobbing on all sides. With both arms, he wrapped himself around a huge piece of ice; the searing chill of the makeshift buoy against the linen of his shirt radiating through his chest and hardened his lungs. He kicked his heavy leather boots and pointed himself at Orance. "Hold on," he called, swallowing a few gulps of water and a half dozen pea-sized shards of ice in the process. Orance, floating in a distance, didn't respond.

Josime hardly moved, his weak legs doing little to propel him through the muck of slush. "Hang on, boy," he whispered then coughed, stymied and desperate. Pushed around by the waves, the eerie sound of ice sheets grinding at each other, he shuddered at the thought, *Cling to the ice flows, freeze, and drown. Or, let go and manoeuvre yourself toward the boy.* He squeezed his eyes shut, moaned, and released his right hand from his makeshift lifesaver. Fumbling, he slapped at the water, feeling his way through, grabbing at large lumps of ice as they drifted by. Slowly, he moved forward along the flows till he got close enough to hear Orance's voice. The boy was muttering something, sounding almost as if he were humming.

Josime had nearly reached his grandson when his left shoulder and arm locked; spasmic pain had short-circuited his muscles. He felt his jawbone crack, his teeth mashing at each other, his tongue slipping back into his throat. "Orance," he managed to grunt. "I've ... I've got ... got you, boy," he managed to say before his forehead dipped below the slush.

Orance, barely fifteen feet away, mouthed the words, *grandpa, grandpa*, till the old man disappeared. The boy fought the current and looked out into the river to see if the old man would surface, but the flow of ice had sucked him in. Pain pulsed through every cell in Orance's body, his swollen joints seeming to tear with each movement, a cold vice crimping the nape of his neck had turned his lungs to stone.

The boy's cheek sat on the flat part of his ice raft and his toe dragged along a rock. Instinctively, he kicked his feet till his heel connected with the sharp edges of submerged granite. He saw the shore, the pain rising from his frozen feet no match for the sudden burst of hope that had revived him. The current nudged him in closer and his knee bumped into a submerged rock. Finding purchase, he lunged forward and latched onto whatever seemed connected to the shore before rolling himself out from the St. Lawrence. Crawling, calling to his grandfather, the pain of the searing cold lifted, and he slipped into unconsciousness.

-10-

"You see him? Right there ... I saw him. I'm sure it was him," Siméon told his brother, poking furiously at the spot where he thought he'd seen his grandfather. "Stay with

Orance, I'll go get grampa."

"I'm going, too. I can't let you go out there on your own," Charles said. "Dad'll be back soon. Anyway, Orance is all bundled-up … he'll be okay," he added, both of them pulling their boots off before bouncing along the jetty's jagged stones and stepping into the water.

Urbin raced along the water's edge, working hard at nurturing thoughts of his father having been rescued. "Dad!" He hollered, breathless, the wind slicing through him. Surrounded by silence, he slapped at his thighs. Gathering clouds had dampened the moon's brightness and nearly caused him to step on Orance; the boy wrapped in two dark navy coats, his head on Urbin's wool jacket, nearly invisible lying amongst the stones. "Where's your brothers?" He asked, kneeling next to his unconscious boy. Shaking—nearly vibrating—he lifted his son's head, removed the coat that had served as a pillow, and used it to cover the boy's feet.

"Dad. Charles. Siméon," Urbin shouted at the horizon, Orance held tightly to his chest. After an eternity of seconds, of nothing but the sound of mushy waves brushing against the rocks, he dropped to his knees, his boy in his lap. "I'm sorry," he whispered, turning away and climbing up the jetty on his way back to *The Flats*.

His energy nearly consumed, Urbin walked up and over the jetty. Along *The Flats*, feet crunching into the snow, the weight of Orance having set his shoulders and biceps on fire, he trudged toward the faint lights of Griffintown. Along the way, he paused to glance back and cursed at the sky. Eroded by the cold, frittered by the wind, he kept moving.

-11-

Some of the Charpentier's ice fishing buddies, though thoroughly inebriated, realized the boys hadn't returned from the river. By sundown, an impromptu search party had assembled to roam through *The Flats*. Regis Bouthillier, icicles hanging off the tips of his long mustache, was the first to spot Urbin and Orance. Urbin had collapsed no more than fifty yards from where his father had left the sled loaded with what used to be their shanty. "Over here," Regis called to his buddies, orange embers flying off his torch dancing in the darkness. "Urbin? Are you with me, Urbin?" Regis asked, patting his friend's chest. Soon, a group of men arrived at the scene. They knocked the shanty's remains off the sled and lay Urbin and Orance on a pile of blankets that some of the guys had brought.

-12-

Urbin opened his eyes, looked up at his wife, at his daughters, and scanned every corner of his hospital room. "Dad?" He asked, his voice no louder than a whisper. "Siméon... Charles?" Uriette kissed his forehead, her tears dripping onto her husband's temples. He closed his eyes when Dahlia started bawling and turned his bandaged head into the pillow, unaware his right ear, along with four of his toes, had been amputated. "Orance?" He asked, looking out the window.

"Doctor said he'll be fine ... a miracle, they said." Urbin looked at his daughters, doing his best to smile with his eyes while in his gut, a strange kind of anger boiled. A kind of anger he knew nothing about. His youngest boy had ruined his life; ended his father's life. Two of his sons were somewhere at the bottom of the St. Lawrence. Urbin imagined them drifting in the cold water, wishing he was with them. He believed—he'd always believe—that Orance should feel the same way.

Chapter 4

-1-

July 1896

Walking through the large doors at the main entrance of Sohmer Park, Eugénie thought she could pass for Élisabeth Rousset, the *Boule de Suif* heroine from her favourite Guy de Maupassant novel. She and Orance mingled with the large crowd, everyone anticipating famed baritone Victor Occellier's entrance as the orchestra performed Viennese waltzes. Eugénie watched others dance, twirling on the grass, as Orance steered her toward the grandstand. She sat, hands on her umbrella's handle, hoping Orance would ask though he shifted from cheek to cheek, occasionally reaching into his breast pocket and sipping from his flask.

"Isn't that a beautiful sight?" Eugénie asked. "It's like they're all part of the same movement."

"The dancing? Uh, yeah. Yes, it's something to see, for sure it is."

"They look like they're floating on dew."

"Oh yeah, looks pretty good."

"It just seems like such a pleasant thing, on such a beautiful Sunday. Don't you think?"

"Thank goodness it's not raining, is all I can say," Orance said, reaching into his jacket. "Want a sip?" He asked, dangling his flask. "Caribou. Really good stuff. My dad's own recipe."

"I'm fairly certain a lady wouldn't drink Caribou, especially not from a flask," Eugénie replied, looking at the dancers.

"Of course not. It's just that there's no place to buy spirits here so, I thought it might be a good idea to bring my own, you know, for the both of us."

"Thank you. That's thoughtful, I suppose," Eugénie said, turning to face Orance. "I try to act the way my mother did. There's more to being a lady than what, I think, you understand," she added, looking back at the field and admiring the twirling couples hovering above the grass.

Orance wiped his lips and stuffed his flask back into his jacket, smiling while pondering the right words. "I'll be right back, I have to go to the privy pit," he said and bolted. Eugénie watched him push his way through the crowd, hand on his breast pocket as he disappeared amongst the people.

-2-

Out of sight under the grandstand, Orance properly greased the wheels of his personality. The medicine would soon take full effect and the young man would regroup. Meandering along the kiosks he glanced at trinkets for sale and the many hats and scarves on display. He studied the men, thumbs confidently hooked under the armholes of their waistcoats, doubtless and in control. Others, some as young as he, strolled happily, arm in arm with their beloved, seeming to enjoy the moment.

Dizzy and a bit nauseous, he plopped himself next to a couple sitting on a bench facing the perimeter of the dance area. "Beautiful day," he said, and scooched away down the pine when the lady he had intruded upon glared at him. Looking down at his lap, he reached into his jacket's other breast pocket and pulled out a cameo brooch. He stared at it, gently rubbing the contours of the lady's profile while reflecting upon the proper way of offering such a gift.

Careful not to trip, he made his way up the grandstand and took his seat next to Eugénie. "I thought you'd left," she said, focused on the spectacle below.

"I wouldn't leave you here all alone. Besides, if I'd left, I wouldn't be here to give you this," he said, slowly unfolding his handkerchief.

"I see you've had your fill of Caribou; you smell like a—"

"Never mind, look, I have something for you," Orance said, nodding down at his handkerchief. He smiled when Eugénie blushed at the sight of the intricately carved profile of a woman's face set against a rose background.

"That's so beautiful. How did you get this? How can you afford this?"

"It's my mother's. She gave it to me … to give to you. It used to belong to my grandmother. I always thought it was really nice."

"No. I'm sorry, I can't accept this. It was your grand-mother's. Your grandfather probably gave it to her. I couldn't possibly—"

"No, It's all right. Both my mother and father thought I should give it to you as a keepsake. A memento. Something for you to remember this day, especially since it hasn't been all that I'd hoped it might be for you. You know. I'm sure you've noticed that I've some trouble with … yunno."

"It's beautiful. I'll pin it to my lapel, it'll be perfect with this dress," she said, taking a deep breath.

The young couple sat, listening and watching, the music continuing till five. Eugénie tried as best she could not to touch the brooch, to remain stoic but, every few minutes, she'd look down till her chin brushed her collarbone. As they walked out through the large doors, Eugénie smiled a little smile. When he let her off at her uncle's house—on time— she looked directly into his eyes and caressed the brooch.

-3-

Days past and time spent seeing each other at the butcher shop seemed to transform Orance into a normal young man. Almost. On some days, especially when his father wasn't around to holler and pound at the boy, he seemed more relaxed. Comfortable. Almost.

Everyone at the shop had seen how Urbin would come down hard on his boy. Slapping him, cursing and kicking the backs of his legs. Whenever one of these furious encounters took place on the shop floor, Eugénie looked to Marc for help, hoping her uncle would do something to defuse the situation. No use, Urbin never let up. *Speak up*, Urbin had become accustomed to saying whenever Marc dared to comment about the violence. Then he'd raise his hand up to his missing ear, and with the other, point at his son and add: *can't hear you. Know why? 'Cause of that son of mine.*

-4-

"Can't wait to speak into the telephone. Next Wednesday, right?" Eugénie asked Monsieur Charpentier as he walked into the shop.

"Who told you about that?" Monsieur Charpentier asked, staring at Marc busy wrapping a load of pig's feet for Madame Daoust.

"Uh, Orance," Eugénie answered, lifting her hand to draw Monsieur Charpentier's attention away from her uncle. "He told me you're planning a big day. That you're going to invite clients to come in and try it … preparing a new sign for outside to let people know about how they'll be able to talk to us through the telephone … to order things on the teleph—"

"That boy of mine should learn to shut up. Where is he? In the back?"

"I s'pose. Not sure," Eugénie hesitated before answering, looking at her uncle and fussing with her hair.

Urbin took off toward the back, his limp seemingly worse than usual; boots crackling as they pulverized blood-soaked wood chips underfoot. Eugénie barely managed to get out of his way and skittered behind her register, looking back at his long, greying hair flopping around where his ear used to be. His bulging eyes, like grey soap bubbles about to burst, seemed on the verge of popping out of his face as he stoked his inner embers. Eugénie, instantly regretting having mentioned something she had assumed harmless, felt her heart climbing up her throat as she stood frozen behind her register.

"Get over here, boy. Orance, where are you? Get over here," Urbin said, crossing through the swinging door, the back of his head visible through the porthole. "Didn't I tell you to keep things to yourself? To keep our business private?" His voice spilled out onto the shop's floor.

Orance faced his father and looked at the floor. "Yes," he whispered, wiping his hands along his drenched apron, his forehead creased. "Is there a problem?"

"A problem? *Saint Sacrifice!*" Urbin tilted his head and repeated, sarcastically mimicking his son's nervous pitch. "Yeah, it's a problem if you're gonna talk about the telephone. Or, maybe that you don't even know I'm not getting the installation done till Thursday after next. Won't be hooked up till then. Did you tell anybody else about this? Is anybody else coming by next Wednesday expecting to see a telephone?"

"No. No, sir. I only told Eugénie 'cause I thought Marc would've told her, anyway."

"That's not your business, boy," Urbin said, clutching his son's lapel, a fat finger aimed inches from his boy's nose.

"Sorry," Orance said, leaning back, eyes crossed and staring down the barrel of his father's digit.

Eugénie leaned back, shoulders against the swinging door hoping to muffle the yelling.

"I think you might like the new sausage, Madame Daoust … we case 'em right here … all pork," Marc said.

"I'm sure," Madame Daoust replied, leaning sideways to glance through the swinging door's small, round window.

"How 'bout you, Madame Gendron, did your husband like the blood pudding?"

"*Oh, oui mon cher Monsieur.* Certainly did," the shopper replied as she scurried out.

Loud footsteps drew near and Eugénie stepped aside just as Monsieur Charpentier burst through the swinging door, smoothing his hair to cover the cavity where his ear used to be.

"Come now, let's get sorted here. We've got customers to serve," said Monsieur Charpentier, leaning into Eugénie. "And how are you Madame Daoust? Did you try our new sausage? We case 'em right—"

"The young lady already told me all about it," the customer replied, pointing at Eugénie, her timid smile at odds with her fearful expression.

Urbin shuffled back and forth between the salted meats table and the peameal bacon display, his limp carving a peculiar trail in the sawdust. "Where's he going?" He asked Eugénie, pointing at the swinging door that Marc had just walked through.

"I think he's getting rabbits down in the cellar," she replied stiffly and without hesitation.

"Tell him I need help at the loading dock … got beef carcasses to bring in."

"Uh, yes sir," she replied, nodding at Urbin as he walked past her on his way to the back.

"I'll send that son of mine to help out here till your uncle gets back."

"Thank you," Eugénie said to the still flapping door, looking away, and straightening her hair.

-5-

Orance slowly oozed out the swinging door, eyes fixed on the floor while retightening his apron strings. Eugénie stood shifting from foot to foot, wishing the suddenly empty shop was full of customers.

"My father said you needed help out here till your uncle comes back."

"Well, I *am* alone and I do have to take care of the register but, as you can see, the place's empty. I'll call if I need help."

"No, I better stay here. My father expects me to be out here, so I better stay. Anyway, you heard him. You know what he's like."

Eugénie started to say something, thinking she'd explain all about how she hadn't really heard anything but couldn't find an elegant way to manoeuvre around such a deception.

"My father can be pretty rough, sometimes. A lot of the time, come to think of it."

Eugénie glanced at Orance, then quickly refocused on the register. "Well, I'm sure he appreciates you. The work you do, here at the shop," she said, rubbing her left elbow.

"I suppose. But I've got to admit that it gets pretty intense sometimes. Lately, though, I'm starting to worry that the old man's gonna lose control one of these days. I mean, really lose control... you know?" He said while reorganizing the pile of beef ribs on the table next to the window. "But what's been really scary to me lately is that, sometimes, I start thinking about what I might do, that I might lose *my* temper, too ... like losing control of myself. I know it's stupid but that's how it feels to me sometimes, like there's this other person that crawls up inside me and wants to do things I wouldn't do." He exhaled, looked out the store window and continued repositioning and restacking a mound of pigs' feet. Then, he stopped, turned and looked at Eugénie, staring directly into her eyes. "I know it all sounds pretty crazy, right? Besides, better to remind myself of how lucky I am. That I've got a good job. That I might even own my own shop one of these days."

"Well . . ." Eugénie replied, looking down at the register. "Maybe you have to be the bigger man sometimes and jus' walk away."

Orance snorted and smiled for a second. "I did walk away once, a couple of months ago. Outside, in the yard. He was yelling at me pretty good, his mouth must have been three inches from my face, so I turned away. He started to yell at me even louder: *'Don't turn your back to me,'* he said. So, I stopped and stood there, my back turned to him. He hit me with a stick or something. Hit my neck ... knocked me to the ground. I stayed there for I don't know how long. He left me there. In the yard, in the snow. When I came to, I thought I was going to puke. My shoulder, my left shoulder, the one I must have fell on, hurt even more than my neck."

Eugénie's eyes were round and moist, her lips pinched together tightly as grim images flashed in her brain. She looked up from the register. Orance stared at the beef ribs in his hand, a single tear laying a track along his cheekbones before landing in the bloody sawdust. "I don't know what's worse sometimes: to have your father hurt you, or thinking about revenge? About defending yourself ... hurting your own father?"

Eugénie's mind swirled. The top of her scalp tingled as if her own thoughts were trying to escape. "You think about that? Often?"

Orance paused and, as if waking from a nap, lifted his chin, wiped his face and asked, "What? Think about what?"

"Hurting your father. About him hurting you ... about what you've just said."

"I try not to. Most times, when it gets really hard, I'll have a sip from my flask."

"That helps?"

"Doesn't hurt. It's all I've got, really," he answered, chortling.

Eugénie took a deep breath and considered saying: *I'm here for you*, or *You're not alone*. Instead, she swallowed hard and looked down at the register, imagining the sound of her voice, the sound of those words filling the void.

-6-

Order your Meat Directly by Telephone, read the sign nestled between the pork and beef carcasses hanging just above the shop's window. All day, people came in, pressed the receiver to their ear, and waited for the switchboard operator's voice. "*Allô ... vous m'entendez*? Can you hear me?" Madame Lasonde hollered into the mouthpiece. For hours, customers took turns talking with a woman's disembodied voice, some lady, out there, somewhere in the ether.

Though few of the *Boucherie Salaison Charpentier* customers owned a telephone, Urbin believed in the new technology and how it would eventually catch on. How, one day, the cost of having to spend nearly thirty-five dollars each year for this type of gadget would—eventually—pay off. *One day, people from all over the neighbourhood are gonna call in their orders*, he'd say.

"Imagine this, my friends," Urbin said, while balancing atop a crate and holding on to the wall, receiver in hand. "You're in your kitchen preparing to cook your family's supper when, suddenly, you realize you're lacking in some necessity: a roast, sausages, or maybe even a fine cut of steak. Too busy to come all the way here? Well, all you need do is pick up your telephone's receiver, tell us what you need, and my boy here," he added, using the receiver to point at Seamus, who was leaning on the counter. "My boy, Seamus here, will hop on his bicycle and have it in your icebox before you know it. Wouldn't that be a miracle, folks?" Urbin pitched as effortlessly as any carnival barker.

The twenty or so people crammed in the shop applauded the prospect of living in a world of such cutting-edge technology. Urbin, lit up as he mixed and mingled with his clients, slapped backs, shook hands, and encouraged everyone to *get themselves one of these wonderful machines*.

"Where's Orance?" Urbin, surrounded by some of his most loyal patrons, asked Eugénie. "He missed the whole thing."

"I don't know, I didn't see him. I suppose he's still in the back. Maybe he's unloading a cart or something."

"Well, if you see him, tell him to come out here and see this," Urbin said, before returning to his customers.

Eugénie, eager to address a few words to the switchboard operator (by now, everyone knew her name was Azilda, all of them asking the same questions as soon as they were handed the mouthpiece: *Is this Azilda? Can you hear me? Azilda, I'm in a butcher shop on Hochelaga street*) looked sideways through the round window—from time to time—looking to see if Orance was back there. Marc, folding brown paper around a mound of ground pork, noticed Eugénie's contortions while keeping her place in line.

"What're you looking for?" Marc asked her from across the shop's floor.

"D'you see Orance?"

"Nope. He's probably in the back."

Eugénie, who stood three spots behind Madame Lasonde—the old lady hogged the telephone, talking louder and louder into the mouthpiece despite patrons tugging at her sleeve—looked at the round window, shook her head, and finally decided to abandon her place in line. She looked through the porthole before pushing the swinging door open. Alone in the back, the butcher block and counters free from the usual carcasses and bony discards, she opened the loading dock's large black door. As usual, the high-pitched squeaking noise of the counterweight dropping as the door slid open drew the attention of several neighbourhood dogs. Orance, whenever able to take a break, often escaped outside and watched as Seamus flung bones and meat scraps at local mutts. But, though dogs begged and yelped, Eugénie had nothing to offer them. The loading dock was empty.

She turned her back to the dogs and walked back in, tiptoeing, trying to avoid getting blood on her beloved Edwardian Oxford shoes, elbows tucked in safely away from the stained counters that lined either side of the narrow aisle. She had nearly cleared the bloodiest zone when, as she carefully pulled her dress up and away from the mess, the tip of her foot got jammed in the cellar's trap door. Monsieur Charpentier had always insisted that whoever went to the cellar ring the bell—the big, brass bell attached to the underside of the trap door—before pushing it up and climbing out. Whoever had opened the trap door had disregarded that rule.

Eugénie tripped and dropped on the trap door, slamming it shut to the sound of a loud clapping sound reverberating throughout the back. She lay on her side, stunned, her dress blood-stained. Spitting away wood chips that had gotten stuck to her lips, she felt the trap door push up against her ribs. "Wait … wait a minute," she said, pushing herself to her knees. "You're supposed to ring the bell before opening the door," she said, slamming the side of her balled-up fist onto it.

She stood and began stomping her heel on the door, the move causing more wood chips to fall off her dress. "S … sorry. I'm so sorry," Orance's muffled voice wafted up from under the floorboards. She stepped away and watched Orance's head slowly pop up as the door opened. He wore a pitiful look, eyes unfocussed, one hand holding the door over him, the other grasping a nearly empty bottle of his father's Caribou. "I'm … I'm really sorry. I didn't see you up t … there," he repeated.

"Didn't see me? How could you have seen me? You're in the cellar. The door was closed, of course, you couldn't see me," she said, looking down at her dress and brushing away more of the sawdust. "People are worried, looking for you and, as it turns out, you're getting drunk down in the cellar!" She said, as Orance smiled meekly, and chuckled.

"Come up here," she insisted. "Let's go outside. You need fresh air … you can't stay in the cellar all day."

Orance, clutching his bottle, reached for Eugénie's extended hand and, though he managed to maneuver himself through the hatch, his foot slipped off the top step and nearly pulled Eugénie down with him. Outside, sitting along the edge of the loading dock, Orance held on to his bottle with both hands, ranting about his father, about the telephone, about his deceased brothers.

"Maybe you should lie down here for a while. Jus' give me the Caribou and rest. You're in no position to see anyone right now," she said, reaching for his bottle.

"Leave me be ... let go my bottle, there's plenty left in there," he said, wrestling the bottle away from Eugénie, Caribou spilling on his chin when his hand sprung back as Eugénie lost her grip.

-7-

The sound of voices on the loading dock drew the usual suspects. Three or four mutts mooched around, crying and barking, hoping to snatch a primo delicacy. "Get outta here," Orance snarled at a beige and brown dog nipping at his boots, downing what remained in his bottle and kicking at the beggar's snout.

"Leave them alone. They did nothing to you, they jus' think you'll have treats for them," Eugénie warned Orance, slapping at his shoulder while trying to shoo the dogs away.

"Consarn you mongrels," he said, stomping at the air, leaning forward, and swinging his empty bottle at the dogs. "I'm not Seamus, get away from me," he slurred, eyelids heavy. With every flourish, the dogs would retreat and then regroup. One of the larger ones, likely the hungriest, moved in closer and barked. "I said, get away from me," he yelled, swinging his weapon at the rachitic dog. The impact made a ghastly thudding sound as the bottle's hard base connected right between the animal's eyes. The dog yelped, dropped to the ground and started to shake. Orance leaned forward to look at the unconscious wretch, slipped off the dock and fell on the dog. "Consarn all you God-forsaken hounds," he muttered, kicking and flailing at the other dogs congregating around the bizarre couple.

"Stop. What are you doing? Stop," Eugénie said, palms to her temples. "They didn't do anything. They're jus' gonna bite you. Stop being such an idiot."

"Mutts, they're all mutts," he said, smiling groggily. "Mutts. They don't do nothing. They're just beggars ... mutts is all they are," he repeated, staring up at the clouds, Caribou bottle still in hand while dogs bit and tugged at his blood-drenched apron. Eugénie ran inside and returned with Seamus in tow. Seamus looked down and saw Orance, stretched out on his side and swinging his bottle at dogs clawing and pulling at his clothes. Seamus shook his head, walked inside, grabbed bones and fat from the garbage bin and threw the mess of it in the alley, away from where Orance lay.

Eugénie watched as dogs growled at each other, competing for the few pieces of scattered food laying in the alley. Then, looking back at Orance sprawled all over the dead dog, a kind of quake rippled up her back. *'Was Orance any different from his father?'* She thought. *'Where would his violence end?'*

-8-

Seamus jumped off the dock and reached for Orance but had to stand back when the tosspot started kicking at his shins. "Get away. Leave me be," Orance said, his words gurgled in drool.

"I can't leave you here lying in the alley," Seamus persisted, offering his hand to his boss's last remaining son.

"Can you jus' get him up here," Eugénie said atop the loading dock, looking back in fear that Monsieur Charpentier would come looking for his son.

Seamus grabbed hold of Orance's wrists and dragged him off the dead dog. "Nah ... this is no good," Seamus said and shook his head at the sight of one of his frequent clients; a tame fellow with a black patch under his left eye. "What happened here? Did he fall on the dog?" He asked, his puzzled face looking up at Eugénie.

"Uh, no," Eugénie said, looking down the alley, arms folded over her chest.

"How did he end up on the dog? Why's he dead?" Seamus

asked, manhandling Orance up on the dock.

"The dog attacked him so—"

"That dog never attacked nobody. Never attacked me. You're saying this dog attacked Orance?" Seamus asked, breathless, struggling to push Orance over the steel edge of the loading dock's cement floor.

"Orance," Eugénie said, biting her thumb's fingernail. "The dog," she started over, hoping to reconstruct the scene. "The dog," she bent over and pointed at the dog. "It's the dog that attacked him. Orance jus' defended himself … with the bottle. He hit him with the bottle. Had no choice. Really, he didn't. It was more of an accident, I'd say."

"Get that mutt away from me," Orance repeated, slumped on the loading dock, his chin sunken into his chest.

Seamus looked up at Eugénie and scratched his chin. "Really? Defending himself?"

"Never mind, it's not important. Can you pull him back inside?" She asked Seamus, looking in through the large door.

"Don't leave me here," Orance said, his oily eyes looking up at Seamus.

"I won't, but I can't get you inside. Not alone, I can't. You're gonna have to get up if you want to come back in."

Seamus scrunched down low, put his arms around Orance's chest and helped him to his feet. "My Cabou. Where's my Carbou?" Orance garbled. "Need my Caribou … I'm not leaving without my Caribou."

Seamus managed to pin Orance against the door. "Stay here. Don't move, I'll get your bottle." Orance grabbed the bottle from Seamus's hand, brought it to his lips and, when a single drop landed on his tongue, threw the bottle at the dogs still milling near the dock.

"What're you doing?" Eugénie cried. "What's wrong with you?"

Seamus held onto Orance and aimed his limp body towards the opened door.

"Ok, I'm gonna let go of you. You all right? Can you walk

on your own?" Seamus asked.

"I know how to walk … no n-need to hold me … I'm not a b-baby," Orance said, pushing his elbows out, working to release himself from Seamus's hold.

Orance's knees folded and, seemingly invertebrate, dropped to the cement like a crumbling house of cards.

"Let's grab his arms and pull him in," Eugénie suggested.

"*Non, non, non. Bout d'viarge*," Monsieur Charpentier said, rubbing his forehead and shaking his head till a long strand of hair flopped over his cheek. "What in thunderation is going on out here?"

Eugénie let go of Orance's wrist as if realizing she had been holding onto a snake and stepped away. Seamus, still hanging on to Orance's forearm, looked at his boss and shrugged.

"No problems here sir. Looks like your son's had just a bit too much to drink, sir," Seamus said after finally letting go, scratching his shoulder and pointing down at Orance.

Urbin, his lower teeth pulling at his upper lip, looked down at his son and turned to Eugénie. Eugénie, bent slightly at the waist, looked down at Orance.

"Help me get him in," Urbin, frowning, told Seamus, smoothing his long strand of hair back over the side of his head.

They dragged Orance inside, his nose and chin scraping along the dock's cement floor and dropped him in the sawdust, face down, arms extended on either side of his body. "You're a fine one," Urbin said looking down at him. "A fine one, indeed. And to think I lost two fine boys at the bottom of that river."

"It was all an accident, Monsieur Charpentier. I'll take care of him … sober him up," Eugénie said. "Seamus will help me … right Seamus?" Seamus walked out, jumped off the dock, picked up the dead dog and walked down the alley.

"That's right, for the love of God, get him out of here. It's not exactly a good idea to have dead dogs lying next to a butcher shop's loading dock," Urbin said. "*Maudit vaurien*," he added, looking down at his comatose son. "A good-for-nothing bugger is all that boy is."

"He jus' had a bit too much to—"

"Never you mind, Eugénie. Go back in the shop, I'll take care of him." Urbin said, rubbing his sleeve across his nose. "And to think that the future of this whole business depends on ... on him," he added, nodding at his son and scraping his palm against the side of his neck.

Eugénie stepped over Orance and looked straight into Monsieur Charpentier's eyes. Fiddling with the buttons of her dress, she said, "You sure? Please, let me help. I can—"

"Please go to the shop. I'll take care of him."

-9-

Weeks passed and the mahogany box that Bell Canada called a *telephone* sat silent. Every morning, Urbin spoke to the switchboard operator asking her to call him back to ensure the machine really worked.

"So, Urbin, ever regret getting a telephone installed?" Marc asked his boss from behind the counter.

"You've got to look to the future. This is new to most everybody. I'm telling you, you'll see, sooner or later, that bell's gonna ring. Mark my words, that bell's gonna ring so much you'll curse the day we ever *got* a telephone."

It had taken nearly seven weeks—forty-seven days to be exact—when on a Friday morning, as the usual hubbub of customers milling and pacing back and forth along the length of the counter was disturbed by the unsolicited sound of a ringer. A clear and sudden noise.

"*Allô!*" Monsieur Charpentier said, his lips kissing the receiver.

"*Allô* ... is this the Boucherie Charpentier?" A woman asked at the other end of the line. An unknown voice from some unknown place.

"Yes ... yes, it's the Boucherie Charpentier. Can you hear me? Why did you call here?" Urbin replied, pointing at the telephone and looking sideways at Eugénie.

Eugénie, aware of the apparently momentous event unfolding, turned and pushed the swinging door open and called to her uncle. "*Mononcle* Marc! Someone's calling on the telephone." Marc, having heard the bell, was already running in, coughing and wiping his hands on his apron.

"Who's calling? Is it the switchboard operator calling back?" Marc asked.

"No. It jus' rang on its own. Someone's calling," Eugénie replied, her face aglow.

"Yes. Oh yes," Urbin said. "Could you speak a bit louder Madame Daoust, I didn't hear the last few words you said ... speak louder ... speak in the receiver. Oh ... OK. That's nice to hear. Call us anytime, dear. Thanks," he said, then delicately deposited the mouthpiece back on its cradle.

"So? Did she order something?" Marc asked, just before starting into another coughing fit.

"No. She just wanted to tell me she had a telephone. We're the only number she knew to call. That's something, I guess."

"For sure it is. You'll see, she'll call in an order later. At least now we know it works."

"Yeah, it works," Urbin repeated, rubbing the back of his neck and pondering the likelihood of having wasted thirty-five dollars; perfectly good money spent on a rich person's toy. "Well, that was exciting," Urbin added, looking out the window. "I suppose we should all get back to whatever we were doing before the bell rang ... we're running a business here."

"You all right?" Eugénie asked, walking toward her uncle, bent over, hacking and coughing. "Let me get you some water?"

Marc looked up, waved at his niece then walked his hands up his legs all the way to his waist till he had finally straightened out. Though his handkerchief covered most of his face, Eugénie recognized the smile in his eyes. The coughing fit over, Marc stuffed his hankie in his pocket and looked back at the assembled crowd, embarrassed. "Must be coming down with something, sorry about that." The words had barely slipped past his lips when he started to cough, again. Then, the coughing stopped, his eyes turned white and he started pawing at his chest.

"Uncle Marc … what's going on?" Eugénie asked, brow furrowed, panic draining the blood from her face as she lunged at her uncle.

"Sit down, man," Urbin said, reaching for the chair in the shop's corner.

"I'm fine," Marc managed to say, the words more coughed than spoken. "Stop … I'll be fine," he repeated, turning sideways and punching at his chest with the side of his fist.

He sat, and his coughing fit morphed into a dizzy spell. Drawing deep breaths, his left hand cupped over his knee, he tried to smile, to calm the atmosphere, his right-hand over his chest.

"Don't know what that was. My chest felt so tight … but I'm all right now … I'm OK."

Eugénie stood behind him and rubbed his shoulders.

"Whoa, whoa … you're making too much of this, my dear," Marc said, gently tapping his niece's knuckles. "Urbin's right. Let's get back to work."

Marc picked up the chair he had sat on and, on his way to placing it back in the corner where it belonged, dropped to the floor, his chest crashing on the chair he was carrying. Marc's heart had stopped beating before he hit the sawdust.

Chapter 5

-1-

September came and Eugénie remained at her post—the family's sole wage earner—her meagre earnings falling short of what was needed to house and feed four people. Months passed before Blanche could hold her tears in front of Ephrem, the boy still unable to process the loss of his father. The landlord had knocked at their door twice already looking to collect the rent money that Marc had always made a point to deliver personally.

"Look here, Madame Albert, you know I'm sorry for your loss, for sure I am. Your husband was a good man … always paid on time. But if you want to keep on living here, you're going to have to pay me in full. I need my money on the first of each month. Every month," Mr Emerson said, looking into the envelope Blanche had given him, sticking his chin into his neck and sighing at how the number of dollar bills fell short of the amount specified on the lease.

"Oh, we'll have it. For certain we will. Eugénie, my niece, she works very hard," Blanche said, the strings from her apron fluttering as she waved at Eugénie from behind her back. "My niece has a job and I've been busy looking for employment, too. Madame Castonguay, my neighbour across the street . . ." Blanche added, pointing past Mr Emerson to one of the doors across the street. "She told me they're looking for people at the gas works … you know, on Harbour Street."

Mr Emerson looked at his feet, his silence making the noise of his hands rubbing along the sides of his pants sound like sandpaper scraping wood. "That's all well and good, Madame Albert. But I'm going to need my rent. In full. Plus, all the money you already owe me. You have one month," he said, his pale grey eyes lasering through Blanche. "You'll have to face the facts," the man added, pointing at Blanche with the envelope. "Three females and an imbecile boy can't afford to live in a ground-floor apartment. Not on their own, they can't. I don't want to throw you out on the street but if you can't pay me then you leave me no choice. You have one month, not a day more ... and I'm being very generous at that."

Blanche thought of telling Mr Emerson: *You can count on me*, or *I'll have your rent money... you'll see*. But she stood there as if rooted into the floor, dwarfed by the mountain in her way. Eugénie, who had stood back in the hallway, looked over her aunt's shoulder and called to Mr Emerson. "Ephrem's not an imbecile. He jus' can't talk good." Her words bursting like soap bubbles as they dribbled past the porch.

Saraphine had watched and listened to the grown-up discussion taking place in the vestibule. "C-c-canna d-d-draw? Saraphine ... draw?" Ephrem asked, his question seeming to snap Saraphine from her trance.

"Yes ... yes, of course you can draw," she told her cousin, handing him a piece of the brown paper Marc used to bring home.

"Don't worry Aunt Blanche, we'll be fine. Maybe I'll be able to get more hours at the shop ... that'll make a difference. You'll see."

"More hours? How could you? You couldn't possibly work more hours, you're there whenever the shop's open." Blanche said, trailing off. She looked at Eugénie for a second, cleared her throat, then her eyes rolled back, her knees unlocked and she dropped as if executed by a firing squad.

"Aunt Blanche," Saraphine called from the kitchen, her face crumpled, hands on her head.

"Ahgg ... ahgg," Ephrem howled, bumping into Saraphine while bolting to his mother.

"Help me, she fainted," Eugénie said, grabbing her aunt's

arm and dragging her into the hallway.

"It's all right … calm down … it's all right," Saraphine bawled at Ephrem, the noise of him slapping at his thighs sounding like applause. "Mamma's gonna be fine, don't worry. Look, Eugénie's taking care of her," she tried to reassure, stroking his back as if trying to douse flames. "She's just asleep … tired is all. It's gonna be fine," the empty words feeding the boy's panic.

"Never mind him for now … help me with Aunt Blanche," Eugénie turned and said.

They dragged Blanche away from the front door and Eugénie held a cold compress to her aunt's forehead while Ephrem bawled—his high-pitched cries bouncing off the walls. One of Blanche's eyes cracked open and she slowly reconnected with the sights and sounds of the moment. She started crying; reality had settled in. Both her nieces buried their chins tightly against her neck and shoulders; Ephrem pulling at her apron. They would have to leave the apartment. They had no idea where to go.

-2-

Orance wrapped beef cubes and handed Eugénie the package as she prepared to leave. "Here. It's just chuck but it's good when you leave it to cook for a while," he said.

"I can't take that. You can't jus' take what you want from the counter and go home with it," Eugénie replied, lips pursed.

"Oh … no, no. My dad said I *could* give you some. He's the one who told me to give you this. He told me I could give you some of the cuts that have been in the counter for longer," he replied, smiling and pointing the brown paper bundle at her.

Eugénie thought of rejecting the offering, of starting into a speech about how she couldn't; wouldn't accept charity. But the thought of Saraphine, Ephrem, and her Aunt Blanche shouted in her mind. She envisioned what was sitting in the icebox at home; thought about how creative their food preparation had become; about how their cheekbones had gained prominence. She stared away and thanked him then looked down at the package; nicely wrapped and tied with a string. "Please, make sure to thank your father when you see him later. We all appreciate the kindness," she felt obliged to add, fearing that Orance might be acting as a kind of Robin Hood.

"Oh no, please, don't worry about it. My dad's happy to help. We all are. Besides, since you've told me about your aunt having a spell … Is she better?"

Eugénie's head bobbed back; surprised by Orance's empathy. "…Yes, thanks for asking. She's still really upset and worried but, we'll see things through."

"Well, see you tomorrow," he added when Eugénie backed out through the door, the sound of the bell resonating throughout the empty shop.

Walking home along the dirt and cobbles of Forsyth Street, the smell of raw meat reminding her of the many times her uncle had arrived home with a large piece of beef, Eugénie pondered a life spent with Orance. The two of them … together. A life that, maybe, could be like what her aunt and uncle had known. A life free of want.

She knew Orance liked her; suspected he loved her. The boy seemed able to be sweet, kind … when sober. Perhaps the time had come to open that door; to be more welcoming of his attention, she thought as blood from the chuck dripped through the gaps in her fingers. She *could* live with him, she thought, pulling her cheeks back and forcing a smile onto her face. Yes, this was possible, provided certain conditions were met.

-3-

On her way to work the next day, walking briskly and staring at the cobbles, Eugénie resolved to be sweeter to the boy, to be open to his kindnesses. *Thank you, kind sir*, she had considered saying when Orance would, once again, open the butchery door for her. But she nearly hit her nose on the door having to pause upon reaching the top step. "Where's Orance?" She asked Monsieur Charpentier, his face framed by the swinging door's round window, the glass fogging as he exhaled.

"Back here with me, loading fat and bones on Mr Stankey's cart for the rendering plant," he answered.

"Mr who?"

"Stankey. He collects fat and bones and delivers it to the David & Davies rendering plant. He's said he's gonna pay us for it instead of us giving it all away for nothing. Do me a favour and bring me ten cents from the register," Monsieur Charpentier asked Eugénie, who was folding her coat neatly beneath the counter.

Eugénie, two nickels in hand, pushed open the large, black door leading to the dock. Her eyes watered and her face contorted as the stench of a horse's rotting corpse lying in Mr Stankey's cart rushed her all at once. The sight of blood pooling all around the nearly decapitated animal—its body covered with fat and bone discards from the shop—nearly brought her to her knees.

"By God's nails, that's awful! How can you stand the stench?" She asked, turning away, her nose jammed into the crook of her elbow. The Charpentier men laughed; the plan to lure her to the back and delight in her disgust having worked the charm.

"Got you good … didn't we?" Orance said, bent over backwards and laughing the loudest. "We knew how you'd react. Don't worry, you'll get used to it eventually," he said, he and his father still wrapped in hilarity while Mr Stankey—sombre and glum—emptied buckets of fat on either side of his quarry.

"Sometimes I wonder about you. You might consider becoming more of a gentleman or to at least act your age,"

Eugénie told Orance, her face still buried in her arm, her watery eyes shooting bullets at the young man.

"We just wanted to make you laugh … that's all," Orance replied, smiling broadly and wiping his mouth on his crimson sleeve.

"The boy didn't mean to offend … just having a bit of a laugh at your expense," Monsieur Charpentier chimed in.

"You certainly did," Eugénie said, throwing the two nickels on the loading dock on her way back to the register.

Back in front, self-conscious and worried the odour would somehow stick to her, Eugénie subtly sniffed at the fabric of her sleeve. "Bonjour, Madame Lalonde," she said, greeting the day's first customer. "We have quite a special on rabbit all of this week," she added, her sinuses still invaded by the foulness. Orance, doing his best to conceal his lingering amusement, burst through the door, grabbed his apron and addressed Madame Lalonde.

"You'll be interested to know we have a nice special on—"

"I've already informed Madame Lalonde that rabbit is on special this week."

"Oh, all right then," Orance responded, brow cocked, his hairline leaning way back atop his head and lips pinched into a smile. "I hope you're not still mad about all that … about Mr Stankey's cart … the smell that is," he said, maladroit, shuffling next to Eugénie till his shoulder bumped hers.

"Sometimes you can be a bit of a rascal and I'm not even sure you realize it."

"I didn't mean to upset you. I don't want to make you angry. It's just something that my dad thought would be funny. Sorry if it—"

"Your dad! What about you? Why did you agree to this?

"I thought that, maybe … if … maybe—"

"Let's jus' forget about it and get on with our day," Eugénie whispered, eyes pointed at Madame Lalonde, whose nose was nearly immersed in the sausage platter sitting on the table next to the window.

Many years would pass before Eugénie would realize that, for those few moments, father and son had enjoyed each other's company.

-4-

All day, Orance stayed out of Eugénie's way, making sure to keep out of trouble—at least till the anger had slowly burned from her system.

"See you tomorrow," Eugénie forced herself to say over the doorbell's chime.

"Yes," Orance said. "Wait. Would you mind if I came by this evening?"

"My aunt isn't feeling well these days so I think it's best if—"

"It's been a while. Isn't she a bit better by now? Besides, maybe my coming by will help her. Maybe, I could come by for supper. I've got pork chops I could bring."

Eugénie drew a long, slow breath till the sting of the inelegantly veiled bribe had sunk in. *Am I being overly judgemental*, she wondered? *Maybe he's jus' trying to be kind*, she tried to reassure herself.

"All right, but come by *after* supper. I'll expect you at seven," she said, not quite certain why she had agreed to his visit while forfeiting a chance at eating pork.

-5-

"I'm looking forward to seeing Orance. Marc always had such good things to say about that boy," Blanche said, clearing the table while Ephrem noisily piled wooden blocks onto the wagon his father had built for him—still unable to recognize the meaning of the letters carved upon each of them.

"I don't remember Uncle Marc having ever said anything about Orance. When did he ever speak to you about him?" Eugénie asked, piling dishes into the sink.

— *89* —

"Oh … often. He'd talk about what they did at work. How he was going to inherit the butchery one of these days … and how hard his father was with him."

"Did he ever mention anything about his drinking?"

"Uh … no. Well, maybe a few times, I suppose he did," Blanche answered, running her hands along her shoulders.

"That's true . . ." Saraphine chimed in. "I remember once when Uncle Marc said that Orance would end up getting everything the old man had worked his whole life to build, so long as he didn't drink it all away."

Eugénie looked sideways at her sister; Saraphine raised her shoulders and nodded up at Eugénie's disapproving glare.

"The way his father treats him, from what I see at work every day, I'd say that he'll have to work pretty hard if he wants to inherit those shops. Besides, you don't realize how much pressure he's under. Maybe that's why he has a drink from time to time," Eugénie raised her chin and responded.

"No, no … of course. He seems like a very nice young man …" Blanche cut in, before hesitating, then adding, "Certainly seems interested in you, though. He's been courting you for quite a while and, to be honest, I'm not seeing any other young men calling on you. Maybe you *should* be more real- istic and see what's right in front of your eyes."

Eugénie continued to put dishes away, her demeanour moving from defensive to reflective.

"He's sweet on you," Saraphine said, smiling, rocking back and forth and pointing at her sister.

"Stop it, Saraphine, that's not nice," Blanche said, lunging forward and swiping her dishcloth at her niece's offending digit. "You're too young to understand what your sister's going through … you know that we're about to get kicked out of this place, don't you?" She added, turning her back to her youngest niece.

"I know. I'm sorry Aunt Blanche," Saraphine said, wide- eyed

"It's not me you should be apologizing to," Blanche added,

wiggling her finger in Eugénie's direction. "You know, some-times a woman has to make sacrifices when it comes to ques-tions of the heart. Your sister here, she knows all about that," Blanche said, turning to face Eugénie. "You do … don't you?"

Eugénie stared at the pile of blocks that Ephrem had stacked and after he knocked them all to the floor, she drew a long breath and said, "What I know is that some men—more so than others who've had everything given to them—need a woman in their lives. That it's possible to reach a boy if there's sweetness in his heart. It's that sweetness that I see, now and then, a sweetness that lets me know I can reach him. I've read a hundred stories about how to do that. A woman can lead a man to better things. I'm sure of that." Then, as if reality had been waving at her from the other side of the room, she shook her head and noticed how Blanche and Sa-raphine had been staring at her, their lips parted and heads to the side.

"You're right," Blanche said, moving in and wrapping her arm around Eugénie's shoulder. "Go fix yourself up. A pretty face is always a welcomed sight for a man. Go in my room and put some of my Latour Almond Complexion Cream on … and plenty of face powder."

"But that was a gift from Uncle Marc. He gave it to you," Eugénie replied, her eyes welling up at the sight of her aunt's quivering chin.

"Go ahead, make yourself pretty, then go sit in the parlour, I'll get some tea ready and you can wait for your gentleman caller. Relax."

-6-

Orance cranked the doorbell at seven sharp.

"Bell—d-doe bell," Ephrem called, his attention momen-tarily drawn away from his pile of blocks.

"Your beau's here," Saraphine said, looking into the parlour as she ran to open the door.

I hope this evening finds you well, is what Orance had intended to say as either Blanche or Eugénie greeted him at the door. Instead, when he saw Saraphine's dimpled cheeks and dark brown eyes smiling at him, the words, "Is your sister here?" dropped from his lips like chunks of broken brick.

"Let Orance in," Blanched yelled, walking down the hallway and wiping the back of her hands on her apron along the way. "Your gentleman caller's here," she told Eugénie, passing by the parlour, arched backwards, her brow pointing at the front door.

"Come … come in Orance, I'm in the parlour," Eugénie called, trying her best to act appropriately; to behave as one of her romantic heroines might.

Away from the butcher shop—the only bridge that had, till now, linked the two of them—Orance was unable to transcend the dullness of vague discussions. Though Eugénie had introduced varied topics of general concern, Orance only managed to nod and agree. Soon enough, he realized that very few minutes remained before he'd have to take his leave, before this evening's window of opportunity would close for yet another day. Looking at the clock ticking away on the shelf, he rubbed his nose, reached for his ankle and, looking up, blurted, "You know, maybe we could go for a walk on Sherbrooke Street this Sunday. Have a picnic at Logan Park. My mum could prepare some—"

"No … *I'll* prepare lunch. I even have the picnic basket my mother used when she and my father would go to St. James Market."

"Swell. So, I'll come by on Sunday. I'll be here at, what? Ten?" Orance asked. Then, smiling broadly, added, "Of course, only if it doesn't rain."

Eugénie grimaced and laughed, unaware she had reached for Orance's elbow.

The feel of her fingers wrapped around the jacket, wrapped around the shirt, which wrapped around his arm, caused his heart to flutter. He looked down just before she let go. He smiled and, in a sudden burst of enthusiasm, considered touching Eugénie's hand, the one that had touched him. But he didn't, and the moment quickly melted into the next. He had lost his opportunity. *Sunday*, he thought. *Sunday will be the day.*

Saraphine, sitting on the porch next to the parlour's open window, crossed her arms and studied her lap as Orance walked out.

"Hope you didn't miss any of our conversation in there," Orance said, having reached the stoop and looking back at Saraphine. "Pretty certain that boys'll be lining up to court a pretty girl like you. You'll see ... in no time," he added and winked.

"I ... I ... it's a nice ... need help in the kitchen Aunt Blanche?" Saraphine yelled, springing from her chair, and running all the way back to the kitchen.

"What did he say?" Blanche asked as Saraphine ran in.

"What d-d-eh," Ephrem added.

"Enough," Eugénie yelped. "He asked me to go for a walk on Sherbrooke Street. We'll have a picnic, that's all," Eugénie said, walking out the parlour.

"So ... what do you think?" Blanche asked, looking at her niece from under her brow.

"About what?" Eugénie replied, glancing away to conceal her smile.

"You know, what do you think?" Blanche said, and snapped her dishrag at Eugénie's bum.

"I think ... I think it'll be a nice outing," Eugénie said, looking away.

"I think it's romantic. A walk ... a picnic ... sounds so wonderful," Saraphine said, absently helping Ephrem pile blocks on his wagon.

The couple walked and walked along Sherbrooke Street, all the way to Logan Park. "Should we have our picnic here?" Eugénie asked, as they walked along the edge of the grass.

"We could, but the timing's a bit off, don't you think? You know, it's not even noon yet. Are you hungry? Maybe we should build more of an appetite before we stop," he suggested, though his concern had nothing to do with food. Orance's mind was a blur; continually searching for the right words while trying to read Eugénie's mind—decipher her every expression. Was this the right day? Was it too soon?

So, they walked - Orance, hoping the exercise would stop him from shaking; that the march would soften her defences - all the way to St. Famille Street, and beyond McGill College. They continued till they stood in the shadows of the ancient stone towers of the Collège de Montréal. Orance, whose right shoulder ached from supporting Eugénie's hand on his elbow, proposed they stop and join other couples having lunch and strolling along the lush grounds of the Collège.

"This is beautiful, let's set ourselves on the grass, right here," Eugénie agreed.

Eugénie, who had carried a small, brown wicker basket neatly packed with pieces of bread, slices of peameal bacon, and sausage, pulled the tablecloth folded atop her *pannier* and turned her back to the breeze before laying the linen on the grass.

"It'll feel good to sit, I didn't think we'd make it this far," Eugénie said, reaching for a jar and spreading beef drippings congealed in fat on a baguette, all the while glancing at a young couple holding hands.

Orance stood and surveyed the site, hands tucked in his pockets. "Such a beautiful day. Not that many left before the leaves start falling, you know," he said, eyes unfocused, staring into the distance, fidgeting and rattling coins.

"Sit. Relax. You must be hungry?"

"Yes. Actually, yes ... very hungry," he replied, suddenly aware of his empty belly. He paused, looked around for an instant and, blam! A flash—something like confidence—shot through him as if a door in his brain had been blown open by a strong gust. His mind had left a tiny space for him to act without thinking. All his fears, thoughts, and insecurities would just sit there for a little while, hidden behind his face. He dropped to his knees, his butt on his heels.

"What are you doing? We're not in church. Sit down, let's eat," Eugénie said, watching him staring at her and noticing the quiver in his lower lip.

Orance mumbled something, pulled his leg out from under himself, reached into his breast pocket, and offered a wad of fabric.

"What's this supposed to be? You won't need that, I brought napkins."

"Wait," he answered, his giant hands trembling while, in an uncharacteristically dainty manner, he carefully picked at the corners of the hanky and unfolded it. Inside, a white gold ring sat on linen. Eugénie, legs folded beneath her skirt, felt as if she were falling backwards and instinctively propped her hand behind her. Expressionless, she stared at the shiny object, mouth agape, her brow raising long, tiny lines up her forehead.

"It would be your ... no, sorry. It would be *my* honour if you accepted to become Mrs Orance Charpentier."

"You want to ... you want us to get married?" She asked, peaking up at him before refocusing on the ring.

"It would be *my* honour if you accepted ... accepted to be my wife."

"I ... I"

"Wait ... wait, wait ... don't say anything ... not now. Think about it ... take all the time you want."

"No, it's not that . . ." Eugénie said, lifting her head and looking into his eyes. "It's not that I don't want to get ... to get married. It's jus' that I—"

"What? You needn't worry. I've got the job at the shop, that's a guarantee. Why, one day, I'll own the whole thing. We'll be comfortable. I'll be able to take care of you. You, and our family."

"You don't understand. It's not about me ... not jus' about me. I have to take care of Saraphine and—"

"Ok ... no, don't worry, that's all right," Orance said, palms raised to the sides of his head. "I know, she can live with us till *she* gets married. She could move in with us. My father's opening a new butchery. That'll be my responsibility. We could live there, in the apartment upstairs ... plenty of space for your sister," he added, eyes wide, trying to read Eugénie's expression.

Eugénie rubbed her shoulders and stared at the grass. Orance, dread dripping off his face, stuck his arm out and held the ring inches from her face, slowly tilting it back and forth hoping the ruby would sparkle in the sun. Eugénie adjusted the comb in her hair. "It's more than that. You don't really understand. You *can't* understand, and it's not your fault that you don't."

"Don't understand? So, tell me. What is it that I don't understand? Please, please explain to me what the problem is. Maybe I *will* understand once you explain what the problem is," Orance pleaded, pushing himself off the ground. "I care for you ... care for you very deeply," he added, leaning down and squeezing her shoulder.

"I have responsibilities. My sister depends on me, but it's not jus' her. My aunt and Ephrem ... I can't jus' leave 'em; they need me."

Orance looked away and slid his hand down Eugénie's arm till it rested on hers. "When I ask if you'll be my wife, well ... it's because I accept everything that implies. There'll be plenty of space for everybody. They can come and live with us. Please. Be my wife?"

"D'you understand what you're saying. You know Ephrem. My aunt has to take care of him. Every day. He can't go to school, so she can't work, she always has to—"

"I know. Please, be my wife."

Eugénie got to her feet and stood, motionless, looking past Orance for what seemed like a full minute. She took a deep breath, let it out slowly and said, "Is that a promise?"

"I promise."

Eugénie's hands dropped from her shoulders. Orance seemed sincere. She looked deeply into his eyes, and, for an instant, the picture that formed in her mind showed her a future where, perhaps, one day, she might learn to love this young man.

"Then, I will. I accept."

Orance cupped his hand on Eugénie's cheek and kissed her on the lips. Eugénie slipped her hand into his, eyes opened wide, imagining how Saraphine would react to the news.

-8-

The couple ate lunch, Eugénie mindful of nibbling daintily at her crust while glancing at her fiancé. Orance sat with his legs crossed, a silly, giddy smile plastered to his face while swallowing huge chunks of his baguette, the bread sliding down his throat like a small mammal slithering down a python's craw. Orance pondered his future; living away from his father; being his own man. Eugénie tried to imagine living with Orance, of founding a family; the intimacy of two people sharing their lives alongside a sister, an aunt and a cousin.

"You're being honest when you suggest that my family can move in with us?" Eugénie asked, snapping out of her daydream.

"Of course," Orance replied, bits of meat bullets flying from his mouth before he wiped his lips with his sleeve. "After all, let's face it, the gang's not going to be together forever," he added, casually. "A fine-looking girl like Saraphine's not going to become an old maid, and … well, your aunt's still young. I'm sure she'll get married again, too."

Eugénie leaned in close to Orance, her neck craned forward. "What if she *does* become an old maid? And, what if my aunt and Ephrem end up living with us for a long time … or forever?" She quizzed, looking directly into his eyes.

"I told you. I promised. I won't let you down. I'm a man of my word," he reassured. Eugénie believed him, instantly, not because of what he had said but because he had placed her hand over his heart.

The walk back seemed to take only minutes. All the way home, they considered potential wedding dates and plotted their future; baby names popped into Eugénie's mind. They talked about how they'd arrange the apartment, about how the people around them would react to their big announcement.

"The new butcher shop's gonna be ready by the end of spring, early summer at the latest. That'll give us time to fix it up and get it ready before we move in."

"So, we'll live in the apartment above the shop?"

"Yes Ma'am, we will. That makes sense … right?"

"Oh, yes, yes. That's wonderful. Makes sense to be living above where we'll be working."

Orance paused. "So, you're planning to continue to work?"

"Makes sense, doesn't it? I'm experienced at it and you won't have to hire additional people—especially now that my uncle's passed."

"I was thinking about a family, about your responsibilities having to deal with that."

"Well, that's wonderful but it won't happen … not right away … at least not for the first nine months. There'll be a little bit of time so, while there is, I could help out. Doesn't that make sense? Anyway, I thought, you know, once we do have a family my aunt could work at the shop, too … and we'd all be there for Ephrem."

Orance seemed to have drifted elsewhere. He stopped

walking and faced Eugénie. Realizing she had processed and anticipated the future—their future—with far greater efficiency and foresight, he said, "That all sounds fine. But what if your aunt *does* remarry? She's not that old, you know … no reason for her to die a widow."

"Oh, my goodness … you weren't sincere. You were lying when you made that promise," Eugénie said, the look on her face morphing from silk to stone. She stepped back and added, "You *can't* be trusted. I hate myself for having believed you. I used to think you were a rascal but … but you, you're jus' a scoundrel."

"No … no, you don't under—"

"Please, leave me alone. I want to walk back on my own."

"No, you've misunderstood, that's not what I meant. Your family can live with us … can live with us as long as they need to … as long as they want to," he said, shaking his palms at the clouds before tripping on the picnic basket Eugénie had thrown at his feet when he tried to follow her.

Eugénie froze and turned to face him. "That's not the point. It's not about them *needing* to live with us. It's about us living together... them *wanting* to live with us, and us *wanting* to live with them. I'm talking about a family, not commerce," she said, jabbing at her palm.

"I thought that, maybe, your aunt would get married again; would *want* to get married again, is all I'm saying. Please, don't put words in my mouth. I apologize for the misunderstanding," he said, despite Eugénie having disappeared amongst the throngs of Sunday strollers. Orance laced his hands over the top of his bowler hat. Surrounded by happy people—happy couples—he reached inside his *other* breast pocket and pulled out his flask. He gulped the Caribou, his father's own recipe, till his leather-covered silver container was empty; his mind whirling, unable to process the shocking turn of events.

On hands and knees, Orance managed to climb the stairs, twenty-three steps leading up to his father's apartment. Having reached the balcony, he sat back against the door and banged his head on the oak panel till his hat fell into his lap. His mother, Uriette, opened the door, and he dropped backwards onto her shins, his head thumping hard on the oilcloth.

"Jesus, Mary and Joseph … what happened?" Uriette said, hands covering her mouth. "Oh, my sweet goodness, thank heavens' your father's not here," she added, struggling to pull him inside. "Get up … get up Orance," she said, unable to move her youngest son.

"What happened," Dahlia and Florie, asked, as yet another episode of *the drunk brother* unfolded.

"You know what happened … come help me … oh my goodness, if your father sees him like this again," Uriette repeated, panic-stricken. The sisters ran, grabbed at Orance's sleeves and pulled till they nearly fell; his jacket having slid over his head. Uriette peeked out hoping none of the neighbours were enjoying the latest show. She lifted her son's legs and pushed as hard as she could. "Come on girls, pull, we've got to get him inside," Uriette whispered loudly, all of them aware of the likely consequences should the boy's father show up and witness the scene.

"Leave me alone," Orance said, his words sounding more like: *leaf be a bone*. "Heeey, stop it," he added, trying to free himself from his sisters' grip.

"Get up, Orance. Let him go, girls. Let's see if he can stand on his own," Uriette said, leaning over the boy and wincing at the aroma drifting up at her.

Orance lay on his back, jammed in the doorway, torso in the kitchen, legs sticking out the door. "Come on, get up … for goodness' sake … get up," Uriette pleaded.

Groaning, he slowly rolled himself onto his side and eventually managed to crawl to the kitchen table. "What happened? How could you let Eugénie see you this way? What's wrong with you?" His mother asked, slapping his hip, her voice pouring out into the neighbourhood.

"Wrong with me?" Orance asked, laughing, clutching the edge of the kitchen table and struggling to get to his feet.

"Help him up," Uriette told her daughters. "Help him get to his room before your father gets back."

"Leave me alone, I said," he yelled, his right arm flailing, holding on to the table with the other. He belched, then added, "You don't know nothing ... you don't . . ." Then, his chin dropped to his chest, shoulders bobbing as he tried to complete his sentence. Unable to speak, he swallowed his words before releasing a series of belches. Through watery eyes, he watched his lunch jump out of him, drifting along a stream of Caribou—his father's own recipe—splashing on his shoes and covering the floor in a kind of purple goo; the kitchen fouled by an iron-melting, sweet stench. Though familiar with the scene, they stood back, ankles warmed and stained. Aghast. Orance unfolded himself, eyes yellow and unfocussed, his head on a swivel. He ran his palm over his mouth, and without warning, released a second stream of the sweet stuff. By now, his diminished gastrointestinal strength had impeded the heaving; the effluent merely bubbling and dribbling down his chin; rivulets of puke sliding along his chest.

"Oh, my goodness ... goodness me," his mother repeated as the sisters shrieked. Uriette tiptoed to the counter, grabbed the newspaper and dropped the day's headlines over the sludge.

"This should take care of the worst of it," she said, under her breath, heading to the pantry for the mop.

Orance, propped up against the kitchen table, vile remnants stuck to his chin, aimed himself at the hallway. He soon stepped onto the imbibed newspapers, slipped and fell; dropping straight back like a severed tree. The nape of his neck slammed on the table, the cracking sound of the impact either due to some shattered bone or splintered wood. Sprawled on his back, hair soaked in his own vomit, he remained unconscious though his mother slapped at his cheek; his sisters doing what they could to push him off the pile of barf he lay in.

"My God. At least his father knows to go to bed when he gets drunk," Uriette said, rubbing her forehead as she spoke.

-10-

Dahlia and Florie cleaned the floor, eyes watering and dry heaving as they persisted. Uriette gingerly plucked chunks of vomit off her son's face and applied a cold compress to his forehead. "His father can't see him this way. He'll kill him," Uriette told her daughters. "We've got to get him to his room and get rid of this smell."

Dahlia and Florie, neither of them strong enough to crush a bug, grabbed their brother's left arm, Uriette pulling from the right side. Orance moaned when they managed to lift his back off the floor. Taking advantage of the minor success, Uriette hurriedly wiped the floor clean and peeled Orance's vest and shirt off his wet skin.

"Gee … Genie doesn't care … she's not gonna marry me," he blurted.

"Did I hear that he's gonna marry Eugénie?" Florie asked.

"Maybe that's why he's like this," Dahlia replied.

"No," Orance said, blubbering. "No, no. She said, no. She hates me."

"Please, try to get up. We'll help you to your room. You've got to get yourself on your feet," his mother said, pushing his back and shoulders forward, hoping to keep him upright.

"I can get up, just leave me alone," he growled, forcing his arms away from his sisters' feeble grip. Sitting on the floor, his back buttressed by his mother's forearms, he looked around for a bit and pushed himself to his knees. Dahlia, wanting to help, took hold of his left elbow. Orance slapped her, his palm striking her cheek sounded like a firecracker.

"Orance! *Maudit*, Orance," Florie screamed, wrapping her arms around her sister.

Uriette hit her son's shoulder and furiously slapped the top of his head. Orance, disoriented and grunting, waved his arms in defence as if trying to repel a fly. As blows kept raining down on him, he jabbed both hands into his mother's belly. She folded like a closed book and fell back onto the hutch.

"Don't you bother me," he said, staggering out of the kitchen, his dirty hand trailing along the wall to keep from falling.

"We were trying to help. *Maudit ivrogne* ... damned drunkard. How could you hurt your sister ... what's wrong with you?" His mother yelled, Dahlia sobbing in her arms.

-11-

Ephrem sat in his usual spot on the porch, waving at passersby and smiling at familiar faces. *Bonjour Madame* or *bonjour monsieur*, he'd say to those who smiled back—words his father had painstakingly taught him to pronounce without stumbling—tipping his cap and tilting his head the way his mother had instructed.

As soon as she turned the corner on Forsyth Street, Eugénie could hear her cousin calling her name. "Eug-Eug-g-gé . . ." he'd repeat, bouncing off his wooden chair and leaning over the porch's wrought iron railing. Eugénie waved, the sight of him—his brilliant smile, his cat-like grey eyes—raising her spirits.

"And how was *your* day, little man?" Eugénie asked.

"Eug . . ." Ephrem replied, his outstretched arms reaching for his adored cousin. Eugénie dropped to her knees and pulled him tightly against her.

"Did you make nice drawings today?"

"C-cats ... T-two c-cats," he replied, pointing at the open doorway.

"My day wasn't so good," Eugénie said, arms crossed, the small of her back leaning onto the porch's balustrade. "You might even say this day was jus' … jus' for the birds. I don't suppose you drew any pictures of birds today."

"O-only c-cats. Two," he replied, smiling brightly.

"That's good," she said, looking down and wiping tears from the corner of her eyes with her fingernail. "For the birds … that's what my day was like. D'you know what that means?"

"That m-means not v-very g-good," Ephrem said, through his fading smile.

"That's about it. We really went at it today. Like cats and dogs, you might say. We're so different from each other," Eugénie said, looking away as she mused. "I think we might all be stuck together, my little man. I'm starting to think that we'll have to find a way to make this work 'cause I don't know who's going to want to marry the lot of us." She said, unconsciously caressing Ephrem's temple. "But, I guess you'll be needing a place to live, won't you?" She asked, looking down at the boy, not really expecting an answer.

-12-

Monday came, and Eugénie mumbled to herself all the way to work, searching and rehearsing the right words to say when she'd walk through the shop's door—the door Orance would likely be holding open for her. From across the street, she paused, peeking through the procession of carriages and carts rolling along Hochelaga Street, spying the spot where Orance usually waited for her. The place seemed empty—no one in sight. Relieved about not having to face him—yet curious as to why *he* should be the angry one—she hurried onto the street, dodging horses and carts. Distracted, she plopped her beloved Oxford directly into a massive pile of manure, some of the muck clinging to her laces and her white cotton tights—the warmth underfoot a testament to the deposit's freshness.

She hopped along on her clean foot, holding her fouled shoe away from her dress while trying to avoid getting trampled by a horse. Arms extended, holding onto her mother's old black and white reticule bag, she bounced and skipped along the sidewalk all the way to the shop's large granite step. Sitting with her back to the door, dirty foot sticking out from her dress, she slowly pulled the tip of her laces, carefully avoiding the shit smeared all over. Looking away, enveloped by that awful odour, she loosened the laces, hooked her heel along the edge of the step and, in one swift movement, yanked the shoe off her foot. With her soiled stocking foot sticking away from her wool serge dress, she looked back through the glass and banged on the door, hoping someone other than Orance would let her in.

She nearly fell backwards into Orance's legs when he opened the door. "Wa hapin? Whash wong wish yo foff?" Orance asked. Eugénie drew a long breath and prepared to launch into a speech about her, him, the future. But, she turned, looked up at his face, and froze. Large, black and purple marks covered his left brow and cheek. His eyes were bloodshot and swollen, his lips inflated like satiated leeches; a necklace of yellow bruises tattooed all around his neck.

Eugénie pulled back and returned the question, "Wa-what happened to your face? Your neck?"

"Nothing I won't get ower … nothing I didn't dewerve. Wa 'bout you? Where's your shoe?"

The details of Eugénie's story made Orance chuckle, his parting lips revealing how some of his teeth had also fallen victim to whatever had mangled his face. His silly, pathetic giggle made Eugénie look away and smile. "May I?" He asked, pointing at her manure-covered shoe sitting on the granite step.

"Be my guest."

Orance maneuvered around Eugénie, found a small stick lying on the sidewalk, picked up her shoe and sat next to her.

He scraped the muck away, occasionally whipping the twig at the side of the step to remove some of the *material* off his tool. Eugénie, hands tented over her nose, watched through tearing eyes as Orance did what he did.

"I'm sharry 'bout what I shaid. I didn't mean it that way. Rearry, I didn't," Orance said, focussing on the shoe.

"Maybe I made a bit too much of what you said," she said, looking straight ahead, her dung-infected foot still extended out beyond her dress.

"On my honour, I swear that I'll be happy to have you as my wife, no matter how many others come along for the ride," he said, pausing from the shit scraping in the hopes of properly emphasizing his genuine intentions.

"I believe you. I do … I believe you."

"Sho?"

"So … yes. I'll marry you," she said, surprised to hear her voice crack—just a bit—as she uttered the words.

Orance pulled up his apron and wiped Eugénie's shoe on it. He smiled at her, loosened the laces around his waist, pulled it over his head, and threw the soiled apron on the street.

Chapter 6

-1-

July 1897

A couple of men—the one with a length of rope holding up his pants seeming way too fat to be perched that high atop a ladder—whacked and tugged at a huge black sign, straining to wrestle it into position. Its freshly painted gold letters spelled out the words Urbin Charpentier had so keenly looked forward to seeing: **Boucherie Salaison Charpentier et Fils**. Of course, Urbin had expected that the *et Fils* portion of the sign would have included his other sons, Siméon and Charles. But, given those boys had long ago become part of the St. Lawrence River, the burden of carrying on the family name had fallen upon Orance.

Urbin, paint splotches all over his new work shoes, had just transformed the red brick of his expanding business into lustrous white.

"The sign's covering up the windows of the apartment ... it's too big for the space," Orance told his father, upon arriving with his new bride.

"Shows what you know about business, my boy. A sign's never big enough. You should know that. People got to see it from all over. Everyone's gotta know there's a new butcher shop in the neighbourhood, right here on the corner of St. Denis and Ontario," Urbin said, wiping his hand on his chest and pointing at other commercial signs with his brush; the small cigar—long ago extinguished—pinched tightly in the corner of his lips bouncing as he spoke.

"Sure, of course," Orance replied, looking at where the brush pointed. "But, the parlour's windows, they're almost completely covered. We'll hardly get any light in the apartment."

"Listen, you're gonna have a butchery to run," Urbin, brow creased, said, moving closer to his son, hobbling along his nearly toeless foot. "Your priority's gonna be the shop. You've got to make this work; this isn't just something else for you to blunder."

Orance took a half step back and shook his head.

"It'll be fine. No need to worry Monsieur Charpentier. I know Orance'll make it work. Anyway, the sign, well … I guess we won't need drapery. It'll keep the sun out in the summer," Eugénie said, taking hold of Orance's arm, eyes bright and looking up at the sign.

"See, she's a smart one. Careful boy, she's gonna take over the family business before you know it," Urbin Charpentier said, smiling and pointing at Eugénie with his wet cigar, a long filament of slaver dangling from its butt. Orance exhaled, looked up at the sign, and led Eugénie toward the apartment's stairs.

"When are your things getting here?" Urbin yelled at the couple's back.

"That new boy you hired to replace Orance—what's his name … Sean, I think—he started loading up the cart when we left, so soon, I suppose," Eugénie replied. "Seamus was helping him. I expect both of 'em will help us move the furniture upstairs."

"Well, watch out for those two, I just finished painting the staircase. The whole place looks like new. Don't want to see them bumpin'n'scratching all the way upstairs."

Eugénie let go of her new husband's arm, turned and looked at her father-in-law, her hand shielding her eyes from the sun. "Yes. We have you to thank for all this. We really appreciate everything you've done for us," she said, tugging at Orance's sleeve. "Don't we?" She added, looking up at her husband, pinching her lips and nodding at him.

"What?" Orance asked, looking up the stairs.

"We appreciate your father's help," Eugénie said, tilting her head and aiming it at her father-in-law.

"Yeah, for sure we do. Thanks for all this," Orance said, turning back and looking down at his shoulder.

-2-

"Doesn't the place look wonderful? All white … it's gleaming," Eugénie said, peeking through the open door atop the long flight of steps.

"Gleaming? It's dark. It's ten in the morning and you'd swear the sun hadn't come up yet."

"It's not that bad. Besides, there's a sink in the kitchen, and water … electricity in every room," Eugénie said, pointing at the lightbulb hanging from the hallway ceiling.

"For sure we'll need those electric lights with that sign covering up all our windows … they'll need to be on all the time. You know how much that'll cost me in electricity?"

"We have a window in the back. That one's not covered," Eugénie said, looking down the hallway into the kitchen.

"G. Rover Cripes, it's like a dungeon in here," he said, stomping down the hallway toward the darkened parlour, pointing at the sign covering the windows up front. Looking back at Eugénie, he said, "Can't you see he's doing this for a reason? He's doing everything he can to let me know this place isn't mine. That this place isn't—"

"Yoo-hoo, anybody up there?" Blanche called from downstairs. "Come, come, follow me," she added, waving at Ephrem and Saraphine.

"We're up here, come on up," Eugénie said, sticking her head in the stairwell, smiling.

"I'm so excited," Blanche said, holding the hem of her dress above the steps as she climbed.

"Where's my room?" Saraphine asked, running back to the kitchen.

"You must be so happy?" Blanched asked, walking toward

the parlour and smiling at Orance.

"It's dark. Way too dark," Orance replied, while standing on tiptoes to look out and over the sign. "There's hardly any light coming into this room."

"But it's so big. How often are you gonna find a place like this with three bedrooms … it's unheard of. And, besides—"

"It's dark," Orance said, face crumpled, the spittle flying from his lips sending Blanche scurrying to the kitchen. "How come I'm the only one who notices that it's dark in here?" He continued, jabbing at his chest, hunched forward, and looking back into the kitchen.

"D-d-dawk," Ephrem said, heading toward the parlour.

"Great. The lunatic's the only one who agrees with me," Orance said, thumping his knuckle at his temple. Blanche's mouth unhinged and she looked back at Eugénie before reaching forward and whisking Ephrem back to the kitchen.

"Don't call him names. What are you doing? Ephrem'll do fine, that's his name. Besides, it so happens that we agree with you, Orance. Sure, it's dark. I guess you could say that we're jus' looking at the bright side of things," Eugénie said, forcing a smile as she stepped in Orance's direction.

"But that's the point. It's not bright. It's dark, is all I'm saying."

"OK. But, there's no reason for you to get angry at Ephrem," Eugénie said, stroking the boy's back. "I think we should be happy and jus' appreciate what we have here."

-3-

The sound of hard soles scratching at treads echoed up from the stairwell. Urbin, curious to hear what the newlyweds had to say about the apartment's updated look, stepped into the hallway, arms crossed, arched back, and grinning. "So? What does everybody think? Looks pretty nice, eh, doesn't it?"

"It's wonderful Monsieur Charpentier, you did a great job," Eugénie replied. "Don't you agree, Blanche?"

"It's absolutely wonderful. Thank you so much, Monsieur Charpentier," Blanche said, searching for the perfectly titrated reaction. "Me and Ephrem, well, we both thank you so much. We're forever in your debt," she added, pressing Ephrem's temple tightly to her hip. "And a big thanks to you too, young man. You have no idea what this means to us," she quickly added, the pitch of her voice raising as she looked at Orance's chin.

"I worked like a dog to finish this on time," Urbin said, slapping his chest. "I'm not just a little proud of this … why I'll bet you that—"

"*We* worked on it," Orance said, looking out the window above the sign.

"What?"

"We," Orance emphasized, pointing at his father, then at himself. "*We* worked on it. I worked to get the shop ready, to get this apartment ready. *We* did all this together. All except this sign. That, I had nothing to do with, and that's why it's so dark in here."

Urbin Charpentier creased his eyes, pulled his smokeless cigar from his lips, and glared at his son. "Certainly. I apologize," he said dramatically, kowtowing, his dirty hand on the wall to keep his balance.

Orance, distracted by the sound of banging coming from outside, waved dismissively at his father. He looked out over the small space between the sign and the top of the window, heels off the floor, trying to see what had caused the sudden ruckus. The fat man on the ladder had started to yell at his partner while frantically clutching at the sign.

"Don't hang on to the sign," his partner on the sidewalk hollered, holding on to the rope while looking up at his plump fellow fumbling while trying to untangle a knot snagged in the pulley.

"Hold on, wait … OK … pull, pull hard, lift it up," the fat man shouted, his hat slipping off his head when he looked down.

The man below, straining to maintain a grip on the coarse rope, yanked the line. "Harder, the knot's untangled, it should come along," the man on the ladder called to his buddy. The mortar gave way and the pulley anchored into it snapped off and pulled the ladder down along with it. In a panic, the fat man grabbed the sign and, together, they crashed onto the pavers, the awful sound of the impact loud enough to be heard all the way back into the apartment's kitchen.

Everyone rushed downstairs. Urbin, hands sliding along the railing, was hopeful the falling sign hadn't broken the shop's large widow. Orance looked down at the scene, face bathed in light, elbows comfortably resting on the window sill.

-4-

The fat man lay sprawled on the ground, blood rushing from a huge gash above his left ear. "Does anyone have a rag?" His colleague asked, looking at the assembled gawkers and pressing his palms against the man's wound; blood pissing out between his fingers.

"My handkerchief," Eugénie said, pulling a small, cotton square from her lap pocket.

Ephrem watched, bug-eyed, cheek stuck to Blanche's hip.

"Let's go back upstairs," she said and covered Ephrem's eyes.

"I'll need more than a hanky," the man tending to his partner shouted at the bystanders.

Seamus, seated up front next to Sean, pulled the reins, jumped off the cart and joined the huddle surrounding the man busily bleeding to death. "What in blazes happened here?" He asked at no one in particular.

Unfazed, Sean casually stepped off the cart, pulled burlap from under the pile of furniture, ripped long strips of the material and tossed them next to the injured man's face.

"There. Roll that 'round his head. Should keep him from

spilling all his blood out," Sean Murphy said, his Irish accent green as clover, the sound of his voice gravelly and parched, his hat floating atop long strands of copper hair.

Eugénie, pale and nauseous, watched as both the man's colleague and her father-in-law wrapped the dirty burlap around the man's head. "Where's Orance?" She asked, turning to her father-in-law.

"Quick, get the furniture off the cart … everything off the cart," Urbin ordered. "We'll have to bring him to the hospital." He declared, pointing at the cart.

Sean and Seamus jumped on the cart and piled what was to be Eugénie and Orance's furnishings all over the sidewalk. "Are we gonna be able to lift this guy on the cart? I've dragged dead horses that were smaller than he is," Sean whispered to Seamus.

"Hurry up fellas, this guy's lost a lot of blood," Monsieur Charpentier said, pressing down on the warm, burlap bandage.

"You sure he's not dead?" Sean asked, looking sideways at the scene while pulling kitchen chairs off the cart.

"Dead? Does he still have a heartbeat?" Monsieur Charpentier asked the man's colleague.

"Doesn't look like he's bleeding no more," Sean added, dropping a chair on the sidewalk and elbowing himself to the front of the crowd, hunched over and hovering. "Once the heart stops the blood just trickles out, yunno … I think he's dead," he added and walked away, bloody footprints left in his wake.

"Put your hand on his neck … can you feel his heart beating?" The fat man's colleague asked Monsieur Charpentier, the knees of his trousers having turned red.

Urbin Charpentier put his finger on the man's neck and lowered his ear to his nose. "No use. He's dead," he said, and then reached for a clean strip of burlap and wiped his hands.

Onlookers leaned in. Eugénie held Saraphine, her chin on her sister's shoulder, and scanned the crowd in search of

Orance. Nowhere in sight, she looked up and saw him staring down at the scene, elbows still perched on the sill. "S'cuse me," Sean said as he and Seamus, a large dresser between them, stepped over the dead man's legs on their way upstairs.

"Careful with that. That's pine," Orance hollered from above.

Eugénie looked at him, unable to keep from shaking her head.

"So, is he all right?" He shouted.

"No."

"Oh," Orance said, pausing a few seconds before adding, "Come up here, you should see how bright it is now that the sign's gone."

Eugénie looked up at Orance, looked down at the dead man, and walked away, arm around Saraphine's shoulder.

"Looks like Orance is pretty ... pretty happy about how things worked out," Saraphine said, looking up at the empty window and tugging at her sister's sleeve, a puzzled look on her face.

"Well . . ." Eugénie answered, looking at the ground and, in turn, squeezing her sister's arm. "Everybody reacts differently to these kinds of situations."

-5-

Sean and Seamus hauled up the last of the happy couple's furnishings, careful not to track blood along the stairs or dirty the walls. The sign maker loaded the damaged sign back into his wagon—it had split in two, some of the letters sheared off as it struck the pavement—assuring Monsieur Charpentier that he'd prepare a new one for him at no cost.

"You better believe you will," Urbin said before darting upstairs.

A constable walking his beat down Sherbrooke Street noticed the gathering and pushed his way through the crowd.

"Anyone here know anybody with a telephone?" The officer asked, prompting some to look at others while a few – more sensitive souls – crossed themselves before shuffling off. By now, children had gathered, pushing and squeezing themselves around the many legs surrounding the scene in order to catch a glimpse of the cadaver.

"He might have killed himself just by tripping on his own laces," a saucebox whispered loudly to a man who snickered at the insensitive remark.

"All right, I think everybody's got something else to do," the officer said, holding his nightstick horizontally, threatening to shove at the gapers. "All of you … be on your way. You've seen enough here … be on your way," he repeated, pushing at the men and pointing at the women.

"Maybe Orance stayed upstairs 'cause he's got so much on his mind, you know, about the new butcher shop and the apartment," Saraphine said, sitting next to her sister on a trunk yet to be hauled upstairs.

"Yes, maybe that's why," Eugénie said, looking up at the empty window. "Wait, the trunk," she added, remembering that the trunk they sat on contained linens. Brusquely, she pulled Saraphine to her feet, opened the lid, and pulled out a white tablecloth she had packed. She approached the officer and handed him the neatly folded fabric.

"Maybe it'd be best to cover him," Eugénie suggested.

Orance, having returned to his perch, watched as Eugénie approached the cop.

"Hey, that'll ruin it. Don't give him that," Orance said, the disembodied voice seeming to pour down from above.

"Mind your business, up there," the cop replied, squinting at the reflections bouncing off windows.

"He's my husband, sir … he didn't mean—"

"Never you mind, she's my wife, so that's mine," Orance said, pointing at the tablecloth. "I don't know exactly what that is, but it's white and that guy's covered in blood … it'll be ruined if you drape it on him."

"Sir, I think the lady did the right thing. She just wanted

to—"

"That lady's my wife," Orance repeated and slapped the window sill.

The officer looked at Eugénie and frowned.

"Please officer, go ahead," she pleaded and handed him the tablecloth.

Still looking up—his forehead wrinkled, struggling against the glare bouncing off the white brick—the officer took the tablecloth and laid it over the man's head and torso. Orance, shoulders up, chortled, "Hope you're satisfied? Now it looks as though you've covered up a pig wearing pants."

Orance snapped his head back inside—the move transforming his laugh into a kind of whooping hiss. Seconds later, the sound of knuckles pounding at skin resonated throughout the empty parlour; the frightful noise attracting the attention of those still lingering beside the corpse. Following a few moments of silence, Monsieur Charpentier appeared through the window.

"Come upstairs, dear. The boys'll finish bringing up your things. There's nothing more you can do down there," Eugénie's father-in-law said.

-6-

That evening, the new family gathered around the dinner table. Silently. Orance, his left eye blackened and nearly shut, sat on his hands and stared at his still-empty plate.

"I've never used a coal oven before … not sure when the meat will be ready."

"It's gonna be fine," Orance told his wife, nose still pointed down at his plate. "None of us have eaten in a while. We're all hungry enough for whatever you come up with."

Orance, though wearing the mark of his subjugation, felt ennobled. Ensconced at the head of the table, lord and master of his household. He would be the ruler. His authority unquestioned. Stonelike, they sat shoulders back, hands on laps, aware of every inhalation. Even Ephrem, smiling as usual, eyes bright, looking for someone to connect with, knew to remain quiet. Saraphine, increasingly aware of how Ephrem's very existence pricked at Orance, slowly took hold of her cousin's hands and pressed them to his thighs, gazing forward as she manoeuvred.

"Wa-what hap-happened t-t-to you're a-eye?" Ephrem asked, looking directly at Orance, prying one of his hands away from his cousin's grip to point at Orance's shiner.

Eugénie, back turned to the table, handling pots and tending to the roast, turned to look at her husband. "He hit his head," she said, looking at Blanche, her raised eyebrow instructing her aunt to short-circuit any further inquiries.

"Why won't you let me help? You don't have to do all the work."

"Stay right where you are, Aunt Blanche. You cooked for us for years," Eugénie replied. "Besides, I want to be the one who prepares the first meal in this kitchen. It's almost ready … a beautiful roast that Monsieur Charpentier gave us."

"R-roost," Ephrem said, clapping, the tip of his shoes banging on the underside of the tabletop, rattling cutlery and tipping over a teacup. They all yelped at the outburst that had slashed through the quiet. Orance sprang to his feet, his chair falling backwards onto the linoleum.

"Consarn that dinlo of yours!" He barked, glaring at Blanche's horrified face and pointing at Ephrem. A look of terror washing over the boy.

"He didn't mean any—"

"Didn't mean what? Didn't mean to be a dinlo. Is that it, Blanche?" Orance said, his puffy, black eye looking blacker than ever.

Blanche, blinking uncontrollably, wrapped her fingers around Ephrem's wrists and held them to the tabletop.

"Roost, roost. What does that even mean? It's roast, not roost or r-r-roost, you dinlo," Orance said, picking his chair off the floor, slamming it down and plopping himself back into it.

"Don't say things like that," Eugénie protested, pointing her large wooden spoon at her new husband.

Orance looked back at Eugénie, sucked his face in and said, "By the way, none of this would've happened if supper had been ready on time."

-7-

Orance pushed away from the table and stuck his thumbnail into his mouth; a belch oozing up his throat as he scraped and jabbed at remnants of beef stuck between his teeth. Downstairs, in his shop, looking at freshly painted white walls, he fidgeted with sharpened knives and re-wiped counters in preparation for the grand opening—now only three days away.

All three women had exhaled at the sight of the stairway door closing behind him. They glanced at each other and then, in synch, scurried to clear the table and wash the dishes. Saraphine handed Ephrem a large sheet of brown paper but he didn't bother to pick up his wax pencil. He sat there and watched them clean and organize the kitchen as the August sun's long, diagonal light beams illuminated the tension.

"I'm sorry about all that … about Ephrem," Blanche pleaded, nodding and looking down at the plate cradled in her dishrag. "I've never heard anyone yell like that … yell at *Ephrem* like that. I didn't know how to react."

"Why doesn't Orance like Ephrem?" Saraphine asked, arm hooked around her cousin, the other on his wrist, helping him trace the contours of some four-legged creature.

Eugénie looked at the ceiling and drew a long breath.

"Besides, what happened to his eye?" Saraphine added. "Did his father do that to him? Is that the noise we heard?"

Eugénie squeezed all of the air from her lungs, fixed her eyes on Blanche, and said, "That's why I can't get too angry at him. He's going through so much these days: the shop opening soon, getting this place ready, all of us moving in … it's a lot for a man to deal with."

"Maybe us being here isn't the ideal solution?" Blanche said, her words barely audible. "Maybe I should think about—"

"No, you've got to stay." Saraphine said.

"I gave you the wrong impression," Eugénie added, tapping her foot in frustration. "Don't worry. Orance wants you here … really does. We discussed this a long time ago. It's our privilege to have you here and I don't want to hear any more about it," she said, cheeks pulled up as high as she could bear.

"It's just that, well, he seems to get so angry sometimes. I'm afraid that he'll—"

"I work with him, Aunt Blanche. I've seen how he is, for real. I know how to handle him. There's jus' no reason to be afraid."

-8-

Downstairs in the shop, Orance sat on the still unmarred butcher block, cleaver in hand, banging its spine on the edge of the end grain. Then, he ran his thumb along the cutting edge of his sharpened tool and cut tiny slices off his fingernail. Looking around the still meatless butchery—empty counters soon to offer varied types of animal constituents; the oversized image of his grandfather hanging on the wall—his face reddened by electrical currents shooting up his spine, setting him a boil, he breathed in and breathed out, hoping the rhythm would curb the trembling.

There were a couple of walls left to be painted, not to mention the opaque coat of wax needing to be scraped off the shop windows. Then there was the swinging door leading in and out of the back (this door too, like the one at his father's place, had a round window in it) that stood leaning against its frame, the hinges still not screwed in place. Yet Orance sat … wandered, looking away from all that needed to be done, swallowing the bile that percolated up from deep in his gut. He walked out through the back and stood on the loading dock and hoped to enjoy the darkness. For several minutes he stayed there, doing his best not to look at the drawer under his workbench, reminding himself about having to be sharp for the big opening; keeping busy, tugging at the back of his neck, rubbing his cheeks and the sides of his legs. Gently running his fingers along the massive bulge over his eye—aware this bluish lump would soon turn a deep, wine colour before morphing into a strong shade of yellow—he conjured a fresh set of misfortunes that would account for this … his latest injury.

-9-

The apartment was dark, everyone asleep. Orance slid his hand along the wall as he laboured up the stairs, moaning and groggily humming some tune while slowly making his way. Twice, he bumped his shoe on the riser, lurched forward and slapped the steps to keep his teeth from smashing onto the hard maple.

Eugénie, awakened by the racket, jumped out of bed, turned the light on in the bedroom and stood in the hallway waiting for her husband to appear. The humming coming from the stairway stopped, then the door blew open and banged on the wall.

"Come in here... everyone's asleep," she whispered between her teeth, waving at him.

"We're all ready for-ffffor the g-gra-grand opening," Orance said, smiling and winking with his non-bruised eye.

"Jus' come in and get to bed. You'll be sleepwalking all day tomorrow, and there's so much left to do."

"All finished. D-done," Orance said, bumping his shoulder onto the door jamb and chuckling.

"You don't *look* like you're in any condition to have done

any work down there. Did you jus' spend all this time drinking? With so much work left, that's what you do?"

"That's what I d-do 'cause that's … that's … just leave me be," he said, dropping his butt on the mattress, bedsprings yelping as he fell on his back.

Eugénie pried the shoes off his feet, loosened his belt and lifted his heavy legs onto the bed. The drunken newlywed, lying atop the covers, fell asleep immediately. Eugénie yanked at the string dangling from the fixture and turned the light off. Lying next to him, his wet, congested breathing making her eyes water, she pulled the cover over her face to filter out his polluted Caribou breath. Lying there, she searched for some pleasant thought to disconnect her mind.

She had almost fallen asleep when the bed creaked. Orance, agitated by the high sugar content of his brew, stirred and turned to face his bride. Slowly, awkwardly, he climbed on her. Lying above the covers, maladroit and repugnant, he pulled away the sheets that Eugénie held to her face and pressed his lips to her mouth. Unable to push away so much dead weight, she clenched her teeth and sealed her lips, hoping the blockade would hold back his pungent tongue. Orance turned his prickly cheek and rubbed it hard against her face, grabbing at her breast, his hand slithering down to her crotch.

"You're drunk. Stop it," Eugénie said, her breathing laboured by the weight crushing her chest.

"Ahhh, what's wrong?"

"You're drunk, you smell."

"We're married. I lo-love you. And, you … you love me," he belched, slipping in and out of consciousness. She wriggled and twisted, trying to lift her knees, to slide out from under him. Hardly able to inhale, his weight compressing her lungs, she watched Orance's head lift up and heard a noise gurgling its way up from deep below his throat; a grumbling … something churning. He coughed and blew Eugénie's hair off her forehead. The gurgling intensified; its origin less remote.

She managed to take a deep breath when he reached to grab the headboard and wiped his mouth on his sleeve; spit dribbling from the corners of his mouth. By now, Eugénie's forehead and cheeks glistened, though she tried to avoid the spillage by turning her face into the sheets. Orance's head suddenly dangled off his shoulders and his chest heaved. Once. Twice. He moved forward, his mouth pulled open and let a torrent of purple puke flow. The effluent splashed in Eugénie's ear; its warmth nearly as nasty as its stench.

Eugénie gasped and strained her neck while attempting to pull away from the toxic puddle. Managing to steady himself by putting both hands on the wall, knees straddling Eugénie's waist, Orance turned and offered a second course. This time, gallantly spewing at the sheets and mattress, colouring what had managed—up until now—to remain white. Eugénie, finally free, catapulted herself from her bed while frantically pulling her soiled hair away from her shoulder and ear. She yanked the light on and saw her husband, face down in the muck—chunks of beef floating in Caribou—laying diagonally across the bed and snoring.

Paralyzed and shocked, she stood at the foot of the bed somehow unable to look away from the abominable spectacle. Slowly, she reached again for the ceiling light's string, eyes watering, and the stink so thick she believed it would forever haunt her sinuses, pulled the string and let the scene fade to black. Feeling her way to her side of the bed, she lay on the floor, eyes opened, and waiting for her vision to adjust to the darkness. All was silent but for the cadence of Orance's disturbed breathing; that raspy flute sound she had already grown accustomed to. She stared at the ceiling wondering if Saraphine had heard … if Aunt Blanche had heard; surprised to realize her eyes had remained dry.

-10-

The sun had hardly cast its first, long shadows by the time

Eugénie had finished drinking her first cup of coffee. She stood in the kitchen, her backside leaning on her new stove. Arms crossed, cup dangling from her index finger, she looked out at the neighbourhood's rooftops; the boiling lump in her stomach overwhelming her usual appreciation for breakfast. She took long, laboured breaths, pushing at her thighs, curling her back in an effort to suck air from the room. She started cutting thick slices of bread—her mother's usual pre-dawn ritual. The pine cupboard's creaking doors sounding the call for others to assemble in the kitchen; Saraphine shuffled her wool slippers along the linoleum and sat, hands cupped over her knees. Ephrem, his face lit up by the prospect of yet another perfect day, dragged his mother out into the kitchen.

The room was silent—everyone had heard, everyone knew—though Ephrem's lips smacking at a piece of bread smothered in headcheese said something about the boy's capacity to sleep through anything.

"Not too much time left before the shop opens," was how Blanche chose to break the stillness—the awkwardness—while looking at no one in particular.

"Yep. Monday's the big day," Eugénie replied, slurping at her third cup of coffee.

The bedroom door swung open, and Orance, suspenders hanging off either side of his trousers, walked out, rubbing at the stubble on his chin. He stood in the hallway for a few seconds; hand on the door frame to steady himself.

"You started without me ... didn't wake me up," he said, the creases at the corners of his lips causing some of the dried puke to flake off as he feigned a smile.

Blanche and Saraphine looked away. Eugénie, hands cradling her large cup, turned her back to him.

"O-Or-Ornce," Ephrem said, pointing his baguette at him, hunks of beef lard sliding off while waving his piece of bread over the table.

Orance shook his head at Ephrem, pulled his suspenders over his shoulders and shuffled toward the kitchen table.

Eugénie, concerned by the smell wafting from her own bedroom, abruptly rushed by her husband and closed the door.

"I guess you're going to need a good, strong coffee this morning," Eugénie said, returning to the kitchen and reaching for the kettle.

"Every day ... every day," Orance replied, eyes darting back and forth, gauging if Saraphine and Blanche had heard the commotion. Unsure, but realizing no one but Ephrem could bare to look at him, he added, "Especially ... you know, with how much work I've got left to do downstairs."

"Well, I hope you'll feel up to it today," Eugénie said, pulling her chair out from the table.

"Hope my coming up late last night didn't disturb any of you? There was just so much to finish last night," he said and winced, the hot coffee he had gulped burning its way down his throat.

"I know *I've* got a lot of cleaning up to do," Eugénie said, the chill in her voice stiffening Saraphine and Blanche's shoulders.

Orance took a large slice of bread, folded it twice, stuffed it in his mouth, and mumbled, "Might as well get an early start." Then he leaned forward, pushed his chair back against the table, muttered something, and headed downstairs.

"Everything all right?" Blanche asked, looking sideways at Eugénie.

"Is he sick?" Saraphine added.

Eugénie wiped her hands on her apron, and said, "I don't think you can really understand what it's like to have a business like this. Orance is under a lot of pressure to make this work and, well, sometimes the pressure is too much to take ... it gets to him, is all."

"Oh. Of course. That's for sure," Blanche said and nodded exaggeratedly. "But what about you? What about the pressure that's on you, not to mention having to endure his ... you know. I don't want to get between the two of you or to—"

"I know Aunt Blanche. It's not like I'm blind ... not deaf.

But we're all here, aren't we? Whatever this is—or isn't—is a whole lot better than the street," Eugénie said, swinging her empty cup on her thigh as she spoke.

Later, while Blanche and Saraphine were helping Orance downstairs at the shop, Eugénie pulled the sheets off her bed, rolling partially digested bits and lumps of yesterday's roast into the coiled cotton.

"Arrgh," Ephrem said, leaning against the dresser and lacing his cousin's rosary beads around his fingers.

"I know … smells awful in here. Go in the kitchen and draw some pictures," Eugénie instructed.

"Ornc … Orance sick?" He asked.

"I don't know. I guess he is," she replied, pausing for a moment when looking down at the huge, disgusting stain on the mattress."

"S-sick?"

"Maybe. But he's okay now."

-11-

Urbin, his father's photograph in his arms, posed alongside his son and daughter-in-law for the local newspaper's photographer. The moment was to be immortalized; the grand opening of a second *Boucherie Salaison Charpentier.* Though, this time, *et Fils* was added to the name.

"How does it feel to know your son's following in your footsteps?" The newsman asked.

"It's all about family. My son, he was born into this business, just like I was," Urbin answered, pointing at his father's photograph. "It's all up to him now to make sure the next generation continues the tradition," he added, squeezing both Orance and Eugénie's shoulders.

Later, after the reporter and photographer had left, Urbin toured the shop, his son trailing a few steps behind him.

"Looks good," Urbin said, scrutinizing every corner of the shop. "I was worried you'd bugger things up, but looks like you didn't."

Orance, hands on his hips, looked at his feet laying tracks in the sawdust he had spread that morning.

"It's all up to you now, *fiston*. What we've got here ... all this ... it's got to work," Urbin said, stopping abruptly, grabbing his son's elbow and pulling him in. "You know, I've come to believe there's a reason why you're here ... why you're *still* here ... the only boy God left me with," he added, his yellow eyes reddening.

Orance nodded and chewed at the inside of his cheek.

"I don't know why what happened, happened. No one does. My father's gone and he's the one who ... and then your brothers—"

"Don't worry dad, I won't—"

"No," Urbin interrupted, tightening the hold on his son's arm while shaking his bicep. "You've got to *make* yourself succeed. This has gotta work. You understand what I'm saying to you?"

"I will ... I guarantee it. I will."

"You can't keep living the way you are ... can't keep heading down that road. *Comprends-tu mon gars*? Huh? D'you understand what I'm telling you here? Cause if you don't, you'll lose this shop, lose everything. We'll all lose everything."

Orance paused, looked beyond his father and saw Eugénie near the window, speaking with customers.

"Yes. I'll take care of everything."

Urbin let go of his son and turned to look at Eugénie. "There's something else you've got to keep in mind. This ..." he said, pointing all around the shop. "All this is yours. You understand? It's all for you and your children."

"Yeah, I understand. This place is—"

"Keep it for yourself. This is not for your wife to own. If something happens to you, it's all coming back to me. Eugénie's great but, be careful. She's all business, that one. Don't let her take over. You're in charge and don't you forget it."

Later, from behind the register, Eugénie grabbed Orance's sleeve as he walked by, a platter of entrails held out in front of him.

"Looks like you had a nice talk with your father earlier."

"Nice talk?"

"Yes ... the two of you. It looked pretty intense. What did you two talk about?"

Orance paused. "Well ... huh ... father, son stuff. You know, the kind of things a father says when he's about to ... you know ... bring his son into the family business."

Eugénie let go of his sleeve. "Gave you advice?"

"I've got to put these in the counter," Orance said, nodding down at his platter. "Besides, he'll be helping out over here all week so I guess there'll be plenty of opportunity to talk some more."

"Jus' curious, I guess. It's important to—"

"Look, this isn't *your* business. Your job is to make sure customers pay in full. I'll deal with my father," he said, sliding the platter inside the counter.

Eugénie smoothed her sleeves and stepped back. "I suppose that's so," she said. "I guess we'll see how well you handle all of this ... on your own."

-12-

Weeks passed, and the bell atop the shop's door jangled and clanged till shades were drawn. Locals loved the latest addition to the neighbourhood; loved the quality of the meats; the service. Loved Eugénie. Customers had lined up before Thanksgiving and Christmas. By now, Eugénie—the face of the new Charpentier butcher shop—managed staff, inventory, paid bills, and made sure each sale was properly transacted. She greeted customers by name and knew what the ladies' husbands loved to eat.

Despite his initial misgivings, Urbin couldn't help but notice Eugénie's skill, her business acumen. After all, she's the one who had suggested stocking pickles, olives, tea leaves, and spices. She listened to customers and responded to their needs. Soon, whatever changes were made at her ... at Orance's shop, Urbin soon introduced at his. She learned that, when it came to making business decisions, it was best to by-pass Orance and speak directly with her father-in-law who, in most cases, believed she knew best. She was the boss. The leader. The brains.

"Has your father arrived yet? He was supposed to bring two more beef carcasses today," Eugénie asked Orance on his way to the back.

"I have to go slice pork bellies, not sure when he's coming by."

"Lemme know when he gets here, I have to—"

"No . . ." Orance said. "*I* have to. *I* have to speak with him. This is *my* butcher shop. *I* have to speak with *my* father," em-phasizing each word, his finger spearing at the floor as if striking periods at the end of each of his sentences.

Eugénie turned away and looked down at her register. The women in the shop, at least four or five of them milling and talking amongst themselves, tried as best they could to make believe they hadn't witnessed the sharp exchange. Eugénie smoothed the fabric of her skirt, plastered a *public* smile on her lips, and said, "Can I help any of you ladies?"

"I've got beef coming in that's as fresh as today," Orance announced, looking into the shop through the swinging door's round window, a large tray of ground beef held shoulder high.

"I thought you had to slice bacon," Eugénie said while mil-ling amongst customers.

"Could you help me with something in the back," Orance said, pulling her backwards through the swinging door as soon as she got near him.

"You're making it sound as if you owned this place," he said, making sure to lower his voice down to a menacing whisper. "*I* don't even own this place. I'm gonna owe my father for years before I can call it my own," he added, releasing Eugénie's upper arm.

"I'll appreciate you not grabbing me again, especially not in front of my customers," Eugénie said, running her hand down her wrinkled sleeve.

"But that's the point; they're not *your* customers. They're not even *my* customers. They're *our* customers. They come here to buy meat. They're not here to see you."

"I'm not insinuating anything by calling them *my customers*. I happen to know these people ... by name. Besides, they also happen to know *my* name. I have a relationship with them. I'm not trying to make you look bad or to imply I'm the owner. Besides, isn't it *your* name that's painted on that sign?" She retorted, pointing at the front of the shop, at the (new) sign, outside, suspended above the door (well below the parlour's windows).

Orance leaned back on the butcher block and wiped his hands on his dirty apron. He cleared his throat, looked at Eugénie who, arms crossed, looked away from him, and he said, "Look, I'm trying to make this work, here. There's a lot of pressure to make this thing work."

"I'm not pressuring you to do anything. The last thing I wanna do is—"

"I'm not saying you're pressuring me but you know how it is. My father's expecting this business to work. Really work. He's put everything into this and if it doesn't work," he explained, looking at the ceiling and holding the heels of his hands to his temples. "If it doesn't, that'll mean he's been right all along; right about thinking the way he does about me."

Eugénie placed her hand on her husband's forearm, pinched her lips together, and said, "Nobody's out front. I have to go." Walking away, she couldn't help but shake her head ... nearly imperceptibly. She flung the door open, smiled brightly, clapped a few times and said, "Who needs my help?"

Chapter 7

Easter had finally passed and lent-starved regulars had returned in search of flesh, fat, and sizzle. Melting snow had transformed the macadam streets' diamond-hard consistency into slimy mud and, despite the sawdust on the floor, a pair of slippery soles were probably to blame when a lady dressed as if she was a dancer from some downtown review fell straight down on her derrière; legs stretched out in front of her to the ring-a-ding of the little bell chiming above the door she had just walked through. A whooping sound shot up from her chest that seemed to harmonize with the lingering ringtone as she unceremoniously collapsed.

"P-P-POW!" Ephrem yelled. "POW-P-POW!" He repeated, giggling and hiding behind his mother. By now, Blanche had been recruited to help out at the register—Ephrem in tow—the boy now used to spending his days drawing battleships and looking at customers' distorted shapes through the counter's bowed glass front.

"Help me, Blanche," Eugénie said, clutching the lady's arm, the back of her fancy dress covered in wet sawdust.

"Oh, my goodness ... oh, my goodness," Blanche repeated, running from behind the register to help.

"POW-P-POW!" Ephrem kept saying, tears of laughter in his eyes, standing on a stool to look over the counter.

They helped the woman to her feet; Eugénie felt the gilded lady's luxuriant fabric and assumed this customer wasn't from the neighbourhood.

"Are you all right?" Eugénie asked.

The lady smiled broadly and ran her gloved hands along her backside, sending sawdust to rain on the floor.

"Oh, I'll be fine, my dear. Thanks for the help."

"Pow," Ephrem repeated, banging his pencil on the counter's wooden edge.

"Enough. Ephrem, stop that. Be a gentleman," Blanche warned, letting go of the lady's arm to rejoin her son behind the register.

"Please, sit down for a while and make sure you haven't caused yourself any harm," Eugénie insisted, dragging a small chair behind the clumsy lady's legs.

"No, please, don't make a fuss on my account. I'm just glad no man was in here to witness all this," the lady said as other customers gathered around her.

"I'm the proprietor's wife, Eugénie."

"*Enchanté*. I'm Anna ... Anna Déry," she said, pulling at her sleeves and readjusting her broad hat. "I wasn't expecting to make such a spectacle of myself, but I must admit, this is not the first time I've been saved by my jacksie," she added, her powdered face and smirking red lips seeming out of place in a butcher shop.

"Did you suffer a spell?" Eugénie asked, taken aback by Anna's admission.

"No. My balance is fine," Anna said, surveying the damage, her chin pushed into her chest. "Don't concern yourself with my well-being. I'm fine ... please, attend to your other customers. The ones who managed to remain on their feet, that is," she added and winked.

Eugénie walked away, curious about this finely—if not daringly—attired lady who had made the worst of entrances.

"Hey, Eugénie, I need help back here," Orance said, poking out sideways from the partly opened swinging door behind the register. Before returning to the back, he turned to Blanche and said, "By the way, why's the dinlo yelling in the shop? I told you; you can bring him in here but he's gotta stay quiet," his left hand shoved under his right armpit while pointing at Ephrem with the other.

"A lady fell. It was just a reaction. It's the noise, he was laughing at the noise of it all. It's no problem."

"It *is* a problem when an imbecile ridicules customers. We can't let that happen."

"Don't call him that!" Eugénie snapped at Orance as she walked into the back.

Orance shoved both hands in his armpit holsters and looked at Eugénie.

"Don't call him that. Don't be unkind. He's fine out in front. He never disturbs anyone," she added, turning away abruptly, her beating heart ringing in the back of her eyeballs.

-2-

Orance's razor-sharp cleaver, the one his father had intended to give his late son, Siméon—the ebony handle with abalone inlay worn smooth and comfortable—felt as if it was part of his own hand as the instrument sliced smoothly through pork bellies, freeing thin tongues of bacon corded on the butcher block's end grain. Standing behind the door—slight tremors travelling up and down his arms, a weighty load of bacon neatly arranged on a steel platter in hand—he gazed out the round widow at the many customers inside the shop. Face hardening. Tightly. Tighter. He watched, unblinking, lips curled as he surveyed the activity; how his wife's graceful waltz with customers seemed natural, pleasant. Easy.

"Tell Orance to come on the floor?" He heard his wife ask Blanche, Eugénie no longer able to keep up with the crowd.

Blanche, ringing up orders and pulling the register's handle, yelled, "Orance, you're needed in front!" She then kicked her leg back at the swinging door, all the while focussed on making change for Madame Gendron who stood before her. The door smashed onto Orance's platter, sending bacon strips flying all over his face and chest. The meat hadn't yet hit the floor before Blanche realized she had broken the golden rule; the one that stipulates anyone opening the door dividing the back from the front should look through the round window first to ensure no one was attempting to do the same from the other side.

The reaction was immediate. The thumping sound of the door hitting the platter, the metallic clatter as everything hit the floor ... all this racket could hardly compete with Orance's bellowing. Everything stopped. Everyone Froze.

"*Tabarnak!*" He yelled. "*Osti d'câlisse de tabarnak!*"

Ephrem, who would usually respond to loud noises by contributing some of his own, looked up from his brown paper drawings and plastered himself into the corner. Orance, covered in bacon slices, pushed the door open and stood in the doorway, shoulders rising and falling, breath hissing from his nostrils like a bull about to rush. Blanche, partially pinned by the opened door, managed to wiggle free and positioned herself in front of her son.

Orance swatted strips of meat off his shoulders as if brushing snow after coming in from a storm. He moved forward and faced Blanche, the empty platter pinched between his index finger and thumb, a single slice of bacon left clinging to his lapel.

"Could you come back here—later—when the dinlo's done snivelling behind you?" He said, pointing back at the door with his thumb, the blank look on his face highlighting the stillness of his gaze.

Blanche bit her knuckle and nodded—slowly—shuffling backwards till she connected with Ephrem. Orance pushed the door open with his butt, tapped the platter against his thigh and left. Eugénie, who ordinarily, would never leave the shop unattended, followed right behind him.

"I jus' asked you not to use that word. His name's Ephrem. Ephrem! It's not hard to remember and pretty easy to pronounce," she challenged her husband, looking straight up at him, her finger angled at his chin.

Orance slapped her finger away with the back of his hand, crouched down and picked bacon strips off the floor.

"He's Blanche's son ... Marc's son. We all love him. Very

much. He's a person, a person with a name. Ephrem."

Orance flicked wood chips off the bacon strips, dust clinging to the white, fatty parts. "Correct me if I'm wrong but, I believe Blanche is alone out there. Never you mind what I called him. Get back on the floor. Now," Orance said, piling bacon strips on his platter.

The door cracked open and part of Blanche's face appeared in the small opening. "I'm so … so sorry about this. I apologize. We were so busy, I had to deal with the register and when Eugénie asked me to call you, I—"

"Mind your business, Blanche. I'll deal with you later," Orance said, throwing a slice of bacon in her direction; the meat sticking to the door.

"What's ailing you? Have you gone mad?" Eugénie confronted her husband while Blanche disappeared behind the swinging door, its back-and-forth momentum making the suspended slice of bacon wiggle like a worm on a hook.

"Why don't you just get back out there to those customers you say you love so much," Orance said, staring menacingly at Eugénie, his lower lip pulling away from his teeth.

Eugénie gasped, pushed the door hard on her way out and inadvertently swung it on Blanche's hip—the impact causing the bacon strip to lose its grip and fall to the floor.

"Sorry. You all right?" Eugénie asked, wrapping her arms around her aunt and winking at Ephrem.

"She's fine," Orance replied, walking out front, holding the door opened behind him. "Everyone, please, everything's fine here … just a little family squabble, that's all," he said, hands on his hips. "After all, this is what a family business is all about. Am I right?" He added, smiling and chuckling.

-3-

"You go along, I've got lots left to do here," Eugénie told Blanche as she locked the shop's door.

"I'll get supper ready; don't you worry about anything.

Your supper'll be waiting for you, on the table, as soon as you come up," Blanche insisted.

"Don't worry 'bout me. Just make sure Ephrem eats. I'll deal with things once I come up,"

Blanche paused for a second, then called Ephrem who ran to her and locked his arms around her waist.

"Sorry again for what happened earlier. I don't know what came over me ... I know I'm not supposed to open the door when—"

"Don't torment yourself with any of this, Aunt Blanche. It's jus' as much my fault. I should've been the one to call Orance. Jus' go upstairs, Ephrem's gonna want to play with his toys."

"Eugénie," Orance hollered from the back.

Eugénie smiled at Blanche and walked away. Blanche looked back at her niece then wrapped her arms tightly around her son. "She'll be all right," Blanche told Ephrem looking down at him and running her fingers through the boy's thin, blonde hair.

"Did you finish cleaning up out there?" Orance asked.

"Everything's ready for tomorrow. Might as well go upstairs and eat. There'll be plenty of time—"

"You go, I've got lots left to do here. Besides, I don't wanna go to bed late again tonight, I want to make sure things get done, now."

"Ok, but I can help. Besides, Aunt Blanche said she'd get supper ready for us."

"I'm not sure that woman can get anything done right. Besides, she'll probably try to poison me."

Eugénie, sweeping soiled sawdust off the floor, paused and looked at her husband, rubbing his chin with his shoulder while cranking the meat grinder's handle and stuffing beef cubes into its mouth.

"Can't you stop talking about my aunt that way? She's really a wonderful person, you know. She saved Saraphine and me ... took us in. We owe everything to them, my Aunt

Blanche and my Uncle Marc," Eugénie said, her words coated in a soothing, conciliatory tone.

"I'll tell you what; a man's what she needs. She needs to get married ... take care of her own man."

"But she helps out right here. If it wasn't for her, you'd have to pay someone to do the same work. Look at all she does for us. Why, she's upstairs—right now—getting supper ready. Isn't that important? Isn't that—"

"True enough. But won't Saraphine be done with her schooling soon? When will she start working here full-time? She does fine when she helps out on Saturdays. Besides, if she worked here that'd mean we wouldn't have to deal with that crazy dinlo all the time. You heard him again, today? He makes everyone uncomfortable. No one feels right around a freak."

"Don't call him that! He's got trouble speaking, he's a stutterer, not a freak. Jus' because it takes him longer to understand things, that he's a bit slower than others, that doesn't mean you can call him nasty names," she ranted, slamming the broom's bristles on the floor.

"A retard's a retard ... and he's a retard," he said, hands cupped on the sides of his mouth and shouting at his wife.

Eugénie moved-in close, broom in hand, and slapped his shoulder with it.

"Stop that," he said, brushing sawdust off of himself.

"Don't call him that. His name's Ephrem," she repeated, her white knuckles choking the broom handle.

"Ephrem-the-retard ... call him by his full name. Yeah, maybe that's what I should do?" He teased, looking down into the meat grinder's gullet while absentmindedly spinning the handle and smiling.

Eugénie took three more steps, lifted the broom over her shoulders and smacked Orance on the head. "Stop it!" she cautioned.

Orance kept his hand on the grinder's handle but stopped spinning it. He took a deep breath, looked at his wife, and said, "Don't do that again. Don't *ever* hit me again."

Eugénie dropped the broom at his feet. "I'll be having supper," she said, on her way to the staircase. "Spend as much time down here as you want. I think I'd rather be with people who aren't as angry as you are."

"It's my house, I'll go up whenever I want," Orance said at Eugénie's back. "By the way, this also happens to be *my* business. Maybe you should remember that. Not yours … mine. I'll run it anyway I want to. My father and me … we're the family business. Maybe you should just do what you're told and stay out of things that don't concern you."

Eugénie stopped and, without turning back to look at Orance, said, "Maybe I should and let your father see how truly useless you are."

-4-

Mumbling something to herself while slapping at her hip, Eugénie somehow managed to slow her breathing and calm herself—she thought—by the time she reached the top of the staircase. She sat in her spot at the table and offered a nod and a smile. Saraphine smiled back at her sister while Blanche loaded Eugénie's plate. Eugénie ripped a piece of bread from the half-loaf that remained on the table and looked at both of them—Ephrem having never taken his eyes off his drawing.

"That stew was terrific, Aunt Blanche … wasn't that good?" Saraphine told her aunt then shook Ephrem's elbow in order to pull his attention away from the critter he had been working on.

"G-good," he answered over the sound of his grease pencil gliding along his large sheet of brown paper.

Just then, Eugénie thought of saying something, of complaining about her husband, but didn't. Instead, she looked at her plate and managed to eat everything on it. "That was succulent, Aunt Blanche," she remarked, pulled up a corner of the table cloth and wiped her mouth. She looked at her cousin and asked, "How did you enjoy your supper, young man?"

Ephrem looked up, puzzled. "I t-told a-already … g-good … good s-s-supper"

"Maybe we can play cards after the dishes?" Saraphine suggested and rubbed the back of Ephrem's neck.

"I'm tired," Eugénie said. "It's you and Ephrem tonight. Your aunt and I had a really hard day."

"So, maybe I could help downstairs. School's almost over … surely, there must be something I can help with at the shop. Besides, you're the one who says that there's always something left to do."

The door in the hallway creaked and Orance walked in, his shirt stained with blood that had soaked through his apron.

"You made it just in time. We were about to do the dishes, but there's plenty left," Saraphine said. Eugénie and Blanche exchanged a quick glance before looking at their laps.

"Something smells good. I'll have plenty of whatever that is."

"I'll have to go back downstairs … still have lots to do down there." Eugénie said, taking off her apron and tucking her chair under the table. "I'm hoping I can count on you two to do the dishes?" She added, eyes moist glancing at Saraphine and Blanche as she walked out the kitchen.

"There's nothing left to do … took care of everything," Orance said, reaching for his wife's arm as she tried to squeeze by him.

"The counters need to be cleaned. You're always thinking about what needs to be done in the back … what *you* have to do. There happens to be plenty more that needs to be done, things you don't really seem to care about," she said, staring up into her husband's face, arm locked in her husband's grip.

"I say you can finish whatever needs to be done, tomorrow. For now, we're going to spend our evening upstairs."

Eugénie yanked her arm loose, ran her hand along her

sleeve's fabric, walked into her bedroom and closed the door.

Orance watched as his wife walked away, then, turning to look back at Blanche, said, "So, what about me having a nice, big plate of whatever smells so good," tucking himself in his spot at the table's end.

Orance didn't react at the sound of the bedroom door banging against the wall, and Eugénie never looked back before she stomped down the stairway. Orance, the thick vein in his neck having turned purple, belched, its resonance startling Saraphine. Ephrem giggled, then promptly answered by offering a juicy one of his own.

"So, Blanche, what about supper?"

Blanche looked down the hallway, eyes clasped into tiny slits, trying to make herself small as she loaded up a plate and placed it under Orance's face.

"Did the dinlo eat?" He asked, nodding in Ephrem's direction.

Saraphine slid her hand beneath the table, took hold of her cousin's forearm and smiled at him. "I think your drawing's pretty much finished. Why don't we go play with your blocks," she said, and dragged Ephrem behind her.

-5-

"You're a real wizard in the kitchen, Blanche. What is this, anyway?"

Blanche looked into the dish-filled basin, a humourless smile pasted on her face, playing along with Orance's exaggerated appreciation for the ordinary supper.

"Just stew. I cook it real slow, you know, to bring out the taste. Marc always enjoyed having it prepared that way," she said, the sound of clanking dishes in the sink nearly drowned out by Orance's loud chewing.

"Marc was a good guy. A real gentleman," he said, mouth full and smacking. "Did you know that he helped me … that he's the reason why me and her got together in the first place," he added, pointing his fork over his shoulder, drops of gravy landing on his shirt.

"Um, no … wait … yes … maybe. What did he do?"

"Just helped. You know, greased the wheels you might say."

She hurried to finish cleaning up, eager to join her son in the parlour—away from the danger zone. Orance, having sopped up all the gravy from his plate with his bread crust, abruptly lifted himself off his chair.

"Well, I guess it's not fair to let the wife do all the work. I should go down there and see what she's up to," he said, wiping the corners of his mouth with the cuff of his sleeve.

Blanche quickly plucked his plate off the table and dunked it in the murky dishwater. Trying to sound casual, she said, "Oh, all right then," her brow wrinkling, the back of her neck tingling at the thought of what might happen below. Hands dripping, she scuttled behind Orance, grabbed the door before it had closed, and yelled down the stairwell, "Maybe I should join you two? Can't I do anything to help?"

Orance, halfway down the steps, looked back and waved dismissively.

"You don't need to come down here jus' 'cause *I've* got work to do," Eugénie said, looking up into the stairwell.

"Just wanted to check for myself to see what was so urgent that it needed to be done tonight," Orance added, his voice fading behind the door he had closed behind him.

"Like I told you, jus' the usual *to-dos*," Eugénie said, rubbing a vinegar-soaked rag along the counter's glass front.

"It's those kids," he said, holding the swinging door ajar with his elbow, his face squeezed in the opening.

"What? What kids?" Eugénie asked, wiping and rubbing.

"Mothers, with their children. They point at everything in the counter and leave all those fingermarks on the glass."

"I guess. They jus' needed cleaning."

"Well, I'm here so I might as well make myself useful," he said, pushing away from the door.

He stood at his bench, reached down under the second shelf, and pulled out a rag twisted around a half-full bottle of Caribou. He spent nearly ninety minutes carefully disassembling his large meat grinder, sucking back a gulp of Caribou for each part he managed to extricate from the tool's body. Eugénie moved back and forth along the counter subtly peeking through the round window, watching her husband, his back turned, the nearly empty bottle sitting next to him on the counter.

"You almost finished in there?" She asked, trying to infuse her voice with some kind of positive inflection. "Orance, you all right?"

Pacing behind the shop's counter, wiping and re-wiping every surface, Eugénie finally walked through the door. Orance, sprawled on his bench, head down on his right arm—empty bottle in hand—snored and drooled; spit bubbles forming and bursting from the corner of his mouth. She stood there a few seconds; hand glued to the door; the pathetic scene requiring some time to fully sink in. She let go of the door, absentmindedly wiped her forehead with her vinegary rag, slipped her shoes off, and slid her feet along the floor in order to avoid crunching woodchips underfoot from waking him up. Shoes in hand, she looked back at the long tracks she had left behind, silently closed the door and tiptoed upstairs.

The large skylight atop the stairwell did little on this moonless night to illuminate the long, narrow space. She had climbed eight of the fourteen steps when the door behind her rattled and flung open. Startled, she looked down at his backlit silhouette; drunk, unsteady, and rocking from side to side. Squinting down at him, she sat and put on her shoes. "What're you doing? I thought you were asleep," she said, looking back at the steps left to climb.

"You're finished w-with your w-w-work? I'm not finished.

Why don't you h-help me? You shouldn't go upstairs …
there's s-still lots to do down here," he pleaded, a long spit
ribbon dancing from his lower lip.

"I think maybe you should come up with me. You need to
go to bed. You've done enough for—"

"Get down here," he said, lumbering up the stairs. "There's
lots to do, still," he added then—pow—lunged at Eugénie,
grabbed her ankle and yanked hard. She skidded down the
steps, her left hip bearing the brunt of the impacts; shocked
by the drunkard's burst of speed and agility.

"Let's see what *you* can do to help *me* down here. That
meat you sell up front, somebody's gotta butcher all that, you
know. Somebody's gotta get it all ready. *C'est ma job* … it's
what I do," Orance said, hands around Eugénie's forearms;
bile and sugars merging in the back of his throat blowing
noxious fumes from his lips.

"What're you saying? I know that. Don't you think I—"

"No. I think that you think I do nothing 'round here."

"I don't think that. I never—"

"Shut up, stop it. I know what you think. You think the
same thing my f-father thinks. Well … you're wrong. I do
plenty 'round here. This place is all about me," Orance said,
releasing one of Eugénie's arms to point at all parts of the
shop.

Eugénie wrestled away from him, the strength of her move
surprising Orance and shutting him up for a second.

"You're drunk. Again."

"I happen to be tired, I'm not—"

"You're drunk and beastly. That's what happens whenever
you drink. You're like that Mr Hide character," Eugénie said,
her fingertip inches from Orance's nose and banging her heel
on the floor.

Orance, startled by the retaliation, fell back on his bench,
scoffed and dismissively waved at her.

"Enough drama. You're like one of those actresses at the
Empire."

"Don't you see how you upset everyone when you drink? You're not yourself anymore. You must—"

"Must what? What exactly?" Orance asked, pushing his butt off the bench and moving in; closing the gap between his face and Eugénie's finger that she kept aimed at him.

Eugénie stepped back, stuck her hands on her hips and said, "There's no point in me trying to reason with you when you're like this; in the state you're in … might as well jus' go to bed."

"Yeah, sure, maybe that's a good idea."

"We'll speak tomorrow when the Hyde drains out of your blood."

"What're you t-talking about? What's a Hyde?"

"Never mind, it's not important anymore. I'm going to—"

"*I* mind," Orance said, his scalp sliding back along his head; his tone ratcheted up to its most menacing. "You think I'm a muttonhead, like that dinlo you all love so much up there," he added, pointing up at the stairwell with his eyes.

"Don't call him that," Eugénie warned, her finger pulled from her holster and pointed back at his face.

Orance turned away and shook his head.

Eugénie clenched her teeth, sucked her lips into her mouth, leaned forward, and stared through him. "I said … don't call him—"

Orance drove the heels of his hands into her chest. Air hissed from her lungs as she slid along the sawdust before finally crashing into the door jamb. There she lay, propped up against the wall, head drooping sideways and spilling blood onto her shoulder. He stood over her mouthing soundless words, wiped his hands on his chest, reached over his unconscious wife, turned the light off, stepped over Eugénie's legs, and climbed the stairs.

-7-

Blanche had been sitting upstairs, ear to the door, monitoring the latest skirmish till the sound of Orance's heavy boots fumbling up the stairs sent her scurrying to her room. Sitting at the foot of Ephrem's bed, she waited till the snoring started—drunk, Orance's nightly sawing of logs morphed into a kind of animalistic, guttural gurgle—before going back to check on her niece. She pulled her door open, synchronizing the sound of the creaking hinges with Orance's vocalizations, and slid along her woollen slippers. There, across from Orance's bedroom door, she whispered down the stairwell.

"Eugénie," she called, hanging on to the doorknob, bent at the waist and pushing her mouth as far forward as she could. "Psst ... Eugénie, *chérie*, can you hear me?" She whispered, looking back at Orance's closed bedroom door, stalked by his proximity, and trembling at the thought of her niece having been injured. Beaten.

Over and over, she whispered Eugénie's name, chewing her lips, droplets of cool sweat sliding down her back. "Eugénie," she repeated, her accelerating heartbeat driven by imagination.

"*Matante?*" Saraphine asked, standing in the kitchen, rubbing her forehead with the heel of her palm and looking perplexed at the sight of her aunt sitting in the hallway in the middle of the night.

Blanche's eyes popped. She glided toward her niece and leaned forward; finger crossed over her pursed lips and shushing frantically.

"Just checking ... making sure everything's all right down at the shop," she told Saraphine as she rushed her back into her room.

"Something wrong at the shop?"

"No, nothing. I just woke up, thought I heard a noise, down there. It's nothing."

"Why don't you wake up Orance? He'll go down there. You shouldn't—"

"No, everything's fine. It's probably Orance's crazy snoring that woke me up. Back to sleep, you go," Blanche said, pulling the covers over her niece. "Anyway, I don't want to wake Ephrem. You know how he is when he wakes up in the middle of the night."

Blanche backed away, thinking Saraphine—a teenager about to leave high school— looked smaller than ever tucked under a pile of covers. Walking out of the bedroom, her sleeve got snagged by the skeleton key sitting in the lockset. She tugged the fabric loose; her eyes lit up.

She pulled the key out and locked Saraphine's door from the kitchen. Key in hand, she tiptoed to Orance's bedroom and locked him in. Standing still, very still, she stared at the knob and didn't move till she heard him snoring then hurried to do the same for her own door and locked her son away from Orance.

"Eugénie, Eugénie … *t'es où ma belle?*" She asked, having reached the bottom of the steps. "Where are you?" She repeated, groping the wall in search of the light switch. Feeling nothing but plaster, she walked in and tripped over Eugénie's legs, swallowing the yell that had sprung inside her as she fell.

"*Ahh non,*" she whispered in the darkness, pressing down on her knees to lift herself back on her feet. She found the switch and illuminated the scene; Eugénie, her nose buried in sawdust, bleeding. Blanche's eyes nearly sprung from her head.

"Eugénie," Blanche said, brushing her niece's hair off her forehead. "*Non, non, non.*"

She rolled Eugénie's sleeves around her hands, dragged her away from the door and laid her back against the workbench's drawers.

"Eugénie," she called again, her niece's hand sandwiched between her own. "Can you hear me? *Réveile-toi ma petite.*"

"Blanche," she answered, her voice faint and distant, her chin rolling on her chest as if her spine were made of cotton.

"*Dit pas rien, ma p'tite … essaye pas d'parler,*" Blanche said, tears clinging to her lower lashes. "Don't say nothing."

Eugénie tried to look up at her aunt but her head fell back and thumped the bench's drawer fronts. Her thick, chestnut hair and left ear were bloodied, the red spill having flowed down her neck and shoulder.

"I'll get water and clean that cut. Stay here … stay there," Blanche said, furiously patting Eugénie's hand.

"Wait, wait," Eugénie said, squeezing her aunt's wrist. "Jus' help me up … get on my feet."

"What happened? What did that worthless man do to you? *Maudit vaurien*." Blanche cried, struggling to help her niece to her feet. Though wobbly and needing Blanche's hand to steady herself, Eugénie's eyes darted in all directions.

"Where is he?" She asked, feeling the side of her head; her cold fingers warmed by her own blood.

"Sleeping … locked in his room. I locked Ephrem and Saraphine in their rooms, too. He can't get out. We're safe … we're all safe."

"You locked who? What?" Eugénie, eyes squeezed shut from the pain and stroking her temple, asked.

"I took the keys out of the locks and—"

A loud bang avalanched down the staircase.

"Lemme out of here," Orance shouted, the meaty sides of his fists pounding on the door.

Seconds later, shattered from their slumber, the frantic voices of Saraphine and Ephrem added to the mayhem. "Why's the door locked, let me out," Saraphine hollered in terror while Ephrem cried and howled.

"I'll go let them out, they don't know about any of this," Blanche said, twirling and pointing her finger at Eugénie.

Blanche ran upstairs, turned on the hallway light and rushed past Orance's door, her body turned sideways as if avoiding a wild animal's lunging paw.

"Lemme out. Don't you leave me here. I'm telling you, I'm gonna break this door down. I swear, I'm gonna break it down." Orance screamed at the noise of footsteps running past his door.

Having let Ephrem out—the boy had immediately wrapped himself around his mother's arm—Blanche, hyperventilating, dropped to her knees in front of Saraphine's bedroom door, and fumbled to insert the key into the keyhole.

"What's happening," Saraphine wailed from inside, the sound of her cries pushing every drop of blood in Blanche's body into her throbbing skull. The bedroom door swung open and they clumped together as if trying to meld themselves into a single being. Orance hollered and cursed. They held on tighter.

"What's the matter? What happened? Did something happen to Eugénie?" Saraphine asked—the look on her aunt's face having terrified her—Ephrem now wrapped around Saraphine's legs.

"Everything's all right but we have to go downstairs," Blanche said, pushing back from them and looking deeply into their eyes.

"Downstairs? Why downstairs? What's going on?" Saraphine cried.

"We have to go downst—"

"Somebody, unlock this damn door," Orance exploded.

Saraphine looked down the hallway, then at her aunt, mouth agape. "Why's he locked in his room?" She asked, wiping snot from her nose. "Why were we locked in?"

"Just follow me and don't pay any attention to Orance or anything he says. We're going downstairs," Blanche said, chin up though failing to look fearless. She took hold of Saraphine and Ephrem's hands and got up from her knees. "Come on, we're going downstairs," she repeated, the three of them hugging the wall as they slunk by Orance's door.

The sound of Orance, soused and unsteady, his back to the door, kicking at the bottom panel with the sole of his heavy shoe, caused Saraphine to quietly yelp as they hurried past.

"Hurry. Please, hurry," Eugénie called weakly up the stairwell.

"Eugénie," Saraphine shouted. "Are you okay? What's

happened to you?"

Blanche corralled them down the stairs. Once landed in the butcher shop they rushed to Eugénie and dropped to their knees around her, all of them locked in an embrace.

"Lemme out of here, now!" Orance screamed.

"Close the door . . ." Eugénie said. "No need to keep on hearing this."

They ran through the swinging door—Eugénie having to rely on Blanche and Saraphine to keep her balance—and stood in the moonlit shop, breathless, hams suspended on strings pinned to the top of the large window, casting strange shadows on the floor.

"Why are we leaving? Where're we going?" Saraphine asked.

Eugénie and Blanche looked at each other, slack-jawed.

"Monsieur Charpentier's house. That's it, we're going to Monsieur Charpentier's house," Eugénie blurted. "He'll take us in … for a little while … maybe."

"We can't leave like this," Blanche said, the reality of the situation flooding over her as she looked down at her *chemise de nuit*. "I'm in my nightgown … slippers on my feet. Saraphine and Ephrem, they're barefoot."

"I don't understand why we've got to go to Monsieur Charpentier's house. It's the middle of the night," Saraphine asked, on the verge of tears.

"Listen," Eugénie said, taking hold of her sister's shoulders. "It's dangerous for us to stay here. Orance is drunk … sick … dangerous. I can't deny it any more, none of us can. It's what happens to him when he drinks and he drinks all the time. You know, you both know that we've got to leave."

Saraphine stared blankly at her sister, looked back at her aunt and nodded, slowly.

"Wait here, I'll go get some of our things," Blanche said, clapping her hands before aiming her palms at the other refugees. "I'll be right back."

Blanche picked-up Ephrem's shoes and plucked Saraphine's coat from off its hook; sprinting in all directions and grabbing stuff they'd need for their nocturnal march. Arms full, she scanned opened drawers trying to figure out what she had forgotten to snatch up. She dumped everything on the bed and bundled the mess in her sheet, pausing every once in a while to look out into the hallway to make sure Orance had remained locked in.

Slowly, she walked out into the kitchen; her neck craned forward, staring down the hallway. Moving toward the stairwell—one tiny step at a time—she slid her wool slippers along the floor, shortening her strides as she approached Orance's closed bedroom door. Shoulders up to her earlobes, she glided by. In the blink of an eye, the door had crashed upon her, shards of wood flying all around. He had charged the door, the full weight of his body ripping out the jambs.

Blanche felt her breath wheeze up her throat when body slammed into the wall, the impact of the crash busting a large crater into the plaster. Orance, drunk and dazed, lay on top of her, blood dripping from his forehead. Blanche, the shock of the event anesthetizing the pain she would later feel, bounced to her feet, arms flailing while frantically slapping off remnants of the heavy oak door from her shoulders and chest. Orance, flat on his back, moaned and coughed.

"Stay there," she yelled, showing her palms as if holding up an invisible wall.

"Blanche," Saraphine and Eugénie screamed from downstairs. "Blanche, are you all right?" Saraphine repeated, running up the stairs.

"I'm coming … coming," Blanche answered, reaching down for her bundled sheet.

"Why'd you lock me in? Why'd you do that?" Orance said, rubbing his knees as he tried to get back on his feet, his butt against the broken wall.

"Don't you move … don't you touch me," Blanche warned, bent at the waist, struggling to retrieve her loaded sheet pinned under the shattered door.

Orance wiped his face, eyes narrowing at the sight of his own blood. "Look at me," he said, blood trickling from his nose mingling with mucus dripping off his chin.

"What's going on up there? Blanche? You all right?" Eugénie and Saraphine continued to holler.

"I'm hurt. I think my nose's broken," Orance answered.

Blanche, desperately yanking at the sheet, surprised herself by thinking Orance sounded like a battered child—as if unaware of the circumstances leading to this moment.

Orance, suddenly realizing the voices were coming from downstairs, straightened and pushed himself off the floor. "You're not gonna take the egg on this one, Eugénie. You better learn discipline," he shouted at the stairwell's open door, spit and blood raining on Blanche as he started yanking at her bundled sheet.

"Get out of there, Blanche … jus' get down here," said Eugénie.

Orance stomped at the broken door—elbows jerking up and down as he thrust, moves reminiscent of some juvenile dance—the repeated impacts setting free Blanche's sheet. Pushing past Blanche, he took a few unsteady steps toward the staircase, took hold of the doorframe, and looked down at his wife's darkened silhouette. "Get up here right now … now, this minute!"

Eugénie, Saraphine behind her, looked up the stairwell, neither of them able to see through the dimness.

"I'm not gonna say it again, if I go down there, the *both* of you are g-gonna get what you got coming," he said, pointing down, his voice sounding malevolently detached from his own body. Then he sneered, his upper lip lifting up against his nose, and banged the side of his fist on the wall. "I said, get up here. Now! The two of you, get—"

Orance was airborne. Flying clear over eight steps, his chest landed a few feet above Eugénie, his limp body sliding down the rest of the way, a bloody skid mark left behind his heels. Atop the staircase, sheet flung over her shoulder, Blanche stood breathless.

Eugénie and Saraphine looked down at Orance and up at their aunt, necks craned, squinting and struggling to see her expression. "Blanche?" Eugénie asked, sounding calm and shocked all at once. Saraphine looked at her sister, wiped her eyes, and looked back up the stairwell.

"Guess we better go," Blanche said, walking down the stairs and nearly stepping on Orance's hand sidestepping around him. "M-m-mom," she heard Ephrem call. She let the bundle drop from her shoulder, ran to her son and held him to her chest.

-9-

Saraphine clutched at her sister's arm with both hands. Blanche and Eugénie took a few turns carrying Ephrem on their backs. They trekked through the rain, north along St. Denis Street. Wet and dirty, refugees on the move. Silent. Together. They walked ... walked by men, passed out, lying on flattened crates and discarded rugs—indigents wearing summer clothes in late fall, huddled around steel barrels loaded with burning garbage. Some of the men looked at them; this strange troupe of wanderers, their ghostly demeanour seeming to immunize them from peril.

Urbin pinched the curtain rod and slid the door's dainty lace curtain just far enough to poke an eye out at the balcony. It took a few seconds, but he soon recognized who had knocked at his door—out there, in the cold, at four in the morning. He stepped back, nearly losing his balance and needing to steady himself by grabbing at the doorknob. He stood before them, stock-still, aghast at the sight of them wearing nothing but nightgowns and balled-up linens. Eugénie's hair was knotted in bloody clumps … a tragedy had occurred

It took some time before Eugénie could calm down and describe the scene; to adequately convey the danger, the menace, while Urbin looked down and tapped his knuckles on the table and listened. Now and then, he'd run his hand over his mouth, his gritty chin nearly setting his palm alight. Eyes unfocused, lost, he tried to conjure a plan, some way of managing his son; of dealing with the fact that he had a business to keep afloat. Scenes popped up in his mind; the suffering he had endured to save this boy from the water. They talked and talked (he mostly listened), images coming into clear focus. Through all the words, explanations and graphic descriptions, he struggled to keep his mind from wandering … struggled to understand why Orance had to have been his Moses.

PART II

Chapter 8

Orance came too, flat on his chest, one arm tucked under his body, his yawning mouth immersed in a small, red puddle; his feet propped up on the stairs sending blood rushing down into his head. He opened one eye—his ears buzzed—convinced his brain was trying to bust out of his skull. He coughed saliva from his lips that formed into bubbling, white islands drifting along the sanguine mess. Despite the fantastic discomfort of his situation, he feared moving any part of his body, overwhelmed by the thought of having to rely on what he suspected was a number of broken bones to get himself off the floor. Motionless, he scanned his body from top to bottom before slowly wiggling his ankles, bending knees and shrugging shoulders; building up an inventory of working parts. Minutes passed before he could roll off the floor—steadying himself on jellified legs and clutching at the walls on either side of him—feeling like a newborn fawn. He gasped and bent over slightly, gently touching his chest, wincing when he felt the swelling and discombobulated shards of bone beneath his skin.

Considering himself lucky that a few broken ribs were the only casualties of his express trip down the stairs, he stepped out, moving as if afraid he'd fall through rice paper. Breathing slowly, deliberately, his chest cinched up into a fist, the rising of his lungs rubbing against his ribcage feeling like a lash whipping at his insides; he held on to the doorframe and clutched at his side, looking as if trying to keep his ribs from falling through his shirt.

Shocked and still drunk, he wondered. *How could all this have happened? How did this all start?* Taking in shallow breaths and struggling to swallow, he gasped and recoiled from the pain. Just then, the story came clear. There, at the bottom of the door frame, a blackening, crimson stain, long chestnut hairs mingling within it. His wife, the woman he had nearly killed, had escaped. In a flash, last night's events came jetting into his budding sobriety. He, he had done this. He was the source of fear, of pain, of violence. The aggressor. The monster. What yesterdays had been—and none of them had been great—would never be again. This he knew for certain.

He looked at the clock; customers would soon be at his door. He reached for his apron on the hook next to his bench and tied it behind his back—the move igniting his broken ribs like fireworks—and used it to wipe the blood off his nose and mouth; just another red stain hanging off his chest. He looked through the swinging door's round window, into the shop, and saw no one waiting at the steps. A pillow case and a sock lay amongst the sawdust next to the front door. Like an old man, he put his left hand on his knee, bent down—slowly— and picked up the blood-stained material. He felt the fabric, looked out the window, balled up and tossed everything into the bin. Reaching for the door, he noticed it had remained partially opened. Visions of his wife, Saraphine, Blanche, and Ephrem appeared in his mind. People he had terrorized and injured. A family fleeing into the night to save themselves from the violence, to save themselves from him.

-2-

Urbin sat at the corner of his kitchen table, the smoke from his pipe curling back through his yellowing, greying hair. He sat still except for his left leg which he couldn't keep from bouncing, the toes on his good foot mechanically pumping his knee up and down. Arms folded over his chest, he stared into the still-dark room, trying to envision his next step. Trying to deal with his drunk of a son. How to tame the boy's violent edge?

"I'm sorry about all this," Eugénie said, sitting next to the kitchen counter, her voice cutting through the stillness.

Urbin stood and pulled the chain dangling from the ceiling's light fixture.

"*You're* sorry?" He said, noticing patches of dried blood on Eugénie's neck.

"I couldn't think of anywhere else to go. I don't have anyone else to turn to. None of us do … I don't think—"

"Come and sit over here," he said, pulling a chair out from the table. "Sit, let's have a chat."

Eugénie sat and stretched her arms over the tabletop, nervously sliding her fingertips on the surface as if polishing the wood.

"Let me get you something to eat, you must be hungry."

"Y-yes, f-food … b-bread," Ephrem answered, his mother reaching out to take hold of his waving hands.

"It's okay," Eugénie said, looking at her sister and shaking her head.

They sat, neither of them knowing how to initiate this type of conversation. She tried to smile, uncomfortably. Urbin got up, tapped his pipe on the stove's ash pan, took his tobacco pouch out from the sticky drawer and reloaded his pipe's chamber. Eugénie, nails tapping on the tabletop, looked down at her scraped knuckles.

"What'd you want me to do, dear?" He asked, seemingly mesmerized by the contents of his tobacco pouch.

Eugénie looked at her sister, looked at Blanche but they just looked down at their fingers. "Do?" She echoed Urbin's question.

"Yes. *Do*. What can *I* do in all of this?" Urbin repeated, the light and sound of the match he struck serving to accentuate the pertinence—or impertinence—of his question; a huge plume of smoke rising as he shook the flame off the little piece of wood.

Eugénie shrugged and said, "I don't know, you've spoken

with him before. The good Lord knows *I* have. I've pleaded with him to act like a gentleman but, he jus' doesn't ... not when he gets to the drink, anyway.

"But that's not how I raised him. Believe it or not, he *was* raised to be a gentleman. He's the chosen one. His whole life's a miracle. I don't understand what's happened here. Maybe you could . . ."

"What?"

Urbin sighed and rubbed his prickly jaw. "Maybe you could help him control his liquor. Isn't that the real problem that we're dealing with here?"

Eugénie looked away, breathing in, tapping her knuckles on the table. "You're right, his drinking *is* the problem," she said, words muffled by her hands covering her face. "But, what I'm really afraid of is that he's . . . that, one of these days, he's gonna beat me, beat me real bad. That he's gonna kill me, or my sister ... Ephrem or my aunt. Over and over, I've asked him to stop, but it's jus' not in his temperament to be sober. He's got bottles hidden all over the shop and stashed upstairs. I don't dare get rid of 'em; I don't want *him* to know that *I* know where he's hiding his booze. Sometimes, I pour a little bit out from the bottles so that when he gets to them, there won't be enough left for him to get drunk on. But he jus' finds other bottles and downs whatever's left in those."

Urbin looked at Eugénie, blinking through the smoke billowing from his mouth. He pushed away from the table, mumbled something then limped off—downhearted at his failure to offer reassuring words, at his failure to be a father to his son.

"I never know when he's gonna start drinking, or when he's gonna start with the hitting. I can't fight him. Maybe, if *you* talked to him Monsieur Charpentier ... maybe *you* could—"

"For the love of Christ, that boy needs more than a stern talking-to," Urbin coiled around and said, rubbing his temples till his hair stuck out from the sides of his head like some weird stork. "Besides, there's been way too much talking going on here. That boy needs a taste of his own medicine if he's ever gonna change. Everybody's the same, we all keep acting the same way 'til we get a lesson we don't forget," he added, waving his fist.

Eugénie's cheeks puffed up like balloons and her eyes grew wide. "You really think that hurting him, again … that pummelling him is gonna make a difference?"

"Listen girl, nothing else's worked," he said, running his thumbs the length of his suspenders. "Maybe if I had the parish priest speak with him. Maybe he'd be able to—"

"Don't. It's bad enough our own customers look at me the way they do. I'd rather we keep this in the family."

Urbin moved to the back of Eugénie's chair and dropped his hand on her shoulder. "Leave it to me. All of you can stay here. Tomorrow, me and him are gonna have a talk. Trust me, I'll make him see reason," he said, patting his daughter-in-law's shoulder before walking down the hallway, the sound of his bedroom door closing behind him.

Blanche went to the breadbox and pulled out a large loaf. Saraphine opened a few cabinet doors before finding plates that she carefully placed on the table. Looking through the icebox, she found a jar of drippings, remnants of a pork roast—a thick layer of fat sealing the tasty brown sludge at the bottom—that they spread on pieces of crust.

"I'm sorry," Eugénie said, looking down at her plate.

"It's not your fault," Saraphine said, corralling crumbs into the corner of her mouth with her thumbnail.

"Of course not," Blanche added. "It's him. He's the one. How can you possibly say that you're the one who's—"

"What, Aunt Blanche? The one to blame? The one who's sorry? Well, I am … both those things. I'm to blame 'cause *I* married that man. I'm to blame 'cause I insisted on bringing you all into this hell. Sorry? You better believe I'm sorry. Sorry for the both of you," she added, pointing at Saraphine and her aunt. "It's like we're all stuck in a jail without bars.

What are we supposed to do, exactly? Live out there, home-less?" She added, nodding at the door.

They sat. Saraphine looked at her cousin who seemed to be enjoying his portion of the bread. Blanche reached for Eugénie's wrist but she withdrew her hand and sprang to her feet.

"That's just the thing," she said, walking across the kitchen and leaning on the counter. "There's no answer. He's got no solutions," she said, pointing down the corridor. "There's nothing to do ... nobody that can really help us."

Ephrem looked up at his cousin Eugénie and said, "S-sit. C-come and s-sit. It's o-o-okay. To-tomorrow, he s-said. To-morrow."

Blanche, eyes wide, looked at Saraphine then turned to her son, stroked his hair and said, "That's right, boy."

-3-

Orance—swollen nose, dark blue and mustard circles below his eyes—was ringing-up customers when his father walked into the shop. Noticing the three people at the display, Urbin took his hat off, grabbed one of the aprons hanging next to the steel-top table, and set himself behind the counter.

"Thanks, dad," Orance said. "And I'll be right with you," he told the ladies waiting to be served.

"Where's everybody?" Urbin asked his son.

"And how can I help you, today?" Orance addressed the lady at the front of the line.

Urbin pulled a pork roast from inside the counter, wrapped it, tied a string around the package and wrote the price on the waxed paper with a grease pen. "Anything else for you, my dear lady?" He asked before making his way to the register.

"Where's Blanche? Why isn't she at the register? Where's your wife?" Urbin insisted.

Orance wiped his hands on his apron. "I'll go get that for you right away, Madame ... just need to go prepare those out back."

Urbin excused himself and followed his son through the swinging door.

"The ice's almost all gone … meat platters aren't cold. Why didn't you add some ice? What's going on? Where's Sean?" Urbin asked, looking at his son's back, Orance's elbow moving to and fro as he cut thin slices with his cleaver.

"He's coming in after lunch," Orance said, looking down at his work.

Urbin leaned on the wall next to the swinging door and glared at Orance. Looking around, he noticed blotchy, red streaks that had dripped along the door frame leading upstairs. The sight of blood in a butcher shop, especially out back where the butchering happens, was as familiar as snow in winter. But those stains—on that spot—conjured images of the violence that had spilled that blood. Urbin drew a deep breath and held it in for a few seconds before returning out front.

-4-

Having taken a few minutes to cool down while chatting with customers, Urbin stuck his face in the back, the door resting on his cheek, and resumed his interrogation. "You know your mother's the one that has to take care of everything at *my* shop now, right? Now that I have to be here all day to help you, it's just her and Seamus … alone. All day. You better get yourself right boy, 'cause I—"

"Thanks for giving me a hand, Dad. I appreciate it. But could you please take care of the customers while I'm back here? We'll talk later."

All afternoon, during those rare and brief intervals not busy serving or chatting up customers, Urbin stood behind the counter, elbows perched on the cast iron scale, rooting around unchartered tracts in his mind in search of a strategy—a way of communicating with his increasingly ferocious son. Contemplating some type of remedy; a plan to stop him from drinking himself further down into malevolence.

By the end of the day, enjoying a rare moment of mindful idleness, Urbin stood at the window watching folks heading home. "*Bonjour Madame*," he said, disturbed out of his reverie and opening the door for a lady, the sound of the little brass doorbell still ringing by the time she had asked, "Where's Eugénie?" Madame Déry, her braided cinnamon hair crowned by a silk, periwinkle turban, had drawn Urbin's attention. "I've never been here without saying hello to my darling, Eugénie. Be a dear and tell her I'm here," she insisted, placing her gloved hand on Monsieur Charpentier's shoulder and applying a barely noticeable squeeze.

Urbin, a man not known for his ability to think on his feet, stammered, "Rest … uh, resting. She's finally decided to take a day to rest. We all deserve that once in a while, don't we?"

"Not ill, is she?" Madame Déry asked, head crooked to one side, the look of concern on her face transforming her powdered face and red lips into a sad puppet. "Well, make sure and give her my best," she added and waved her fingers.

"Yes, for sure. She's fine, she'll be back real soon, without a doubt. But, what can *I* do for you?" Urbin said, running his palms along his trousers' back pockets.

"Nothing, really. Just wanted to say hello. I was on my way home and thought … please wish her well for me. Tell her Anna stopped by. Can you do that for me, dear?" She said, then looked over Urbin's shoulder and waved. "Hello Sean. Nice to see you again."

Sean stood frozen, his shoulder against the swinging door, then reversed course.

Urbin looked back at Sean then turned to Madame Déry.

"What a nice boy," she said, pointing a raised eyebrow on her way out.

Urbin nodded, looked at the wall clock and locked the door behind her.

"Thanks again for helping out," Orance said, from behind

the register, lips moving while counting coins and bills.

Urbin leaned back against the front door and stared at his son. Then, as Sean walked out from the back and reached for the door on his way out, said, "And what's with you? You don't act like that with customers. You were rude to that lady. You shouldn't talk that—"

"Just let him go, he's not why you came here, right?"

Sean walked out and as Urbin locked the door behind him, said to his son, "You've got one last chance to tell me what happened here last night. Your wife's with your mother. All of 'em are with her … landed on my doorstep in the middle of the night. For the love of God, seeing them there, outside my door, I thought your house had burned to the ground, or something. But then I found out that they all had to run away from you. What happened? What did you do?"

Orance, eyes locked on the register's open drawer, counted and recounted, adding up the day's take. "I don't know what to do here. Eugénie's always the one who deals with the money at the end of the day. I don't even know how to close out the register. Isn't that something, you'd think that—"

"Shut up, boy! What happened? What did you do to them?" Urbin repeated, walking away from the door and pounding his fist into his clammy palm, each blow more forceful, menacing.

"So, you'll just take their word over mine. It's not always *my* fault, you know," he replied, slapping his chest and wincing from the pain inflicted upon his fractured ribs.

"All right. So, tell me. What happened?" Urbin asked, poking at the counter's wooden top.

Orance leaned back on the swinging door and pushed it open. "Lemme get some ice, first."

Urbin followed his son to the back. "You pack the ice and I'll refill the trays," he said, hoping to get the ball rolling; to cap off some of the pressure he felt bubbling up in his gut.

"So?" Urbin asked, swiping strips of fat off the bloody workbench.

"You keep asking *me* what happened ... asking about what *I* did. But you never asked about my face. Look at me, I copped a mouse. It's like I was run over by the tramway," Orance said, pointing at his nose. "You never give me the benefit of the doubt, it's as if—"

"Are you saying that Eugénie's the one who did that to you? Or was it, Blanche? Or ... maybe it was Ephrem, the retarded lad? That's it ... the retard beat you up. Right?"

Orance hooked his hands on his hips and exhaled a long, drawn-out breath.

"Or, maybe the lot of 'em ganged up on you? Blanche, Ephrem ... your wife? An unprovoked attack. Right? Answer me," Urbin asked, his whitening face making his ear look even redder. Hotter.

"Of all people you're the one who should know about losing your temper. When I look like this it's usually because of what you've done," Orance said, a fillet of blood re-emerging from his left nostril.

"Don't you talk about me. All I've ever done is—"

"What?" Orance shouted, his finger aimed at his father, spittle spritzing from his lips.

"Whatever happened between us was never due to me being drunk. You deserved everything you got. Everything." Urbin said, looking down at his son's shoes.

"Deserve," Orance said sarcastically, walking around the workbench to face his father, shaking his head and wincing at the word. "I know what you think I *deserve*, pop. Don't you think I do?" Then he turned and pointed at the window. "You know what? I even know where you think I should be," he said, his other hand clutching at his throat.

Urbin stepped forward and slapped him, the heel of his leathery palm connecting with his son's jaw. Orance's head swivelled back, hard, causing the trickle from his nose to gush. He smiled, looked at the stairwell, at the bloody stains along the doorframe, and slowly pivoted toward his father. "That's it ol' man. You can hit me all you want, but next time,

I'm hitting back," he said, whispering, the blood dripping off his chin and landing on his apron mingling with the rest of the day's work.

"Look at you. Ingrate. Look at everything you've got. You think you'd be standing here if it weren't for me? You think you'd be the boss of this place if it weren't for me?" Urbin said angrily, shaking the numbness from his hand, secretly impressed by his son's capacity to take a hit. "This has got to stop. You've got to get off the booze. You've got to be a man. It's time you—"

"A man? G. Rover Cripes! You don't respect me, never have ... never will. There's nothing I can do that's gonna change that," Orance said through clenched teeth, slapping at his temple. "I can't change what you think of me, and I certainly can't change the past."

"To hell with the past, I'm talking about now, about last night. About your drinking. That's got nothing to do with the past. It's got nothing to do with—"

"Nothing to do with the past? Then maybe I should be telling you all about how my *past* has something to do with my boozing."

"You're not even making sense. All you're trying to do is avoid the subject. For the love of God, look at those blood stains on your wall. Doesn't that tell you something about where your life's at right now?"

"Don't sell me a dog, you liar," Orance said, blood smeared on his lips and chin. "I don't know how you can look at yourself in the mirror and not feel . . ." he paused and breathed through his teeth, "not feel at least an ounce—just one ounce—of the burden I've had to carry. My whole life I've had three dead bodies chained round my neck while you flogged me, kicked me ... making me feel undeserving of anything. Unworthy of living. Right? Isn't that what you really think?"

Urbin rubbed the back of his hand along his expressionless face and limped away. "I don't know what to tell your wife.

She asked me to talk to you, to straighten you out. I don't know what to do," he said, the swinging door flapping behind him.

"Why don't you take 'em all in? You wanna do that? You're such a better man than me anyway, right? Eugénie's gonna be better off with you," Orance yelled at the still swinging door.

"Can't you at least try to be sober for a while? Lay off the—"

The door swung open behind Urbin, hitting the wall and knocking one of the signs off its hook. "Why don't *you* stay sober, ol' man. Maybe *you* should have been sober," Orance replied, stuttering, his bulging eyeballs nearly jumping out of their sockets, the colour of his face—those parts not covered in blood or bruises—pink as cooked ham.

"You're not even making sense. You know what, you're beginning to sound like Blanche's retarded son. You're not worth me—"

"*You* should've been sober. *You!*" Orance screamed. "That's right, Dad. *You* should have been sober. You. granddad, Siméon, Charles ... all of you should have been sober. They'd all be alive today if they'd been sober," Orance said, the sound of his voice lowering with each name he listed, leaning over the counter and looking sideways at the register.

Urbin looked back at his son, lips pursed, puzzled.

"They're all gone because of you ... because of me. You're just as much to blame as I am," Orance said, his tears turning red.

Urbin pulled the door open, the cheery chime of the doorbell sounding absurd. "I'm coming back here tomorrow ... and I'm bringing all of 'em with me ... we're all gonna have a talk.

-5-

Uriette had been washing dishes when Urbin walked in.

"How did it go with the boy? What did he say?" She asked, wiping her hands.

Urbin limped to the table and dropped his butt on the chair as if springs in his legs had given way.

"Can I have something to eat? I didn't even have lunch," he answered, inspecting stuff in his fingernail he'd just scraped from deep inside the hole where his ear used to be.

She stared at Urbin and reached for a plate in the cupboard, filled it with whatever had remained in the pan and dropped it in front of her husband. Urbin grabbed his fork, holding it as if it were a hammer, and stabbed at the overcooked, brownish meat.

-6-

Eugénie, her mother-in-law's scarf twisted over her temple covering the lump on the side of her head, helped her sister tie the buttons along the cuffs of her sleeves. They tried to stay calm by recounting stories about their mother and sharing sweet—naïve—scenarios of how their lives would unfold.

"I think your father-in-law's back," Saraphine said, listening. "Maybe he managed to straighten things out," she added, pulling her hair back.

"Let him eat. Give him a chance to relax before we go in and see what he's got to say," Eugénie told her sister, rubbing the soreness from her shoulders while smiling a counterfeit smile.

Urbin always planned ahead during mealtime making sure to save a crust or two to soak-up whatever gravy remained on his plate. Tonight was different. Left with no bread, he dragged his finger along the bottom of his plate, brought his grey fingertip to his mouth, and sucked whatever leftover juices he could salvage.

"There's a demon in that son of yours," he said, transiting gravy to his mouth, his lips wrapped around his finger.

"When I talk to him, it's almost as if the words don't make it directly into his ears," he explained, looking at his wife.

Uriette, having joined her husband at the table, scowled. "Don't you say that about my boy," she said, pinching his elbow. "He's our son. There's nothing unholy about him. He's just gonna have to make some changes … you know, change his ways. No man can be in charge of himself till he gets off the bottle. You know that."

"A man's gotta *want* to change, Uriette," he said, pulling his arm away. "A man's gotta face himself first. Really look at himself and be honest about what he sees before he can move away from whatever he doesn't wanna be."

"Exactly. I know Orance for what he is. He's a good man and I'm sure he's—"

"What should I do?" Eugénie asked, standing in the doorway, her silhouette backlit by the hallway's dim light.

"Don't worry dear, Urbin had a nice talk with your husband," Uriette answered, rubbing and patting her husband's hairy forearm.

Urbin pushed back from the table and balanced himself on the chair's back legs.

"Maybe the best thing to do would be for all of you to go back tomorrow morning … all of *us*, actually. We'll all go back and clear the air. Start anew. You'll see, we'll have a talk, all of us, together," Urbin suggested, letting his chair drop to the floor—the bang meant to emphasize his positivity. "It's time to put all this misery behind us. I think we need to be positive and look to the future. Don't you?"

Blanche, who had joined her niece, her fingers on Ephrem's neck, walked ahead of Eugénie and stepped into the kitchen.

"I'm the one who pushed your son down the stairs. I did it 'cause I thought he'd kill Eugénie. Kill the lot of us. I can't go back there. You've got to realize that I can't take my son there and—"

"Don't be so sure. I *spoke* with him, Blanche," Urbin said, springing to his feet, hobbling, seeming to have forgotten he had but one good foot to stand on. "I'm his father, and a father knows something about his son. We looked straight at each other and confronted the issues," he insisted.

"Well . . ." Blanche said, looking down at Ephrem and pulling at Eugénie's dress. "I've got to take my own son into consideration here. You weren't there last night. I thought we were all gonna die. That we'd all get killed," she added, looking directly into Uriette's eyes.

"But I'm gonna be there with you. Uriette's gonna come with us, too ... right?" Urbin asked, turning to his wife and reaching for her hand. She, unable to look at Blanche, slid her other hand against her forearm and looked at the linoleum.

"I've got to agree with Aunt Blanche, Monsieur Charpentier. There's no way of knowing how Orance is going to treat us once you're gone. Besides, I'm not sure you realize how Orance gets once he's drunk ... really drunk," Eugénie said, her sister's arms on her shoulders.

"Orance gets mean, like a madman. Orance isn't Orance when he's drunk. He scares us," Dahlia, Orance's sister, standing in the hallway's shadow said, arms wrapped tightly around herself.

Urbin looked back and scowled at his daughter then dragged the heel of his palm from his chin all the way to the back of his neck. Shaking his head, surprised by the sound of Dahlia's matter-of-fact description of his son's shameful ways, he dropped his head, stared at the floor, reached into his pocket and pulled out his pipe. Holding it clenched between his teeth, he looked sideways at Eugénie and took a long, deep ... deep breath. "Look, how about we all sleep on this? We can talk some more in the morning. We'll all have a good breakfast, you'll see, we'll all feel a lot better in the morning," he said while abruptly slashing his match along the back of his leg, the smoke from the ignition making him look like a magician intending to vanish into a cloud.

Ephrem sat sandwiched tightly between Urbin and his mother, upfront on the spring seat, holding the reins, giggling, and hoping people strolling by would look at him.

Rolling along St. Denis Street, Eugénie and Saraphine, legs dangling limply off the back, squinting at the sun's morning orange beams, spoke in whispers while Uriette—rosary beads laced around her hands—strained to overhear.

"I find it helps to leave space in my life for the Lord to fill," Uriette finally decided to say, leaning in and crossing herself.

Saraphine turned and half-smiled. Eugénie kept her head down, looking at the road scrolling along below her feet.

"I'm praying the Lord will give my husband the wisdom to find the right words, the right way into our boy's heart … to release him from his craving for the drink. We should all pray together," Uriette said, fingers laced together and bound by rosary beads.

"Thanks," Eugénie said, hunched over, focused on the road. "Let's hope so … maybe this'll all end well," she added, comforted by the feel of her sister's hand running up and down her back; though sad at the thought of her husband having never—not once—touched her in a way anyone could describe as tenderly.

"I believe my husband will find the right words," Uriette added, pushing her head between the sisters. "My word of advice to you," she added, lips inches from Eugénie's ear, "is that you pledge yourself to God. Pledge yourself to ensuring your husband isn't pushed to the bottle … that you don't give him any reasons to drink. You understand what I'm saying to you?"

Eugénie paused and breathed in through her teeth. "I've done all *I* can to keep your son from being the way he is," she replied, turning slowly to face her mother-in-law. "Fact is . . ." she added, her finger running circles around her thumb's knuckle, "…it's the drinking that brings out the evil in him and he knows that bottle's filled with a potion … a poison that turns him into what he becomes. So, as far as I'm concerned, he's in control. He *wants* to do what he does. Satan's not in the bottle. Satan's the one holding the bottle."

Uriette snapped her head back and crossed herself. "I always liked you, Eugénie, but you're making a mistake thinking like that. That boy was saved from the water. He's *my* Moses and he's being tested. It's up to us, all of us, to make sure he gets the help he needs," Uriette said, swiftly crossing herself again, her rosary beads clinking and rattling as her hand moved from shoulder to forehead.

-8-

"Wait here, let me go up first," Urbin said, turning into the alley and stopping behind his son's butchery.

"G-gid-giddy up," Ephrem said at the horses, halted by the cart's hand brake.

"We're here, Ephrem. The horses have to rest now," Blanche told her son, rubbing his small round shoulders and looking back at Uriette. "I don't know what your husband is planning on saying to Orance, but—"

"Don't worry, Blanche. None of you should worry," Uriette said, looking at each of them in succession and pointing at the small crucifix dangling off the end of her rosary beads. "My husband knows his son, how to speak with him, to convince him. Besides, Orance is a good boy, has a good soul. It's the bottle that's taken over his character. You'll see. Urbin will know exactly how to steer him in the right direction. He always has."

"Maybe so, but after what he did to his wife … leaving her there, downstairs . . ." Blanche said, looking back at Eugénie, Ephrem pulled tightly to her side, "… leaving her there to die, to bleed to death. We know what he's capable of."

Expressionless, Uriette turned to Blanche. "Orance did none of that, you've got to believe me. It's the drink. Once he stops drinking, I'm sure that all this . . ." she paused, fumbling as she stored her beads into a small pouch she kept in her purse, ". . .all this commotion will come to an end."

They waited for Urbin to come back. To tell them about the plan. Thirty minutes. Forty-five minutes. Soon, images flooded Eugénie's mind. Maybe he had learned a hard lesson about his son. Had Orance already started drinking? Could he have hurt his own father? Blanche, alone upfront, tried not to think. She watched Ephrem scratch shallow holes into the hard, tamped ground. Uriette mouthed silently, hands resting on her purse. "H-hello," Ephrem said when the shop's large, tin-covered back door squealed open; the piercing noise sending a pulsing bolt of electricity through Eugénie's body. Urbin cussed at the weight of the door, struggling against the resistance of torn metal rubbing on the wooden deck. Looking past her father-in-law, Eugénie saw him—Orance—lurking behind his father, his right eye swollen shut, his face purple and burgundy. He stood reclined on his workbench, compulsively pumping his heel up and down, arms crossed and chewing at his lower lip.

"Come, come, it's all gonna be fine," Urbin said, reaching down at Ephrem from the loading dock. "Come on young man, it's all gonna be all right," he repeated to the smiling boy.

"Stay right there," his mother ordered, her tone flat and direct.

"I got him, Blanche. It's all gonna be okay. You've got my word," Urbin replied, the reassuring look on his face nearly disarming Blanche.

Blanche looked at her son, "Go with Monsieur Charpentier," she said, her voice wet and fearful.

"Ladies, ladies, this is the beginning of a new day for all of you ... all of us," Uriette said, hands clasped.

Saraphine stood without letting go of Eugénie's elbow.

Eugénie followed, absently drawn by her sister's momentum. Eugénie noticed Ephrem on the deck gleefully waving them in … saw Blanche's face, bleached and expressionless. Sideways, she glanced inside the shop, looking for clues. "You're all gonna stay for a while, right?" Eugénie asked her in-laws.

"I told you, dear, we're gonna make things right, show you how this boy of mine's gonna change," Urbin tried to reassure Eugénie, jumping off the loading dock and hobbling before reaching up to help her off the cart.

They huddled round the workbench. Orance was nowhere to be seen. Ephrem ran through the swinging door, plopped himself on his stool behind the register, tore a long strip of brown paper off the roll and, just like that, the swooshing sound of his grease pencil gave life to images of cannons and battleships.

"What now?" Eugénie asked, looking right, looking left.

Urbin walked to the stairwell; Eugénie noticed her blood had been washed off the wall.

"Come on down!" He yelled. "He'll be down in no time," Urbin said, rejoining the group, his thumb pointed back over his shoulder. "So, don't nobody start up with too many questions," Urbin whispered, motioning up and down as if putting out an imaginary fire. "Let me speak first and that'll give you an idea of what my plan is all about."

Eugénie's spine nearly fused at the sound of her husband's boots thumping down the staircase. Having arrived downstairs, Orance stood in the doorframe for a long few seconds, rubbing his nose and slowly bobbing his head.

"Huh, hello everyone. Hello Blanche," he said, looking at her and squeezing his lips together with enough force to crinkle his abraded chin. "Saraphine," he added, up nodding at her while slipping his left hand in his pocket. "Eugénie. You can look at me, I won't do anything," he added, letting go of the doorframe and tentatively walking toward the assembled group as if a sudden move on his part would send them scurrying.

"Now, isn't this better? All of us here, together, talking again," Urbin said, his forced enthusiasm cutting through the tension like a dull blade tearing through a vein. "We spoke, talked about the future and what's needed for all of you to live together. For us to live like a family," he added, meeting his son and placing his hand on his shoulder; swivelling his head sideways and looking intensely into his eyes.

Eugénie, upon hearing the word 'family', looked at Saraphine and slid her palm down her sister's head and neck.

"This boy of mine was under a spell. Taken prisoner. And you know what? He never even realized how deeply he'd fallen into the … the very grips of the devil," Urbin said, patting his son's shoulders, eyebrows knit together. "All this misery, this pain, all of it because of this spell, the spell of the drink. I know it. Orance knows it. But alcohol won't be the undoing of this family," he added, turning to face the group. "You see, Orance and me made a pledge. Both of us swore to each other, and to God, that we'd never have another drop of alcohol ever again. No more booze! Right son?" He exclaimed, turning back to look at Orance, his arm around his son.

Uriette, unaware of the agreement, flinched and snapped her chin at her husband. Eyes wide, oblivious to the fact her jaw had slackened, she gasped. "Never again? Urbin, never again?" She asked, fingers woven into a tight ball held over her chest.

"Never again!" Urbin repeated, eyes bright and wide. "We made a pact, a promise to each other, and that's why things are going to change around here."

Eugénie, Saraphine in tow, walked around the workbench to join her aunt. "So, if I forgive you for what you've done— will you forgive, too? Are we all letting bygones be bygones here? Is that it?" Eugénie asked, her face pointed at her husband like a spear.

"The past is the past. This is all about looking forward and starting things over. I promise you that—"

"That's fine Monsieur Charpentier, but I need to hear those words coming from Orance, I need *him* to make that pledge," Eugénie said. "Are we forgiving each other? Is everyone here being forgiven … for whatever they've done?" She emphasized, taking her aunt's hand.

Orance, looking at his wife's forehead through bloodshot eyes, nodded an almost imperceptible nod.

"Come on son, tell your wife you forgive her," Urbin insisted, his voice dialled into a pleading, nearly begging tone.

"I'm not the one looking for forgiveness, Monsieur Charpentier. I'm jus' trying to survive here. That's what we're all trying to do. Ephrem, my sister, Aunt Blanche … we're jus' wanting to continue living."

"We're starting fresh, turning over a new—"

"Let me hear *you* say it, Orance. Tell Aunt Blanche you forgive her … that you understand why she did what she did. Otherwise, I don't see how we can all come back to living in this house together unless you—"

"I forgive you, Blanche," Orance said, staring at his laces. "We'll … uh … we'll make things work."

-9-

Uriette and Urbin helped out all day at their son's butcher shop, filling in every awkward silence and—when called upon—acting as unofficial intermediaries. Orance had camped out in the back and though feeling the pain from his fractured ribs, hacked at meat, lugged ice, tended to his father's horse, and unloaded crates. Eugénie, whose joy had always been to serve customers, returned to the floor, Saraphine by her side. Blanche stood behind the counter ringing up orders and supplying all the brown paper Ephrem needed for his art, chills running up her spine at the thought of the man she had nearly killed standing a few feet from her—back there—slicing and slashing away on the other side of the swinging door.

"So, you kids seem to have done all right," Urbin said, locking the front door. "We'll be on our way, now. But remember, it's gonna take a little while before things get back to normal," he warned, smiling like a disturbed mannequin.

Eugénie and Blanche offered forced smiles in return.

"You go on up and get supper ready," Urbin instructed his daughter-in-law. "After all, nothing says normal like a good supper. Right?" He added, pushing through the swinging door on his way outside.

"You're gonna bring ice for the trays?" Eugénie asked Orance, keenly aware those were the first words she had spoken to him all day.

"There you go. Your wife's gonna make you a great supper. All of you, enjoy. Enjoy the evening knowing that tomorrow's gonna be even better. You'll see," Urbin said, limping out the big, steel door.

"Remember your pledge, son. Never, ever forget," Uriette told Orance, kneading his forearm, looking up at him while her husband, reigns in hand, his foot poised to knock off the wheel brake, waited in the wagon.

-10-

They said nothing during the ride home. Urbin watched his wife climb down and he put the horse and cart away. Uriette, aware her husband expected each meal to be prepared on time, beelined past her daughters and started on supper. "You think they'll be all right?" Uriette, slowly spinning her big ladle through soup, asked her husband once he finally walked into the kitchen. "After all, looking at them and—"

Psssssst … the familiar sound pierced through her like a hot bullet. She coiled and inadvertently pulled the ladle along for the ride spilling broth all over the counter and floor.

"What're you doing?" She asked, mouth open wide, eyes like billiard balls.

Urbin, leaning on the back legs of his arrowback chair, a

Molson's beer in hand, casually replied, "Having a beer, dear. That's what I do after a tough day."

"The pledge. My God, the pledge. You swore you'd … you'd—"

"I swore I'd help the boy, and I did. The way I figure it, I had to say whatever I had to say to make things better … make sure he was on the right track, so, I said what I said," he replied, raising his bottle before bringing it to his lips and downing half its contents in one long gulp.

Uriette, unaware the contents of the ladle she held in front of her continued dripping on the floor, pulled out a chair and joined her husband at the table. "But you made a pledge that you'd support him, that you'd do the same."

"Yes. That's what I said."

"So, what about that? What about the pledge?"

Urbin lifted his feet and let the chair drop to the floor. Elbows on the table, he took another hit from his bottle, ran his sleeve along his lips, and said, "Look, I'm not the one with the problem. I'm not beating *you* up, right?"

Uriette squinted, blinked, and suddenly noticed the ladle she had pointed at her husband.

"You better get back to your soup. You know how much you hate scraping burnt stuff from the bottom of your pot. Anyway, it won't be any good if it's all tasting burnt. Right?"

Zombie-like, Uriette pushed herself away from the table, returned to the stove, dipped her ladle into the broth, stirred and stared at the wall.

"*Ah Calvaire*, Uriette. Don't be like that. I did what I had to do. The boy's gonna be all right. Besides, I'm not gonna drink when I'm around him. As far as he's concerned, I've given it up," Urbin said, pointing his bottle at his wife, the deepening lines across his forehead suggesting he no longer considered the topic open for discussion.

Chapter 9

January, 1902

For hours Eugénie and Ephrem scraped and shovelled their way through a huge wall of snow that gangs of city workers had piled along the sidewalk—hundreds of men reclaiming the city's streets, shovel load by shovel load, spending the night opening lanes for horses and tramways brought idle by a January storm. The butchery's light bulbs shining through the front window illuminated clouds of mist rising from their hot lungs and sweaty clothes. Customers' endless craving for fresh meat having to be satiated, they also had to clear the congested alley; make it passable again in order for deliveries to make it through.

The sun had hardly peeked over the distant St. Lawrence River when Monsieur Charpentier's sled arrived fully loaded with huge sides of beef, ten whole pigs and three crates over-filled with live rabbits. Orance, his apron hanging below his jacket, helped haul in the meat. They went through the front—the snow in the alley still too deep—dragging the sides of beef along the snow; deep, bloody grooves left along the sidewalk and stairs advertising the latest arrivals. Ephrem, eager to help and now nearly as tall as Monsieur Charpentier, stacked three crates and carried them all the way to the back, his boots leaving a wet trail in the sawdust.

Blanche, arms gathered against her chest, fed the wood-stove, opened and closed the front door on cue and made sure to slap her boy's back as he walked by; a proud mother happy to see her son contributing to the shop's routine.

"Who says a dinlo can't be useful, eh Blanche?" Orance

said, holding his side of a huge crate as he climbed backwards up the granite steps and through the front door she had held open for him.

Blanche rolled her eyes, breathed in, deeply, slowly, then looked away. Ephrem returned from the back, and she reached out to pat his head as he walked by, the young man's face beaming with pride, his lower teeth shining from behind his smile. Eugénie, still warring with the snow, struggling to widen the narrow opening along the sidewalk, had felt the damned word pierce through her like a dull hatpin. Resting on her shovel's handle, she looked into the shop, at Blanche's pained face. She lifted her tuque off her eyes, sniffed the snot up her sinuses and, reenergized by anger, gripped her shovel's heavy, wooden handle and pressed on.

"Last one left," Monsieur Charpentier said, looking into the sled and pointing at the large side of beef leaning on the box board. Eugénie stepped away as the men walked by, pulled her shovel back, and smacked Orance with the sharp end of her scraper right at the beefy part of his calf. Orance yelled and dropped his end of the carcass in the slushy snow.

"Ahhrg... G. Rover Cripes! Why'd you do that? You crazy? Why'd you try to chop my leg off?" Orance cried, rubbing his leg and hopping around.

"Come on boy, it can't be that bad," his father said, wiping his mouth with the back of his hand to conceal his smile. "She's trying to shovel a path for us. It was an accident. Right, Eugénie?" He added, winking at Blanche who had watched, smiling at the spectacle.

"Sure, yeah. A mistake. I'm sure," Orance agreed, bent over and rubbing his leg while staring at his wife's back who, despite the hubbub, had resumed shovelling.

"Almost done, dear?" Blanche asked her niece while reaching for her shawl.

"Get back inside, you're not dressed warm," Eugénie ordered.

"Back in-inside," Ephrem added, frozen slime that had

clung to his upper lip breaking off from under his nose.

"Don't worry about me, I've been standing next to the stove all morning," Blanche said, shrugging. "Anyway, listen, there's something I've got to tell you. I've made a decision. I've … I've decided . . ."

"What're you saying, jus' tell me. What is it?" Eugénie quizzed, climbing the stairs, her wet mitten wrapped around her aunt's elbow—Blanche's warm, trembling arm suggesting she might not appreciate what she was about to hear.

"I've told you about my brother, right? Uncle Jean? You know, the one that lives in the States."

Eugénie sighed and stared into Blanche's pale face, thick puffs of mist merging between them.

"Anyway, I told you before, he lives in Winooski, in Vermont. He told me that I could get a job at a plant there, they make wool or textiles, or both. Not sure. He said we could live with him. You know, since his wife died last year and all."

"You're leaving? You and Ephrem? Leaving?" She asked disbelievingly, dropping her hand off Blanche's elbow. "When?"

"Anytime, he said. Told me it was up to us to decide. But I can stay a while longer. Don't worry, it's not like I'm gonna leave you with all this work," Blanche whispered, stepping back to let Ephrem walk by. "Please, don't make a big thing about this. You know how things are. It's been what, four, five years since we've moved in? That whole *pledge* thing with Orance, that didn't work. Look at the bruise on your neck," she added, her fingers running along Eugénie's jaw. "I'm not saying that I'm leaving tomorrow. I'll stay long enough to make sure you find someone to replace me and the boy."

"I suppose Ephrem doesn't know anything about this."

"Course not. Besides, I'm not sure he'd be wanting to go, he's never been anywhere other than here, you know, around the neighbourhood."

Eugénie took a step back, wiped her nose, and looked at her aunt's feet. "Can't say I blame you. I understand. Things haven't been easy 'round here. Believe me, I know. I wish I could jus' take off, too," she said, leaning her shovel on the wall and taking her aunt's hands. "It's gonna be good for Ephrem. Good for you. A new start and all."

"You'll be okay, too. We've been nothing but trouble for you," Blanche said, looking back at the swinging door. "You know how Orance hates Ephrem ... can't stand to be around him. Now you won't have to deal with that kind of tension, with any more of the—"

"Thanks, Aunt Blanche. Thanks for everything. For taking us in. For saving my life. Jus' tell me how I can help," Eugénie said, tugging at her aunt's arms. "By the way, Orance doesn't hate your son. He's jus' a small man, he's afraid of him," she added, then kissed her aunt's hands and walked away.

-2-

"Why was your sister crying again today? I could hear her all the way from upstairs," Orance asked, pulling his suspenders off his shoulders as he readied himself for bed.

"She's sad 'cause she's losing her cousin," Eugénie replied, sitting on her side of the bed and pushing the heel of her shoe off with her toes.

"What? What losing?"

"She's leaving ... Blanche is. Going to the States, to work somewhere in Vermont."

Orance, bug-eyed, walked around the bed and bent down to face his wife. "She's going to the States? Where's she gonna live?"

Eugénie pushed herself off the bed, shoes dangling off her fingertips. "What'd you care about where she's gonna live?" She snapped, angling her way past her husband.

"What's so wrong about me asking?"

"'Cause you don't care. Anyway, don't you worry about it. She told me she'd help out here till we find someone to replace them."

"No need for that. Your sister's doing fine since she's left school, she gets the job done at the register. She'll do," he said, kicking his pants to the corner of the room. "So, where *are* they gonna live?"

"Her brother's got room for her. He lost his wife a little while back."

"Her and the dinlo?"

Eugénie's shoes dropped from her hand. "Of course. Aunt Blanche won't abandon her son. I'm assuming he's got room since he's the one who invited them."

"But does he know about the dinlo? You know, that he's a retard and all."

Eugénie shoved Orance out of her way and slid under the sheets. "I need to sleep. I started shovelling at four this morning. They're leaving. That's all you need to know."

Orance chuckled.

-3-

The early spring had dissolved much of the snow into puddles but Orance had other reasons to account for the grin on his face. Walking briskly back and forth, he loaded his wagon full of crates—the ones usually crammed with rabbit carcasses—filled with clothes, boots, dishware, and most everything Blanche had brought with her after her husband had died. On this day, a person could have actually mistaken Orance for a happy fella. Everything cinched snuggly into the wagon, he sat, reigns in hand, waiting to drive his wife's family to Bonaventure Station on their way to board the Grand Trunk train line to Vermont.

Eugénie and Blanche stood side by each while Saraphine sat, elbows on the workbench, unconsciously leafing through Ephrem's favourite Jules Verne book, the one with beautiful illustrations of spaceships and moonscapes. Everyone made sure to smile the way people do when they're trying not to cry. They said things, words spoken mechanically; the heartache of this last interaction shared mostly through the melancholy in their eyes.

"It's hard to believe we've been living together since ninety-four ... how old was Ephrem then? Five ... six?" Eugénie said, fiddling with her aunt's shirt collar and folding it neatly over her coat.

"Yeah, eight years. Got to admit, I never thought we'd be together for that long, that I'd be here and working at the shop that long. Thanks for everything. I really—"

"No, thank *you*," Eugénie said, waving dismissively at her aunt.

"We both thank you," Saraphine added, her hand on Ephrem's shoulder as they inched forward toward the big, steel door at the back.

Ephrem sat on a crate behind his mother. They waved till the wagon turned on Ontario Street and disappeared. The sisters were on their own again. Eugénie pushed the big door open and looked back at Saraphine before walking in.

"Coming?" She asked her sister. "We've got to get to work."

-4-

Saraphine was in the back fetching a roast for a customer when the sound of a horse's shoes reverberated in the alley.

"Everything all right? Did they get on the train?" She asked.

"Dunno. I dropped them off at the station and came right back, unloaded the crates and all. The big dinlo just stood there, didn't lift a finger and Blanche never told him to help, either. Besides, I can't stay away all day when there's so much to do here. Right?"

Saraphine wrapped the roast in brown paper and went out

front, staring back at Orance as she left.

"Wait. Is that the roast I tied for Madame Charbonneau?" Orance asked, lighting his pipe.

"She's here, I came to get it for her."

"Wait," Orance said, dropping his dirty apron over his shoulders and knotting the strings over his belly. "Now that it's just me and the two of you," he added, pointing at Saraphine and the swinging door. "I'm gonna expect that you earn your keep. You understand?" Saraphine froze as blood from the roast trickled down her wrist and dripped into the sawdust. "You understand what I mean, right?" He added, swooping toward his sister-in-law, his nose inches from her forehead and looking down into her eyes.

Saraphine fumbled backwards and nodded.

"You're seventeen. Pretty soon, you'll be on your way, married and all. But for now, you're here and you've got a job to do, and I'm gonna expect that you're gonna do it, and do it right. You understand?" He repeated, moving forward, cupping her shoulder and poking his finger at her forehead. "Your sister's my wife, but you're not living in *her* house. You're living in *my* house," he said, now pointing at his chest. "You're not working for her; you're working for me... so I expect you to obey *my* orders, and I don't need you talking to Eugénie all day long. Got it?"

Saraphine, looking at the roast, took a long step backwards till her shoulders pushed the swinging door open.

"There it is," Madame Charbonneau said, clapping in a silly, overjoyed manner.

"Everything ok?" Eugénie asked, looking back at her sister.

"Yeah, yeah ... fine. Everything's fine," Saraphine answered, placing the roast on a sheet of paper, having to start over twice before finally stringing it tightly into a bundle.

By June, Saraphine was ensconced behind the register; ringing up orders and ensuring each transaction was completed smoothly. At the end of each business day, Eugénie tallied up sales and stashed the day's earnings in the bank's deposit drawer. Though the butcher shop hadn't changed its name, most customers now referred to it as *Les Deux Soeurs*. Business was good and Eugénie orchestrated the growth masterfully. She had improved the shop's layout and regularly painted information about daily specials on the window. A banner was installed below the big black sign proclaiming: *Only Locally Grown Meats Raised by Local Farmers*. Sean Murphy, Urbin's former apprentice, was now working full-time at Orance's shop and took on all the extra work needed to maintain inventory. Despite his awkward (some would have said disturbing) manner with people, he could even be called upon, in a pinch, to help out front with customers.

Monsieur Charpentier appreciated his daughter-in-law's innovations and had implemented similar changes at his location. Eugénie, relying on the newly installed telephone, spent nearly as much time taking orders on the phone as she did helping clients on site. Saraphine soon learned to do the same, both of them sharing time at the register. Increased sales meant that Orance had nearly doubled his payments to his father for his share of the business. Money flowed in and every indicator pointed north.

"Could you put the chops on ice while I go make my deposit?" Eugénie, counting bills and writing totals down on the deposit slip, asked her sister.

"In the counter or d'you want me to bring 'em in the back?" Saraphine asked.

"No, jus' want to make sure everything's on ice for the weekend, you can leave 'em in the display," Eugénie answered, wrapping bills and coins in a brown paper bag and lacing the package to look like a piece of meat; a trick she had learned from her Uncle Marc back when *he* used to bring the day's earnings to the bank.

"Sean, could you bring some more ice out here for the displays?" Saraphine asked, yelling at the swinging door.

"He's gone. What's it you want?" Orance replied.

"Ice. Eugénie wants me to put the chops on ice for the weekend."

Orance, shoulders strained by the weight of two metal pails, pushed his back through the door, the jerky motion causing pieces of ice to fall and disappear into the sawdust.

"Just under the chops or everywhere?" He asked.

"What?" Saraphine, who didn't seem to understand what he said, asked, pulling her head from inside the display.

"D'you want me to spread ice all over, or just under the chops?" He tried to sound clearer.

"The chops, she only mentioned the chops."

Orance emptied both buckets and slid the display's door shut. On his way to the back, he stepped on a piece of ice buried under sawdust and crashed to the floor.

"Orance!" Saraphine yelped, bumping her head on the counter's edge as she jerked up. "You all right?"

"My ankle. *Câlisse* … I hurt my ankle. Help me up."

Saraphine stood over Orance, leaned forward and reached for his outstretched hands.

"Careful not to strain your ankle … I'll help you up," Saraphine said, doubting she had the corpulence to provide the counterbalance needed to pull such a large man to his feet.

"OK, just a minute. I'll count to three and you pull me up … OK … you ready?"

"Ready."

"One … two," Orance stopped short and pulled Saraphine down on him, her neck snapping back from the force of his tug. He laughed and held her tightly to his chest. Saraphine, arms locked to her sides, strained to peel herself off him; the blood from his apron transferring to her dress.

"You really thought you'd be able to pull me off the floor?" Orance said, squeezing tighter.

"Lemme go. I thought you were hurt. Lemme go," Saraphine squirmed, waves of panic roused by the feeling of captivity.

"Is it so bad to be close to your brother-in-law?"

"The blood … it's getting all over me. Let me go!" She repeated. Shocked. Angry. Terrified.

He rolled over and pinned Saraphine's wrists to the floor. He looked down at her, his laughter heightening her frustration; drool dangling from his lower lip releasing into a long stream that pooled onto her neck.

"You two are the same. Always fighting, always wanting to have things your way."

Saraphine stiffened herself, lifted her chin, and swung her knee into Orance's crotch. The connection was directly on target. He rolled off her, grunting and squealing, the noises oozing from him sounding as if the impact had collapsed his lungs. Arms around his knees, he rocked from side to side like a giant, apron-wearing fetus. Bits of sawdust fell from his lips while struggling to say, "Was just playing … having fun. What's the matter with you? Just like your sister … you never wanna have fun."

Breathless and light-headed from having been pinned down by such weight, she sprang to her feet and ran through the swinging door.

"What's going on?" Sean asked as Saraphine whooshed by his workbench and up the stairs.

Upstairs, in her room, Saraphine sat on her bed frantically chewing skin off her fingertips while staring at the key in the door's lockset. Hours seemed to go by—staring at that key—waiting for her sister to return from the bank. She sprung off the mattress and paced the room before deciding to sit on the floor, her back against the door, clutching the doorknob and listening for the sound of Eugénie's shoes scraping the treads of the staircase. Unable to stay put, she peeked out the bedroom door. Slowly, she tiptoed down the hallway and perched herself atop the stairway, waiting to hear her sister's voice.

-6-

"You've got sawdust all over your face," Eugénie observed, perplexed, walking toward the register, her right cheek rising up to meet her eyebrow.

"Ah, it's nothing. I tripped on a piece of ice," Orance replied, rubbing his forearm along the side of his face, spitting small pieces of wood from his mouth as if trying to get rid of a hair stuck on his tongue.

"You fell? What happened?"

"He slid on a piece of ice walking through the door. I asked him to bring ice for the counters, some of it must've fallen from his bucket … he stepped on it, I guess," Saraphine, standing in the doorway, answered.

"Oh. You, Okay?" Eugénie asked, eyes shifting from Orance to Saraphine. "We need to be careful with things like that. Can you imagine if that happened to a customer?"

"I'm fine. Everything's fine," Orance said, glancing back at his sister-in-law, smiling, nodding, empty buckets hanging from his hands.

"Well, if it's all right, I'll be leaving now," Sean said, compulsively wringing his tweed hat and swaying from side to side trying to see beyond Saraphine who stood blocking the doorway.

"Sure. Of course," Eugénie answered, waving at her sister to move out of Sean's way. "Let Sean go by," she said to no avail. "Saraphine! Sean has to leave, could you please let him get by," she repeated, seeming to startle Saraphine out of a spell. "Mind locking the door?" Eugénie asked her sister. Saraphine followed Sean, locked the door behind him and watched longingly as he disappeared into the crowd. Eugénie stared at her sister's back, then pivoted to face her husband.

"So, somebody tell me about it … what happened here?"

Saraphine—having seemed mesmerized by the sight of Sean walking across Ontario Street, fingers on the latch, absentmindedly feeling for the key sticking out from the lock—took a deep breath before dropping the key in her pocket.

"What happened?" Saraphine slightly mimicked her sister's words, nose pressed against the wavy glass. "Sorry, what're you saying? What d'you mean? When?" She added as she turned to face her sister.

"Why do *you* have sawdust on your back? There's sawdust stuck to your dress. What happened? How did it get there?"

Saraphine's expression petrified into a sad smile. Chin up though looking down, she sidled away from the door, glanced at Orance then looked back at her sister. "I … huh … I helped him off the floor … pulled him up. He said his back was pretty sore … fell pretty hard, you know."

"I know, but why do you have sawdust on *your* back? *He* fell. You didn't. Right? I don't understand."

Saraphine sidestepped behind the counter and started wiping the glass.

"Your husband's a big guy, you know. I was pulling, you know, pulling him up and … he's too heavy. I lost my grip and fell backwards," Saraphine answered, mimicking the tale; head snapping back, arms flailing.

Eugénie stared at her sister, lips parted, her crimped left brow burrowing thin lines on her forehead. "D'you hurt yourself? You all right?"

"*Ben oui* … of course, I'm fine. I just slid on my *derrière*. That's it, that's all."

Eugénie stepped toward the swinging door and held it open with her bum. "Go up, would you mind? There's a few things I want to discuss with Orance. Jus' start supper and we'll be up soon."

"I'm telling you, I'm fine. There's nothing to worry about. My hands slipped and I fell, is all. He's a heavy man, your husband," Saraphine insisted, turning sideways, forearms pulled tightly to her chest as she squeezed by Orance and ran up the stairs.

Eugénie shuffled toward her husband, her tongue poking at her cheek. She looked at him for a while as he sliced strips of fat off a rump, tossing the long, white strands in a pale.

"So, what happened here?" She asked, tapping her fingernails on the workbench.

"What?" Orance asked, looking at the rump, grinning, and shaking his head.

Eugénie, unwilling to answer her husband's smile, bent down to meet his gaze.

"Saraphine told me something about helping you get up. About you slipping and falling."

"Yeah. That's right. That's it. I was on my back. I was hurt. She tried to help me get to my feet. What's the issue here? What's the—"

"You never mentioned anything about her helping you. You'd think that her falling while trying to help you is a pretty important part of the story. Wouldn't you?" Eugénie asked, looking back at him as she headed toward the stairwell.

-7-

Saraphine had started setting the table when Eugénie walked in.

"You sure you're all right?" Eugénie, standing at the kitchen's doorway, asked.

"Yeah. Of course. Stop worrying for nothing," Saraphine answered while placing napkins next to plates and setting cutlery on them.

"'Cause you know you can talk to me, tell me anything. We don't keep secrets, right?" Eugénie tried to speak directly into her sister's heart, walking into the kitchen and running the back of her hand along her sister's forearm; caressing. "Neither of us should ever keep secrets. We've got to stick together. Help each other," she added, looking down, her eyebrows pushing her ears back while attempting to read her sister's expression. Saraphine looked back at her sister, nodded and positioned another napkin down on the table. "D'you have anything else you wanna tell me ... that you want to talk about?" Eugénie gently insisted.

"Stop worrying yourself all the time. You've got enough to handle here with the shop. With Orance. I'm old enough to take care of myself," Saraphine answered, hands on the table and staring at the place setting she had prepared.

Eugénie tried to meet her sister's eye. "You'll tell me if there's something wrong, right?" She asked, wanting assurance. Her head turned to look down the hallway.

Orance, his long knife that he'd used to carve the pork still in hand, looked up the stairwell, trying to listen in on the sisters' conversation, his neck stretched out into the darkness, hoping that Saraphine had stuck to the story. Hearing voices but unable to make out words, he returned to his workbench, pulled open his top drawer, wrenched the false bottom out and peered down at the soldier's row of three full bottles of Caribou. Obedient anesthetists. Medicine. Salvation. The cadence of his heart slowed as he lifted one of the bottles from its bed. He pulled the cork, the popping sound releasing the sweet aroma into his nose and throat. He looked through the amber-coloured distillation before resting the bottle's finish on his lower lip; the sweet liquid sliding down his tongue, warming his chest and mincing his mind.

Chapter 10

If Mondays at the shop tended to be slow, Tuesdays could be counted on to be dull. These were the days for doing what businesses do in order to stay in business: engage with suppliers, repair whatever had conked out, and of course, clean.

On this Tuesday in late July, Saraphine stood behind the counter, pushed her hip against the swinging door and talked … and talked to the boy. Sean—busy disassembling the meat grinder, dropping various components in a tub of soapy hot water, scrubbing and scouring the metal with his wire brush—strained to keep up with the gossip hurled at him. She'd talk about what lady so-and-so was wearing, books she had read, a dress she had seen in a shop's window, and how much she enjoyed going for walks on Sundays.

"Uh, huh … sorry, what? Who's that you're talking about?" Sean would ask every once in a while, the grinder's long auger on his wet apron, the sound of the wire brush brisling back and forth as he diligently scoured and scrubbed.

"Madame Déry. Eugénie calls her Anna. You know, the lady with the big cinnamon hair, those big, big hats she wears. You've seen her. She comes by all the time to see Eugénie. I saw her smoking once, a kind of little cigar," she answered, hands held high over her head to give an exaggerated sense of the lady's large chapeaus. "Anyway, don't repeat this, but I've heard she might be a *dame de maison*," she added, parted fingers covering her lips, eyes darting back into the shop, making sure no one had walked in.

"A *dame* … what?" Sean asked, up to his elbows fishing for the remaining grinder parts sunken at the bottom of the tub.

"You know, *une femme galante,* a strumpet," Saraphine said, giggling, head swivelling back and forth between Sean and the shop.

"Really. A whore," Sean said, wiping his hands on the sides of his trousers, chin cocked up and staring across his body at Saraphine. "Pardon my frankness, but I don't think you should have anything to do with this woman. A woman like that's a disease. A scourge on society. It's nothing to giggle about," he added, wiping his forehead before turning his attention back to his work.

The large steel door squealed open, its creaking hinges sounding like a stepped-on cat. "Aren't you finished cleaning that?" Orance asked, bursting in from the loading dock, arms outstretched and locked in front of him like battering rams.

Sean, startled by the noise, instinctively flung the heavy auger he'd been cleaning at Orance. The metal piece flew near his boss's ear before clanking on a bone saw's blade hanging from the ceiling, the clatter of metal on metal nearly melodious.

"You trying to kill me?" Orance asked, fully aware he was to blame for Sean's defensive reflex.

"So sorry. I was holding on to that … then, when you came in … the noise … I just…"

"Relax. I knew you'd be in here. I was just trying to get a rise out of you, that's all. But I've got to say, I didn't think you'd try to kill me," Orance said, jaw unhinged, head bobbing and laughing.

"Well … I'm really sorry. It was just a reaction."

"Forget it and just make sure to finish cleaning that. I'll need it later. There's a lot coming in this afternoon."

Saraphine, eyes ablaze at the sight, had scurried back to her post behind the register, keeping the door from swinging as it closed behind her. Orance, noticing the move, barrelled through the door, arms cocked, applying the same battering ram technique.

"Not too busy, uh?" He said, picking at his thumbnail.

"It isn't usually, not this early in the week. Got a few orders on the telephone, though. Anyway, customers tend to come in later on Tuesdays. After lunch. I wouldn't worry about it."

"Oh, for sure. That's the way it is. It was always that way at my dad's place, too," Orance said, hands stuffed in his trousers pockets.

"Eugénie asked me to sweep the steps, and I already did that," Saraphine, feeling the need to fill in an awkward silence said, pointing at the street. Orance slowly walked to the front door and looked out, seeming to enjoy what remained of the early morning's golden sunbeams.

"Eugénie's still at the … where is she anyway?"

"At Monsieur Charpentier's place. Remember? She told me that you'd asked her to talk to your father about our signs, about us having the same signs in our windows at the same time. Same specials, same prices," she said.

"Oh yeah, yeah, I remember," Orance said, watching buggies and wagons rolling along Ontario Street. "Sean," he added, looking back at Saraphine. "Nice guy, eh?"

Saraphine turned to look at the door behind her, slowly rocking on the balls of her feet.

"I've noticed you two talk a lot. He's a really nice young man," Orance added, turning his attention back to the outside world. "You seem to be quite taken by him. Am I wrong?"

Saraphine stopped rocking. "He's nice. A gentleman," she said, stepping away from the register before speaking, hoping her words wouldn't bleed through the door.

"Yes, yes, yes," Orance said, walking all the way back and through the swinging door, nodding, lips pursed.

"Hey, Sean, do me a favour and take the bone saws to the sharpeners; that place along the canal. The saw that fell when you threw the auger at it probably needed work, anyway. Use the wagon, take all three of 'em and make sure to tell Réjean to get 'em done by tomorrow morning. Like I said before, there's a lot coming in and I wanna be ready for it."

"All three? You don't want to keep one here in case we

need it?"

"What did I say? All three … yes, please," Orance said, lifting the saws off their hooks and pointing them in Sean's direction. Happy to abandon his scrubbing duties and take a ride in the sunlight, Sean dropped the metal handle he was working on into the tub, removed his apron, grabbed the saws and headed out.

"You stay out here 'cause I'm gonna have to take over for Sean in the back," Orance, his face poking out the door, told Saraphine.

"Cleaning grinders?" Saraphine asked, contorting her face, surprised Orance would take over a job everyone knew he'd rather delegate.

"Never mind what I'm doing. I've got plenty other things to do back there."

-2-

Saraphine stood outside, leaning back on the door, squinting at the sun and waving at familiar faces. Bored, she broomed the already clean steps, parts of the sidewalk and swept the debris into the street.

"Saraphine," Orance hollered from the back. "Could you come here?" She closed the front door behind her and hurried to the back.

"What is it?" She asked, balanced on the tip of her shoes, looking through the door's round window.

"Lock the register and come back here. I need help with something."

Saraphine secured the register's drawer and slipped the key under the big scale.

"What is it?" She asked again, the opened door pressing against her shoulder.

Orance, his large, bulbous head sticking up through the trap door, said, "Hand me those crates, one at a time? I need to stack 'em down here," while pointing with his chin at five large wooden crates piled next to his workbench.

"But no one's in front. Should I go lock the door, first?"

"Yeah, right. Lock it and hang the *back in five minutes* sign. Quick," he said, looking down into the cellar.

Saraphine hung the sign in the window just as Madame Dufresne had started up the steps.

"Oh please, I just need a small roast for tonight. I won't be a minute," Madame Dufresne asked, the rim of her hat inadvertently tapping on the glass as she tried to convince Saraphine to open the door.

"It's just going to be a couple of minutes, Madame. I need to help out in the back. I'll open the door in no time," Saraphine replied, her breath fogging the window.

"But it's just a roast. It won't take long."

"Wait, let me see," Saraphine replied, then turned and yelled, "Can I just get a roast for Madame Dufresne before I help you back there?"

"Tell her to come back. It's just gonna be a couple of minutes."

"I'm sorry, Madame. Would you mind coming back in a little while?"

"Never mind, I heard him. I'll come back," the lady said, stepping off and pursing her lips while foraging through her small purse.

Saraphine ran through the swinging door and stood next to the crates.

"Is she waiting? Did she leave?"

"Yeah. She didn't look too happy, though ... but she said she'd come back."

"All right then, push those close enough for me to grab 'em," Orance said, pointing at the crates. Saraphine pushed the crates along the floor, grunting, struggling to bring them near enough so Orance could haul them into the cellar.

"Is that it? Is that all of 'em?" Orance asked from the bottom of the stairs. "Saraphine!" He yelled. "I can't hear you. Any more crates?"

Saraphine moved to the edge of the trap door and leaned forward to look down into the darkness. "That's it, all done," she responded, out of breath, hands on the small of her back.

"You should see some of the rats down here, they're the size of beavers," Orance, sounding far away, shouted up.

"Rats!" Saraphine yelped, hands on her crumpled nose. "Can you see any of 'em now?" She asked, leaning farther over the opening, looking without wanting to see. "Orance? You all right?"

Something gripped her ankle and pulled at her leg. She screamed and bounced on her free foot till Orance's laughing face appeared up the ladder, his hand still wrapped around her ankle.

"Lemme go. How could you do that?" She yelled, leaning on Sean's workbench, her pulse pounding in her neck and temples. "I was worried about you. How could you do that?" She added, watching him rise up through the hatch. Smiling. Proud of his prank. She turned away from him and took a step, but Orance locked his arms around her chest and pinned her elbows to her sides till she gasped from the tightness of his grip.

"I can feel your heartbeat. I guess I really scared you, didn't I?" She heard him whisper, his cheek against her ear, his hands cupped over her breasts as she struggled to inhale.

"Don't," she grunted, twisting her body; her stomping feet aiming at crushing one of his toes. "Don't do that. Stop it," she repeated, breaking away from his grasp.

"Not too ladylike?" Orance said.

"What?" She asked, pushing her back through the swinging door.

"I could see right up your dress. You were standing right there, right at the edge of the trap door and let me look up your dress."

Saraphine let the door close behind her and stood there a few seconds, looking back through the round window, making sure he wouldn't come to the front.

"You shouldn't tempt a married man like that," he added, talking at the door.

"I wanted to help. I couldn't see you down there. I was worried about the rats," she answered, beads of perspiration forming on her forehead like August dew; arms wrapped tightly around her chest. "I've got to unlock the door and let customers in."

"Relax. I was having a bit of fun. I know you couldn't see me down there," he said, laughing while dropping his apron over his head. "Don't you know that I've noticed how Sean looks at you from back here? Staring at your backside through the window," he added, stepping toward the swinging door—Saraphine having moved to the other side of the counter. "You know, men are all alike. Young ones. Old ones, we're all alike. You should know that. These are the facts of life. Besides, you don't have a father to tell you about things like that," he said, his nose pressed to the window, bits of spittle clinging to the round glass.

"Eugénie's always been there for me. We've always been there for each other and that's never gonna change."

"Of course. Sure. I'm just saying that when you work around young men—young men like Sean—you always have to be on guard," Orance said, walking backwards and knocking the trap door closed with the heel of his shoe; the heavy oak panel slamming shut making Saraphine flinch. "Just trying to teach you a bit of a lesson. Be careful how you handle yourself around men. That's all," he added, rubbing his hands along the front of his apron before opening the large steel door, lighting his pipe and stepping out onto the loading dock.

Saraphine took a deep, long breath, rested her elbows on the counter, looked up at the poster of the pig—its body mapped out into various cuts of meat—and waited till blood had drained from her brain. *Tack, tack, tack,* the sound of metal clicking on glass jarred Saraphine back into reality. She bounced and rushed to pull the sign off the window and unlocked the door.

"About ready, now?" Madame Dufresne asked, sarcastically.

"Yes, oh yes. Sorry. We have so much to get ready … we're expecting a lot of—"

"I need a little pork roast for tonight."

More customers walked in and Saraphine, surrounded by familiar faces, started to breathe normally. The little bell rang again and Eugénie, armed with big rolls of paper, walked in, her face partially covered by the load she carried.

"*Excusez-moi*," Eugénie said, walking blindly toward the back while trying to avoid colliding with a customer and thrusting a hip at the swinging door. "Where's Sean?" She muttered to herself, looking around at the empty space. "Saraphine, where's Sean? Where's Orance?"

Saraphine excused herself. "Probably on the deck, smoking," she said, three thick rib eyes loaded onto a sheet of brown paper in her hands. "Sean's at the sharpeners. Could you come out here, it's pretty busy," she added, hoping Eugénie wouldn't speak with Orance before she had spoken to her, first.

-3-

Saraphine sat in her usual spot, facing Orance, aligning and realigning the utensils on either side of her plate; clumsily mimicking how people act when sitting at the kitchen table.

"You sure I can't help? You walked all the way to Monsieur Charpentier's place today, you must be tired. Why don't you get off your feet and let me help."

"I'm fine. I'm not an old woman. I can prepare supper on my own. Besides, it's my turn, anyway. You've been cooking way too much lately," Eugénie answered her sister, buoyed by her latest initiatives aimed at promoting the shop.

"So, what about all that stuff you brought back today? We're gonna start putting more signs in the window now? Is that it?" Orance asked, his face aimed at his wife while his strained eyeballs stared at Saraphine.

"That's it. Exactly. We'll promote sales, sell more of our older meats. You'll see, it'll make us more money. Your father told me that he's gonna do the same," Eugénie replied, beaming with enthusiasm. "We can have weekly specials, you know, try and get rid of whatever's about to go bad. Sure, we'll sell it for less—but won't get caught with so much rotting meat," she added, brow lifted, wide-eyed while swivelling around to look at Orance.

"Makes sense, I s'pose. What d'you think?" Orance asked Saraphine, pointing his knife at his sister-in-law.

"What?" Saraphine asked, blinking, obviously unaware of what had just been said.

"You all right?" Eugénie asked, twisting away from the stove to look at her sister. She dropped her big spoon in the pot, walked behind Saraphine's chair and rubbed her shoulders. "My God, you're shaking. What's wrong?" Eugénie asked, leaning over, her face next to her sister's cheek.

"You're probably coming down with something?" Orance mumbled, leaning on his forearms and picking at his teeth, a look of concern poorly drawn on his face. "Hope not, 'cause we're gonna need you in the shop. Eugénie especially is gonna need help."

"Stop that. Maybe she *is* sick. I don't care about the shop," Eugénie said. "What you need is a good meal. Wait till you get a taste of this," she insisted, reaching to pull the spoon from the pot and offering it for Saraphine to lick as she resumed kneading the back of her sister's neck.

"Maybe she strained too hard today when she helped me in the back," Orance suggested, biting down on a large crust of bread, flaky crumbs sticking to the corners of his lips. "Sometimes I forget she's a girl ... that, yunno, she doesn't have a man's strength," he added and winked when noticing Eugénie wasn't paying him any attention.

Saraphine looked back at her sister, nodded and said,

"That's not true. I can push crates across the floor just fine."

"Pushing crates? Where? Why?" Eugénie asked, glaring across the table at Orance.

"Never you mind. Forget about all that, I'm fine. Let's eat," Saraphine added, glancing briefly at Orance before stroking her sister's forearm and pushing her toward the stove.

-4-

The open window next to Saraphine's bed did nothing to cool her clammy skin. Drapes cinched tightly at each end of the curtain rod, still and heavy, let in all of the full moon's light; silver beams reflecting in her watery, black eyes. It seemed tonight would be a calm one, not a peep from her sister's room. No grunts or groans from Orance, no shouting or banging on walls, and, best of all, no *claps* ... that horrific sound of fists pounding at flesh.

She lay staring at backlit clouds moving along the skyline. Compulsively, she'd turn to look at the key—securely engaged—blocking access to her door's keyhole. Sucking in long, unsatisfying breaths, she blew air down her chest and flapped the front of her nightgown—her efforts failing to cool her salty skin did, nonetheless, allow her over-oxygenated blood to make her woozy enough to eventually drift off.

Saraphine had learned to sleep lightly, rousing a sentry in her mind to patrol the night's stillness. Dried tears that had soldered her eyelids shut gave way at the sound of nails faintly scratching at her door's varnished grain. She spun her legs off the mattress and knelt at the foot of the door, fingers laced around the knob.

"Eugénie?" She whispered.

"Open the door," Eugénie replied.

Eugénie slid her bare feet along the floorboards, pushed the lone cover off the bed and lay on her side, her back against the window sill, the outline of her silhouette sharpened by the night's silver light.

"I'm worried about you. There's something—something wrong that you're not telling me," Eugénie said, spooning her sister tightly.

"You know how it is. Nothing's changed. You know that," Saraphine replied, looking back at her sister's shaded face.

"I know, but I get the feeling there's something you're not saying, that you're holding back. Did anything happen to you? Is it Sean? I don't know what to think about it. I don't want you to—"

"It's not Sean. Sean doesn't care about me. I doubt that he knows anything about me. Besides, all he does lately is rant about how Anna's no good … that women like her are a scourge."

"So?" Eugénie asked, chin in her palm, elbow resting on her sister's shoulder.

"So … so nothing. You've got enough to deal with already. The last thing I want is for you to worry about *me*."

"So, there *is* something wrong. Tell me. We don't keep secrets. Tell me," Eugénie insisted, her index and thumb pinching her sister's chin.

Saraphine lay back, hands behind her neck, looking up into nothing.

"What aren't you telling me?"

"It's been a couple of times now that … that your husband's been," Saraphine stammered, nudging herself closer to her sister.

"What? It's about Orance? What's he done to you?" Eugénie asked, her voice growing dangerously louder.

"He's been a bit too … too close to me. Too familiar. A couple of times is all. Just too familiar. You know?" Saraphine said, talking into the sheets.

"He touched you?" Eugénie asked, veins in her neck pulsing.

Saraphine turned abruptly. "Don't be worried about this. It's my problem. I should be gone already, have a life of my own," she snapped, clutching her sister's arm unaware of how tightly she was squeezing.

"Jus' tell me what's on your mind. Tell me what he did." Eugénie said, slowly, emphasizing each syllable of each word.

Saraphine told her sister—about how he had touched her, had groped her. About how he had spoken to her. About how she feared him. But, most of all, she told Eugénie about how guilty he made her feel and how badly she felt for her sister.

Eugénie cramped up, the pain in the back of her neck feeling as though someone had smashed a hammer at her spine.

"I'm so sorry," she mumbled, breathlessly. "I'm the one responsible for this, and I'll make sure it stops."

"No," Saraphine said, spinning to her knees and frantically looking down at her sister's face. "No, don't do anything. Please, don't *say* anything. Don't you see? That's exactly what I'm afraid of. He's gonna hurt you … hurt both of us."

Eugénie lifted herself on her elbows, glanced sideways at her sister and instantly recognized the desperation in her eyes—feeling as if she were looking at a reflection of herself. "Okay. Don't worry about that," she said and shook her head.

"You've got to promise you won't tell him that I told you about this. I can handle myself. Handle him. I'll make sure to keep away from him."

"We'll be all right. Don't worry. I won't let anything happen to you," Eugénie said, burying her face in the pillow.

"These things he's done, the touching … does he do that only when he's been drinking?"

"I don't think so. It's mostly while we're working. When you're gone. I don't know if he snuck a drink or two before. I didn't smell it on him, anyway … or is it that I've gotten used to the smell?"

"Don't give it another thought," Eugénie persuaded, and took hold of her sister's elbow. "I'm not gonna say anything and I'm gonna find a way of dealing with this. For now, jus' keep away from him as much as you can and I promise I won't leave you alone with him."

They lay side-by-side till the night's shadows gave way to a bright yellow, July sunrise.

"Remember when mom used to come in our room at night when one of us was sick or when we were—"

"Afraid," Eugénie said, pointing at her sister. "You always found something to be afraid of. Remember when the pattern on the drapes used to scare you?"

"They looked like ghouls, evil faces staring at me. Anyway, I was probably five the last time that happened," Saraphine said, a tiny smile lifting the corners of her lips.

"Remember, sometimes all three of us ended up sleeping in the same little bed? I never slept better. I'd fall asleep as if cradled in God's hands," Saraphine added, sounding distant.

Eugénie felt her sister's body loosen.

"I'm sure mom didn't fall asleep so easily, stuck in that little bed, the both of us wrapped around her."

Eugénie looked out the window, the cresting sun turning the neighbourhood windows orange. Orance would soon be up, the caw of crows calling him to work.

-5-

Eugénie looked at Orance as he lumbered into the kitchen, suspenders dangling to his sides and brushing against his calves.

"She still asleep?" He asked, motioning at Saraphine's door as he walked by.

"It's early still. She's not usually up at a quarter past five, anyway."

"Yeah, but we've got a lot to do today. We're all gonna have to be on our toes," Orance said, the gritty rasping of his palm rubbing his stubble sounding like a hissing snake.

"You always say that. Every day's a big day for you."

"Anyway," he replied, gesturing dramatically, head craned forward, "we do have to get ready for the day. It always gets busy 'round the end of the week," he added, reaching for his suspenders and snapping them over his shoulders before sitting.

The half-pound of bacon sizzling in the pan made Orance's tongue moisten. He stared at the stovetop, leaned back in his chair and tapped his fingers on the table.

"Where's the bread?"

"The breadbox, where else?" Eugénie replied, lifting her shoulders up to her earlobes, her cheeks curled up to her eyes.

"Lemme have some bread, will 'ya?" He said, looking in the general vicinity of the breadbox. "The bread should be on the table by the time I get up."

"You're jus' sitting there. *Maudit*! Can't you get up and get it yourself?" She replied, reaching to open the breadbox's door.

She piled a dozen or so bacon strips on a plate and shoved it all under her husband's chin. He picked at the bacon, cringing from the hot grease, seemingly unaware of the utensils on either side of his plate.

"I got a letter from Blanche the other day. Seems like she's doing pretty well over there, you know, in the States."

"Aw yeah ... that's good," he replied while chewing.

"She's working steady now, weaving, sewing ... or something. Actually, she told me that the company sells a lot of what it makes back to us here, in Canada. Isn't that something?" She asked, a piece of bread pinched between her fingers while poking her fork at her plate.

"Yeah, I guess."

Eugénie stared at her husband for a few seconds, pointed at him with her crust and said, "Anyway, I was thinking that, maybe, that company would be a good place for Saraphine to work. You know, a steady job. She could stay with Blanche."

"What?" Orance asked, snapping his head back. "She'd work, where?"

"In the States, where Aunt Blanche works," she replied, though Blanche had never made any such offer.

"What about the work that needs to be done here?" He queried, jabbing at the floor with his eyes and pushing down on the tabletop, oily imprints glistening on the wood. "Oh no, we're not gonna lose her too. We need more people here, not less."

"It was jus' an idea," she said, slotting strands of hair behind her ear. "I'm trying to think about what's best for her. She's not gonna work here forever, yunno."

"Maybe, but there's no point in us letting her go. Not now."

"Letting who go?" Saraphine asked, standing in her bedroom doorway, arms folded over her chest and looking at her sister.

"Your sister says Blanche wants you to go work with her in the States, that place, where was it?" He asked, turning to his wife.

"Um ... Winooski ... it's in Vermont," Eugénie replied, picking bits of food off her apron.

"Well, wherever it is, you're not going," Orance said, wagging a finger while sopping up bacon grease with his bread crust.

Saraphine blinked slowly and asked, "When did you hear from Aunt Blanche?" Her brow crumpled, puzzled; her sister hadn't relayed the latest news from her aunt and her beloved Ephrem.

"I must have jus' forgot to mention it. We're so busy round here, these days," Eugénie said, sighing and pushing herself off her chair. "Want some bacon? The bread's on the table."

"Can I see the letter?" Saraphine asked, sliding into her familiar spot across the table from Orance.

"How 'bout later? Never mind for now," Eugénie said, loading her sister's plate. "It was just a crazy notion, anyway. It's not like I—"

"I'm not leaving ... not leaving you," Saraphine said, looking at her sister while Orance looked up at Saraphine. "Anyway, I'm not going to the States, I don't even speak good English."

"Your English's pretty good when you're 'round our Irish friend, Sean. You two seem to communicate pretty clearly," Orance chimed in, smirking, droplets of bacon grease clinging to his thick, black mustache.

"Couldn't you leave her alone," Eugénie said, digging her nails into the table's pine top.

"That's my personal business, anyway," Saraphine said, springing from her chair, her sudden motion rocking the table and rattling the dishes.

"No need for dramatics," Orance said, shrugging as Saraphine slammed her bedroom door behind her. Eugénie wiped her forehead and mumbled something—disappointed by her clumsy attempt at distancing her sister from her husband.

"Saraphine, come back and eat your breakfast. Your gonna have to eat," Eugénie said, her nose inches from the bedroom door.

"Never mind her, she'll eat when she comes out. Just make sure the both of you are on time … lots to do today," Orance said, then squeegeed his lips with his thumb and headed downstairs.

-6-

Eugénie looked like a starfish, stretched out and reaching up in all directions to pull a sign off the big window up front.

"You shouldn't stand on a chair to do that," Saraphine said, hurrying through the swinging door to help her sister. "Why didn't you wait for me? I told you that I'd help with this."

"I wasn't sure you'd come down this morning knowing how mad you were at me. I thought for sure you'd—"

"Not mad … I'm worried. I don't know why you didn't tell me about Aunt Blanche … about Ephrem? Besides, how's *he* doing? What's the situation like over there?"

Eugénie stepped off the chair and pulled Saraphine close. She crooked her head over her sister's shoulder and looked at the swinging door to make sure they were alone then looked into Saraphine's eyes and said, "I didn't get a letter, didn't hear from Aunt Blanche ... not recently, anyway."

"I don't understand. Why does Orance think that? Why's he talking about me going there to work?"

"Because I lied to him," she said, turning again, rechecking that the swinging door hadn't swung. "I was jus' bringing up the possibility, you know, to see how he'd react. That's all. I was thinking that, maybe, it would be a good idea for you to go there, to work with Aunt Blanche. Besides, you'd be with Ephrem ... I know how much you love him. Besides, Aunt Blanche really cares for you."

"But none of that's true. Right? Besides, I don't *want* to go to the States and, even if I did, who knows if I'd actually find a job there? You don't even know that Uncle Jean or Aunt Blanche would want me there. It's all make-believe," Saraphine replied, squeezing back at her sister's hands before turning to look at the swinging door.

"I know. I was fishing, looking for some way of getting you out of this poisoned place. Maybe I'll write Aunt Blanche. Maybe that's the best way to move forward."

"No," Saraphine said, pushing Eugénie's hands away, her tone sharp and unequivocal. "I'm seventeen. I know how to take care of myself. You've got enough on your plate," she whispered through her teeth. "Let's just get these signs down before customers arrive."

Eugénie faced the window, stepped on the chair, and pulled the paper away from the glass while Saraphine held onto the hem of her dress.

-7-

Sean burst through the shop's door to the sound of the little bell's lament. Visor cap in hand, his head on a swivel, he strutted past Saraphine just as she—seemingly entranced by yet another of Anna Déry's tall tales—tried hard to focus on the lady recounting details of how she had recently returned from some exotic destination. Saraphine, face frozen into a smile, looked back at Sean as he thrust himself through the swinging door. Noticing Sean looking back at them through the round window, she subtly waved at him, her hand tucked in tightly to her hip.

"Sean, come out here. Have you met dear Madame Déry?" Saraphine asked, putting down some ground veal and breaking away from the lady's stare.

Sean pushed the swinging door open and, while looking away, pinched his lips and nodded up at the colourful lady. "Pleasure to meet you," Madame Déry said, reaching over the counter, her gloved hand extended in the boy's direction.

Sean, beads of perspiration clinging to his upper lip, the skin under his rusty freckles having turned pink, gave Saraphine a look before turning away abruptly, looking over his shoulder as he kicked the swinging door nearly off its hinges.

"The boy's obviously busy," Madame Déry said, her hand having remained hovering over the counter.

"Yeah ... busy, lots to do back there, you know," Saraphine offered, ears pushed back as a result of her maintaining such a prolonged fake smile. "Well, I guess I should wrap that up for you," is all she could think to add, looking down at a lump of ground veal sitting on a square of waxed paper.

The register's bell rang just as Madame Déry—intent on fully recounting the minutia of her most recent adventure— had reached the climax of her story involving some Parisian man she had spoken to, or met, or danced with ... or something.

"That's going to be eighty-five cents, Madame," Saraphine said, looking over her shoulder at the round window.

"Hope this veal is as good as the last one you—"

"Oh yes, no doubt."

"Hope that boy's a gentleman," Madame Déry whispered, bent at the waist and looking up at Saraphine, tapping the counter with her gloved knuckle as she backed away.

Saraphine smiled awkwardly and watched the lady exit.

She closed the register's drawer and stuck her face in the round window, the tip of her nose imprinted on the glass, hoping Sean would look back at her. He looked up, flung his apron over his shoulders and waved as if swatting at a fly.

"Everything all right?" She asked, her face poking in through the door's small opening.

"I told you about whores. I don't think she's the type of … the type of *woman* you should be talking to," Sean said, while Orance, smoking on the deck, pretended not to listen.

"You don't know her. She's a very interesting lady. She travels to Europe; she was just telling me that—"

"She's a whore. Don't you understand? A whore!" Sean yelled, as if vomiting the words, grinding through each syllable and spitting as he spoke.

Saraphine's head snapped back as if struck. She stared at the door a few seconds then tiptoed sideways behind the register.

-8-

"I see we both like the same kind of ladies," Orance said, his voice barging in from outside.

"I beg your pardon," Sean said, eyes unfocussed, unaware he had taken a few steps in his boss's direction.

"Saraphine. You're sweet on her, right?" He asked, rolling down his sleeves, a crooked smile hanging from his lips.

"Oh, sorry. I thought you were talking about … that depends. Did she say anything to you? To Eugénie?" Sean's expression had transformed while reinterpreting the question; a fragile look of anticipation washing over him.

"You'd have to be blind not to see she's sweet on *you,* my friend," Orance said, slapping dirt from his hands. "But, I'm gonna have to tell you this, too. If you intend to court that young lady, you're gonna have to find yourself another job. I won't tolerate romance at the workplace. You've got to understand, I need everyone here to be one hundred percent focused. I know I can't stop you from courting her but, well, you'll have to find yourself another job if you do," he added before burying his head into a crate. "Give me a hand over here," Orance shouted. "Unless you plan on quitting right away, that is."

Sean, picking at something stuck in the corner of his mouth, glanced back at the swinging door's empty window. He bit at the inside of his lip then, still looking back at the swinging door, slowly joined his boss on the dock, lugging pork carcasses out of the crate before hanging them on hooks.

Sean avoided Saraphine all morning. At lunchtime, he sat outside legs dangling off the dock, devouring his sandwich and ruminating over his boss's instructions, his warning.

"Sorry Sean," Eugénie's voice broke through his thoughts. "Would you mind slicing some pork chops for my customer? Orance is at his father's shop—delivering the old man's payment, you know—and the lady's in a rush."

"Oh, sure, of course," he replied, bounding to his feet and patting the dust off the seat of his heavy denim pants.

Sean walked through the swinging door; a paper-lined tray loaded with chops in hand.

"There he is. How many did you say you'll need?" Eugénie asked her customer. Sean, holding the tray up to his chest, peeked in Saraphine's direction.

"Can I have a word with you? Later, when it's not so busy," Sean leaned towards Eugénie and asked.

"Certainly, of course. I've got a few customers to serve still, but don't worry, I'll go and see you after," she answered, pointing at the still busy shop.

For the rest of the afternoon, he stared at the door hoping Eugénie would walk in before Orance had returned from his father's butchery.

"So, what can I do for you?" Eugénie asked, wiping her palms along her backside.

Sean looked up, his arm moving back and forth like a whirligig as he sawed a round off a cow's hind leg—the raw meat moistened by droplets of sweat sliding off his jaw—suddenly unsure if his idea to speak with the boss's wife was a good one.

"Yes," Sean said, dropped his saw on the bench and ran his forearm along his face. "I was speaking with Orance earlier, and ... he ... I guess what I want to know is ... is your sister interested in me?" He asked, fighting to draw a breath as he stepped out from behind his workbench.

Eugénie's eyes flew open and she twisted around, pointing at the swinging door while staring back at him. "You ... you're saying you're interested in my little sister?" She returned the question to Sean who, by now, had decided to speak plainly.

"I am. I like her. I think she's a wonderful person and, well, I'd very much like to court her."

"Rest assured. You have my blessing."

"That's great. That's really great news," he said, the pained look on his face seeming out of place. "But, there's a problem. I'm not supposed to court her. I can't," he said, clearing his throat, steadying himself before facing the next hurdle.

"Saraphine likes you, I'm sure. I'm her sister and sisters know about things like that," Eugénie replied, smiling as she moved closer to him.

Sean cleared his throat—this time loudly enough to make Eugénie flinch—stepped back, and rubbed his forehead till the tendons in his neck popped out like ropes. "Your husband ... Orance ... he said this kind of thing wasn't allowed, that I couldn't court your sister while I worked here, that I'd ... I would have to quit if I wanted to court her."

Eugénie leaned on the workbench and crossed her arms. "Well, I wasn't aware we had that type of policy here. I guess, from where I stand, it's not too logical to enforce that type of rule, you know, especially since I'm married to him ... that we work together."

"I'll admit, that kind of came to mind for me too ... I mean, that I thought it was strange for Orance to say what he said given, well, that you two are married and all … and met at work."

"All right," Eugénie said, raising her voice a bit as she stared out the door's porthole before swinging it open. "Jus' let me speak with him. Leave it to me."

"Before you do, know that I'll leave, that I'll quit if I have to … if he won't allow it, that is," Sean said, looking directly at Eugénie.

"Good to know," she replied, walking out, reassured—at least—that the young man was serious about her sister.

-9-

Orance backed his wagon next to the dock.

"Supper's nearly ready," Eugénie announced, pushing the heavy, steel door ajar on her way to dumping the bloodied sawdust she had swept off the shop's floor. "What took you so long? Problems at your father's place?" She asked, immersed in a cloud of rusty dust.

"Huh?" Orance replied, unhitching his large, white horse from the cart.

"Was there a problem?" She repeated, stepping back and swatting at the filth rising from the overflowing steel drum.

He waved his hand a couple of times and shook his head as he pulled the horse's reins, leading him to the shed across the alley. "You know how he is; the old man likes to take his time when telling me how to run my life," he said, his head turned to the side.

"Well, anyway, you better come up if you want your supper to be hot."

Saraphine heard Eugénie's footsteps echoing up the stairwell and shouted down the hallway, "You're late. I couldn't wait, I started without you."

"Yeah, yeah. Of course. Sorry, I'm late. Had to wait for Orance," Eugénie replied, looking down at the steps as she climbed.

"I guess Orance'll be on his way up soon, too?" Saraphine added.

"He's putting the horse away, he'll be up in no time," Eugénie answered, Saraphine serving up plates loaded with sausage, boiled potatoes, peas and sliced carrots.

The sisters ate, the sound of utensils scraping at plates seeming louder in the absence of the usual chatter. Eugénie peeked down the hallway—Saraphine peeking at her peeking— wondering why her husband hadn't yet run up the stairs. Why this man—a man who regularly choked from swallowing before chewing—wasn't already sitting at the table?

Resigned to the silence, Saraphine decided to enjoy the unusually peaceful meal while continuing to glance at her sister who, every few minutes, winked and smiled back at her.

"I should go see what's keeping him," Eugénie finally said, pushing herself away from the table, the linen napkin falling from her lap.

"What? You think something happened?" Saraphine asked.

Eugénie looked back at her sister, holding on to the stairway's doorframe. "No, no, jus' wanna go see what's keeping him."

Eugénie yelled down the stairwell, "Come up already, we're almost finished with supper."

She stood in the doorway looking back into the kitchen till the silence below drew her downstairs. Orance leaned forward on the butcher block—focussed—slowly honing his long carving knife; dragging it carefully, purposefully along an oiled sharpening stone.

"What?" He asked, eyes on his knife.

"Couldn't you say something? I've been calling you. Supper's ready," Eugénie said, clasping the doorframe, her left foot braced behind her.

"Just so happens that *I've* also got things to do," he said, riveted by the sight of his long blade's finely honed edge.

"It's up to you. If you don't want supper, that's fine with

me. But don't get mad when you come up and nothing's left," Eugénie said, maintaining her hold on the doorframe, poised and ready to run up the stairs.

"Fine," he replied, the smooth sound of the blade gliding along the oiled stone sending shivers up Eugénie's back.

Eugénie swallowed hard and took a step in her husband's direction, adding, "Lemme ask you something before I go back up."

"What?" He looked up from his sharpening stone long enough to get a read on his wife's face—her eyes—assessing if Sean had shared any of their discussion. If Saraphine had talked with her sister.

"Sean spoke to me earlier. He said you wouldn't allow him to court Saraphine," she said, walking toward the dock, ensuring her voice wouldn't carry upstairs.

He looked at the ceiling, shoulders pushed up by a long, deep inhalation, wiped the oil off his knife and placed it delicately on his bench. Turning back to his wife, he removed his apron, wiped his hands on it and said, "Yeah. Of course, I did… makes sense, right? That's the kind of thing that's not allowed in a place of business. You know that as much as I do."

"I can't believe you," she said, stomping her heel and jabbing at her palm. "What do you think this is? We're a family business. We don't have rules like that. Sean's a nice young man. Saraphine likes him and it certainly seems that he likes her. Why don't you leave them alone?" She added, pointing at the doorway leading upstairs.

Orance, stone-faced, looked directly into his wife's eyes till, all at once, his entire countenance relaxed. His face slackened—softened—trying to suppress a laugh. Giggling, he clapped.

"You drunk? What's going on?"

"Women. You got no sense of humour. I was pulling Sean's leg," he said, hands on his waist and bent over.

"What? That's not funny. Do you know that Sean said he'd

quit? That's not good business. Losing employees is no joke," she said, crimping her lips and pointing her chin at her husband who remained bent over and chuckling.

"Ok, no point in getting all upset about this," Orance said, his expression shifting back to its standard glum, menacing register. "Take it easy, I'll tell him it's okay when I see him tomorrow. I'll tell him it was all a joke. He'll understand."

Eugénie turned, dress flying and puffing up as she stomped away, her heavy heels crunching wood chips underfoot seeming to emphasize her frustration.

"Hey!" Orance yelled up at his wife. "You better tell your sister to stop talking with that Anna lady. Yeah, it looks like Sean ain't too keen on whores. Besides, maybe you'd do well to spend less time with her, too," he added, fists clenched as he hollered.

-10-

Orance reached into his top drawer, yanked the false bottom out, and grabbed a nearly empty bottle of whiskey; the black label with gold lettering staring back at him. He pulled the cork, making sure to mute the *pop,* the wafting aroma melding into the shop's meaty atmosphere. He lifted the bottle up to his eyes, looked at the doorway through the glass's amber tint and slowly rested the bottle on his lower lip. He let the potion linger in his mouth for a few seconds before lifting his tongue and guiding the elixir down his throat. The alcohol that had raced down to his gut felt as though it had caressed his ribs as it passed, the sweet sting reminding him he hadn't eaten in hours. A kind of warmth pushed up through his chest and percolated up to his brain, gently—so gently— toasting the back of his eyeballs along the way.

"That's it, your last chance. I'm putting everything away unless you come up now," Eugénie called down.

"Yeah, coming!" He screamed, the tightly coiled tendons under his chin cramping his neck.

He put the bottle back in its hiding place, climbed up the stairs, and plopped himself down in his usual spot at the table.

"So, where's supper?" He asked, tapping his knuckles on the table while leaning forward on his chair to better see through the side panel curtains fluttering over the small kitchen window. Resting back on his chair, he shoved his little finger in his ear, scraping at whatever he could find; carefully inspecting what he had managed to fish out.

"Right here," Eugénie replied, the sausage and boiled potatoes nearly bouncing out of the plate she had dropped in front of him.

Orance twisted his body to look back into the hallway and noticed the light was on in the parlour.

"Don't you worry yourself. Nobody's gonna come between you and your precious beau," Orance said, aiming his words at the parlour beyond the darkened hallway.

"Leave her alone," Eugénie said, smacking the heel of her palm at his shoulder.

"It was a joke, a prank," Orance repeated, reaching out and slapping back at his wife's hand, his giant fingers smashing at the back of her wrist.

Eugénie rubbed and cradled her hand. "There's no point being around you when you're in a mood," she snapped, walking away to join her sister in the parlour.

Eugénie and Saraphine sat on the couch, legs curled under them. Eugénie read. Saraphine, cockeyed, poked and pulled colourful threads through her needlepoint pattern. Orance, who had twice refilled his plate, offered a massive belch on his way back down to the butchery. Relieved by her husband's departure, Eugénie's shoulders loosened as Orance's digestive vocalizations faded into silence. She dropped her hands a few inches, just enough to see over her book and smiled at her sister. Saraphine exhaled, pushed her shoes off, stretched her legs along the cushions and jammed her toes under her sister's thighs.

Eugénie's head was on Saraphine's knee when she was

awakened by a loud noise. The floor seemed to shake. Orance, sitting on the bottom step, had started yelling while banging at the stairwell's wall. Eugénie sprang to her feet, wiped the drool off her cheek, and ran to look down the stairway.

"What's going on down there?" She asked, aware her husband was drunk. "You better come on up while you still can."

"You'll sleep in my room tonight," Saraphine told her sister, hands wrapped around Eugénie's arm.

Orance babbled in the dark, rocking side to side, his weakened neck causing his cheek and temple to bang on the wall every time he jerked and lurched.

"I'm not gonna help you out. You're gonna have to sleep downstairs, again," she said, scratching her scalp.

"Leave him there. Come on, let's just go in my room," Saraphine begged, tugging at her sister's elbow.

Chapter 11

Evening dissolved into night, undisturbed; soothing tranquillity that had allowed the sisters to eventually fall asleep. As usual, Eugénie woke first—a dot of light sliding along the bed cover had landed on her eyelid a full ten minutes before the neighbourhood's urban roosters had punched in. She carefully pulled her foot from under Saraphine's calf and rolled from under the cover. She stood at the bedroom door, ear to the panel, listening for the sounds people make when having breakfast—or when vomiting. Reassured by the tranquility, she turned the key, stuck her head out, looked down the hallway, and noticed her bedroom door was ajar.

Cool air coming through the kitchen window drifted softly through the room and flapped her nightgown gently along her perspiring skin. She tiptoed down the couloir, aiming to pull her bedroom door shut, hoping her husband would sleep through the morning, long enough, anyway, for the alcohol to lose its hold on his mind. Better to deal with his retched hangover temperament rather than his drunken violence.

She reached for the doorknob, cheeks puffed out and holding her breath to avoid inhaling the odour that would billow from her husband's gaping mouth. She exhaled at the sight of her empty bed; covers left undisturbed.

She noticed the stairwell's door shuttling in the breeze; the same cool air slipping down into the butchery. She pulled it open with her nails, the creaking hinges echoing down the dark chute. Holding on with her right hand, she leaned sideways and looked down the staircase. He lay at the bottom, sprawled on his back, a fly moving in and out of his nostrils. No one had pushed him. Not Blanche. Not Saraphine. He had probably tumbled back on his way to bed, a victim of his own inebriated stupor.

Eugénie's skin tingled. Her heart raced. Sweat beaded in her armpits as the draft rushed along her bare feet. She stared down at him for nearly a full minute. Inanimate. Deathly still. She stepped down, her palm on her chest.

Maybe he's dead, she thought. In a flash, she glimpsed a future without him, without fear. Her name atop the sign. She rubbed her cheek and tried to knock the thought from her mind—but it stuck. Grew stronger. More detailed. Stepping down closer to the body, she focussed on his chest. *Was he breathing?* Another thought shot through her brain like a cannonball skipping through the enemy's legs. *What if he's not dead? What if he's just knocked out? Maybe I could find something heavy enough down in the shop to bash at his skull? Finish the job? Nobody would know. No one would ever find out.* The invading notion terrified her and sent a shiver down her sweaty skin till she was nauseous.

She looked at him and wedged her feet in between his arm and ribcage. She then bent over and placed her hand on his chest. Though faint, she felt the rise and fall of still-active lungs. The proximity to his mouth made her eyes water and confirmed the source of his current predicament.

"Oh, my lord," Saraphine's words, muffled by hands tented over her mouth, startled Eugénie.

Expressionless, Eugénie looked up at her sister.

"Is he dead?" Saraphine whispered.

"He's breathing, but he hasn't moved. I think he's jus' knocked out. He must have banged his head all the way down the stairs."

"What're we gonna do?"

They looked at each other, aware of the other's thoughts. Aware that *doing nothing* was a valid option. A good option. That going back to bed—unaware of the unfortunate accident—was a plausible alternative. Eugénie, bent forward and hovering over him, looked carefully at his face, at his chest, then straightened up and said, "I'll call Dr. Emond," then turned to her sister and offered a bit of a shrug. "What else are we gonna do?"

"Of course. Yes, of course," Saraphine said, walking sideways down the staircase and clinging to the handrail. "Now?" She added, staring into her sister's eyes.

Eugénie looked away and nodded. "Jus' help me. We've got to get him out of here. Grab an arm and we'll drag him into the shop," They pulled Orance along the shop floor, the floorboards clean of sawdust in his wake.

"Urgg," he moaned, his left eye half opened.

"Orance. Can you hear me?" Eugénie, crouching, her nightgown tucked tightly onto the back of her thighs, said in his ear. Saraphine, biting the corner of her lower lip, clapped her hands a few inches away from his nose as if a hypnotist stirring a lackey out from a trance. Eugénie, startled by her sister's unexpected exuberance, took Saraphine's wrists and held them to her lap.

"Jus' call Dr. Emond," she said, looking down at him. Inanimate. Helpless.

"But it's not even five yet. He probably won't be up so early."

"Jus' call him. That's why telephones ring," Eugénie said, shooting an angry look at Saraphine and feeling as though bottled inside an alternate dimension; going through the motions, fulfilling the requirements expected from a dutiful wife or, at the very least, a concerned bystander.

-2-

Having returned from Hôtel Dieu hospital—his room a few doors from where he had convalesced those long days recovering from his time in the river—Orance had been instructed to follow Doctor's orders. That meant being continually reminded to remain off his feet and to avoid alcohol. It also required he let Sean take care of the butchering in the back while Eugénie and Saraphine did their thing up front; keeping the shop's momentum moving forward.

Clad in bloomers, Saraphine delivered orders, drawing looks as she pedalled along the neighbourhood, the basket hanging from the handlebars filled with neatly wrapped roasts and cutlets. This had been Sean's job, but with Orance on the mend, he was now responsible for butchering all of the meats. Orance, given his almost constant migraines, had soon developed an appreciation for spending his days under the sheets. Eugénie, ever the dutiful caregiver, made certain to bring him his acetylsalicylic acid powder—which she carefully diluted for him—like clockwork, every four hours.

By mid-October, Dr. Emond had determined that the patient's condition had improved to the point where he could spend a few hours on his feet. Every day before lunch, Sean helped Orance down the stairs where he sat in an overstuffed chair they had lugged down from the parlour—his crooked, broken nose whistling whenever he tried to talk—spending mornings smoking and criticizing the goings-on. Soon enough, the brightness of the day electrified his headache into a migraine and chased him back to his dark bedroom, snug under the covers and falling asleep easily.

Sometimes on those rare occasions when Orance found himself alone downstairs (Uriette dropped-in to check on her boy nearly every day), he felt a kind of pull from his top drawer like a lasso slipping over his shoulders and dragging him against his will. Looking all around to make sure no one could see him, he'd yank his bottle from its hideout and drain a few gulps of his preferred therapy. Besides, Sean was always available to refill his supply. Could the boy refuse his boss?

-3-

"*V'là ma belle fille*," Madame Déry said, her voice hardly defeated by the pane of glass between them. Eugénie spun away from her customer, eyes catching fire at the sight of Anna's big lips, redder than hot peppers—the gaudy lady smiling and tapping her umbrella's handle at the glass. "Is that my beautiful girl I see in there?" She repeated, making Eugénie feel as if she were on display.

Eugénie waved and kissed both her rouge-laden cheeks as soon as the lady walked in.

"We haven't seen you in so long," Eugénie said, arms around the beautifully exuberant woman. They both stood for a while, locked together, cheek-to-cheek, looking at Saraphine while Saraphine smiled back at them.

"I've just returned from Paris, *mon enfant*," the lady said, gently stabbing her umbrella at the floor with both hands.

"Paris," Saraphine said, hands on her cheeks. "You went to France?"

"That's where Paris is, girl. All of October and November. It was wonderful … saw everything, met everyone," Anna Déry said, hugging herself, eyes rolled back.

"I'm going upstairs," Orance's nasally voice spilled through the barely opened swinging door.

The sisters—locked in a state of suspended animation, hanging off Madame Déry's every word—paid no attention to the whistling voice coming from the back. "*La Seine, ma chérie. La tour Eiffel … mon Dieu.* And the show they put on at *Le Moulin Rouge … pas croyable*! And, you know what? It was a lot like the one we did, right here, at the Empire. Oh, it was amazing, girls."

"Hey!" Orance yelped, his voice exploding through the shop like a grenade. "D'you hear me? I said Sean's gonna take me upstairs. I've got to rest. I don't feel so great," his face poking through the barely opened door sneering back at the smile that had remained suspended on his wife's lips.

"Fine. We'll be fine. Sean'll come back down, right?" Eugénie responded, nodding while waving the back of her hand at the swinging door as she turned to face Anna.

"Don't forget my powder. I've got the usual migraine,

don't forget it," Orance ordered before disappearing behind the swinging door. "Your girl's with that whore again. Looks like they're having a great time out there," Orance told Sean.

"It's no laughing matter. Those types of women are … there's no place for women like that in a Christian world," Sean answered, looking through the round window and stuffing a rag in his back pocket.

"Really? I guess we'll have to disagree on that one," Orance said and snapped his fingers impatiently, waiting for the boy to help him up the stairs.

"You'll have to come by my place. I can't wait to show you all the things I brought back. I got something called a stereoscope that makes pictures look like the real thing, as if you were there. I bought drapes … I even found a—"

"Why didn't you send a postcard? It would've been such a delight to receive that kind of news in the mail, to have a postage stamp from France," Eugénie said, frowning.

"I did. Sent three. I bought them in a dispensing machine. I put coins in a silver machine, pulled a lever, and cards dropped out. Like magic. One of them had a photograph of the Eiffel tower, the other was of the Notre-Dame Cathedral, and I think the other one had a picture of The Arc de triomphe. I don't know why you didn't receive *any* of them, dear," Madame Déry said, smiling though looking puzzled.

"We didn't," Saraphine responded, her round eyes focused on her sister's.

"Huh. Strange," Eugénie added, looking back at the swinging door.

"Well, anyway. I'm back, and it was wonderful," Anna said, her pinched lips forming a thin, red line below her powdered nose. "Besides, all the more reason for you to come by and look at what I brought back. There're tons of stories I could tell you about it … about what it was like in the old country."

"Orance is yelling about his powder . . ." Sean said, opening the swinging door with his shoulder, "…said you'd bring him his powder."

"Is it time, already?" Eugénie said, still consumed by Anna's tales.

"Why, hello my boy," Anna said, tilting her head to catch a better glimpse of Sean.

Sean looked at Eugénie. "He's sounding like he's got a pretty bad headache," he said, before following the door's momentum and disappearing into the back.

"I agree. We're both going to go and visit you. Right, Eugénie? Can't wait to see all you've brought back," Saraphine said, looking back at the swinging door while stroking Madame Déry's silky sleeve.

"Yes, yes, of course, you must," Madame Déry insisted, squeezing Saraphine's cheeks and forcing her lips into a pout. "For now, though, I'm needing to refill my icebox with some choice cuts of meat."

"Without a doubt," Eugénie said, Anna's fingers still locked on her sister's chin.

Eugénie walked behind the counter and readied herself to prepare Madame Déry's order.

"What about Orance's powder?" Saraphine asked, nodding at the back and blinking.

"What?"

"The powder. Orance. Sean said Orance was—"

"Yes, right. Huh, would *you* mind bringing him the power?" Eugénie asked, her exaggerated smile and crumpled-up nose letting her know she was aware of the imposition. "You'll have to measure it with the spoon that's in there. I usually leave it in the cabinet with the aprons and rags in the back," she added, pointing at the swinging door while listening to Madame Déry reading her list of carnivorous delights. "You can just leave it for him and come right back."

"Well ... uh ... I suppose I can," she replied, cheeks inflated. "Yes, of course. How much does he need?"

"A spoonful from the bag, mix it in a glass of water."

"I don't know where the powder is, if that's what you're looking for?" Sean said, not looking up when Saraphine walked in, his blade slicing effortlessly through muscle and gristle.

"Eugénie said it's with the rags and aprons," Saraphine said, leaning forward, hoping he'd look back at her. "D'you know where the rags are stored?" She added, seeming to skate along the wood chips and sawdust as she moved closer to Sean.

"The cabinet, right behind you," he responded, pointing over Saraphine and smiling at her—finally—his grey eyes sparkling and mischievous.

Saraphine bowed, palms together as if in prayer, the deliberateness of the move intended to emphasize her sarcasm. "Why, thank you dear sir," she said, walking backwards and smiling, still bent forward as she withdrew.

"Very funny. Why don't you make sure to—"

"My powder! Where's my powder? I'm in pain here," Orance hollered, his words rumbling down the stairwell like an avalanche.

"I think you better get up there," Sean said, rubbing his forehead and pointing at the stairwell with his knife.

Saraphine took the small, white paper bag sitting next to the glass, scooped in a tablespoon of powder, and rushed up the staircase.

-5-

"I know I'll need to dilute this in water, d'you want me to fill the glass up or, say, leave it half full, maybe?" Saraphine asked, hurrying past Orance's bedroom door on her way to the kitchen basin.

"Did you put a full teaspoon in? Make sure it's a whole teaspoon 'cause it hurts ... hurts really bad," Orance said, hand on his forehead, his voice down to a whisper.

Saraphine, glass full of murky, foggy liquid in hand, stood at Orance's door. She looked down at him, noticing how her brother-in-law suddenly looked small under the covers, seeming weak without being drunk. Though Eugénie liked to wear perfume, Orance's smell—his odor—had overtaken the room. She couldn't stop herself from staring at the man in the bed, eyes closed, his forearm over his head.

"I think it's about right. The mix, I mean. I think I poured just the right amount of water in it," she said, pushing her chin forward, trying to inform without disturbing, a tremor moving up her shoulder as if burdened by the weight of a small glass.

"Thank the Lord. Finally," he replied, eyes still closed. "Glad *somebody* cares enough to bring me my medicine."

"We ... huh ... we all care about you," she said, toneless, feeling the need to respond. "Eugénie's really busy in the shop, you know ... and Sean, well, obviously, he's carrying the load on his own. So, here I am . . ." she added, words spewing out like bullets from a machine gun while looking down at the glass, "...so, it's not that nobody cares. It's just that everybody's pretty busy, you know, at this time of day ... you know how . . ."

"My wife doesn't care. You know that. I know you two talk all the time. She doesn't care ... not anymore. She doesn't."

Unable to respond yet unwilling to lie, she said, "So, should I leave this on the dresser?" Noticing her foot had stepped into *his* bedroom—a man's bedroom—she half expected the sole of her shoe would catch fire. She stood there, pointing the glass at her brother-in-law, hoping the tremor running down her arm wouldn't cause her to drop the medicine.

Orance slowly lifted himself on his elbow, the movement seeming burdensome. He wiped his face from top to bottom, the friction of his hand rubbing against his lips making a squishy, wet sound. "Come on, bring it to me. I won't bite," he said, arm outstretched, a glossy hand dangling off his wrist like a maple leaf in late November.

Saraphine stiffened and placed her fingers under the glass, hoping the move would dampen her shaking. "I'll leave it here," she said, pointing at the dresser with her brow. "You can take it whenever you're ready."

"You know, when I really think about things, you're the only one in this house that cares anything about me," he said, swinging his hairy legs out of bed and dragging the covers down on the floor.

Saraphine darted forward, tiptoeing over the covers and put the glass on the dresser, the impact causing some of the liquid to spill.

"Wait, wait," he said, lunging forward and grabbing Saraphine's wrist before she could retreat out of range. "I'm trying to thank you here, trying to be nice. There's no reason for you to be worried about me ... afraid of me, I mean."

Saraphine felt as if her head had inflated to twice its size as a burning current of electricity funnelled up her spine. Her throat closed and locked all sounds deep in her chest. Orance, suddenly dynamic, quickly took hold of her other wrist and pulled himself out of bed, the thin fabric of his underwear no match for his erection.

"Sean!" Saraphine yelled, turning to aim her voice at the opened bedroom door.

Orance, seemingly fully recovered from his migraine, spun around and threw Saraphine on the bed. "Never mind Sean ... all good up here," he said, looking down at Saraphine before kicking the door closed with his heel.

Saraphine watched, eyes watering, lips quivering as Orance leaned back against the door and turned the key. Dozens of thoughts shot through her mind; every nerve in her body was alight. She looked at the door, hoping to hear Sean's voice on the other side. Hoping. Waiting.

"Nothing's gonna happen here that both of us didn't think about before, am I right? You were curious, I know that. I've seen how you've reacted when we played together before."

None of Orance's words registered. All she could see were his lips moving; his eyes consuming her. She clutched the sheets, waiting to see which side of the bed he'd flank; waiting to see if she would have to go right. Go left. Trying to remember in which direction to turn the key ... toward the door frame? Away from it? Thinking about how quickly she could manage the whole process.

"Sean!" She screamed, staring into Orance's eyes, her teeth vibrating as air rushed from her chest.

Orance's face relaxed. He smiled and arched his upper body way back, his kneecaps pressed tightly against the foot of the mattress. For an instant, a half-second at most, Saraphine thought that maybe ... maybe the scenario wouldn't unfold as she feared. Maybe, just maybe, Orance would stop and, maybe—

He lunged forward and slammed his hand over her mouth, the move sending Saraphine's head smashing into the wall. She struggled to breathe through the leathery palm covering the bottom of her face, unsure if the cracking sound she heard was due to the wall's plaster breaking off its keys or if her skull had fractured. The blow shot lightning through her eyes and numbed her shoulders. She looked into her brother-in-law's eyes, realizing she had never before been so close to his mustache, his nose; subcutaneous pus held back by an army of blackheads. His hand tasted like vinegar.

Dazed and fighting to remain conscious, she found herself face down; Orance's giant paw pushing against the back of her head, driving her face into the mattress. *I've got to take a deep breath, fill my lungs and scream as loudly as I can*, she thought, but a growl is all she could manage. "Help! Eugénie! Sean! Help!" The words barely escaped from her lips.

The physical and psychic pain of being raped merged into a cataclysmic horror. Saraphine's entire body was on fire. She screamed.

Finding purchase in Saraphine's fine hair, he pulled her head back and thrust her face into the pillow sealing her nose and mouth tightly against the fabric. She felt her neck cracking with each of his thrusts—bolts of pain shooting up and down her body. Unable to breathe, her asphyxiated mind shut down. The pain stopped. She was no longer in that moment.

-6-

"Was it so bad?" The words trickled in from somewhere outside Saraphine's mind as her spirit rose from the abyss. Through a fog, she saw an empty glass held upside down over her face as cool droplets of acetylsalicylic acid-laced water landed on her forehead and cheeks. She wiped her face. Orance belched.

"This stuff's pretty good, but nothing beats a good lay. Am I right?" He teased, looking at the empty glass he held up to his eyes. Jovial. Kindly. Oblivious.

Lying on her side and arched back, she sucked in all the oxygen her lungs could hold. Slowly regaining control of her body, she swept her legs off the bed. Bursts of pain exploded from her pelvis as if shrapnel had gouged the tender flesh inside. A torrent of images rushed into her consciousness and spread inside her like an infernal panic. Electrified, she jumped off the mattress and felt a terrific jolt of pain flow up her back like lava. She froze. Groaned. Anguished that her attacker now enjoyed the satisfaction of watching her suffer, she noticed her drawers hanging off the top of her right shoe. Slowly, hands braced to her knees, she pulled them up while he watched, smiling.

She looked at him and felt a flow of energy. At first, she thought it was shame that coursed through her but soon realized the ignition had been fuelled by pure hatred.

"No reason why *we* can't have some fun. It's all in the family, right?" His voice unfamiliar. "So . . ." he added, whirling his empty glass on the dresser with his index finger, "all this, our bit of private time together, don't you worry, it's all gonna stay between us. I'm not gonna say anything to your sister." Then, looking into the empty glass, he sat on the edge of the bed and crossed his legs. "Why a young woman would go in a man's bedroom … well … maybe your sister would find that hard to understand? But who's to tell, right? I know how jealous women can get so, like I said, I promise to keep quiet about this," his sudden fatherly tone contrasting with the monstrous nature of his threat. He leaned forward and took a closer look at Saraphine, hoping to gauge her reaction.

Saraphine stepped toward the door. Orance lurched in front of her and turned the key. She watched, noticing he had turned it away from the doorframe.

-7-

Every part of her body seemed disconnected from her brain. Shaky, she clutched at the stairway's railing. Labouring to slide her feet down the steps, the impact of each footfall seemed to detonate mines buried in her spine. *How long have I been up there? Fifteen minutes? An hour? What am I gonna tell Eugénie? How can I explain—*

Something warm slithered down her inner thigh, stinging her abraded skin along the way to her knee. She stuck her hand up her dress and spooned the ejaculate into her palm. She stood there, frozen. Looking back. Looking down. She reached into her pocket for a handkerchief but found none so rubbed the semen on the step till the worn wood had absorbed most of the evidence. The pulsing pain worsened with each passing minute. *I won't be able to pretend that nothing happened … Eugénie will know. They'll all know,* she thought, trying to control her breathing.

She placed her foot down on the next step and nearly lost her balance, the herky-jerky move making it feel as if her vertebrae had cracked. She slapped her hand over her mouth and bit her palm. She thought of sitting on the step till the pain subsided but, instead, a competing thought bullied its way through her muddied mind.

She took a couple of deep breaths, bent her knees, screamed, and flung herself down the nine remaining steps.

-8-

Saraphine heard Eugénie's voice coming from some distant place; words jumbled as if bouncing in an echo chamber. She opened her eyes and flinched at the sight of Dr. Emond's face hovering over her.

"Ance . . ." Saraphine mumbled.

"So, you've decided to join us," Dr. Emond said, his thick, gray mustache covering his upper lip making his words sound strangely telepathic.

"She's awake!" Eugénie said, reacting to her sister's voice. "Saraphine, oh my goodness. Saraphine," she added, unaware she had nearly pushed Dr. Emond to the floor as she reached for her sister's hand.

Adrift in a heroin haze, Saraphine saw ghostly figures milling around her, unsure why they were there.

"Let's leave these two for a little bit," the Doctor said, corralling his doctorly implements back into his bag.

"Thanks for everything, doctor," Saraphine heard Orance say. In a flash, every second of her recent past rammed its way into her consciousness; every detail, all at once, blowing up inside her brain.

"What happened? Did you trip on your dress, slip on something? Was it too dark?"

"Am I all right? Am I gonna be all right?" Saraphine asked, reaching for her sister's forearm.

"The doctor said you'd be fine. You've got a big bump on your head. Said you fractured your skull, and ... and . . ." Eugénie paused, combed her fingers through her sister's hair, "...hurt your knees and scraped your legs."

— 232 —

"But, I'm all right?" Saraphine asked, lifting her shoulder to gauge how much of the pain would persist.

"Yes. He said that the drugs he gave you will take away the pain till you're all healed up."

Saraphine closed her eyes and drifted away.

-9-

Saraphine stood at her post behind the register, shoulders back, making sure not to slouch as Dr. Emond had ordered.

Orance, cheeks sucked in, opened the swinging door with his head and whispered to her, "Could you come back here; Sean's out on a delivery and I need help with the grinder."

The voice—the whispering—hollowed out Saraphine's gut. She dashed across the shop, her stilted walk making her look like a wind-up toy on a mission and grabbed Eugénie's arm. "Your husband wants me to help him in the back. I can't do that; I don't want to hurt myself. Please tell him that I can't help him back there."

"What? Of course. I told him ... specifically told him you couldn't do anything other than ring up sales," Eugénie said, a vein inside her forehead ghosting a deep blue line though she tried to douse her anger while surrounded by customers. "I'll go talk to him as soon as I'm finished with this lady," she added, patting her sister's hands before prying them from her forearm.

"Here you go, Madame Sauvé. Like I said, make sure to braise it before putting it in the oven," Eugénie told the lady, wrapping the meat and handing it to her sister. "Let me know what your husband thinks about it," she added before bursting through the swinging door.

"I asked you to make sure Saraphine didn't exert herself. Why'd you ask her to help you back here?"

"Sean's on a delivery. You know the grinder's screw's stripped. I need someone to feed the meat into it or else I can't hold it and turn the lever at the same time. I was just gonna

— 233 —

ask her to drop beef cubes into the mouth of the machine. How's that gonna hurt her?" Orance said, reaching back for the grinder and pointing at the broken screw.

"Jus' leave her alone. She can't help you, not now."

"Yeah well, maybe you should tell *her* that," Orance said, under his breath, smiling and nodding.

Eugénie's expression morphed from puzzlement to anger. She walked slowly toward her husband and looked up at his mustache. "What'd you say?"

Orance stepped back, leaned forward and answered, "I said, why don't you tell *her* that."

"What? What, exactly, am I supposed to *tell* her?"

"To leave me alone, that's what," he said, turning away and pawing at his grinder.

Eugénie's shoulders slumped. She took a deep breath through her nose, one of her nostrils whistling as air rushed in. "You want *her* to leave *you* alone. That's what you're saying?" She asked, pointing at the swinging door before pointing back at her husband who continued to fidadle with his grinder, mumbling something while keeping his hands busy.

"Leave *you* alone? She's afraid of you, Orance. I suppose you haven't noticed that. Saraphine, my sister out there, she's *afraid* of you," she reemphasized, biting her lower lip and pointing once more—this time with even more vigour—at the swinging door. "She's not in the least interested in getting *closer* to you so jus' leave her alone. *I'll* tell her what to do," she said, pounding the swinging door open and returning out front.

PART III

Chapter 12

By October's gloom, Saraphine's nights were spent scanning through obscurity at the shiny, round key's bow tucked under the doorknob. She would eventually succumb to exhaustion and fall asleep—sometimes as many as three hours—till, startled out of her restless slumber, breathless, as if having plunged off the edge of a thousand-foot cliff, she would bolt to her feet and stare at the key. Stare at the key … stare.

On this particular night, she woke to the sound of her heart booming in her ears, her tongue scraping her dried-out pallet; her clinging, drenched nightdress making her shiver. Though the nightmare she escaped from hadn't been real, the world all around her was; trapped in a life where every minute of every day was spent worrying. On guard. Anxious. Having to live and work with a man who could—who would—at any given moment, attack.

Having finally caught her breath, she coiled her knees to her chest and scrunched herself into a ball. Later, cramped and stiff, she paced the room, eyes trained on the key. This grind could last for hours. Round trip turnabouts in a room that had become a squirrel's cage. Sometimes she'd sit on the floor, her back against the door, and look out the window, staring at smoke puffing from distant chimneys while waiting to hear those familiar, friendly sounds from the kitchen; Eugénie's clatter as breakfast was made ready.

"D'you sleep well?" Eugénie asked, yawning while getting bacon and sausages out from the icebox.

"We're running outta bread," Saraphine answered, reaching into the breadbox before collecting plates from the cabinet.

Eugénie, as she had been doing a lot lately, peeked sideways at her sister, undetected (or so she thought), assessing her sister's movements. Had she fully recovered from her fall? Had her body healed?

"You feeling better these days?" She asked, knees bent sliding lumps of coal into the oven with a small steel shovel.

"Better? I suppose. My neck's getting better, that's something."

"Good," Eugénie said, looking back at her sister while returning the shovel to its hook. "What about your legs?" She added, eyes darting down the hallway and rubbing the back of her arm.

"My legs?"

"Your knees and those scratches the doctor mentioned. He said you had scratches along the inside of your legs. You remember how that happened?"

"Well, I fell down the stairs, so … I suppose it's when I fell against the steps. Anyway, they're all gone. Healed up good with the ointment he gave me," Saraphine answered, running her hands down the back of her nightdress.

Eugénie hardly noticed anymore those sounds Orance made when rising—hacking up a lung, his big shoes scraping the floor as he forced his giant feet into them. For Saraphine, however, those noises had become a signal to initiate her newly established morning routine. Coffee in hand, she'd grab a piece of bread and scurry back into her room.

"I'm gonna go and get dressed," she'd say, looking down the hallway, then into her huge, brimming full mug.

Used to the new pattern, (though unwilling to confront her sister about it) Eugénie watched her sister flee to her room knowing she'd soon hear the key pushing the deadbolt into the door frame. "I'm off. Getting an early start," Saraphine would then say, bursting from her room, looking straight ahead and fiddling with her hair, beelining down the hallway and down the stairs.

"Careful not to fall," Orance had gotten used to yelling as

she'd race by. He'd smile, somehow unaware of his callousness. Every morning, she'd walk by a bit faster, hoping to make it downstairs before being struck by those words—but they never failed to land.

Early one morning, late in November, Saraphine sat in her usual spot alone behind the register. Staring down at a book Eugénie had passed on, absentmindedly rereading passages—sometimes whole paragraphs, the words failing to register in her mind—she peeked at the clock looking forward to unlocking the front door, to chatting with regulars, to leaving her thoughts behind. While blankly gawking at one of the pages in her book, she was startled by the sound of Sean wrapping a knuckle on the front door's glass. Swallowing a gagging noise down her throat, she looked up.

"It's just me," Sean said, his mouth inches from the glass, his breath fogging up the window, the lower part of his face partially concealed by the mist.

"Sorry. I guess I was really involved in my book," she said, looking down at her hand while closing the door behind him.

"You look like you've seen a phantom. Must be a scary book."

Saraphine returned to her stool behind the register and smiled without looking at him.

"I've been working a lot lately. That's probably why you think that."

"Oh, that wasn't meant as an insult," he said, swiping his cap off and holding it in front of him with both hands, his long hair dangling off his shoulders. "I was just meaning that—"

"Is that my apprentice I hear out there?" Orance's voice came crashing in from the back.

Sean looked at the swinging door and then back at Saraphine.

"I'm sorry if I was insensitive, it's not that I—"

"Let's get to work. There's a lot to do today. First of all, you're going to go get rabbits at my father's place," Orance said, dropping both his hands on Sean's shoulders. "You two starting pretty early this morning," he added, looking at Saraphine while slapping Sean's back. "At least you're not on the clock yet," he added and winked, pushing Sean into Saraphine and causing her to drop her book.

Keeping her back straight, Saraphine slowly bent her knees and picked it up, dusted the sawdust off, and pressed on the register's *no-sale* key. The bell rang, and the cash drawer slid out.

"Eugénie's gonna have to get rolls of change at the bank. All I've got is mostly bills in here," she said, hoping Orance would soon disappear into the back.

-2-

"You need coins?" Eugénie said walking into the shop. "Which ones? How much?"

Saraphine opened the cash drawer and pulled out a bill. "Quarters and dimes. A couple of rolls of each should do fine."

Eugénie unlocked the front door, tightened the hair net that corralled the big bulge of hair hanging from behind her head, and said, "Give the money to Sean. He'll go to the bank. I'm not leaving you on the floor all by your lonesome."

Saraphine reached back, slapped the swinging door open and, just as she prepared to call Sean, smells of meat and fat, blood and sawdust rushed at her as if the entire room had belched. Those familiar scents—odours that had swirled all around her for years—suddenly brought a flood of saliva to her mouth. Lightheaded and nauseous, she bent over and dry heaved. Holding on to the doorframe, she looked up and saw Orance and Sean staring at her. She took a long, deep breath and lifted her chin up at them, but the move sent most of the blood in her body racing up to her head. She ran through the back, grabbed the big, steel door's handle with both hands and dragged it open. Kneeling, hands braced along the edge of the deck, she nearly fainted as that morning's breakfast streamed past her lips.

Sean, lips puckered, his round eyes pushing at his forehead forming a deep, horizontal crease amongst his freckles, watched her spew. He considered a few options but couldn't think of anything to say. Orance picked up a long stick with skinned rabbits skewered all along the length of it, and casually joined Sean at his workbench.

"Eugénie! Eugénie!" Sean yelled, turning to face the shop, his rusty, Irish cheeks turning purple and red.

Busy with customers, Eugénie heard nothing.

"Your sister's sick as a dog, back here," Orance said, pushing the door open, not waiting for Eugénie's reaction before letting it close in front of him.

Saraphine sat at the edge of the loading dock and rocked, beads of perspiration dripping on her lap.

"Go stand behind the register," Eugénie told Sean as she wiped her hands on her apron, chin up to look through the door's round window.

She sat next to her sister and wiped her forehead with her sleeve.

"It's the pork from last night. I knew it as soon as I ate it," Saraphine said, nervously swaying back and forth.

"You all right? Is it passed?" Eugénie asked, the smell from the puddle below wafting up.

"Yeah, I'll be fine. Some water would be nice,"

"Orance," Eugénie called, looking back through the still-open door. "Get me some cold water from the ice box's tray."

Orance tilted the melt tray into a glass, walked out and handed it to Eugénie.

"None of *us* are sick, though. We all had the same meal. You know how much Orance likes his pork, and *he* doesn't look sick. Maybe it's more a question of … maybe it's 'cause of you having—"

"Maybe it wasn't the pork, but *something* made me sick. Anyway, who cares? I'm fine now. Let's get back to work,"

Saraphine said, looking away and rubbing her palms along her thighs.

"Oh no. You go lie down. Rest a bit. Go to your room. You must be weak after all this."

"I'm fine. Let's just get back to work," Saraphine answered, turning brusquely, the look on her face suggesting Eugénie had, somehow, been responsible for poisoning her.

Eugénie lifted her apron from her lap and wiped more perspiration off her sister's face.

"Whatever you want. If you feel up to it. Let's all get back to work."

Eugénie helped her sister to her feet and looked at Orance looking back at them.

-3-

For hours Saraphine watched moonbeams curl around her bedroom's back wall while images shot through her mind like meteors. She sat on the floor leaning back against the door and clutched the doorknob till her white knuckles ached. Near dawn, her hand slipped off, plopped on her leg, and startled her out of a shallow sleep. Breathing in long, slow breaths, she barely succeeded at keeping her mind from reaching speeds she feared she couldn't handle. By now, her every nerve ending had been set on high alert. She rubbed her twitching muscles hoping to keep them from shaking. Nausea, ever-present, a constant reminder that whatever she had ingested was readying itself to escape. During supper that evening, her sister had begged her to eat but she had hardly pecked at her plate—the food she used to love now seemed repulsive; the thought of swallowing any of it was repellent.

Her eyes twitched from staring at the darkness. Though the room was cold, drops of sweat running down her back made her shiver. Kneeling on the mattress, she reached down and cracked the window open, the night's air cooling her growling belly. She paused, sat on her heels, and pushed the sash all the way up; the dark opening before her felt welcoming. Serene.

She leaned forward and looked down, suspended in the cool breeze, her leg's goose-pimpled flesh feeling taut, hands braced on the ledge. Fresh air filled her lungs and the brisk dryness offered a pleasant, gentle sting. Calm. Peaceful. She slid her knees closer to the window's edge so she could taste the burning coal and wood swirling down from the many chimneys; smoke rushing up and down the narrow alley. She closed her eyes, let go of all the air in her chest and raised her hands along the sides of the window. Just then, the faint sound of fingernails sliding along her door's panel rang as loudly as a raging river.

"You awake?" Her sister whispered.

Saraphine looked down into the alley, sat back on her heels, and closed the window sash. The sight of Eugénie's face liquefied every muscle in her body. She fell to her knees and sobbed into her palms.

"*Mon Dieu, qu'est-ce qui se passe?*" Eugénie asked, tears sliding down her cheeks. "What happened? What's wrong?"

Saraphine babbled, gasped; tears leaking through her fingers. Eugénie bent to face her sister, laced her arms around her while leading her back to bed.

"Everything's gonna be all right. Jus' tell me what's wrong," Eugénie said, leaving her sister to close and lock the door.

Saraphine buried her face in the pillow while Eugénie rubbed her back, waiting till the agony had poured out.

"It's not what you think. I c-c-can't," Saraphine said, bouncing to her knees, her words coming out in little hiccups.

"I'm not thinking anything. Jus' tell me what's upset you so," Eugénie said, gently pulling her sister's hands from her face to catch a glimpse of her eyes.

Saraphine wrapped her arms around her chest and looked up at her sister's outline—moonbeams reflected by tiny tears clinging to her lashes and twinkling in the dark. "Funny, all of a sudden this all feels like when you used to calm me down whenever I had a nightmare. Remember? You'd come to sleep with me and I'd fall asleep."

"Sure, I do. I'll sleep here the rest of the night if that'll help?"

Saraphine smiled but her eyes dimmed. "I don't suppose all this is because of a nightmare," Eugénie said, leaning in closer.

Saraphine, still holding on to herself, scooched to the edge of the bed. Eugénie pulled the blanket off, sat next to her sister and bundled the both of them under the cover. She put her arm around Saraphine's shoulders and drew her in tightly. They rocked back and forth a few minutes, the silent, slow movement seeming to soothe Saraphine.

-4-

"I remember—I think it's the very first thing I remember—Mother sat me in the parlour, I had my lilac dress on, the one with the little buttons along the bottom of the sleeves. Remember? You ended up wearing it too when I grew out of it. Then again, you ended up with all my clothes, didn't you? I wasn't even four yet. She put you on my lap ... so gently, and said, *little babies are made of flower petals. That's why you've got to be very careful with them.* Then, she took my arms and carefully placed them around you. You were such a little, tiny thing, lost in the middle of a soft blanket. She opened up that little bundle and you looked up at me. I'll never forget that," Eugénie recounted, staring out into nothing, eyes wide open and smiling at the past.

"I don't remember *that*," Saraphine replied, looking at her sister's profile, unsure why Eugénie had decided to recount the oft-told story.

"I know, jus' wanted to remind you that I was always there for you, and always will. No matter—"

"I think there's a baby in me," Saraphine heard herself say, the words moving through her as if on a mission of their own.

Eugénie took hold of Saraphine's face, her expression cloaked in darkness. Dozens of obvious clues, signs from the past month flashed in her mind. Seconds passed before she asked—her dry mouth struggling to pronounce the word, "Sean?"

"No," she answered, gently swinging Eugénie's hands from side to side.

Eugénie's thumping heart felt as if squeezed in a vice. She swallowed the heap of bile that had splashed up her throat and added, "What happened? Who is it? Do I know the person ... surely, I—"

"Yes."

Saraphine bent over and covered her face, the sound of air rushing in and out of her mouth whooshing through her fingers like a storm.

"Who?"

Saraphine lurched forward and wrapped herself around her sister, bawling till Eugénie's neck glistened. Finally, after breathing in long, deep gulps of air, Saraphine hooked her chin across her sister's shoulder; each feeling the other's heartbeat.

"The powder. It's when I brought him the powder," she whispered into her sister's ear.

Puzzled by the non sequitur, Eugénie replied, "Powder? What powder?"

Saraphine pushed back, took hold of her sister's wrists, looked into Eugénie's eyes and waited. Waited for the meaning of the word to land. Waited for the word *powder* to trigger Eugénie's understanding of the situation.

"Powder? You're not making sense. What happened? Jus' tell me what it is you're trying to . . . ."

The word landed. Eugénie's jaw unhooked. A single tear slid down her cheek as if fleeing the anger in her eyes.

"Orance," she exhaled his name as her chin dropped to her chest.

"I'm so sorry," Saraphine cried, craning her neck down to meet her sister's gaze.

"So … so Orance? He's … he's the—"

"I'm sorry," Saraphine repeated, her forehead pressed to her sister's cheek, disappointed for having become a burden and feeling such shame … for having cursed her own sister. "I feel like I've died a thousand times and now … now it's like I've killed you, too," she added, rubbing her palms along her temples, unable to find refuge in any part of her mind.

-5-

"You falling down the stairs, was that part of it?" Eugénie asked, kneeling in front of her sister and biting her lip. "Did *he* push you down the stairs?"

"What am I gonna do now?" Saraphine said, pulling the cover over her shoulders.

"Don't worry about that now, we'll think about this … what to do about this," Eugénie answered, unconsciously looking down at Saraphine's belly.

Ideas burst in and out of Eugénie's mind—each one worse than the last. She nearly mentioned the possibility—the thought surviving no longer than a second—of her raising the child with Orance. Her sister's rapist. Then, aware of how Saraphine felt about Sean, she said, "Sean … maybe you two could—"

"No," Saraphine said. "I called for him, screamed his name. I'm sure he could hear me; the door was still open. He didn't do anything. He ignored me, ignored the yelling, and believe me, I yelled."

Eugénie imagined how Saraphine had screamed, that bit of reality adding to the pictures that now furnished huge galleries in her brain. "I'm so, so sorry for all this, to have brought you into all this. It's my fault. I should've known. How could I let this happen? How could I let—"

"Stop. It's not your fault. Don't blame yourself. He told

me that he'd tell you that *I* was the one to blame for all this. That *I* was responsible for what happened because I went to his room to bring him the powder. But he … he was lying there. Suffering. I put the glass on your dresser and he—"

"Stop that. *He's* the monster here. Don't blame yourself. Besides, I'm the one who asked you to bring him the powder," Eugénie said, cupping her sister's cheeks, Saraphine's lips puckered up in her sister's grip.

"What're we gonna do? I've got nowhere to go. I've got no one else to turn to. I'm always afraid now. I hate being near him … working with him. I can't sleep … it's like I can't control what I think anymore … it's just fear. All the time. Fear … like I'm gonna die inside my own mind … all the time," Saraphine said, staring out the window, the words seeming to drip from her lips as she took deep breaths between each sentence. "Sometimes I even think that … that not being here would be the best thing of all. The best solution, you know," she added, looking out at silvery backlit clouds.

Eugénie stroked Saraphine's back, listened and looked back at the door, unable to conjure a bright future.

"I don't know what's going to be the solution for us right now," Eugénie said, both their faces illuminated by the night's brightness. "What I do know is that it's the two of us now. I don't consider myself married to that man anymore, and I won't let you out of my sight."

Saraphine forced a smile and lay back on the bed. Eugénie did the same. They fell asleep, legs dangling off the edge.

-6-

Saraphine held on to her sister's elbow while high-stepping along De Montigny Street, eyes peeled, navigating along the manure-stained snow. A jovial man and his son with a Christmas tree in tow tipped their hats as they walked by. "*Joyeux Noël*," the gentleman said, over the sound of the sled's wood runners slicing through slush.

Big red letters pierced through the day's greyness. *De Montigny Boarding House* the sign read, dangling off a couple of chains hooked to the soffit animated by the winter's breeze as if waving to passersby. The sisters—Saraphine's face now completely buried in Eugénie's armpit—hadn't yet made it up the seven steps when the door opened and Madame Déry's imposing figure filled the space and warmed the air.

"I thought you wouldn't come, not in all this muck," Anna said, the hem of her velvety red dress brushing the snow.

"We said we would, so we did," Eugénie replied, looking up at the lady through eyelids welded shut by the sleet, both of them struggling to maintain their balance atop the slippery boards.

"Come, come, it's warm inside. Monsieur Lafleur's been stoking the furnace all morning," the lady said, her redder-than-red lips seeming festive.

"Some of the girls are still having lunch, you want something to eat? D'you have lunch yet?" Madame Déry offered, herding the sisters through the foyer toward a long, deep olive-green Chesterfield.

"No, no, both of us had a hearty lunch before we left. We knew we'd need something in our bellies before going out on a day like this," Eugénie answered for the both of them.

"Of course, what am I saying? No one's ever gone hungry living in a butcher shop. Am I right?" She teased, waving her hand over her head as if swatting an invisible bug.

"*Oui*, Madame Déry," a young woman—a huge mound of coral hair atop her head— responded to Anna's gesticulations.

"But I'm sure you won't say no to a nice hot cup of tea. That'll knock the cold right out of you," Madame Déry said, hand still suspended above her head.

"Sounds nice," Eugénie said, looking at her sister who, eyes round, nodded shyly at the young woman standing behind Madame Déry.

The young woman stepped away and disappeared into the kitchen.

"Wait till you see the postcards I brought back and the stereoscope, and the dress I bought at *Le Bon Marché* ... it's all silk. Real silk," she said, sitting at the edge of her elegantly upholstered Bergère chair. The sisters—eyes darting all over the room, at the drapery, the huge Persian rug, the large bust sitting on an intricately carved sideboard—smiled and nodded awkwardly.

"Look through here and you'll see *La Seine*. I'll tell you, it's as if you were there. And *I* was there!" Madame Déry instructed before carefully handing over the stereoscope.

The doorbell rang and the rumble of heavy boots stomping at the vestibule's floor resonated throughout the parlour. "*Y fa' frette*," a man said. "It's that wind out there, I swear ... blasts straight through you."

"Excuse me, girls," Madame Déry said and jumped off her chair to go meet the man who had burst in. "Monsieur Lafleur," she called, looking down the hallway.

"*Oui Madame*," Monsieur Lafleur answered, stepping into the parlour, his oversized neck making his cranium look no larger than a snowball.

"Could you please inform whomever it may concern that a gentleman is here for his appointment," Madame Déry told Monsieur Lafleur.

"*Absolument* ... right away."

"Could you also make sure to answer the bell," she whispered to him, hand to her cheek to shield her words from her guests. "So, what were we talking about, girls?" Anna asked, eyes bright as she made her way back and plopped herself on the *bergère*.

"I was looking at the picture, the stereoscope. Pretty amazing," Eugénie said.

"Amazing," Saraphine repeated, looking at Eugénie and nodding.

"Isn't it? The things you can find in the old country," Anna said, clearing her throat.

"This certainly is a beautiful place," Saraphine said, her voice barely reaching Madame Déry.

"Thank you. I did it all … all this," she said, turning slowly to look all over the room, seeming to take inventory of the artwork and decor items all around them. "That clock, the one on the mantle, I brought that back from New Orleans. It's by Seth Thomas, a veneered piece, it's adamantine. It's not natural at all but I love it. Anyway, it's all butter on bacon. None of it really matters. But, enough of all that. How are you two? You both look positively radiant," Madame Déry asked, scooching nearer the edge of her chair.

"Well, the cold probably has a lot to do with the radiance," Eugénie said, smiling, looking at Saraphine whose expression had turned glum.

"Yes. Radiant. I'll tell you, for a minute there I thought that, maybe, you had been stung by a serpent," Anna said, looking at Saraphine then Eugénie under her eyebrows while playfully twirling and jabbing her finger at them.

Both of them looked at their laps. Saraphine wiped her nose then peeked up at Anna and smiled; her white lips fused shut.

"That's a gift I haven't yet received," Eugénie said, squeezing her sister's wrist.

"That was never in the cards for me," Anna said, looking back at the young woman returning from the kitchen, a silver tray in hand loaded with three cups of tea, a sugar bowl and lemon wedges.

"Oh, my goodness. Lemons in December?" Saraphine said, picking up her cup and quickly squeezing as much juice into it as she could.

"I know a man who works at the train yards. He gets all sorts of things for me … me and my boarders," she winked.

Both sisters took big sips of the tea while looking up at Anna, the lemony hot liquid tasting like sunbeams.

A man walked down the stairs ahead of a trail of thick, white smoke, a gigantic cigar pinched in the corner of his mouth.

"*À la prochaine, les filles*," he shouted up at the staircase, his smiling lips barely visible through his ample, door-knocker beard.

The man's voice had startled the sisters who watched as Monsieur Lafleur handed him his hat and overcoat.

"Don't mind him. Some of the boarders tend to make merry on Saturdays," Anna said. "Louise, Louise," she called and the young lady reappeared.

"Wouldn't you love some cookies? I have biscuits that come from Germany ... sweet, creamy wafers. You'll love 'em," Anna said, pumping her eyebrows while clutching at Louise's wrist as if she had intended to escape.

"She the maid?" Eugénie asked once Louise had gone to fetch the treats.

"I guess you could call her that. Took her in a few years ago. Her husband left her, just left her, the bastard. Always drunk, a real skilamalink, a scoundrel if you know my meaning. I have thirteen girls living here with me. Most of 'em have the same kind of story to tell ... all of 'em now able to provide for themselves."

The sisters drained whatever tea was left in their cups and sucked on the remains of the lemon wedges. Faces slightly knotted, they smiled at the thought of all those girls living together.

"What about you Madame Déry, ever been married?" Saraphine asked, looking at Eugénie to gauge the appropriateness of her question.

Madame Déry slid back into her chair and looked at the ceiling as if seeing through it.

"Oscar," she said, appearing to have dipped herself into a stream of memories. "He passed away long ago. My memories of us together feel so distant, almost as if it had all happened to someone else."

"Passed away?" Saraphine asked, screwing up and unscrewing her face as the words escaped through her lips.

"The grippe. Strong as a horse, he was. Big fat fingers … strong hands … had mitts like anvils sticking out of his sleeves. Worked at the docks," she replied, her gaze focussed inwards.

"I'm so sorry," Eugénie said.

"I was left all alone. I was sixteen when he died. He's buried somewhere in potter's field at Mount-Royal cemetery. We'd left Caraquet to come live here, the both of us, all alone. Had no choice. I was in the family way and, well … had no choice. Had to leave, couldn't stay there. Thank goodness he was enough of a man to stay with me. We had a real love between us. A bond, yunno."

The sisters listened, eyes wide, lips parted, saddened at the thought of Anna's broken heart.

"What happened to the baby?" Eugénie whispered, lips barely moving as the words tumbled from her lips.

Madame Déry's demeanour suddenly grew stricter. "I was sixteen, child. Alone. Homeless. I couldn't afford a baby. Couldn't care for one. It was unthinkable. I was dependent on the kindness of strangers and, believe you me, you soon find out most strangers aren't so kind. I did … did what needed to be done," she said, pointing her nose up slightly.

Eugénie squeezed her sister's hand, neither of them able to improvise a segue to guide them away from the suddenly sombre recollection; Anna's confession.

"Madame," Louise said, her tray filled with delightfully colourful biscuits and cookies.

"Oh, you'll have to try these. They're so good. Right, Louise? You love 'em as much as I do, I know you do," Anna told Louise, taking the tray from her and presenting it to her guests.

Slightly jarred by Anna's renewed ebullience, the sisters each picked a biscuit off the tray, one of which had stuck to the doily.

"Sorry," Saraphine said, fumbling, trying to keep the delicacies from sliding all over the tray.

"Hogwash, dear. Take a handful of 'em. They're truly divine," Anna said, looking up, leaning forward and insisting they empty the tray. "Louise, have a couple of these," she said, turning to face the young woman.

"That's kind of you, truly, you've been so gracious," Eugénie said, pushing and elbowing herself out from the velvety Chesterfield's grasp.

"You can't be leaving so soon. I haven't shown you my postcards … the dress I bought."

"My husband's gonna expect food on the table, and I know that it'll take us quite a while to make it back home so—"

"Monsieur Lafleur can hitch up the horses. He'll make sure the both of you make it back in time."

"No. Thank you for the offer, but we'll be fine. Won't we?" Eugénie said, looking back at Saraphine.

Saraphine smiled and, in turn, inched her way to the edge of the huge couch.

"Are you quite certain that you have it in you? It's a long trek and it's so cold," Madame Déry said, looking at Saraphine whose expression seemed to suggest she'd appreciate a sleigh ride.

"We'll be fine. After all, we made it here without any real problems," Saraphine responded, twisted around to look through the window and the snowy street beyond.

Madame Déry sprung off her chair, wedged herself between the sisters, and wrapped her arms around them; their nostrils stinging from the fragrance wafting from her perfumed wrists.

"I've got to tell you something before you leave. When I look at you two … I see myself. A couple of young women who understand commerce; who know how to deal with people … how to keep a business afloat … the importance of keeping customers satisfied. My girls here, they know that, too. They're all involved in the same business, and we all understand that we've got to rely on each other. To stand behind each other. We're all survivors and know how to take care of ourselves," Madame Déry said, looking back and forth at Eugénie and Saraphine.

"Thanks? That's nice of you to say."

"Just let me say this. Eugénie," Anna said, her face inches from Eugénie's. "I don't know exactly how long you've been married, or why you've never had children—I'm sure the parish priest isn't shy about reminding you about that—but as a married woman, having children, well, that's part of your life."

"Uh uh," Eugénie replied, head tilted sideways, shoulder raised as she nodded.

"But you, my dear, you're in a different situation . . ." she turned and told Saraphine. "I've met dozens of young women like you. I can see it in your eyes, something that looks like fear, and I'm here to tell you I can help. Help you the way I helped Louise, Nahomée, Winona, and many, many other girls that live here and others that lived here in the past. You understand what I'm saying to you?" Anna asked, pulling Saraphine tightly to her shoulder.

"Yes, oh yes. Certainly, I do," Saraphine said, squirming while looking across to her sister for help, hoping she might have deciphered Anna's message and offer a kind of coherent retort.

"Thank you very much, Anna," Eugénie said, reaching for the Madam's fingers that had dug into her shoulder. "I understand your meaning, your offer … I really do. As of now, Saraphine hasn't made any decisions. We've thought a lot about this, about different ways of dealing with . . ." she added, unable to continue or look Anna in the eyes or to face her sister.

Anna jumped to her feet, turned to face her guests and said, "We've had a nice day, haven't we?"

Saraphine looked at Eugénie and then up at Anna.

"Thank you, again. It was all a delight," Eugénie said.

"A delight. Oh yes," Saraphine repeated, instinctively rubbing her belly while massaging the spot where Anna had gripped her shoulder.

The walk back home was as difficult as expected. They held hands, leaning on each other to maintain their balance atop the ice that had formed under the snow.

"Quite a lady," Saraphine finally broke the silence, her face surrounded by a white cloud.

"Oh, yeah. Always the same, she is. Quite a lady, a real enterprising woman … almost like a businessman," Eugénie said, smiling.

Nearly twenty minutes passed before Saraphine finally got around to asking, "What exactly was she talking about back there?"

"About what?"

"At the end, when she sat between us. What she said about her *girls* ... about how she helped them, about how she can help us?"

"Well, she was offering to help you the way she helped some of the girls living with her, you know, all of 'em who were in the same *situation* as you."

For a while, Saraphine looked at her boots punching craters into the snow, then started to say something but stopped herself. Then, a few minutes later, she yanked her sister back, turned and asked, "Is that what you think I should do?"

Eugénie wiped the snot from her nose then put her mitt on her sister's shoulder. "I'm not sure," she said, neither of them able to find anything else to say.

-8-

Orance, reading his newspaper at his usual spot in the kitchen, his back turned to the stairwell, didn't acknowledge his wife's arrival when she stepped into the hallway.

"Oof, felt as though we'd never make it back," Eugénie said looking down at her boots, the tilt of her hat letting a little snow drift that had clung to its brim avalanche down to the floor.

"What about supper? It's almost six," he replied, face glued to his paper, surrounded by smoke rising from his pipe.

"Won't take long. Jus' a matter of me getting the stove ready," she said, before whispering to Saraphine, "Go to your room. I'll knock when it's ready."

The three of them ate in silence. Every once in a while, Saraphine carefully peeked up—in between bites—trying to read Orance's face, to assess the level of tension crackling in his mind. Eugénie, seeming distant, looked at her plate and chewed. Saraphine suspected her sister envied Anna. After all, this was a woman beholding to no one and responsible for maintaining a business. Her own business. Confident. Strong. Beautiful. Dominant.

Orance reached into his vest pocket readying to reload his pipe.

"Not so fast," Eugénie said, pulling away from a daydream. "I brought back dessert. Our friend gave it to us as a gift," she added, reaching for the small paper bag she had stashed in the cupboard next to the stove. She reached into the bag, and one by one, carefully positioned each biscuit on a dish. Saraphine, surprised Eugénie would share this delicacy with *him*, abruptly stood and marched to her room.

"Don't you want any?" Eugénie asked, rising slightly off her chair.

"Let her go, it'll leave more for us," Orance said, glancing sideways at the closed bedroom door. "What's the matter with her, now?" He asked, looking back at his wife, the sound of the bolt pushed into the lock adding a punctuation mark to his question. "Always something with that one."

His pipe clenched between his teeth, Orance reached for one of the biscuits just as Saraphine burst from her room and plucked half the cookies off the plate, nearly knocking

Orance's pipe from his mouth in the process. Handful of cookies in hand, she looked at her sister and said, "This is my half. The other half's yours. She gave those to us. Not him." She returned to her room, walking backwards, a half-dozen cookies hammocked in the front of her dress.

"So, she's turned against *you* now," Orance said, nodding as if to confirm the veracity of his comment. "Where'd you get these, anyway? Where'd you go?"

"A friend," she answered, staring at her sister's locked door, blood squeezed from her white lips and slumped back on her chair.

"Can't say I didn't warn you. She's pretty particular, that sister of yours," he said, grabbing four of the six remaining cookies and shoving them into his mouth.

-9-

The sound of Eugénie's nail rubbing along Saraphine's door came earlier than usual that night.

"I'm sorry about the cookies," she whispered at the door, her forehead on the panel, lips nearly brushing the wood. The sound of the key disengaging the deadbolt came seconds after Eugénie had spoken.

"No, I'm sorry … really sorry about all that," Saraphine said, the features of her face barely visible in the darkened room.

Eugénie walked in and carefully swung the door closed.

"I don't know why I took out those biscuits. I didn't realize I was giving him your share. I guess I jus' wanted a peaceful evening. You know, to keep things calm. To keep *him* calm. I thought the cookies would be a good way to … I guess I wanted—"

"It's not you. You don't have anything to apologize for. It's that … well … those were ours and … I don't know," Saraphine replied, running her fingers through her hair, the friction causing small sparks to prick at the darkness, her sister's startled reaction making Eugénie giggle.

"You going to sleep here?" Saraphine asked.

"Yeah. He's fast asleep. He doesn't even know I'm gone. He drank in the parlour all evening, more than usual. He'll be out till morning."

They lay in bed looking out through the garden of frost that had grown along the edges of the divided glass window. A slowly melting layer of snow that had formed along the top of the frame leaked icy water drops on the sheets.

"You awake?" Saraphine whispered, looking at the ceiling.

"Uh, uh," Eugénie responded, turning to face her sister.

"You never really answered my question. You know, about what Madame Déry was talking about … all her *girls* … all of 'em in the same business together."

Eugénie, propping herself on her elbows, said, "Well, I suppose it's exactly what you think it is."

"So, it's true … she's a strumpet. Anna's a whore."

Eugénie faced Saraphine. "I think the girls living there with her, are. I'm not sure that Anna is, or was one. Not sure. I think it's her place, though. She's the madam, I suppose. She certainly seemed to be the boss of the place. Even that man, Monsieur Lafleur, did what she told him to do."

"So, we spent an afternoon in a cathouse."

"'Spose so. You and me in a bordello," Eugénie said and chuckled.

The smiles drained all of the tension that had remained between them. They lay quietly for a while, nearly long enough to fall asleep.

"I never would've thought that a bordello would look like that," Saraphine said.

"I know. It was beautiful. The furniture … did you see the piano in the corner of the room? It was so … so upper crust. Fancy."

Saraphine spun her legs out from the covers and sat along the edge of the bed.

"How come you've never … never, um."

"Never what?" Eugénie asked, sitting up, knees pulled tightly to her chest.

"You've been married for years now and you've never been ... never been *expecting*. Is something wrong with Orance?"

"Well, I'd say it's pretty obvious the problem isn't with him," Eugénie replied, looking down at her sister's belly.

"Of course," Saraphine sighed.

"Truth be said, there is, in a way, something wrong with him ... I guess you could say that."

"What?"

Eugénie looked out the nearly opaque window, her breath adding to the sheet of frost laminating the glass. "It happened twice ... twice I've been expecting. But, each time, he hurt me so bad that I lost it. Both times," she said, monotonically.

"When?"

"It's been almost a year now since the last time. I don't know if what he's done to me is permanent or not, but that was the last time he punched a baby out of me."

Saraphine placed her arm around her sister while cupping her own belly. "I really hate your husband," she said, looking down at herself.

Eugénie held her gaze on the nubilous window, bit the inside of her lip and nodded. "I know. Aunt Blanche did too," she said, then looked at her sister. "I hate him too ... isn't that merry ... we all hate him."

They sat bundled in a wrap of covers till their breathing synchronized.

"I don't think it's gonna be possible for me ... not possible for me to ..."

"To what?"

"Love this baby," Saraphine said, the words dribbling from her lips as she broke down.

Eugénie pinched her eyes shut and grimaced at the pain her hatred had caused; that feeling of having acid burn a hole through her gut; of feeling the back of her head going numb.

"I'm so sorry for all this. It's my fault. I'm the one who got you stuck in this. I promise I'll find a way to—"

"Stop it … stop saying that, it's not your fault. Where else was I supposed to go? Where else could I live? How could you know about all this? You couldn't predict it."

"I've been thinking about how I'll react when I see the baby. That baby that's been … been beaten into you by my own husband. I jus' don't know how *I'll* feel. *What* I'll feel. A baby's a baby, but I've got to admit, this one's gonna be … hard to love."

Chapter 13

-1-

Eugénie and Saraphine fell asleep, each relying on the other's body heat for comfort. Orance, whose responsibility it was to stoke the stove overnight, had apparently relinquished his duties—the boozy coma he had fallen into making it imposs-ible for him to revive the exhausted coals.

The snow had started again, and by midnight, nearly a foot had accumulated on the balcony. Saraphine, no longer able to sleep deeply when alone, had finally fallen into sweet ob-livion. Eugénie, aroused by the faint sound of hallway boards creaking, turned over, carefully pushed the covers off and stared at the darkened walls. Tiptoeing to the door, she placed her ear to the panel and assessed the creeks and cracks coming from the kitchen. Was it just the cooling stove pipe squawking? Or had Orance regained consciousness?

"Damnation, it's cold in here," Orance's voice broke the stillness.

Saraphine sprang up as if prodded by electrodes; heart thumping and out of breath.

"Shhh," Eugénie insisted, finger crossed over her pursed lips and waving at her sister.

"Come back to bed," Orance, his voice nearer, slurred.

Eugénie waved her sister down as she started to slide out of bed.

"Hey, I know you're in there again."

Eugénie, hands on the door, jumped back when Orance banged at it with his hammer fists and boots. *He's fallen asleep in his clothes again*, she thought.

"Come back to bed. A wife's meant to sleep with her hus-band. I've had it with you two being against me," he said, banging the back of his elbow on the door.

Eugénie, having retreated to the bed and sitting with her sister, rubbed a porthole into the frosty window and looked out at the accumulated snow.

"Aye, *tabarnak* ... open the door, lemme in."

Eugénie jumped off the bed and ran to the door. "Why won't you leave us alone and go back to bed, you're drunk," she said, ear pressed to the panel. The sound of Orance dragging his feet and the whine of the stove's hopper being opened reassured her he had given up.

"What's he doing?" Saraphine whispered.

"I think he's loading coal in the stove. He's probably gonna fall asleep in the kitchen," Eugénie said, listening for clues.

"What's he doing now?" Saraphine repeated.

"Not sure ... think he's stoking the stove."

-2-

Her back to the door, Eugénie listened, her finger sticking up next to her temple like an antenna. The kitchen had been silent for a while but now she heard loud, heavy footsteps rushing at her. Orance—who had taken a running start—flew through the door and crashed in amongst shards of splintered wood. Knocked unconscious by the exploding door, Eugénie lay on the floor, bleeding, moaning, Orance sprawled all over her.

Saraphine screamed and immediately stomped Orance's head; the man's huge body now fully smothering his unconscious wife.

"Eugénie, Eugénie," Saraphine repeated. "Eugen—" Orance swiped at Saraphine's hip. Her head bounced off the wall and she fell on her side. "Leave her alone," she said as blood collected in the back of her throat.

"You. You're coming back to bed," he said, pointing down at his wife before grabbing the back of her nightdress and dragging her along the floor.

Barely aware, head dangling as if unhinged from her shoulders, Eugénie managed to look up at Saraphine pulling Orance's hair while screaming and slapping wildly at his temples—stabbing her finger into his eye. Grunting, he lost his grip on Eugénie as he tried to bat Saraphine's hand away. Disoriented and groggy, he fell back through the doorway and into the kitchen. Eugénie's head thumped on the floor as he let go of her, the back of her skull sounding like a hammer pounding at a sunken nail.

"Eugénie," Saraphine hollered, covering her sister's face and torso with her body.

"I'm all right," she managed to say.

"Oh no. She's coming with me. She's coming to bed with her husband," Orance, struggling back to his feet, repeated as he grabbed a handful of Saraphine's fine hair.

"Get out of here," Saraphine said, wrapping herself more tightly around her sister.

Orance smashed Saraphine's head into Eugénie's chest then grabbed Saraphine's ankles and yanked, hard.

"Let go. She's my wife," he said, Caribou that had risen up his throat mingling with his saliva before dribbling from his lips.

"Leggo, I'll be all right," Saraphine heard her sister repeat.

Saraphine twisted her legs and kicked her feet, heels aimed at Orance's crotch, hoping to hit paydirt. Fearing she'd lose her grip on her sister, she screamed, "LET GO!" managing to hold on to her sister while being pulled by the ankles. He had nearly yanked them out into the kitchen when Saraphine, out of nowhere, had an idea—a perfectly good idea—that flashed through her mind like a fully realized story. She let go of her sister and the sudden lack of resistance sent Orance flying back. His neck crashed with such impact against the edge of the woodstove that the heavy cast iron appliance shifted off its base, causing the chimney to buckle and the hopper's door to fling open.

"We've got to leave, go downstairs," Saraphine said, pulling her sister's arms.

He came to, flat on his back, dazed, arms flailing while trying to grab at whatever he could reach. Saraphine helped Eugénie to her feet but Orance kicked the side of her knee and dropped her to the floor. Suddenly swift, he crawled over and viced both hands around Eugénie's throat, oblivious to Saraphine's nails gouging his cheeks and forehead.

"You're coming with me, tonight," he said, sounding sober, his nose inches from Eugénie's beet-coloured cheeks.

Saraphine, nails dug in deeply into his neck—his punctured skin and flowing blood feeling perfectly satisfying—never saw his elbow as he whirled around and smashed her jaw. She dropped to the floor next to her sister.

Temporarily released from his grip, Eugénie coughed and gagged. Lying there, struggling to breathe, she saw lines of white smoke rising to the ceiling as chunks of coal that had fallen from the stove's hopper slowly burned their way through the floor's linoleum.

"Stop," Eugénie tried to say, her squashed vocal cords allowing for little more than a guttural groan to escape.

Orance stood over Saraphine and stomped her ribs.

"Stop, Orance. Stop," Eugénie said, her faint cries seeming to energize him. "She's with child, stop," she begged, reaching up and pulling at his dangling suspenders.

He stopped and looked at Eugénie.

"Sean?" He asked, shockingly conversational, like someone learning some happy news during some happy lunch.

"You, you bastard. It's yours. You raped my sister, and now she's gonna have your baby," she said, punching wildly at his calf.

Orance leaned over Saraphine who lay balled up to shield her ribs from his boot. He wiped blood off his face, took a half-step back, lifted his foot and stomped her abdomen. Saraphine let out a throaty grunt as pain exploded through her. Eugénie screamed and rolled over on her knees.

"That's no baby of mine," he said, dead-eyed, holding

Eugénie back with one hand to give himself the space needed to relaunch the tip of his boot into Saraphine's belly. But, Saraphine rolled to her side and let the heavy, leather toe strike her lower spine.

"Stop, you're gonna kill her, stop," Eugénie pleaded, slapping and punching his hip. She looked through the dark—through the thickening smoke in search of a weapon. A knife, the big one she used for cutting bone, had fallen to the floor when Orance had landed in the kitchen. She got herself up on her hands and knees—coughing from having been choked and the increasingly stifling smoke filling the room—and grabbed the knife just as Orance was cocking his leg, seconds away from landing the fatal blow. The blade sliced through his shoulder just as the heel of his big shoe slammed into Saraphine's pelvis.

The blade tore through Orance's flesh, struck his shoulder bone, and flew from Eugénie's hand. Stunned, he flung his good arm across his body and smacked Eugénie on the temple. She dropped to the floor. Punch-drunk, hands folded over her chest, she watched the ceiling smolder and flames rising all around the stove. Orance, clutching at his shoulder, moved in on his wife, dropped to his knees, lifted his fist ...

The eleven-inch blade pierced through the back of his ribcage and heart. He fell, the momentum of his punching motion pulling him down onto his wife. The leading edge of the blade protruding from his chest severed Eugénie's index finger and pierced through her right breast.

-3-

Saraphine struggled to roll Orance off her sister. She wailed and pummelled his lifeless face with the sides of her fists, his gaping mouth still smelling of Caribou; his fish eyes staring out into nothing.

Saraphine stumbled to the kitchen window—blood crawling down her inner thighs—the heels of her palms sliding off as she struggled to lift the sash open, then gathered a handful of snow and rubbed it on Eugénie's forehead and chest.

"We've got to get out. Eugénie, we've got to get out," she said, massaging snow on her sister's forehead and temples, hoping the shock of cold would revive her.

"Is he gone? Where is he?" Eugénie asked, a terrified look washing over her previously vacant expression.

"He's gone. Gone," Saraphine said, gagging from the smoke. "We've got to leave. The whole place's gonna burn down."

Saraphine, suddenly aware of the warm blood trickling down her legs, knelt behind her sister and pushed her shoulders up.

"Can't we put it out?" Eugénie asked, looking back at the stove, the accumulating smoke curling down from the ceiling like inverted waves.

"It's too late. We've got to get out."

They hobbled along the hallway and down the stairs, hunched over from the pain. Eugénie howled when the stump where her finger used to be touched the wall. The blood-covered sisters drew a grim trail along the walls; their hands sliding on the plaster and railing to steady themselves as they escaped.

"Where are we gonna go?" Saraphine asked, leaning on Sean's workbench, out of breath, dry heaving as diluted shots of adrenaline slowed her pulse. "All our things are upstairs. We're covered in blood. We don't even have our coats. We've got to go back and get what we can … we can't go outside like this."

"We can't. It's all gonna go up in flames."

"There's still time," Saraphine said, both terrified and comforted by the blood hemorrhaging down her legs.

"There's cash in the safe and fur pelts in the sleigh. That's all we need. We can't go back up there, not again," Eugénie said, her injured hand held cradled in the other, chest warmed by the blood flowing from her breast.

Eugénie stumbled to the staircase and slammed the door to keep the smoke from cascading downstairs. "Empty the register; I'll go get what's in the safe."

Saraphine pressed the *no-sale* key and grunted when the drawer slid out and hit her just above the abdomen. "I think the float was fifteen dollars, yesterday," she managed to shout.

Eugénie spun the safe's dial and watched tiny numbers whiz by; her damp eyes straining to see the digits through dimness. Three times she tried before her shaky fingers managed to land on all the right numbers. She reached in, tossed documents on the floor, and pulled the yellow envelope out, the one with an elastic tied around a sort of leathery knob. "There's more than seventy dollars in here," she answered her sister. "Seventy-seven, in all." More than enough to keep them afloat for at least a couple of months, maybe even till summer.

Eugénie stuck her head through the swinging door. "I'll go get the sleigh ready; you jus' wait here."

"Why do we need the sleigh? Where are we going? We should call the fire station."

"And what? Have them find Orance with a knife in his back? We've got to get out of here or else we're going to be in big trouble," Eugénie said as she dropped the envelope on the workbench, her bloody hand stuffed in her armpit.

Saraphine sat behind the register, took the rag off the display's counter and wiped blood off her knees and calves.

-4-

Eugénie returned from the small stable across the alley and stood on the loading dock looking through long strands of hair that had fallen over her face. Wearing nothing but winter boots—stored out back for when needing to go outside and unload deliveries—and a bloody nightgown glued to her chest, she felt air whistling in to feed the flames. "You okay?"

Eugénie asked, her voice aged by the smoke.

Bent over on her chair, Saraphine nodded and barely managed a wave, unable to stifle a high-pitched squeal rising from her gut.

"D'you get the money from the register?"

"Thirteen and change," Saraphine said, looking back at her sister. "Where in the world are we supposed to go? It's the middle of the night ... full of snow out there. What's the plan?"

"We've got to go ... go somewhere before the whole place burns down," Eugénie said through a grimace, looking up at puffs of black smoke seeping down through narrow ceiling slats.

Saraphine stepped into a pair of huge boots stored near the back door, took Eugénie's arm, and they hobbled outside to the loading dock.

"Wait . . ." Eugénie said and let go of her sister, "...got to get something." Eugénie ran back in and had soon disappeared into the smoke like a magician's assistant.

"Don't be stupid, get back here, come—"

"The picture ... got it," Eugénie said, holding up the small framed photo of the two sisters standing in front of the butcher shop. Saraphine nodded and waved her sister out. They climbed down the loading dock just as the rush of cold air swooshing in ignited the ceiling; flames dancing and sliding along the white, thin oak boards.

Peachy coloured light from the kitchen window lit up the alley and transformed snowflakes into embers. It was past two in the morning when they escaped the fire. Escaped the smells, the flesh, the bones. Away from him. Away from it all.

-5-

Glass shattered as flames escaped through windows but neither of them looked back. They moved east, buried under piles of fur and cowhides, cheeks brushed by the night's cold wind. Snow cracking beneath the sleigh's runners, crunching and creaking, they slid along the night's deserted streets.

"Shit," Eugénie said, cradling her bloody hand. "The money's back in there, on the bench. Oh, my God, what're we gonna do?"

"It's too late, anyway. We're out. Alive." Saraphine, the shock of combat having dulled her senses, said, flatly. "So?"

Eugénie looked at Saraphine, "So?"

"So ... where are we going? We can't just ride to nowhere."

Eugénie wrestled cowhides up under her chin and leaned forward to look at her sister—her eyes suddenly bright.

"How 'bout Anna's place? I can't think of—"

"Madame Déry?" Saraphine said, lifting her head off her sister's shoulder, her voice charged and energized.

"*She'll* take us in. You heard what she said about her boarders, those girls she talked about," she replied, looking ahead, the faint yellow light from the streetlights seeming to highlight her look of determination.

"Eugénie," Saraphine said, staring at the side of her sister's face, "those girls, the borders, they're ... all of 'em ... you're the one who told me ... they're night flowers. What're you saying? What are you suggesting we do there?"

Eugénie, chin up and holding her gaze upon the snow-covered street, said, "That's what it looks like, and I'm pretty sure that's what it is. But those girls... those girls are toffers... you know... able to care for themselves."

"I can't believe what I'm hearing," Saraphine said, "I'm expec . . ." she stopped herself from saying the word, hoping the blood that warmed her seat had resolved the situation.

Eugénie pulled her sister in close, the move causing the pain in her severed finger to shoot up her arm and all the way to her neck.

"Careful. That must be so painful. We both need to see a doctor," Saraphine said, resting her temple on her sister's shoulder.

"I jus' think Anna's gonna help us. I've known her for a couple of years now. We talked a lot. I know her well enough to believe that what she did for those girls was ... she tried to help them out of terrible situations. I trust her. I trust she'll help us, too," Eugénie said, gently snapping the reigns and looking ahead. "Anyway, I can't think of anywhere else for us to run to. Can you?"

-6-

The windows of the *De Montigny Boarding House* were unusually dark on this Saturday night (early Sunday). Maybe snow had worked to restrict some of the regulars' hormonal drive but, by four in the morning, much of the business had either been concluded or escorted out. The snow-covered steps, trackless and untouched, seemed to corroborate that the evening had been a slow one. Eugénie, shivering from the ice water that had seeped into her boots, draped in a cowhide, started up the stairs. Saraphine, invisible under piles of fur, looked for signs that someone inside the mansion might still be up.

"See anything in there?" Saraphine's muffled voice called through the many layers covering her.

"It's all dark, can't see a thing," she replied, forehead pressed against the door's leaded window. "Should I ring the bell?" She asked, moving to the edge of the huge porch and leaning over the railing.

"Maybe you should."

The light inside the foyer turned on and Eugénie swallowed hard before turning to face the door. A man, the one with the huge neck, wearing nothing but long johns and a scruffy chin, cracked the door open.

"*Bonsoir ... Monsieur Lafleur, je crois?*"

"What? We're closed."

"Maybe you remember me, we were here this afternoon.

We met with Anna … Madame Déry. Sat in the parlour … jus' this afternoon," she said, pointing at the parlour's windows.

"Whadda you want? Told you, we're closed, it's the middle of the night, for chrissakes," Monsieur Lafleur replied, his right cheek pushing at his ear, swatting at the air with his huge hand and holding on to the knob with the other.

"We're friends of Anna … we've got nowhere else to go. I … we're . . ." she stammered, looking back at her sister in the sleigh, "wondering if we could speak with Madame Déry. *S'il vous plait… je 'vous en prie.*"

"Friends? Friends don't show up at this time of night. Besides, Madame Déry's my superior and I'm not gonna be the one who wakes her up to tell her she's got guests at this time of night."

"I understand, but we're jus' here to ask if—"

"Bring your horse in the stable out back and stay there till the morning, if you want, but I'm not gonna wake her up," he said, and nearly pinched his nose in the door as he closed it in Eugénie's face.

The light turned off. Eugénie turned back. They fell asleep in the sleigh, huddled together under a mound of skins and a mountain of pain.

-7-

A crescent of light slid along Eugénie's forehead down to her eye, the prick of brightness forcing reality back into her thoughts. The snow had stopped, but looking through the stable's small window, she noticed the sleigh's tracks had disappeared.

"Saraphine, I think it's late," Eugénie said, shaking her sister's shoulder till she woke. Saraphine, away from her room and having fatally stabbed her tormentor, had slept deeply, the way she remembered sleeping as a child.

"How late?"

"We better go and knock, I'm sure Anna's up by now," Eugénie said while pushing the hides off of them.

Bells from a hundred steeples called parishioners to church. Four women walked down the Boarding House's steps; arms locked and dressed in their Sunday best.

"*Allô!*," one of the ladies called to the sisters when, hearing voices coming from the stable, they saw them stepping off the sleigh. Then, noticing the streaks of blood that had stained Saraphine's legs, one of the women stepped towards the sisters and said, "Goodness, you all right, lemme help you."

"No, no, we're fine," Eugénie replied while holding out her four fingered hand in front of her like a shield.

The four women—hands on cheeks, mouths agape—backed away. The one nearest the staircase, ran up calling Madame Déry's name.

Saraphine looked at Eugénie, head drawn into her shoulders.

"There you are … come," Anna, dismissively waving away the girl that had run up the stairs, welcomed the sisters from atop the porch steps.

Surprised. Ashamed. They looked at their boots buried in snow, at their bodies covered in fur and hides. They hesitated—just a bit—then made their way up the steps leading into the Boarding House.

"Monsieur Lafleur told me about you two, just now. I can't believe all this. You slept in the stable? Oh, my goodness," Madame Déry said, palms together while watching the sisters climb—stepping neatly in others' footsteps to keep from slipping in the snow.

"Please, come, there's plenty for breakfast. Go sit by the fireplace and we'll get all that ready for you," Anna said. Saraphine, hunched over and holding on to her sister's elbow, smiled at the lady as she walked by.

They sat in a huge, ridiculously overstuffed chair, toes flirting with the andirons, coals prickling at their frozen skin.

"Here you go, girls," Anna said, bursting from the kitchen

with two pairs of navy, hand-knitted slippers in hand; tops laced in a white, silk ribbon. "Louise is preparing breakfast for you. It should be ready in . . ."

Madame Déry, leaning over Saraphine to hand Eugénie her slippers, noticed the bloody nightshirt peeking down under the cowhide.

"What happened?" She whispered; unaware the slippers had dropped from her fingers.

Startled, Saraphine looked down and realized what Anna had seen.

"Oh, goodness. I apologize. I'm so sorry, I didn't realize … I mean, I forgot that … oh my goodness," Saraphine said. She strained to get to her feet but the sudden movement set off a burst of pain; the powerful spasm causing her to let out a tiny yelp.

Eugénie jumped off the chair and wrapped her arms around Saraphine's chest.

"We're so sorry, Anna. It's been quite a night," Eugénie said, leading her sister back onto the chair and noticing the bloody stain they had left on the upholstery.

"You lost the baby," Anna said, leaning down low and looking up into Saraphine's eyes.

"I don't know how you managed to know that?" Eugénie said.

"It's part of the business I'm in. It's something I've come to recognize sooner than most," she said. "Come with me, both of you. You'll have a nice hot bath. Breakfast can wait. You'll see, hot water'll make you feel a lot better."

-8-

"We left a little picture on the sleigh's bench," Eugénie mentioned, her finger wrapped neatly into a bud of cotton, her blood-streaked skin washed clean. She leaned forward, her injured hand under the table, eating slowly despite loud and frequent bouts of borborygmi.

"Monsieur Lafleur took it to your room and, don't worry about your horse, it's in the stable with your sleigh. Don't trouble yourselves about anything. Everything's been taken care of."

"We don't have anything, really. No money," Saraphine said, glancing at her sister.

Eugénie swallowed hard and coughed; the crushing thought of being penniless tightening her chest as reality settled in. Puzzled, Madame Déry smiled at them. Arms crossed over her bosom, she leaned forward, wiped her chin with the table cloth, took a deep breath and pushed herself to her feet. "None of my girls had any money when they showed up at my door," she said, pointing at the ceiling. "So, don't worry, I'll find some way for you to come up with whatever you need. Besides, that story you told me, the things you had to do last night: your husband, the fire, it all tells me something about you girls … something about your ability to survive. So, I'm not worried about either of you. You've got what it takes to stay on your feet and that's something that's not given to everybody," she added, like a colonel addressing troops.

"We can't thank you enough for what you've done for us," Eugénie said, lips sucked into her mouth, her gut cramping at the idea of having let the little money they had burn to ashes. "I told Saraphine yesterday, not knowing what to do or where we'd end up … I told her you'd help us."

Anna picked up the empty plates, brought them to the sink and with her back to them, said, "You two finish your tea, then I'll show you to your room. You've got to rest. Especially you, Saraphine, with everything you've been through. Both of you'll feel better once you've slept for a good long while."

Down the stairs they went lurching forward into obscurity, smells of mould, coal dust, and smoke growing more intense as they descended. This subterranean hideout would be reassuring. Comforting. Here, they'd sleep. Alone.

"Obviously, there's no bathroom down here, no water. You'll have to go upstairs for that. But you've got a room over there, two beds," she said, pointing at a wall in the cellar's far end. "Just one of 'em is set up for now but Monsieur Lafleur'll bring another bed down in a little while," Madame Déry instructed, looking back at the sisters as her foot landed on the cement floor.

The room, a partitioned space next to a huge cast iron furnace, was illuminated by a single bulb suspended from a wire hanging off a ceiling joist. Their little picture had already been placed on the six-drawer, cream and yellow dresser that sat next to a narrow door equipped with a rusted barrel lock.

"Again, we can't thank you enough for what you've done for us," Eugénie felt compelled to repeat.

"Get some rest," Anna replied and caressed Eugénie's cheek. "We haven't used this room in a while. It's been less popular lately; you can never tell what clients are looking for these days. Just as well, it'll work out for you two, right?" She added, pulling the door closed behind her. Seconds later, the door cracked open and Madame Déry stuck her face in.

"Just wanted to make sure, again … nobody knows you're here? Right?" She asked.

"Like we said, we left in the middle of the night. They'll think we died in the fire," Eugénie answered while Saraphine, looking up over her sister's shoulder, studied the lady's expression.

"That's good … good. It's for the best, really," Anna said. "It's all good," the sisters heard Anna repeat, the lady's shoes scraping the steps as she ascended.

-9-

"Why'd she think that … that this was all for the best?" Saraphine asked.

"People jus' say things, sometimes."

Saraphine sat on the bed and bounced as the springs

creaked. "You sure this was the best place to go? Maybe we could have—"

"What? Where? There wasn't anywhere else to go. There's no family left. I jus' don't know where else we could have gone. You don't know either," she answered, the springs screeching and squealing anew.

"What's gonna happen to us? We can't live here forever. We're going to need to know what's—"

"We'll figure it out. We'll know what to do—at some point, we will. Right now, we've jus' got to stick together and take advantage of this situation; this kindness that's been offered us. Stop worrying, I tell you, we'll figure things out soon enough," Eugénie said, wincing at the pain of pulling the covers over her shoulder, her mind spinning at the thought of imagining the uncertain future.

Neither knew how long they had napped when the sound of metal screeching against cement sent them jumping off the thin mattress.

"Got your bed, here . . ." a man knocking at the door said, "I'll set it up for you." Monsieur Lafleur, bed in tow and leading with his rear end, pushed the door open; the seized steel casters nearly sparking as they grinded along the floor. "Sorry, didn't mean to startle you," he apologized, looking back at them and noticing the terrified look on their faces.

"No, no, it's our fault. We fell asleep. Not sure for how long, but we both jus' fell asleep," Eugénie explained, smoothing the fabric of her borrowed dress.

"You couldn't be sleeping for too long. I went and got this from the back as soon as Madame Déry told me to."

Monsieur Lafleur unfolded the heavy metal frame, the long springs and tight wires screaming as each half of the corroded contraption came unhinged. He wrangled the beds on either side of a small table and rested his hands on his lower back.

"So, that's it. Madame Déry told me to tell you to let her know if you need anything else." They looked at Monsieur Lafleur, crimped their lips and nodded. "So, I guess I'll leave

you two to yourselves," he added and stepped out. "Oh, yes
… either me or Madame Déry's gonna bring the linens for
the other bed," he added, pulling the door closed. Eugénie
and Saraphine slept till their growling stomachs were too
painful to ignore.

Chapter 14

When the firemen from Station 16 bolted off their cots, the flames rising from the butcher shop could already be seen from all around. Clouds of moisture rising from the team of six horses hauling the heavy steam-powered pumping wagon along snow-covered streets made it look as if *they* had caught fire. Arrived at the scene, they aimed their hoses at neighbouring structures, the burning building having already started to crumble.

That Sunday, Urbin started off as he always did on the Lord's Day. He'd inhale his usual artery-clogging breakfast, followed by some quality time spent in his favourite padded chair angled to allow for a perfect view from out the parlour window. Sitting, relaxing, he'd puff away at his favourite pipe, read his newspaper and fall back asleep. By seven, he'd reach into his closet, pull out his Sunday suit and get ready for the eight o'clock mass. This Sunday, however, would be different. Twice, while eating, Urbin and Uriette heard the telephone ringing downstairs in the butchery. *Who would be calling the shop on a Sunday?* They asked themselves. Over and over, it rang.

"Should I go down and answer it?" his daughter Dahlia, asked.

"The shop's closed. Anyway, you won't make it down in time to answer it," Uriette said, looking at her husband and shrugging.

Urbin was getting dressed when Dahlia knocked at her father's bedroom door.

"It's ringing again, daddy. Mom told me to go down in the shop and answer it if it rings again," she said before running down the stairs.

Urbin was rubbing a rag down the side of his shoe when Dahlia came back, out of breath, rambling.

"A man's on the phone ... something's wrong at Orance's place... something... he said something."

"Saint sacrifice!" Urbin said, running his fingers through his thinning hair on his way to answering the telephone. "*Allô!*" He said into the mouthpiece before picking up the receiver. "*Oui... Allô,*" he repeated, his right suspender held hitched over his thumb frozen over his shoulder. His finger let go and the prick of his suspenders snapping down on his shoulder seemed to wake him up. He brought his lips together till they disappeared into his mouth, and asked, "Did you see my son? His wife ... anyone?"

He thanked whoever was on the other end of the call, dropped the handset on its cradle, and looked at Dahlia.

"What's wrong?" She asked, eyes moistening at the thought of bad news.

-2-

On his way to his son's home—his son's business—he pondered the work, all that work to get a second shop off the ground. To make it a success. His son. The struggles, the pain of carrying his boy to safety; to save him from the water. His two other sons, the ones lost at the bottom of the river.

More than a mile from Orance's butchery, heading down along St. Denis Street, the smell of charred wood already pricked at his sinuses. Looking at the calcined building, icicles dripping along the blackened beams, the sign hanging down over the shattered windows, he imagined the last few minutes the three of them had spent, trapped upstairs, unable to escape the flames. The smoke.

He walked around to the alley, his calves cramping up from having to lift his feet out from the small, slushy bowls he created. Milling amongst the many spectators distractedly looking and pointing at the wreckage, he slipped and fell on his ass when the entire second floor collapsed into the shop.

Sitting in the snow he noticed the deck hadn't burned, the big steel door having kept the fire locked inside. Transfixed by the wreck, a large clump of masonry dangling precariously from the neighbour's adjoining wall let go and crashed, sending brick dust to settle like a kind of maroon skin on the snow. Flames, fed by a renewed supply of crumbling dry wood, shot from the wreckage and transformed winter into a furnace. Urbin moved away till his back was to the butcher shop's stable across the alley. The door was ajar. He pushed it open. Looking in, his vision temporarily impaired by the snow's brilliance, he soon realized the place was empty. No horse. No sleigh. The harness … gone. Had someone stolen these things and set fire to the house? Had someone survived and fled?

He moved quickly, trying to find someone to alert. A cop. The fire chief.

"The sleigh, the horse … they're gone. Someone … maybe all of 'em made it out … left. There's no other reason for the horse and sleigh to be gone," Urbin told the police Officer who stood, arms crossed, his foot on the pumping wagon's step.

"I'll tell you, that's interesting, and I hope you're right," the Officer said, a toothpick hanging from his lips bouncing as if a maestro waving a baton. "Right now though, nothing says they're the ones who're responsible for any missing horses or sleighs. It could have been someone from around here—someone who saw the fire and took advantage of the situation to steal all of those things," the policeman said, rubbing his backside from left to right against the pump's wheel.

"All right. Maybe. But isn't it also possible that my son left, or his wife, or all three of 'em?" Urbin asked, looking back and pointing at the stable.

The Officer looked sideways, reached into his jacket, pulled out a pad and pencil and jerked himself forward with his shoulders.

"OK, so I'll take note of this, make a report. But I've got to say the chances of anyone making it out of that fire alive … well, chances aren't in their favour," the Officer said, looking down at his pad before looking back up at what was left of the building.

-3-

Eugénie and Saraphine opened the door of their small basement pen. A bunch of clotheslines had appeared while they had napped, the full length of them covered by women's apparel; undergarments mostly. A dripping wet dress weighed down the braided cordage, the cuffs of its sleeves caressing the coarse floor. A small stream had formed below the canopy of fineries that had divided into several tributaries, each spilling into holes and cracks that scarred the cement surface. They walked under and around the lines, careful not to step in wet spots along their way to the stairs.

Atop the staircase, feet strategically placed along the edges of the steps to keep the dried-out boards from creaking, Eugénie stuck her ear against the door, listening for voices, sounds, anything to give her a sense of what might be waiting for them on the other side.

"Hear anything?" Saraphine whispered, her mouth inches from her sister's lobe.

"I think someone's in the kitchen … doing something," Eugénie whispered back.

"What should we do? Can you tell if it's Anna?"

Eugénie, ear still on the door's panel, pinched her eyes closed straining to make out words.

"*C'pas d'ma faute … I sentait la marde … puait*," she heard a woman saying.

"Did she say someone smelled? Smelled like … like shit?" Saraphine asked.

"Yes. It sounded like a young . . ."

A slap, that unmistakable sound of a palm connecting flush with someone's cheek, followed by the clanking of utensils or some other metal implements falling to the floor, rang loudly through the door. Eugénie jumped and bumped the side of her head on the oak door. Their knees buckled. They sat on the stairs and looked at each other. Though too dark for either of them to notice, both their faces had turned scarlet red as the scene beyond the door replayed in their minds. The gruesome familiarity of that sound sent panic spilling down through their bodies. Had they wandered to where they had run from?

"I can't go out there," Saraphine said, shaking her head from shoulder to shoulder as she pulled at Eugénie's sleeve.

"Wait. Jus' wait, will you?" Eugénie replied, squinting through the keyhole while Saraphine dissected the silence.

"*Assez!*" Madame Déry, standing on the staircase located just above where they sat, yelled and stomped, the lady's heavy heels making it sound as if they were encased inside a kettledrum.

"It's Anna," Eugénie mouthed, frowning and waving at her sister. Saraphine placed her hand over her mouth and pulled Eugénie... tried to pull her back down into their basement dungeon.

"Let's come back later. We shouldn't get in the middle of whatever's going on up here," Saraphine said, tiptoeing her way down the stairs, looking back and waving at her sister to join her.

Sitting on the edge of the bed, they wondered how they'd manage to return upstairs, searching for some appropriate thing to say once they got there.

"Remember when you told me about going to live with Aunt Blanche, about me going down there and maybe finding a job. Well, why don't *we* do that? We could write to her and see if she'd be willing to take us in ... for a while, anyway," Saraphine said, her face lighting up at the prospect.

Eugénie looked at the photo on the dresser and rubbed her

thighs.

"Maybe. I'm not sure about her brother, though. I know he's our uncle but, we don't know him. I don't know what he'd think about the two of us showing up there. We'd have to find jobs, never mind that neither of us speak English too good."

"Wouldn't it be great to see Ephrem again? All of us, together?" Saraphine said, the imagined reunion soothing her mind for a few seconds. "Let's send a letter as soon as we—"

"*Les filles,* I think it's time for you two to wake up," Madame Déry's voice barged in on their shared reverie.

Saraphine, her demeanour dissolved into reality, grabbed Eugénie's wrist and lurched forward to look at her sister; to anticipate Eugénie's response.

"What do we do?" Saraphine whispered.

Eugénie waved her free hand at her sister.

"Coming, right away," Eugénie turned and yelled at the narrow door.

-4-

Urbin held the reins pinched between his fingers, elbows tucked tightly against his ribs, forearms on his thighs. Lost in thought—his face pale as the horizon, ears poking out from his tuque looking like pink flames—he absently stared down Hochelaga Street, contemplating the possibility that his son had escaped the fire. Orance, running down the stairs, his wife and Saraphine in his arms, defying the smoky incandescence erupting from all sides. A hero.

Roused from his trance, he noticed a woman pulling at his shop's closed door. He stood, yelled, and waved at her. "Wait, I'll take care of you. We're open! We're open!" He repeated and flailed. The lady leaned in—her forehead nearly on the *Chicken Livers* sign (the one Eugénie had proposed and painted), her gloved hands up by the side of her temples like blinders—then walked away.

Urbin commanded his horse to trot, but the heavy snow had been too much for the equine. Arriving behind his home and butcher shop, he unhitched his sleigh, flew from the stable, ran up the stairs, burst through the kitchen door, and hollered into the empty room, "The shop's front door's closed. Locked. Nobody can come in. People think we're closed." Uriette, cheeks soaked, her daughters wrapped around her, looked at her husband and wiped her eyes. "Why's the shop closed? Why aren't you at work?" He insisted, struggling to catch his breath and pushing at the front of his waist to make way for oxygen to fill his burning lungs.

Uriette caressed Florie's hair and kissed Dahlia's hand. "People have been calling downstairs all morning, offering condolences," she said, turning away to look outside, tears clinging to her chin. "It's Sunday ... nobody's open today ... all this ... it's all too much for you, old man."

Urbin spun and went to his room, bumping his shoulder on the parlour's door frame as he turned. "Never mind those consarn telephone calls," he said, turning back and pointing at the window. "Those people don't know nothing. They don't know the horse and sleigh are gone from the stable. Who do you think was in that sleigh, huh? I'm gonna get the police involved in this. Oh yes, I'm gonna find out what happened over there—even if those bumbling cops can't ... I'm gonna find out," he said, stomping back and forth down the hallway, looking through the window as if addressing some unseen onlookers.

"You saying they made it out?" Uriette asked, brow drooping, head shaking.

"Don't know. But why's his horse gone? Why's his—"

"You think Orance's alive?" Dahlia asked, letting go of her mother's arm to run her sleeve along her nostrils.

"I don't, all I know is what I said. Me, I'm gonna go down and call the police and talk to somebody about all this."

"So, you're the girls we've been hearing about. Sisters, right?" A young woman asked, hands resting on the back of Saraphine's chair.

"I'm Eugénie. That's my sister Saraphine," she said, swallowing a mouthful of beans that Madame Déry had prepared for herself.

"I suppose you won't be working for a while … not if Anna's giving you her franks and beans for supper," the woman said, turning to look at two other women standing just outside the kitchen and laughing.

"Hey, these girls are hungry. They're having an early supper … been through hell these two … so leave 'em alone," Madame Déry said, wiping her hands on a dishcloth before flinging it at the laughing women. "Don't you let those demons bother you. They've been here too long. They don't even remember what it was like before I found 'em," Madame Déry said, joining the sisters at the table.

Eugénie and Saraphine looked at each other without turning their heads. Saraphine, a dangling piece of frankfurter speared on her fork, turned to Anna.

"What did they mean about working? What kind of work?"

"You two have as much as you want. I've got two full iceboxes here and another one in the summer kitchen. Nobody here goes without food. Everybody gets three meals a day and dessert on Sundays. You'll get all the rest you need … you'll get back on your feet, and we'll talk then," the lady said as she pushed herself away from the table.

"The work, though. What types of jobs are we talking about? The two of us have only ever worked in a butcher shop. We both had schooling but neither of us has experience doing anything else," Eugénie asked, carefully placing her utensils down next to her plate.

"A job's a job. Am I right?" Anna said, raising her

shoulders into her neck and walking away from the table. "Anyway, we all have to earn our keep. And you two ... you two know what it's like to run a business, and that's important," she added, walking out to the front parlour.

Saraphine bit into a frankfurter and chewed slowly.

"We're gonna have to find some sort of job if we're gonna survive," Eugénie said, using the side of her thumb to corral some remaining beans onto her spoon, the bloody wrap on her partially severed index finger starting to unravel.

Saraphine, mouth full of beans, lifted her head and froze as if cast into a trance. Managing to swallow, she looked down at her plate and wiped her forehead. Something had moved. Something—inside her—had moved. Slowly, she slid her hand down onto her belly and peeked at her sister. Had she noticed something? Her reaction? Eugénie, face down, continued to eat. Saraphine left her hand on her belly expecting—fearing something would happen.

"I think I'm gonna go down to the room ... maybe just lay on the bed for a while," Saraphine said, looking away and wiping her mouth.

"Wait, I'm almost finished, don't leave me here by myself."

"Take your time. I just want to go down and, uh, you know."

"I'll go with you, jus' wait a—"

"That's all right. Be right back," Saraphine said, scurrying out, hands cupped around her belly.

She sat on the bed, glided her palms along the slightly curved contour of her dress and listened with her hands, unsure what to hope for. *What was that?* Her insides were still; quiet to the touch.

"Everything OK?" Eugénie asked, leaning in through the narrow doorway.

"Fine," Saraphine said, smoothing her dress.

"Good. Once we get settled down maybe we'll have a talk with Anna and figure out where we're going from here,"

Eugénie said, her outline visible through the darkened doorway.

"What did the police say?" Uriette asked as soon as Urbin walked into the shop, banged his feet on the floor, and slapped his hat on his leg; the falling snow immediately absorbed into the sawdust.

"They didn't. They just said that the horse and sleigh—the fact they're missing—didn't really mean anything," he answered, reaching for his apron dangling from a hook.

"They're not going to do anything about it? They're just gonna … gonna do what, exactly?"

"The cop I spoke with said they'd talk with neighbours. Ask questions to see if anyone saw anything. He didn't seem really—"

"He didn't care that Orance might still be alive? That Eugénie and Saraphine—"

"That's not it, not exactly," he said, looking at the back of the shop as he rubbed his hand over the crown of his head.

"What? What is it then?" Uriette asked, moving toward her husband and waving her fists on either side of her face.

Urbin took a deep breath and looked at his wife. "He said the next step was to see if anything, any remains are found in the debris. I told him that three people lived upstairs from the shop so he said that if three bodies showed up, well, then there wouldn't be no need to go on with any type of investigation. You know, no need to question anybody about what happened," Urbin said, looking up at his father's photograph.

"Right, of course. I guess that makes sense," Uriette managed to say, a handkerchief appearing from inside her sleeve to dab her eyes.

Urbin, facing away, paused.

"No matter what, somebody took that sleigh and the horse. It's either theft or it's something else," he added, driving his shoulder into the swinging door.

At his bench, he pulled out the knife he had jabbed into the butcher block, grabbed the biggest pig's leg he could find, and started slashing and hacking at it. Then, as the meat flew, he paused, seeming lost in thought, and put the knife down.

"Uriette," he yelled at the front. "I'll be gone for a while."

He returned to his son's place—what was left of it—and started knocking on neighbours' doors. "I'm the father of the man who lived upstairs from the butchery," he told the lady peering at him through the small gap in the door she had cracked open. "I was wondering if maybe you saw anybody leave through the back last night. Someone that might have taken our horse and sleigh from the stable."

With her back turned to shield her baby from the cold air rushing in, she fumbled while trying to keep a curious young girl from squeezing through. "*Oh, misère.* Yes. That was quite something, that fire. It woke us up in the middle of the night."

"Yes, but because your house is right behind where my son's house is—where it used to be—I was wondering if you saw anyone, or if—"

"All we saw was the fire. We didn't see no horses … no people," she said, frowning as she stepped back and closed the door.

All afternoon, Urbin went from porch to porch querying his son's neighbours. Back home, well after sunset, he had convinced himself that someone had made it out alive; that someone had something to hide.

-7-

"We'll manage … get our heads above water. We jus' need to figure things out," Eugénie said, the bandage on her severed finger falling to the floor.

"Oh, my goodness … your finger … you all right?" Saraphine asked, fishing for the bandage. "Got it, here you go," she said, on her knees, holding the red ball of cotton up to her sister.

Eugénie carefully slipped the wrap back on her bleeding stump, her face pruned by pain.

"Any chance we'll ever see a doctor about that?" Saraphine asked, lifting herself off the floor and gently rubbing her sister's shoulder.

"Dunno. But never mind me, what about you? It's not like *you* don't need a doctor. You lost a lot of blood. Besides, has the bleeding stopped?"

"It's better. I'm sure that the baby's gone. I don't think it's possible to bleed that much and not lose the baby, right?" Saraphine asked, looking for confirmation in her sister's expression.

"Suppose not. Don't really know."

Saraphine pushed her sister back onto the bed.

"Relax for a bit. Don't use your hand. The pain will go away soon."

"It hurts all the time, throbs and burns like something wanting to explode out from my fingertip," Eugénie said, cradling the bandage.

"Too bad we don't have any more of that acetyl … acecelycit … that powder that Dr. Emond gave Orance, that'd be good."

"It'd be good for you, too. You still cramping up?"

Saraphine looked down at her abdomen. "What if I told you that I felt something. Like as if something was still in there."

"When? Like quickening?"

"Upstairs, at the table. I felt something … something move," her brow scrunching up as she spoke, feeling somehow the need to apologize.

"D'you still feel it now? Has it happened again?" Eugénie asked, looking down at her sister's midsection.

"No. But that wasn't more than fifteen minutes ago. Maybe it'll happen again. What if it does, what would that mean?"

"Only one thing . . ." she answered, scratching her scalp

while tilting her head forward "…that the baby survived. Somehow."

"After all that blood … Orance stomping on my stomach. Doesn't sound possible."

"Who knows, maybe you were carrying twins and jus' one of 'em survived," Eugénie said, looking again at her sister's belly before lifting her eyes to meet her gaze, struggling to manufacture a smile.

They sat for a few minutes, Saraphine chewing at her lower lip while Eugénie ran her hand up and down her back.

"But *what if* I'm still expecting? What then? What am I supposed to do?"

Eugénie looked away as if trying to see through the wall.

-8-

"I got the linens for the other bed," Madame Déry said, ducking unmentionables hanging from the many clotheslines, a large bundle of light blue cotton sheets and wool blankets in her arms.

"Please, let me help you," Eugénie said, noticing a bustier dangling off the Madam's right shoulder.

"No, no, your finger's still bleeding. You'll hurt yourself and stain the sheets," Madame Déry replied, tiptoeing around the puddles on the floor. The sisters stood, their backs to the wall, watching as Madame Déry prepared the second bed, moving briskly from side to side, tucking in sheets, smoothing the heavy blanket such as a skilled chambermaid would.

"There you go. You two'll be fine down here," Madame Déry said, the bed screeching when she sat on it. "Sit, sit girls, let's talk a bit, you two've been through so much. Let's chat," she added, the three of them facing each other; Saraphine and Eugénie knee to knee across from Madame Déry.

"Again, we can't thank you enough for what you've done for us," Eugénie said. "Taking us in and letting us—"

"You know, I'm taking quite a risk by having you two stay

here," Madame Déry interrupted, her voice taking on a slow, authoritative tone; blood seeming to drain from under the brushed on pink powder on her cheeks. "You're fugitives from the law. Wanted by the police, you know." she added, leaning forward and softly tapping her thigh.

Eugénie and Saraphine stared back at the lady sitting mere inches away, seized by the madam's sudden change in attitude.

"You two could be tried for murder," she said, quietly, sliding yet closer to the sisters, her perfume making their noses tingle. "Now, don't misunderstand what I'm saying here. I'm not blaming you for anything, and I'm not saying I wouldn't've done the same thing. Believe you me, I'm not. But you'll have to agree that having you here, well ... that makes me an accessory. Me and everybody else in this house is an accessory," she added, pointing at her chest before circling her finger at the ceiling.

"But ... but you know that we never intended to do any such thing. We jus' thought ... we hoped that you'd help us. We never—"

"No need for apologies. That's not important. What *is* important is for you to figure out what you're gonna do from here on in," Madame Déry said, leaning in, looking up at the sisters, her brow pushed up as she scrutinized them. "The way I see things, you have a choice to make and that choice breaks down into two simple options. Either you give yourselves up to the police and accept whatever comes from that decision. Or, you stay here, with me, and start working on a new life."

Saraphine turned to her sister, her expression the same as when she had listened to Eugénie reading their father's note, arms clasped tightly over her chest to keep from quivering. Eugénie looked sideways at Madame Déry, the realness of the situation rushing through her mind. Bewildered by her friend's new persona, she inhaled deeply, slowly, hoping to keep her heart from banging in her ears. "Maybe what's best is for us to move out. We've got an aunt in the States, she'd be willing to take us in. We won't need to take up any more of your time."

"But you see, that's the problem I'm faced with," Madame Déry said, scooching forward along the edge of the bed, her legs against their knees. "I know what you two did and, well … fact is, I let you stay here. I'm complicit and that makes me responsible for you. I have no choice. If I let you go, I'll have to call the police and tell them what you've done, or else, all of us here are gonna be in as much trouble as you two are … except, we won't be hiding in the States," she said, reaching out and gently tapping the sisters' laps.

"That's not why we came here. We didn't come here to become … 'cause we wanted to be … be like you," Saraphine said, jumping off the bed, back turned to the lady.

Madame Déry leaned back on her hands and smiled. "Come, come now. No one who lives here ever expected to … had ever planned for this life. I know neither of *you* did. *I* didn't. I was a chorus girl at the Empire before I . . ."

Eugénie reached back, took hold of Saraphine's forearm and said, "You'll have to excuse me, but it sounds a bit like you're blackmailing us."

"The sooner you make peace with this new situation, the better it'll be for you and me … for all of us," Madame Déry said, stroking her lap. "Now, you've been fed and you've got a lot to take in, so have a good night's sleep and we'll talk some more tomorrow." Madame Déry closed the door behind her and slid the barrel lock into the latch from the other side.

"You're locking us in here? Anna, why are you locking the door?" Eugénie said, slapping at the door with her good hand.

"Like I said, I'm responsible for you and I don't want you going anywhere till you wrap your minds around what we've talked about," Madame Déry yelled at the closed door while climbing the stairs. "By the way, make sure to lock the door on your side, too. We'll be busy tonight and I don't want anybody wandering down here to bother you."

Saraphine rushed to the door, locked it and looked through a small crack in the frame; nothing to see but darkness and the faint glow of yellow flames; the furnace steadily digesting some remaining lumps of coal.

Chapter 15

Eugénie and Saraphine lay on their beds and looked at the ceiling, bits of dust floating down as it creaked and squealed. Revellers—johns—heels and soles hammering at the hardwood to the sound of happy melodies attesting to the merriment upstairs.

"Sounds like a good time up there," Saraphine said, her words gurgling through phlegm.

"I'm sure the *men* are."

"Hey! You the new girls in there," a voice—a woman's voice - from just outside the door, asked.

The sisters looked at each other and sprang to their feet.

"Hey, in there," the woman called again.

Eugénie shook her head at her sister and then stared at the door.

"OK, I guess you're sleeping. I'm Sheilagh, by the way. We met earlier, I'm the one that made the joke about you two eating beans. Remember?"

"Please, leave us alone. We're trying to sleep," Eugénie said, a faint light illuminating the door's perimeter.

"She locked you in, eh. Well, I guess that's about right. You'll see, it gets better. Just be happy you're not in Griffintown," Sheilagh said, the corset she had come to fetch slung over her shoulder.

"What's in Griffintown?" Eugénie asked.

"Griffintown? That's the place that makes this place feel like . . ."

"Like what?"

"Like a place you don't want to run away from. Yeah, that's it," Sheilagh said, sounding surprised at having found the right words. "Anyway, you'll see. Soon enough, you'll see."

Saraphine slid into her sister's bed and took hold of her arm. "It happened again. Stronger this time, something's still inside me."

"How could that be? After what happened, how could anything survive? You bled for hours. It can't be that, how could anything still be alive?"

"It's moving. I can feel it," Saraphine said. "Touch. Put your hand on my belly. You'll feel it."

Saraphine pressed Eugénie's hand to her belly. Eugénie listened with her palm and looked up at her sister. It took a few seconds, but then, her eyes grew wide and her jaw dropped. "What're we gonna do?" She asked. She too had felt something … something that had survived inside her sister.

Saraphine, suddenly enveloped by the idea of life's miraculous persistence, smiled.

"The idea of you bringing a baby into the world right now is the worst situation I can imagine."

"What if it's special?" Saraphine said, dropping back and covering her face, words muffled as they slipped through her fingers.

"What could be special about another bastard coming into this world? My *husband's* bastard, to boot," she said, lifting herself to her knees and looking down at her sister.

Saraphine turned to face the wall. "You … you said it yourself. How could anything survive through such a thing? Doesn't *that* make it special? A tiny life, surviving through it all?"

"Don't you realize the situation we're in? There's nothing special happening here. We're in no position to take on any extra responsibilities right now. Not you, not me. Having to take care of … of a bastard child, on top of everything else … well, that's jus' impossible. Oh no, we're gonna have to get rid of it. Besides, I'm sure Anna must know something about how to do that," Eugénie said, pointing her bandaged hand at the ceiling.

"No, please don't tell Madame Déry about this. Not right now," Saraphine begged, clutching at her sister's good hand.

Eugénie pushed Saraphine back and squeezed her arm. "You're not thinking right, sister. Best for us to speak about all this tomorrow. You know I'm right. Doing this is gonna be the best thing for you; the best thing!"

-2-

Eugénie nearly fell when she bounced from her bed at the sound of Monsieur Lafleur banging on the door till the hinges squealed. Her feet hit the cold cement; the windowless room offering no clue as to the time of day.

"Madame Déry wants to speak with you … told me to bring you to her room," he announced as he unlocked his side of the door.

Eugénie, her tongue stuck to the roof of her dried-out mouth, opened the door and offered a quick nod. Saraphine, inches behind her, held onto the bow hanging from the back of her sister's borrowed dress. The many garments hanging from the clotheslines had been removed and made the cellar seem larger—the ceiling higher. Light came through two small windows. It was daytime.

"Come, it's upstairs," the man said. The sisters noticed he wasn't wearing his starched-stiff collar.

Arm in arm they hurriedly stepped through the heavy velour drapes lining the parlour's large entrance. Remnants of the raucousness they had heard shouting down at them through the ceiling were everywhere; everything was a mess: cigar butts piled in ashtrays, cushions on the floor and empty glasses—some spilled over—on each table. Looking back, they climbed the carpeted stairs. Colourful paintings of bathing ladies and men on horses covered the staircase's wall. Upstairs, to the left, a less fancy flight of stairs led to a third floor. To the right, a long corridor dotted by tall, dark doors, seemed to extend out into eternity. Madame Déry stood at the end of this endless hallway in a doorway, backlit by a large window, her floral dress brushing the carpet.

"*Merci,* Monsieur Lafleur. Come, come girls. Let's talk. We'll have a good chat," she said, turning sideways and directing them into her room—or was it her office?

Saraphine stepped on Eugénie's heel trying to keep close to her sister as they walked down the endless hallway. Eugénie turned to look at her, pointing her nose at doors and small plaques along the way, each with a lady's name engraved on it. Madame Déry smiled and stood out of their way to let them in. She closed the door behind her, the resonating sound of the latch as it sprung crisply into the strike plate caused both of them to jump. Inside, the red and yellow wallpaper seemed to transform the bright morning's sunlight into sunset. An electric / gas light fixture with long golden arms adorned with crystal pendants, hovered above an oversized desk—the kind Eugénie was used to seeing the bank manager sit behind.

"Let's have some tea," Madame Déry said, unwinding a towel from her teapot.

"What, may I ask, do you want to tell us that you haven't already said?" Eugénie asked, clearing her throat before speaking.

"All right, I guess we'll get right to it," Madame Déry said, looking at them as she poured tea into each of the three cups she had pulled from her desk drawer. "This—my girls— is a castle, the best place in the city for a gentleman to enjoy himself, to make merry, relax, and forget the worries of the day. It's beautiful, clean, and we never get any trouble from the cops. You happen to know why?" She asked, pushing one of the cups along the desktop till Saraphine picked it up.

Eugénie pushed herself to the edge of her chair, placed her hands on the desk, and tightened her lips till they nearly disappeared into her mouth.

"I'll tell you why. It's because every one of 'em—at least the ones who patrol around this neighbourhood—are good clients of mine. That's why," she answered, dropping back in her chair, her sigh disturbing the steam casually rising from her cup. "You really should have some of this tea. It's from China. As fine a blend as you'll ever have," she added, lurching forward a bit and lifting the cup in front of her face.

"We don't want to be a burden to you. Again, we're very thankful for all you've done, for taking us in, but our aunt will be waiting for us, and we'll—"

"Here's the reality of the situation," Madame Déry interrupted, cups rattling as she slammed her palm on the oak desk. "You two need a job. This . . ." she said, making a circle with her finger, her palm reddened by the force of the impact, "this is survival now. You're wanted by the police. You work for me, and you'll survive. You take one step outta this place, and I'll call the cops, and the both of you'll be in jail before you know it. Is that what you want? You've gotta understand, I'm offering you something here. Look around, look at my girls, every one of 'em had to drag herself from the dregs. These girls here ... these girls made it. You two are no different."

They stared back, gawking. Eugénie felt pints of blood rocketing up to her head and swallowed hard in an attempt to keep from vomiting.

"Now, I've got this other place in Griffintown. It's not as nice as here, but it's close to the dock and you can start making good money there, real quick. It's where every one of my girls learned this business. You make it there, and I'll know you can make it here. Monsieur Lafleur's gonna take you there this afternoon. Madame Beauchamp, she's in charge there, she'll be expecting you. She runs a tight ship and both of you'll do well to listen to her. You'll have a place to stay, both of you'll be off the streets and—"

"I'm with child," Saraphine said, lurching forward, still holding on to Eugénie's arm.

"She won't be of any use to you, not for that type of work. Not in the condition she's in," Eugénie said, jerking her arm from Saraphine's grip and hovering over Madame Déry's desk.

Madame Déry crooked her head and smiled. "Show's what you've got to learn. Some of my highest-earning girls *are* in that condition. You'd be surprised how often clients specifically ask for girls *in that condition*."

"*Non, non, non ... Eugénie, fait quelque chose, dis-moi quoi faire*," Saraphine said, crying, fearing that—this time—her sister wouldn't find the trap door leading out from this nightmare.

"Listen, if you'd like, I've got a lady that works for me, we call her the turkey lady 'cause that's what she uses, turkey feathers. Anyway, she could take care of you ... your *situation*," Madame Déry said, leaning away from Eugénie to look down at Saraphine's belly.

"It's already quickening. It would be a sin to do that. Eugénie, tell her. It's quickening," Saraphine said, pleading to both of them.

"Girls who want to keep 'em have to give 'em up to La Crèche. That's the deal here. They work till they can't work no more and then, well, we just drop 'em off. The sisters take care of 'em; those bastard babies that show up at their door every day."

Saraphine fell back in her chair, wiped the snot dripping from her nose and looked down at her knuckles.

-3-

Eugénie and Saraphine's legs dangled off the back of the sleigh, their faces covered by a spiralling scarf rising from their necks leaving but a small opening for them to look through. Their breath, forcing its way through the woollen garments, condensed all around their mouths and formed a puck-sized ring of ice that grew larger and thicker as they rode. Large chunks of snow and ice pushed at their heels as they slid along the yet-to-be-cleared streets leading to Griffintown. Down St. Lawrence Street, along Craig and down again on McGill, they finally reached Madame Beauchamp's place on Prince Street: an old, colourless, wood-clad building with a pitched roof - the ages having long ago tortured its every atom of paint into oblivion.

"Go in, ask for Suzanne," Monsieur Lafleur said running his sleeve across his nose.

Eugénie jumped off, reached in, and dragged the burlap bags Madame Déry had packed for them. Saraphine inched forward and took her sister's hand before letting her feet drop.

"Suzanne?" Eugénie asked. "In there?" She pointed at the old, wooden door, a metal grill covering a small window.

"Yep," Monsieur Lafleur answered, pointing his mitt at the door, clucking while snapping the reins till the horses responded, the sound of hundreds of seagulls squawking overhead.

The rickety door flew open just as Eugénie reached for the handle. Three men—young men—dressed in naval uniforms, burst out laughing. One of them, skinny and tiddley, tripped on the burlap bag Saraphine dragged behind her in the snow.

"Watch it, lady," the sailor said.

"Leave 'em alone, you're half-rats, anyway. You should've watched where you're going instead of being indelicate toward these fine cherries," one of the sailors' pals told his buddy while pulling him to his feet. The door cracked open and a woman poked her face out into the cold.

"You the two girls from the Boarding House? Madame Déry sent you here?"

Saraphine looked at Eugénie. Eugénie looked at the woman and nodded.

"OK. So. Come on, come in. Door's open," Suzanne said, long, flammable, grey hair hanging down in front of her shoulders like frayed steel cables. She wore a thin, beige tunic over her emaciated body, shoulders borrowed from a stick figure.

"So, you're sisters. You two are?" Suzanne asked, her tobacco-singed voice grumbling.

"I'm Eugénie, this is my sister Saraphine," she said, looking past the lady, down the hallway and up the dark stairs.

"I'm the bricky who keeps this place going ... takes care of all the girls here. I've been around for twenty-seven years, and if you do what I say, you're gonna have no troubles with me," Suzanne said, smiling at the sisters, a row of baked bean teeth peeking from behind thin, blueish lips. "Madame Beauchamp's the one who's gonna tell you all about how things work here ... the rules and what not ... what's expected from you girls."

Eugénie, head bobbing while probing the dark room, unwound her scarf, removed her hat, and let a small pile of snow slide off and plop onto the bare, worn-out floor.

"This is not something either of us has ever done. Ever ... never thought we'd ... we're not ... not . . ."

"Wait here. Madame Beauchamp's gonna call you in," she interrupted, climbing the stairs and pausing midway, shoulders pumping as she wheezed air into her dried-out lungs.

The bordello's door blew open. Two men looking like merchant mariners, one of them pinching a small card between his fingers, walked in.

"We in the right place? A kid gave us this card. Said we'd have a good time at this address. This the place?" One of the men asked, a clownish smile stretched across his face as he waved the business card in front of his face.

Saraphine stepped behind Eugénie. Eugénie looked away and pointed up the stairs.

"Yeah, yeah, you've come to the right place. Come on up," Suzanne said, panting. The men ran up, straddling two and three steps at a time.

A large woman—the friction sound of her thighs rubbing like matches striking slate—appeared from the shadows. She walked up to the sisters till she stood mere inches away.

"You come from Madame Déry's place?" She asked,

breathing heavily.

Eugénie nodded.

"Come with me," the fat lady said, the drooping skin under her chin wobbling to the rhythm of her steps.

They entered a small office, the ancient floor creaking under the madam's weight.

"Sit," she said, pointing at an old, torn Chesterfield facing her small desk.

They watched the woman shoehorn her bottom into an office chair, the solid wood armrests doing the lion's share of the work; harnessing much of the woman's girth that had wedged in, overflow oozing from every crevasse.

"I'm Madame Beauchamp. The girls here call me Tubs. That's 'cause I'm fat," she said, looking up and smirking. "So, you two'll call me Tubs, too," she said, looking down at her desk, absentmindedly running her thumb along the spaces between her fingers. "Here's what we expect from you: ten johns a day, every day, all of the three hundred and sixty-five days of the year. You get paid twenty cents per lay (Eugénie's heart skipped when a voice in her head suddenly reminded her that she had charged three cents per pound for ground pork). You keep half that. The other half's ours; pays for your room and board. We supply some booze—you'll get some most Sundays if you don't give us no problems. You get ten cigarettes a day if you smoke, the rest you pay us for—plus, we'll give you the clothes you need," Tubs said, staring up at the sisters while tapping her nails on the desktop. "That's a lot better than what any girl's gonna get working at a factory … a shitload better than hunting for johns on the street."

"But, I'm expecting," Saraphine whispered, words struggling to escape her dry mouth.

"We'll get rid of that, no problem. It's part of what we do for our girls."

"She wanted to keep it," Eugénie said, then quickly added, "She'll give it away to La Creche once it arrives."

Tubs leaned forward, pushed down on the desktop and scowled at Eugénie, her clenched, black unibrow looking as if it would crawl off her forehead. "What she saying?" She asked Saraphine, her lower teeth pushing at her upper lip, leaving space enough for her boozy breath to blow over their faces. "You do what *we* tell you to. You get me ten johns a day and we've got no problems. If that's a problem, it's gonna be a problem. A problem for *you*. Got it?" She emphasized; her fingers balled into doughy fists.

Saraphine nodded—quick, little nods that she struggled to rein in. Eugénie fell back in her chair.

"From now on, you deal with Suzanne. If *I* have to see you, if *I* have to talk to you, that'll mean we have a problem. Now, are either of you gonna give me problems?" She asked, her chin tucked into another chin.

The sisters shook their heads.

"That's it, then. Get out. Suzanne'll take care of you."

They walked out of the office and jumped when Tubs screamed Suzanne's name.

"Come get these two. They're ready," Tubs said, her deep voice nearly pulling the worn plaster off the walls.

-4-

Eugénie and Saraphine—engulfed in a trail of Player's Navy Cut cigarette smoke—followed Suzanne upstairs. The staircase, carpeted by a mélange of mismatched pieces of fabric loosely thumbtacked to the treads, creaked and shook with each footfall. Eugénie slid her hand along the wall's crevassed plaster, long, yellowed strips of peeling wallpaper providing for much of the building's structural integrity. All the cocottes (that's what Suzanne called her working girls) slept in the attic on one of thirty cots squeezed into a small dormitory. Two, huge dressers on the far wall provided a drawer's worth of space for each girl in which to store all of their worldly possessions.

Reaching the third-floor attic meant having experienced the variety of blended odours the residence had to offer: the ever-present fragrance of body odour drenched in cheap perfume; oily hair mingling with eau de musty fabrics, decaying wood, wet plaster and, of course, spittoons and chamber pots. A single lightbulb dangling at the centre of this penthouse dungeon cast long shadows creeping along the ceiling and knee walls.

"Here's your card. You two know how to read?" Suzanne asked. "Your name's on it. You come to me and I punch it when you're done. Like Tubs told you, I need to see ten holes punched in this every day. That's how you get paid," Suzanne said, a cigarette bouncing off the corner of her lips dropping ashes on her chest.

"Up here's where you relax between tricks. When I've got someone for you, I'll call your name and tell you which room to go to. The john'll be waiting in there," Suzanne said while looking around at some of the other girls lying on cots.

"We never did anything like this. We've got no—"

"Listen, just do whatever he wants, sweetheart. Don't worry, he'll tell you. It's not complicated," Suzanne said, hoicking a loogie and, with a sniper's precision, shooting it at a spittoon. "Make these ladies feel welcomed," she added, then snapped her bony fingers at the room. The few girls lying around paid no attention. "Yeah, yeah," Suzanne said, then climbed backwards down the nearly vertical attic stairs.

Any girl hoping to keep her feet out of the snow knew she had to build a pool of steady johns; to be special. Up to fifty hookers worked the Griffintown bordello at the height of the busy season. Now, during the winter months, with the harbour closed till April or May, no more than twenty prostitutes managed to maintain their spot in the rotation, to keep from having to work the streets. Veterans all. Real earners. Cream of the crop.

The sisters, burlap bags in hand, headed to the end of the room where two vacant bunks sat side-by-each.

"Emma, room seven," Suzanne screeched from downstairs. A girl, fifteen, seventeen at most, swung her legs off her cot and shuffled to the small mirror next to the doorway. Head craned at her reflection, she pinched her cheeks, ran her fingers through her hair, licked her bottom lip, and left to meet her mystery date waiting in room seven.

"You two sisters, come down, too," Suzanne added, her voice horse and gravelly.

Eugénie and Saraphine looked at each other, both failing at projecting strength. Saraphine stared down the staircase, at Suzanne leaning against the ladder's stringer and staring back up at her.

"But you haven't given us our punch cards yet," Saraphine said, hoping the loophole would delay the inevitable.

"No, no. I just wanted to give you these," Suzanne answered, waving two paper bags at them. "Your clothes … things you'll wear for johns. I supposed nothing like this was in those sacs of yours that you showed up with."

Saraphine climbed down hands trailing back along the improvised railings, unaccustomed to the aggressive pitch of the descent.

"I probably won't be calling on either of you till tonight," Suzanne said, shoving the bags at both of them. "Just make sure you're wearing this when you come down."

-5-

The yellow glow from the ceiling's light bulb had taken over from the window's pinkish beams. Emma had returned from below, the sisters surprised by the brevity of her absence. One of the girls, three bunks away from where Eugénie lay, had covered herself from head to toe, knees tucked into her chest. Her coughing and wheezing hadn't stopped since the sisters had arrived. The blanket over her mouth puffed out as she hacked and sneezed into it.

"Hey. Suzanne," a red-headed woman shouted at the ceiling. "Sarah's losing a lung up here … gonna make us all sick as dogs," she yelled, the tendons in her neck stretched like taut ropes.

"Sarah, *la trois* ... Ghislaine, *la une*," Suzanne ordered.

The red-headed woman sat on her hands and continued to yell, "Can't you hear anything? She's sick. She can't even get out of bed. She looks like she's gonna croak."

Eugénie and Saraphine looked sideways at the red-headed woman.

"It's not that hard to understand," she said, noticing the sisters' glance. "That's what's waiting for all of us up here," she added, punching at her thin pillow before lying on her side.

A woman, Ghislaine, Eugénie assumed, headed down the stairs.

"Isn't Sarah up there?" They overheard Suzanne ask Ghislaine.

"Come on Sarah. You're up. Room three. *Enwèye, grouille ... tout suite*," Suzanne growled, her metallic head sticking up through the attic floor's hatch.

"She's fucking dying!" The red-head screamed.

"You OK? Hey, Sarah, you OK?" Suzanne asked the coughing figure under the covers. Suzanne climbed up another step and scanned the room. "All right, then … Maureen, you take it. Room three," she said. "Loosen up there, cutie, I'll be calling on you next," she added, her cigarette pointed at Saraphine as she disappeared below.

The sun had dropped away when two men, one of them wearing nothing but suspenders over his naked torso, pulled the covers off Sarah and yanked her off her cot. Looking like a piece of wallpaper that had flaked off the crevassed plaster, they grabbed her wrists and dragged her limp body along the floor. Then, the bare-chested man flung the girl over his shoulder and climbed down, backwards, Sarah's head banging the edge of each step along the way. Saraphine flinched at the sound of each thump. Eugénie, unwilling to watch, had buried her face in the pillow.

"So, you're Eugénie and you're ... what's your name again?" Suzanne asked, sticking up through the floor and pointing at the sisters with her cigarette pinched between her fingers.

"Me? Saraphine," she said, clearing her throat before speaking.

"Forget that. You're the new Sara. That's it, you're Sara from now on, and Sara, you're up. Room three," Suzanne said, dipping down below, a trail of cigarette smoke wafting up as she dropped. "Oh, and make sure to put on what I gave you ... those things in the bag. Put that on before coming down," she added from under the floorboards.

-6-

Wearing the long—what used to be white—beige nightgown and smelling of others (many others), Saraphine slid her feet along the floor, unable to look back at her sister.

"Down the hallway, room three," Suzanne instructed, bent over and looking down the dark hallway as Saraphine stepped off the last rung of the staircase, unable to release the handrail that she gripped with both hands.

Saraphine stood in front of the door and tried to resist the feeling of Suzanne's glare burning a hole through her soul.

"Go on. Ten a day, sweetheart. Ten a day, every day," she heard Suzanne say just as some unknown switch flipped her mind into neutral and lifted her—anaesthetized her—from her body. *Fifteen minutes*, she thought. *That girl was gone for fifteen minutes. That's all it'll take*, she told herself as she walked in.

Inside, a man, trousers down to his ankles, sat on the bed struggling to push his shoes off. Saraphine closed the door and held onto the knob behind her back.

"You're not the Sarah I'm used to," the man said, glancing up at her. "What's your name? If you're good, I'll ask for you again."

Saraphine looked over the man and said, "I'm Sara, too. Another Sara."

"Well, get over here. Help me get these off."

Arms laced across her chest, she moved toward the man, leaned down and pulled his pants off, the smell from his wet shoes prompting her to slide them under the bed.

"So, anything you're particularly good at? Got some kind of specialty?" He asked, grinning, eyebrows pumping while carefully hanging his shirt and collar on one of the bed's short posts.

She looked back at the door and shook her head.

-7-

Back upstairs, card pinched between her fingers, a single hole perforated through it, Saraphine sat next to Eugénie's empty cot. It was past seven and the night's business was in full swing.

"Angéline, *la trois*. Shannon, room five … let's go, girls, let's go," Suzanne called.

Saraphine looked at the empty cots, laid back, and pulled the cover over her bare shoulders; the heat from the small potbelly stove in the middle of the room hardly enough to counter the freeze sneaking past the loose clapboards.

"Sara, *la quatre*."

Saraphine scanned the room to see who would respond to the call till a bolt of putrid energy reminded her that *she* was Sara. She looked at the single perforation in her card, her mind racing at the thought of the nine additional holes yet to come.

"*J'ai dit la quatre*," Suzanne repeated.

Saraphine, card in hand, let the cover drop off her shoulders and walked down.

"Listen," Suzanne said, grabbing her arm as she reached the bottom of the staircase. "Madame Beauchamp told me to make sure you learn quick. So, this time there's gonna be two guys in there waiting for you. Young guys, not a lot of money, yunno. I won't count it as two tricks—more like one and a half. Besides, they're real drunk so, you'll see, it's gonna be quick and your night's gonna be done sooner."

Saraphine, unable to stop from shivering, explored every crevasse in her mind in search of a foxhole to jump into; for some refuge from reality. Noticing the look on Saraphine's face, Suzanne laughed and slapped her bottom.

"Relax. I told you, just do what they ask for ... you'll see, no problems. Anyway, like I said, they're drunk so you'll be done in no time," she added, taking Saraphine by the shoulders and pushing her toward the door.

It was nearly three in the morning when, from under her cover, Eugénie saw Saraphine emerge from downstairs. She sat up and looked at her sister, barefoot, draped in a worn-out cotton nightgown that clung to her skin like a translucent scab.

"Tough night, dearie?" Some woman's voice broke the silence.

Saraphine sat facing her sister, their eyes meeting for an instant aware of what the other had experienced. She noticed Eugénie's cheeks—abraded and reddened by so many beards and whiskers—and suddenly felt the sting of her own chafed face.

"Ten holes punched," Saraphine held up her small cardboard rectangle. "She told me I'd get credit for one and a half for being with two boys at a time. But she didn't. I went down there ten times."

Eugénie covered her face and said, "All this because of me dragging you in this mess."

"It's just what happened, what was in the stars for us after mom died," Saraphine said, pulling the cover over her sister and spooning her, strangely unaccustomed to being the one providing comfort, at being the balm.

With her sister's bump nestled against the small of her

back, Eugénie felt the baby kicking, poking, as if wanting to intrude on the moment.

"Feel that?" Saraphine asked.

"I do," Eugénie said, fearing her husband's child and looking forward to having it disappear into *La Crèche*.

-8-

"Any luck, d'you hear anything?" Uriette asked her husband before he had a chance to close the door behind him. "Well?"

Urbin walked to the kitchen table, sat and rubbed his elbow. "They found a body, said it was a large body, not a woman's body."

"Orance?" Uriette said, leaning back against the Hoosier's enamelled top.

"Daddy?" Dahlia, walking into the kitchen, asked.

"That's all they found. Said they'd tell us if they found anything else while they demolished the rest of the building. Told me that a fire like that, wasn't unusual for … for remains to just burn away."

Uriette looked at Dahlia, pulled her apron's bib up and craned her head forward to dab a tear from her eye.

"I guess I should write to Blanche, tell 'em what happened, tell her about her nieces. There's no hope left, they're not gonna find—"

"I'm not done. I'm gonna keep on asking people, the neighbours, about what they saw. The horse, that sleigh, they didn't leave on their own, *saint-sacréfice*!" Urbin said, looking out the kitchen window.

PART IV

Chapter 16

-1-

Summer, 1903

Saraphine lay on her back watching as yellow light filtering through cracked louvres put an early end to the moon's grave-yard shift. Sweat beading on her forehead—oozing from every pore—did little to douse her molten body and added to the gallons of salty liquid already sucked up by the brown, stinking cot. Cupping her bulge, she ran her fingertips around her protruding belly button. This child she was making would survive. This child she protected, her rapist's son, hadn't been aborted. She would not be damned.

With summer came large ships, and with large ships came mariners to set the whoring business alight. Montreal, the commercial hub of Canada, was the capital of sin and the sire-land of chlamydia, syphilis, gonorrhea, and crabs. The dorm, usually stocked with skinny young girls scratching away the irritation of bed bugs and lice, was now considered a less vital place to call home by those having opted to work the sun-drenched streets. For most, however, all forty-four of them on this bright morning, a place to sleep and three meals a day were good arguments for staying put. Rows of cots, hardly a foot apart, took up nearly all of the attic's floor space. This summer had been busier than most and Madame Beauchamp—Tubs—had been obliged to abandon her space; Madame Déry having explained that her office would be more profitable if transformed into a room for paying clients. These long days populated by merchant mariners, navy men, and regulars, meant workdays could start as early as ten in the morning and keep going till way past three in the A.M.

Looking at the ceiling, the faint light and shadows highlighting cobwebs clinging to dried-out boards and tin roofing tiles visible through cracks, Saraphine tried as she could to distract her mind away from the fact she had to pee. Again. That she'd have to fetch one of the pee pots—a hopefully empty pee pot—and drain her shrunken bladder. She reached under her cot, hoping one had remained where she had left it but whiffed through space. Lifting herself up on her elbows, she noticed a couple of them next to the water basin near the staircase, the *Whirling Spray Ladies' Syringe's* orange ball sticking out from one of them.

Careful not to bump into anyone's bunk, she slid sideways along the narrow aisles in between cots, tiptoeing through a hotbox packed with forty sleeping women all of whom assumed others smelled worse than they did. Her calves brushed along hands dangling off the side of bunks; feet spilling off cots; painted toenails poking at her skin. Having made her way through, she reached down for one of the white enamelled pots, but as she straightened herself, shards of pain blasted through her as if a muscle deep inside had torn and snapped. The pot fell from her hand, banging and clanking till it rolled down the staircase. She crouched and balled up, hoping to contain the pain; to squeeze the cramp out of her body, but instead, her belly came down against her knees and sent her falling flat on her back. The thud of her head as it connected with the floor rivalled the racket the pot had made. Lying on the dirty boards, she felt a scream rush from her lungs as if someone else had commanded her to do so.

"Saraphine," Eugénie called, instantly alert, searching for her sister through faint light.

"I'm all right. Fine," Saraphine automatically grunted, lying on her side, knees raised, arms belted across her abdomen.

Eugénie rushed to her sister as some of the girls complained.

"What's the commotion ... what's with the benjo?" A girl

not bothering to look up, asked.

One of the new girls, her white, freckled face and red hair illuminated by the morning's early rays, jumped out of bed and yelled, "What's the matter … what's happening?"

"Someone, help me get her back in bed," Eugénie pleaded, her hand held under the back of her sister's head to keep it off the floor.

"It's better now. Just a cramp … just a cramp," Saraphine said, her face contorted, eyes squeezed shut.

Having managed to make it up to her knees, Saraphine said, "Just help me up," arms extended for her sister to take a hold of.

"Oh goodness, I peed all over the floor," Saraphine said, looking down, her feet warmed by the puddle.

"This floor's seen worse," Eugénie said, her forehead to Saraphine's cheek while guiding her back to bed.

"You can't work today. I'm gonna tell Suzanne you can't work till all this is over," Eugénie said, sitting on her bed facing Saraphine.

"It can't be much longer now. I'm sure this baby'll be out soon. I can't get much bigger," Saraphine said through puffed-out cheeks.

-2-

From her cot, Saraphine watched as girls paraded back and forth, down and up the stairs. Thursdays—payday—were always busy, and strangely, rainy days like this one always seemed to bring in even more johns.

"Looks like you've gotten yourself a day off," the red-haired girl said, having returned from room three as she passed by Saraphine's cot.

Saraphine looked up and smiled.

"So, you all better? That's quite a load you're carrying," she added, pointing at Saraphine's belly as she sat on her cot.

"Oh yes, Looking forward to the delivery. Well, maybe not

the delivery, but you know, all this being behind me," Saraphine said, surprised to hear herself admitting as much to a kind of stranger.

"Are you hoping for a boy or a—"

"It's for *La Crèche*. I'll be leaving it at *La Crèche* ... you know, for some other family to raise."

"Oh, for sure ... 'spose that's the best thing to do."

"It's run by the Grey Nuns, you know. They'll do the right thing and make sure this one doesn't end up ... doesn't end up having to become involved with this type of work," Saraphine said, cradling her belly, unsure if the girl was still listening.

"Alice," Suzanne's voice came belting up the stairs. "Alice, number two."

Saraphine let flies tickle her skin as they wandered up and down her sweaty arms and legs.

"Cécille, *la quatre*," Suzanne called up. Cécille crushed her cigarette and shuffled off.

Saraphine had almost fallen asleep by the time Suzanne swiped at her foot. She had climbed up to the attic, a place Suzanne hated to go, especially on such a hot day. A wave of panic swirled through Saraphine's body at the sight of the spindly woman's smoke screened face. Something had happened to Eugénie.

"I know you're not supposed to work today, but one of the clients asked for you. He wants *you* ... you know, the way you are and all," Suzanne said, ashes from her cigarette floating down on Saraphine's toes.

"But ... Eugénie asked that I don't ... all day—"

"I know, I know. But it's like I said. This is a good client, he asked for you. It's Tubs that told me to come and get you. If it was up to me, I would've left you alone today, but you know, just this one and it'll be it for you for the rest of the day."

Relieved that nothing had happened to her sister, she turned to her side and inhaled deeply. She rolled off her cot, waddled to the staircase, pointed the atomizer at her heart, squeezed a puff of perfume along her chest, and put the bottle back on the shelf next to the handrail. Looking back at the dormitory, careful not to bump her belly along the treads and stepped backwards down the staircase, off to meet whoever had requested the honour of her presence—down there—waiting in room one.

-3-

Having found the right facial muscles to command, Saraphine managed to work up a proper smile and pushed the door open; her thin, white nightgown draped over her belly. Inside stood a small man, his back turned to the door, apparently riveted by a faded illustration of some naked, baroque ladies. He turned, feinting having been brusquely jolted from a kind of daydream and offered a look of surprise, as if not expecting someone joining him. She noticed the fabric of his suit jacket, the neatly pressed linen shirt, the monogrammed starched collar and wondered why this man hadn't afforded himself the luxuries of more gracious quarters. He held his straw hat tightly to his chest and rocked slowly from heels to toes. His face, the colour of February, was adorned by a thin mustache and grey eyebrows that seemed awkwardly pencilled in. Unable to respond to Saraphine's circumstantial congeniality, he sat and delicately positioned his hat over his crotch while his eyes diarized her body—pausing along the way to appreciate her protruding belly. She took a few steps toward the man and he pushed his hat to the floor revealing his tented gaberdine pants. This, she thought, might be an easy trick to complete.

She undressed him, moving slowly to ensure he maintained his framework, and guided the man to the bed, his large penis seeming borrowed from some other, more adequately proportioned man. She stepped back, pulled the spaghetti straps off her shoulders and pushed him down onto the

— *317* —

mattress. Lying there, looking like one of the high-masted sloops docked at the wharf, she climbed on, struggling to lift her leg before sitting on his erection; thankful for the uncomplicated, straightforward nature of the assignment.

Lips parted; the john closed his eyes; lids crinkled while tingling under Saraphine's movements. Enjoying the privacy, she glanced at the window's opaque glass; waxed over and grey. She figured the panes under those coats of cloak were likely stained, remnants of beauty long-ago designed to let in yellow and orange light for some family to enjoy. She looked again at the man's clothes lying amongst dust bunnies. Yellowed, skid-marked underpants sitting on his clean jacket. She glanced at the naked bulb dangling off a cotton-covered electrical wire; sunlight a luxury for others to enjoy. She bit her lower lip as the muscles in her legs began to strain—the work of having to maintain the rhythm needed to bring this transaction to a satisfactory conclusion drawing sweat from her pores.

Baby names suddenly surfaced in her mind. This, she thought, would be the only gift she would offer her unborn child. Something of herself for this person to move forward with.

The man below her remained silent and blind. Miles away, she wandered the alphabet, stringing letters into names till the warmth of oozing moisture nudged her back into the room. The transaction had been completed. Looking down, she noticed the man, bug-eyed and staring at intersecting crotches.

"What's this?" He asked, looking up, his expression suggesting he had—or hadn't—enjoyed the deluge.

Saraphine lifted herself off the man's unquenched erection; liquid sliding down her inner thighs dripping on the mattress and onto the john's clothes.

"It's coming," Saraphine whispered to herself, looking back at the door.

She pulled her nightgown off the back of the chair; the

heavy piece of furniture banging against the wall before falling to the floor.

"Sorry ... sorry," she said as she bolted from the room.

"Wait," the man said, penis in hand while reaching for his clothes.

"Suzanne, Suzanne," Saraphine yelled, hopping and running along the hallway toward what used to be Madame Beauchamp's office. "Suzanne," she repeated, not sure why this person would suddenly care.

"Eugénie," she hollered, turning back, the little man holding his clothes over his naked body looking at her from the other end of the hallway.

"Eugénie," she screamed again, pushing the little man against the wall as she rushed past him.

Hands straddling her belly, she climbed the stairs calling out her sister's name. Doors opened; puzzled faces stared out. She climbed to the attic and saw her sister's empty cot.

"She was called a few minutes ago. Room five ... four ... one of those two," one of the girls said.

"Which one? Don't you remember which one?" Saraphine asked, breathless, holding her belly as if it would drop from her nightgown.

"Not sure. You all right?" The girl asked.

"It's happening. Now! It's happening," Saraphine said, looking at Eugénie's cot. "Five or four, you said?" She asked, climbing backwards down the stairs, liquid dripping off her heels.

-4-

"Your sister's about to have her baby. I think she's in labour," one of the girls told Eugénie as soon as she saw her face peek up through the floor's hatch.

"Where is she? Did they take her somewhere?" Eugénie asked, her mouth drying up instantly.

"I'm surprised you didn't see her. She's downstairs, somewhere, looking for you."

Eugénie ran down calling her sister's name, blood thundering through her ears as she raced, feet barely touching the steps.

"Saraphine, are you here?" She called into the second floor's dark hallway. "Saraphine," she repeated, slapping at her sides, screaming and hollering. A door flew open projecting the heavy glass knob into the old plaster, adding half an inch to the depth of the hole already sunken into the wall. A john stuck his head out, his long, grey comb-over hanging off to one side, and glared at her, eyes fully loaded and ready to fire.

"Is Saraphine in there? She with you?" Eugénie asked, pushing the man aside to look inside.

"She's not here, sweetheart," a woman inside said, her butt on her heels, irate at the thought of having to reinitiate the launch sequence.

Eugénie flew from door to door, moving through the hallway and down to the main floor, banging on doors and shouting her sister's name till Suzanne finally responded.

"She's here. I took her outside, out back. Calm down," she said, looking at Eugénie, eyes on fire, cigarette ensconced in the right corner of her mouth.

Eugénie ran to the back porch and saw her sister, barefoot, bent forward, and pacing the small yard. A young man, a sailor, walked out from the outhouse while tucking his shirt back into his pants.

"This place's got everything going on," he said, walking past Saraphine, looking back at her and smiling. Suzanne laughed at the remark then burst into a coughing fit.

"Any labour throes yet?" Eugénie asked.

"Yessssss. Bad ones … getting worse," Saraphine said through clenched teeth, leaning on the outhouse while reaching for her sister's hand.

"We should go inside. She needs to be in bed," Eugénie, hands cupping her sister's elbows, told Suzanne.

"Oh no. Not again. That man she nearly drowned, he complained and ran off without paying … big Rob ran after him … anyway, every room's busy and—"

"My sister's in labour. She's giving birth," Eugénie said, leaning towards Suzanne, her nose inches from her cigarette's embers.

"Not gonna happen. Outside's the best place. She can lie on the porch if you want, but not inside. Too much of a mess … and the clients. Oh no. No, no, no."

"Saraphine!" Eugénie yelled realizing she couldn't hold up her sister any longer. She dropped like a collapsed building, her knees having unlocked, too weak to keep her head from banging along the side of the outhouse as she fell.

"It's coming. I can feel it," Saraphine said, grasping her sister's forearm.

"Pull your knees up," Eugénie said, searching for some reasonable course of action, a hundred thoughts pinging through her brain. "Go get something inside for her to lie on. She can't jus' sit in dirt," Eugénie barked at Suzanne. Suzanne flipped her cigarette into the bushes and half-trotted to the house.

"I'll get a sheet. That's gonna be good. A sheet," Suzanne said.

Saraphine hunched forward and drew quick, staccato breaths. "How long is this supposed to take?"

"Don't know. You said you could feel it coming but I'm not sure I see anything yet," Eugénie said, wiping her sister's forehead with her sleeve.

"Got sheets from downstairs," Suzanne said, waving them as she stepped off the porch.

Eugénie unfolded the sheets and tucked them under Saraphine.

"That's better. At least now the dirt won't—"

Saraphine grunted, the guttural roar sounding as if it had come from deep inside a cave.

"It's here. It's here," Eugénie said, eyes popping from their orbits. The baby's head appeared and Eugénie encircled her fingers around it.

"Holy shit! It's a boy," Suzanne said, arms crossed, bent over and hacking, unaware she was experiencing a few, rare minutes without a cigarette hanging from her lips.

"A boy?" Saraphine asked, breathless, pearls of sweat rolling down her temples.

"A boy," Eugénie answered, gently placing the newborn on Saraphine's belly.

"Arthur," Saraphine said.

"Arthur?" Eugénie asked, looking at the baby and stroking his forehead with the side of her thumb.

"You've got to cut the cord. I've got to get something to cut the cord," Suzanne said, and walked off, striking a match as she climbed onto the porch.

Saraphine placed her hand on Arthur's small body and touched his tiny ear. "Maybe I shouldn't get too attached," she said, looking at Eugénie.

"Why Arthur?" Eugénie asked, lying next to her sister and brushing the hair off her forehead.

"I read that Arthur means *bear*. I figured he'd need that kind of strength to make it out there and ... I don't know . . ." Saraphine said, looking at the baby and shrugging, lips pursed.

"This'll do it," Suzanne said, a piece of wood and knife in hand. "You take it, I'm not doing it," she added, and handed the implements to Eugénie.

Eugénie positioned the piece of wood under the umbilical cord, the knife hovering over it.

"You ready?" She asked, her hairline pushed back.

"I don't think it's supposed to hurt. Does it?" Saraphine asked.

"No, course not, you won't feel anything," Suzanne said, waving her cigarette at the baby.

"Here goes." Eugénie looked down, grit her teeth and cut the cord. "Done." Eugénie handed Suzanne the piece of wood, and from the corner of her eye, noticed the white sheet had turned a deep, dark colour … dirt-stained blood. Saraphine, propped up against the outhouse with the baby pressed to her cheek, let the faint smile dissolve from her face at the sight of her sister's demeanour.

-5-

"What's wrong?" Saraphine asked, "Something wrong?" She repeated, up on her elbows, busily reading her sister's face.

"You're bleeding … a bit … that's all," Eugénie said, rubbing her hands along her thighs and looking back at Suzanne.

"Call a doctor. There must be a doctor somewhere around here," Saraphine said.

"Go get a doctor. A cop. The cop'll know where to find a doctor," Eugénie told Suzanne, who looked down at the scene, hands dug into the small of her back.

"A cop. You think I'm gonna get a cop to come here? You're crazy? This aint the Boarding House," she replied and waved, sparks flying off her cig.

"Get someone. Get a towel … towels," Eugénie yelled, pointing at the door.

"Ok, ok … I'll get towels … ask if anyone knows where to find a doctor 'round here," Suzanne muttered, a trail of smoke wafting behind her.

"Hold your knees in," Eugénie instructed while squeezing her sister's knees together. "I'll take the baby."

Saraphine turned to her side as if to shield Arthur from her sister.

"No. I'll be fine. No need to take him."

Eugénie sat on her heels, looking down at the scene and struggling to fill her lungs.

"I feel so tired … exhausted," Saraphine said through a prolonged exhalation.

"Where is she? Where are those towels?" Eugénie said, mesmerized by the growing red puddle muddying the dirt. She stroked Saraphine's forehead and tried to smother the ris-

— 323 —

ing panic her sister's translucent skin now provoked.

"OK, I got a towel. Some of the girls went out looking for a doc," Suzanne said, waving a long, white towel.

Eugénie pressed the towel to Saraphine's crotch, hoping the pressure would stem the flow—as if she were dealing with some run of the mill cut or gash.

Saraphine, Arthur's head cradled in the crook of her elbow, watched—detached—as her sister bunched a towel into a ball and rotated the imbibed portions away from her skin. Woozy, she scooched away from the outhouse, laid her head on the ground, and watched clouds float by, seagulls circling below them.

"Arthur's a name that people'll respect," she said, struggling to lift her head to look at the porch.

Eugénie, hyperventilating as she continued to press the towel to her sister's crotch, leaned forward and looked into her eyes; the feel of panic's acid searing the back of her throat as her tears dripped onto Arthur's tiny chest.

"You'll be fine. Fine," Eugénie whispered loudly, repeatedly.

"Arthur's a gentleman's name," Saraphine said, no longer able to lift her head off the dirt, though relishing the feel of her baby lying on her chest.

"You'll be all right," Eugénie repeated, unable to dam the saliva flowing from her mouth.

"I'm tired," Saraphine said, clouds reflecting in her glassy eyes.

Eugénie's arms trembled from holding the crimson towel tighter and tighter against the flow of blood, then noticed her sister's unblinking eyes as the soft breeze blew a strand of Saraphine's fine hair along her forehead.

Arthur squealed; his wet face shiny and glowing. Eugénie lay next to her sister and caressed the baby's head.

Suzanne came out onto the porch, paused, then walked back inside.

Some of the girls that had watched from behind windows

walked away at the sight of Eugénie closing her sister's eye-lids.

"I think she's dead," Eugénie heard a girl on the porch whisper.

Eugénie looked at Arthur squirming on his mother's chest, crying, bawling. She leaned forward, brushed Saraphine's hair off her face and started pounding her fist at the side of her leg—screaming incoherently. Aware of the many girls who had, by now, gathered on the porch, Eugénie covered her face and sobbed into her hands. Then, suddenly, she snatched the crying baby and held him suspended in front of her like a wet dog. Grunting and growling, she cursed at the sky and said, "No, no, no. Not again. It's you. You!" and pointed Arthur at the clouds, high above her head till tears dripping from the baby's chin rained on her forehead—the shower seeming to have the effect of a slap across her face.

"*Non* ... Eugénie ... *non, non* ... *Mon Dieu*!" girls on the porch screamed.

Eugénie just stood there for a while, mouth agape, the baby still suspended above her. Then she dropped to her knees and delicately placed Arthur back on her sister's chest. Unaware of the baby's cries, she walked by the girls on the porch and went inside.

-6-

"The girls loved having a baby 'round here for a while but it's time you take him to *La Crèche* ... like Saraphine said she'd do," Tubs told Eugénie, the boss lady wedged behind the kitchen table, her office still unavailable during this seemingly endless summer.

"I'll go today if somebody can bring me there," she said, picking at a scab near her thumbnail.

"The big man here's alone all day but Monsieur Lafleur's supposed to come by around lunch time. I'll ask if he can take you before he goes back to the Boarding House. In any case, you haven't punched a full card in four days. That can't go on," Tubs said, wrapping her big knuckles on the tabletop.

Eugénie, on her way back upstairs, paused at the sound of a man's voice, an Irish man's voice; his words, gravelly and parched had iced her spine. Looking down from the landing, kneeling behind the balustrade, hands wrapped around the spindles like a caricatured prisoner, she watched Suzanne greet what seemed like a familiar customer. There, in this Griffintown bordello, hidden under a bowler hat—strands of red hair like lava spills falling out on either side of his face— stood a man she had known well. Sean Murphy, the whore hater, had come to enjoy the company of sluts. On tiptoes, she stepped back, ran down the hallway and climbed up to the attic dormitory where a bunch of girls stood hunched over and hovering above the infant, relishing this brief opportunity to feel human, taking turns caring for Arthur while she had been away.

"Enjoy while you can, he's leaving today," Eugénie said, toneless, standing behind the gathered crowd.

"Is he going to live with family?" A girl asked, stroking Arthur's back in the hopes of him gurgling up a burp.

"He's going to *La Crèche*. He's got no family to go to. That was the plan all along," Eugénie said, arms crossed and looking back at the staircase.

"I heard the nuns aren't too careful when they take care of those little bastards. Not like they're supposed to, anyway," one of the girls said, lying on her bunk, propped up on her elbow, unmoved by the spectacle.

Eugénie pushed some of the girls out of the way.

"He's got nothing else waiting for him," Eugénie said, taking the baby from the girl's arms. "Besides, maybe he'll be taken in by some rich family, or maybe even a farm family. He'll become a farmer. He'll—"

"Oh, for sure. Those rubes with fourteen kids can't wait to adopt a bastard from the city. I'll tell you, if he goes to a farm it's gonna be because they need another slave to work all day.

Besides, rich folks don't get babies from the nuns," a girl, bent over and knotting her hair into a bun said, snorting.

Eugénie placed Arthur on Saraphine's cot, sat next to him, and resumed picking at her scab.

"Eugénie, *la trois*," Suzanne yelled.

"I can't. Talk to Tubs. I'm going on an errand today … waiting for Monsieur Lafleur," Eugénie said, her stomach twisting at the thought of walking into a bedroom and having Sean see her.

"Maybe *I* should get a baby of my own," a girl sprawled on a nearby cot said.

Eugénie watched Arthur from the corner of her eye, his tiny body contorted by colic. Soon enough, the shrieking started. She shook the cot… almost gently. Arthur, unaffected by the motion, continued to scream and wail. Eugénie shook the cot harder till the bunk's feet rubbed against the old, dried out floor.

"Stop. Enough," Eugénie said, shaking the cot as if wanting to sauté the baby.

"Consarn, pick him up," the red-haired girl said, the racket having forced her to sit up.

Eugénie let go of the cot and … noticed Arthur. The baby's eyes were clasped; his face rippling as if facing a stiff arctic headwind. She picked up the little man and pulled him close. Unaware, she started rocking and stroking his foot, teensy toenails jabbing at her skin, the screech of his blazing howls seeming less strident though his face was mere inches from her ear. She caressed his back and ran the side of her hand all the way up to the base of his neck. She ran the stump of her severed finger along the soft spot on his head, the rough, knobby digit pulling at his fine hair—finer than Saraphine's. He quieted down, and she held him long after he had fallen asleep; spit bubbles bursting from his lips. She lay on her bunk, the baby asleep on her chest, waiting for Monsieur Lafleur to arrive.

"Don't be too long over there, those old crows give me the creeps," Monsieur Lafleur warned as Eugénie climbed up into the back of the wagon.

Eugénie looked down at Arthur and pulled her bonnet over her face to ensure she remained unrecognized as they travelled West along Dorchester Street.

Arthur, wrapped in a towel and wearing a torn sheet as a diaper, had clasped a lock of Eugénie's hair. She looked at his face—sunlight illuminating little veins ghosting through diaphanous skin—and recognized Saraphine's eyes imprisoned inside Orance's face. Monsieur Lafleur said something but she couldn't find a way to listen, noticing instead that the baby's forehead was wet.

She looked up at the people along the sidewalks. People with lives. Some alone. Some in pairs. People on their way to some place they had to be. Others being where they should, doing what they did.

She lifted the baby to her cheek, the smell of new life overcoming the city's stench. She saw a butcher shop, a sign in the window listing pork chop prices, three cents higher than what she remembered. Was this merchant gouging his clients? Routine, banal reflections she used to have. She took a deep breath and held it till she could no more and realized Arthur wasn't only Orance's son. Arthur was Saraphine's soul.

"Jus' take us to the Boarding House. We're not going to *La Crèche*."

"That's where Madame Beauchamp told me to bring you … that's where we're going," Monsieur Lafleur said, looking forward, his left elbow propped up on his knee.

"No, please, I need to speak with Madame Déry," Eugénie said, reaching up and pulling at Monsieur Lafleur's coat tails.

He glanced back and said nothing then jiggled the reigns and guided his horse north along Drummond Street. He had acquiesced. A hint of a smile hooked itself onto Eugénie's lips. She lifted her head, the sun's warmth seeming to confirm her decision.

Downstairs, in the same huge Chesterfield she and Saraphine had sat in months ago, she waited while Arthur slept on her knees. Gurgling sounds and baby yelps soon drew girls out from every corner of the place. They sat on either side of Eugénie, made silly faces, held his baby hands, and stroked his baby hair.

"I told her you're here, but I don't know when she's gonna come down," Monsieur Lafleur said, before heading back to his spot next to the staircase. Hours she waited, afternoon sun pouring into the room, July's heat and humidity making the baby feel like a hot kettle on her lap. Some of the girls brought Eugénie pieces of bread from the kitchen but nothing at the Boarding House was fit to accommodate a three-week-old baby. Arthur cried. Shrieked. Wailed.

"OK, follow me," Madame Déry said, stopping midway down the long stairway, hands on the railing and leaning forward as she spoke.

Eugénie gathered the baby and sprang from the Chesterfield, hurrying to keep up with Madame Déry on her way to the kitchen.

"I'm sure one of the girls here should be able to feed this little fellow," Madame Déry said, looking down at Arthur's red face, the crying making it difficult for Eugénie to hear Anna's words.

"There she is, our saviour," Madame Déry said at the sight of a woman, barefoot, with long blonde braids hanging off her shoulders.

"Ever think you'd be able to afford a wet nurse?" Madame Déry asked, gently poking Arthur's wrinkled chin.

Eugénie, unsure as to what Madame Déry meant, clumsily jounced Arthur hoping to squelch the howls jetting from his tiny lungs.

The young woman with braids reached out and smiled at

Eugénie.

"Go ahead. Let her deal with the child. He'll be fed and taken care of while we have a chat," Madame Déry said, stroking the young lady's back.

Smiling, frowning, Eugénie looked at Anna, handed over the screaming infant, and watched the woman leave the kitchen on her way upstairs.

"Don't worry. Don't. Everything's fine. No one's stealing your baby."

"He's not my baby," Eugénie replied, looking out into the foyer, at the woman going up the stairs with Arthur in her arms.

"Of course … right. He's Saraphine's young man."

-8-

"I told you, don't worry. The baby's being well taken care of," Madame Déry said, smoothing her dress along the back of her legs and plopping herself into the parlour's monster sized Chesterfield. "Come, join me. Besides, you haven't even told me the boy's name," she added, patting at the space next to her though Eugénie set herself tightly against the sofa's arm; Madame Déry sliding all the way across nestling herself hip-to-hip against her.

"Arthur. His name's Arthur," Eugénie said, reminding herself of why she had asked Monsieur Lafleur to bring her back to this place. Then, in an instant, images rushed her mind; a hundred thoughts bursting at once: Griffintown, the cold, the filth, the bugs, the smells … the johns, Saraphine lying, dying on the dirt. Breathtaking anxiety sprung Eugénie to her feet and sent her hovering over Madame Déry. Bent at the waist, she looked deeply into the madam's eyes, wet her lips and, just as she was about to speak …

"You want one of these?" She asked, pulling a Panatela from a cigar box on the side table.

Lips parted, looking down at the tiny, long cigar pointed

at her, she said, "Yeah, why not?"

Madame Déry struck a match and lit Eugénie's cigar before lighting hers. Immersed in a cloud of white smoke and speaking loudly in order to overtake the sound of Eugénie's coughing, Anna said, "I just got back from Paris. I know it may seem as though I'm always either there or coming back from there, but I've got to tell you. I went to *Le Théâtre de la Renaissance* to see Gismonda. I'm sure you've heard about that play. Right?"

Eugénie, eyes watering, seized by the seemingly pleasant chat Madame Déry intended to have, felt her mouth had cured like cement into the shape of the first syllable of the first word she had intended to blurt out.

"But that's not the best part. D'you know who was in the play? Who the star was?" She added, eyes aglow, surfing on the silence her question had provoked—having set the stage for the kill shot. "Sarah Bernhardt. The great Sarah Bernhardt. Isn't that something?" She asked, unmoved by the statue before her.

Eugénie's face thawed ... slowly. She stepped forward and dropped herself back on the couch.

"That's ... uh, that's wonderful, Madame Déry," she answered, vacuously, recognizing the strange game she was part of; the kind of need for counterfeit congeniality.

"She's a Jewess, you know," Madame Déry added, lifting her brow and nodding as if sharing a juicy tidbit with someone who cared.

"Saraphine's dead. Died giving birth to the baby. Arthur."

Madame Déry squinted and shook her head. "Arthur?" She asked.

"The baby your girl left with. The baby *I've* been left with ... Arthur."

"Oh, of course, dear, I'd forgotten his name. It's not that I—"

"I've been working in that Griffintown hellhole for months. You told us we'd go there to learn. Well, we've learned. *I* learned. Learned all that I'm gonna learn over there and I'm not going back," Eugénie said, her words coming out all at once.

Madame Déry dropped her back into the cushions and let her granite, business face resurface.

"Why're you telling me this?"

Eugénie looked up the staircase before turning back to look at Madame Déry.

"I want to work here and keep the baby. I know you've done it before. I know you've done that for some of the girls working here."

"And, who gave you that bit of information?" Madame Déry asked, pointing at the staircase while drawing small, imaginary circles in the air. Eugénie crossed her arms and slid all the way to the end of the Chesterfield. "Someone's been lying to you," she added.

"Older ladies who used to work here told me about it. Said you didn't mind so long as it didn't cost you anything … that girls worked together and made sure children would be—"

"That doesn't sound like something I'd do. Do you really think children would be properly taken care of in this type of institution? This type of atmosphere?" The Madam said, pushing herself off the couch to the sound of screeching castors.

Eugénie felt trapped, as if gulped by the Chesterfield, swallowed up by its downy digestive system.

"Saraphine's gone, Anna. I'm alone. I can't go back over there … to Griffintown … I can't. And I can't go to work in a factory 'cause I don't want to go to jail," Eugénie said, looking down at her hands smoothing the fabric covering her knees.

"I know your situation," Madame Déry said, reaching down and ringing the little brass bell that sat on the edge of the coffee table, its sound reminding Eugénie of the customers that had walked through the door of *her* butcher shop.

An older woman walked down the stairs, a crown of charcoal hair atop her head and wearing a long dress made of serge that hung off her shoulders. *That dress is too long*, Eugénie thought, noticing a ring of dust bunnies lining the garment's hem.

"This is Eugénie, the girl I told you about. Prepare the suite for her and bring the crib in there," Anna said. The woman bowed slightly and walked away.

Eugénie looked at Anna, at the grey-haired lady's back as she walked away, unsure how to react.

"Who was that? What was … are you going to—"

"You're right, dear. You've got nothing left to learn from Griffintown."

"Thank you, Anna, thank you. I'll work hard. You know I've got no problems doing ten a day, every day. You can rest assured that I'm—"

"You don't understand. You're out of the game. You're not going to be a night flower no more. Besides, based on what they've been telling me about you, you weren't very good at it. But that's got nothing to do with any of what I'm about to say. No, the thing is, what I appreciate about you … what I always appreciated about you, is your business sense. I needed someone who understands *this* business from the inside out. And now you do. The time you spent in Griffintown, that was your schooling. Now, you're going to run *this* place the way you used to run your butchery. That's been my plan for you ever since you showed up at my doorstep in the middle of the night.

"You know how often I'm gone. You know how much I like spending time in the old country. Now, with you here and running things, I'll be able to keep going over there and have peace of mind knowing everything here's gonna be fine. You're the new manager. The boss. And I'll show you how," Anna said, sitting back, fingers laced together.

A thousand springs tightly coiled inside Eugénie's body released all at once. The icy tension in her shoulders thawed and the low-grade pain that had settled in her body seemed to just slide off her bones. She stared at Anna, the Madam nodding gently as if confirming the plum offering. Eugénie reached into her lap pocket and twirled her finger around Adina's silk ribbon cravat; the one Saraphine's doll used to wear; the one Saraphine used to braid in her hair.

Chapter 17

-1-

February 1914

"Arthur. It's almost ten. Stop being a mule down there," Eugénie Desjardins, leaning forward suspended on the cellar door's knob, bellowed into the darkness while slapping her free hand at the door's rattling panel. "Anybody know when that boy got back last night?" She asked, walking back into the kitchen without looking at any of the five girls sitting around the long table.

"Was almost three when I got done with my last guy, I don't think he'd been back by then," Beatrice said, mouth full, hair dipping into the raspberry preserves she had spread on a slice of bread held close to her cheek.

"Him and his nocturnal runs; collecting dead horses all night with that man. Come to think of it, does Mr Platt ever do any work around here, anymore? Besides, that stink of his … don't know if he's ever taken a bath.

"Who?" A girl covered in a thick, woollen vest asked.

"That man. The one Arthur goes collecting dead horses with. Anyone know him? Mr Platt, he's called."

A couple of girls looked at each other then stared at their plates. Beatrice, bits of sweet preserves dangling off the tips of her hair, shrugged and pursed her lips.

"Cat got your tongues this morning?" Madame Desjardins asked, reaching into the cupboard for a bowl. "Besides, how long does it take you girls to eat breakfast? I've got to eat, too," she said, looking at those who remained focused on their plates. "Make way," she added, nudging herself amongst them to the squeaky sound of chair legs sliding along the floor.

"Somebody, make me breakfast. Bread, maple syrup and a cup of tea, if that's not too much to ask?" Madame Desjardins ordered—not unlike how Orance used to—banging the table hard when none of the ladies acquiesced. The outburst prompted three of the girls to scurry out of the kitchen leaving Beatrice and the girl in the woollen vest to prepare the order.

"You up boy?" Madame Desjardins hollered at the floor while kicking her heels on the linoleum, her flamenco moves rattling the china. "Time to get to work," she added. "Everybody's got to work, am I right?" She asked, pointing her stump at Beatrice, bent over in search of some cream somewhere in the back of the ice box. "Nobody gets a free ride 'round here, especially not a lazy, good-for-nothing boy who doesn't appreciate what's been done for him," she added, much, in the same way, her father-in-law used to describe his only surviving son.

"Sorry, I got to bed late last night. I was out till almost four with Mr Platt. We found two horses and—"

"Don't tell me about last night. Besides, did he pay you? A dime? A nickel? You've got work to do right here, Arthur. You've got to earn your keep. Nothing's free in this life," Madame Desjardins said, elbows on the table and rubbing her hands.

"I know. I'm sorry. It was so cold, we found two horses and had trouble pulling them all the way to—"

"Never mind all that. I expect you to hand out at least a hundred cards today. Those boys, those sailors, they're *your* business. *Our* business. An American navy ship jus' docked. That's a lot of business waiting for us, young man. If those boys don't come here, they'll go somewhere else and then … then you won't have a place to live. Can't you understand that?" She told her nephew, the boy leaning in the kitchen's doorway still in his clothes from the night before. "Have breakfast and get there in a hurry. You understand? Sometimes I can't figure out how you can be so unconcerned about having to earn a living. You're almost eleven now and I can't believe I still have to push and push to get you to do your work. Can't you see all of us work 'round here?" She added, looking sideways at the boy as she eyed the breakfast plate Beatrice had prepared for her.

"Yes, Aunt Eugénie," Arthur said, rubbing his hands along his trousers' back pockets.

"Come, come. Have breakfast, hurry and be on your way," she said, dunking a slice of bread into a puddle of syrup before picking at crumbs that had clung to her bottom lip. "And don't forget to put on your hat. You look so much like your mother, I'd swear people think you're a little girl, sometimes."

"Sit," Beatrice told Arthur as she pulled out one of the kitchen chairs.

"You should've seen those horses last night. They were frozen to the cobbles. Mr Platt had to cut off their legs and—"

"Enough," Madame Desjardins said, running her stump between her eyes. "For the love of goodness, I'm trying to have breakfast and you're telling us about sawing off a horse's legs … a horse who's frozen to the street. Really! Jus' eat and keep quiet," she added, reaching over and slapping at Arthur's knuckles. Arthur pinched his lips and looked at Beatrice from under his raised eyebrows.

"You cold, Helene?" He asked the girl in the woollen vest.

"I think I got the chills," Helene answered and winked at the boy. "And don't you worry, you don't look like a girl; you look like a fine gentleman."

-2-

"Hey, mister!" Arthur barked at men in uniform, ears squished down from the weight of his oversized Homburg hat. With a business card sticking out from the sleeve of his big overcoat, he ran from sailor to sailor, repeating the same question as he approached mariners and others keenly aware of what could be found at the Griffintown Warf, "Want some company?"

Pockets filled with cards, the Boarding House's address printed over a white background, he remembered every man's face and, ever careful not to waste any time, never approached the same person twice.

"Want company?" He jabbed one of his cards at a young man, red cheeks illuminating his white face, eyes bright and grey under his duck cap. "Tell 'em Arthur sent you," he shouted at the sailor who had reached down and taken the card from Arthur while the boy memorized the American's face.

The sailor absently slipped the card into his pocket while staring at the boy—Arthur's face—as if trying to decipher some code the young man had printed on his forehead. He leaned in, took an even closer look and stared into Arthur's eyes nestled just under the rim of his oversized Homburg.

"What's this?" He asked, looking sideways into Arthur's face—or whatever he could see under the boy's deep-seated hat.

"Company ... the address for *company*. Navy men get lonely, that's where you get company," Arthur answered, looking up at the young man and pointing at his pocket where he had stashed the card. "That's where to go to get some company," he added and walked away, scoping faces in the crowd and repeating his spiel.

"No, wait a minute, kid?" The sailor said, bumping into a large man while trying to keep up with Arthur's side winding moves amongst the swarm of people. "Kid? Where's this place? I haven't been around here in a while. Where's this place?" He asked, reaching down and grabbing a handful of Arthur's ample overcoat.

"There. Here," Arthur said, pointing at the address printed on the card. "On De Montigny Street."

"I don't live here anymore. How do I get there from here? Can't you gimme some directions?"

Squinting at the sun's rays bouncing off distant city windows, Arthur looked at the sailor and pointed north. "Up St. Lawrence … right behind the Empire Theatre," he said, jerking his arm free and moving backwards while still pointing north, a business card stuck between his fingers. "Want some company?" He reprised his pitch, turning away and melding into the crowd.

"Hey, kid, what's your name? You look familiar, what's your name?" The sailor asked, shifting from foot to foot as he struggled to maintain eye contact with the boy. Arthur, unused to this type of attention from potential clients, ran off.

"I dunno, he kinda grabbed me and he looked at me as if he knew me. And, he didn't seem to know what *company* meant," Arthur explained to some of his colleagues; three or four boys eating lunch on Island Warf, sitting on a log, legs dangling a few inches above the slushy ice and black water. "Then, he asked me what my name was. That's when I ran … got outta there."

"Was he slow?" One of the boys asked, looking into the bottom of his empty paper bag.

"Guess so, maybe. Dunno. Maybe some guys really dunno what *company* means. What it really means, you know," Arthur said, swallowing the last bit of his sandwich.

"'Cause I heard sometimes they recruit retards in the army," the boy added. "I suppose they do the same thing in the Navy."

"They? Whose *they*?" Arthur mumbled, fingering some chunk of meat stuck in his back teeth.

"Americans. The army. I hear they clean out asylums and all the healthy ones—you know, the ones who don't piss themselves and stuff—have to join the army," he answered, pointing south across the river.

"But this guy was a sailor. He wasn't in the army," Arthur said, bent over and looking past the boy sitting next to him in order to directly address his interlocutor.

"Dunno … just saying, I guess."

"Ahh, you don't know what you're talking about," Arthur said, crumpling his bag and throwing it into the water.

-3-

"Madame, a letter for you, the stamp's from France, from Madame Déry," Maureen said.

Madame Desjardins hurried down and rushed into the parlour. Six or seven girls materialized out of nowhere, all of them waiting to hear the highlights of Madame Déry's latest escapades through Paris and Florence.

"She bought columns, wooden columns that'll be installed right here, in the parlour," Madame Desjardins said, pointing the letter at the mantle. "She went to a place called 98 Boulevard Malesherbes. Says it's one of the most famous brothels in all of Paris. Says the most distinguished courtesans work there ... that it's legal ... they make fortunes 'cause it's legal to be a courtesan ... legal all over France. She's talking here about another brothel ... it's called Chabanais. Says it's where Edward the Seventh goes regularly ... and Toulouse Lautrec, and—"

"Who's too loose?" One of the Irish girls asked, unfazed by the giggling.

"Toulouse, that's his name. I'd tell you who he is, but I don't know. Must be somebody important if Madame Déry mentioned him. Point is, they're successful over there 'cause they work hard at making sure clients are happy with the service, that clients come back ... that they offer a classy type service," Madame Desjardins added, gazing up over the letter in front of her in order to look deeply into the eyes of every woman who had crowded in the parlour.

"I think one of the clients I was with last week—asked for me by name, by the way—might have been a colonel or an admiral, or a general, even. That's pretty good. Right?" One of the girls said, holding her hands along the sides of her head, swinging her hips back and forth and winking.

"All right, back to your rooms. It's almost ten and we'll be getting busy soon," Madame Desjardins ordered, waving her envelope and shooing everyone from the parlour.

The girls were filing up the stairs and she was folding the letter back into its envelope when the bell, the one she insisted be installed over the foyer's door, dinged loudly.

"Eugénie. Where's my Eugénie," a loud, deep voice beckoned.

"Over here," Madame Desjardins answered, arms extended as she beelined toward the man in the foyer. "So grand to see you again."

"Can't stay away. Seems I constantly need to surround myself with beauty. Besides, where else can I go to meet the finest women in all of Montreal?" The man said, grasping the right side of his hat with his left hand and bowing dramatically as Madame Desjardins smiled.

"Ah, Monsieur Dupuis. Always so happy to see you. Please, join me in the parlour. I'll have Marie serve you tea. Or would a spirit be more to your liking?"

"Neither. All I need is for you to call that lovely flower I was with last. Annette. She's here, isn't she?" The man asked, sitting on the edge of the Chesterfield, hands on his knees.

"Of course," she answered, turning to Monsieur Lafleur who, upon hearing the bell, had joined them in the parlour. "Won't you tell Annette a guest is here to see her?"

"So, I hope you're doing well my dear sir," Madame Desjardins asked, turning back to the man.

"Quite. In fact, I only have a short time to spend here. I'll be needed back at work before lunch."

"Busy?"

"These days, especially. As you might guess, the construction of the dam is taking up much of my time lately. Everyone seems in such a rush. I keep having to explain that these things take time. The point is to do it right, or else … well, the city will just get flooded over and over again, am I right?"

"I've seen your name in the paper quite often. You've become quite the celebrity. Maybe one day, we'll have the honour of calling you *Monsieur le Maire*."

"Well, I'm not sure I've got those kinds of ambitions to drive me, but you never know, I suppose."

"Ah, there she is," Madame Desjardins said, jumping off the couch and waving Annette in.

"I think you two have much to discuss," Madame Desjardins said, placing Annette's hand into the man's. "Please, don't let me waste any more of your time. Come, come, it's time for you two to get reacquainted," she added, leading them toward the staircase.

The doorbell chimed again. "I'll get it," Madame Desjardins said as she waved Monsieur Lafleur away. Smiling, she looked at the red-haired man in front of her and froze. The letter pinched between her fingers fell from her hand and her face—the happy, painted-on Madam mask—melted off. Unable to conceal herself, Eugénie—the real Eugénie—burst through and appeared right before the eyes of the motionless man standing in front of her, his hand glued to the knob, staring back at the woman he had once known.

"Eugénie?" He whispered; the man's forehead so creased, his hat nearly slid off the back of his head.

Eugénie stepped back, covered her mouth, wrapped her arm around her chest, and stared back at Sean.

Monsieur Lafleur stepped forward and reached behind the man and closed the door.

"That's all right. I'll take care of this gentleman," Eugénie told Monsieur Lafleur, eyes fixated on Sean as she cleared her throat before repeating the words she had spoken.

"Is Saraphine here?" Sean asked, straightening himself, pulling his hat off and pressing it to his chest.

"Why are you here?" The words slipped from Eugénie's mouth. Shaking her head, she added, "Sorry, how are you? You cut your hair short."

"I thought you were dead. We all thought you'd died in the fire."

"Come in. Come in," she said, walking backwards into the parlour, breathing deeply to keep from panting.

Sean didn't move.

"Where's Saraphine?" He asked again, finally stepping into the foyer and looking up the long staircase, his hand braced on the tall newel post.

"Sit down, I'll explain … explain everything," Eugénie assured him, surprised to hear herself sound the way she used to, unaware of the many girls leaning out from the kitchen doorway.

"Where's Saraphine?" Sean insisted and grasped Eugénie's shoulder.

"Everything all right?" Monsieur Lafleur asked, hands laced in front of himself as he moved in on Sean.

"No, no … fine. It's fine," Eugénie answered, looking at Sean and nodding as she waved Monsieur Lafleur away.

Walking backwards towards the Chesterfield, Eugénie invited Sean to sit and placed herself next to him, eyes round, struggling to fill her lungs to capacity while hoping to counter the sting of old familiar soars. Digging deeply into herself, she manufactured a smile, though her eyes were unable to join in. She offered her hand hoping Sean would take it.

"Answer me. Please, answer me," Sean pleaded, his fingernails scraping at his bowler hat sitting on his lap and looking at Eugénie's damaged hand that had remained suspended in front of him.

Paralyzed—the ticking from the mantel clock sounding like gunshots—Eugénie, absurdly self-conscious, ran her tongue along her teeth and felt her shoulders clenched up to her neck. "The fire took her. Took 'em both. I'm the only one who survived," she finally answered, looking down at Sean's fingers… at the grooves he had gauged into his hat.

"How did *you* get out? How come you didn't—"

"It's not important. I couldn't save either of 'em. All I could manage was to escape through the back and save myself," she said, looking up at Sean from under her brow, lips clamped, bracing for his reaction.

Sean's face relaxed a bit, the ruts in his pale skin smoothing over.

"But why? Why run away after the fire? You disappeared. I don't—"

"You've got to understand. I was afraid Monsieur Charpentier would blame me for having started it … afraid of his reaction. You know how he is, the kind of man he is. I wouldn't have been surprised if he'd gotten me arrested," Eugénie said, unsure how the words forming in her brain managed to escape from her mouth.

"Well, no need to worry about that anymore."

"People don't change. He'd be even madder now. He'd probably make sure I—"

"He's dead. Been dead for nearly two years," Sean said and crossed himself. "Consumption."

-4-

The bell rang again and a man walked in, business card in hand. He offered an open-mouth smile laced by filaments of drool hanging loosely between his upper and lower lips. "Some kid at the wharf told me this was the place where a guy could get acquainted with some company," the sailor said, flicking at his card.

"Just a minute." Monsieur Lafleur waved at the man before turning to face Madame Desjardins. "Everything all right?" He asked again, leaning in.

"Could you wait, jus' a moment? I have to deal with a custo … with this man."

"It's okay. I have to get going, anyways," Sean said, pushing himself off the Chesterfield. "Maybe we'll get to talk a bit more about this another day," he added, moving briskly towards the door, brushing past Monsieur Lafleur and the young sailor.

"What about the shop? How are things going over there?"

Eugénie asked as she picked Madame Déry's letter off the foyer's floor.

Sean stopped abruptly in the doorway, squinted, and carefully placed his bowler hat on his head as if holding a pose.

"His wife owns it. Uriette's the boss now. I'm the butcher," he said, then ran down the seven stairs.

Eugénie ran back to the parlour, knelt on the couch and watched Sean disappear amongst people scurrying along snow-covered De Montigny Street, Madame Déry's letter pressed to her chest.

"Send in the gentleman," she said, absently gazing out the window. "Please, make yourself comfortable," she told the navy man, smoothing her dress, cheeks pulling up the corners of her mouth in order to reinitialize her familiar persona.

"I know jus' the lady who'd like to spend time with one of our valorous *matelots*," Madame Desjardins told the customer, looking back at him as she made her way to the kitchen, fanning herself with the letter.

"You two've heard enough? Satisfied your curiosity? Got enough to gossip about, huh?" She muttered at a couple of girls that had eavesdropped on her conversation with Sean. "You," she said, jabbing her stump at one of the newer girls— sixteen or seventeen years old—in a mint-green dress. "You've got a customer waiting for you in the parlour. Follow me."

She walked back into the parlour, hand in hand with the girl, elbows held high.

"I'd like you to meet Fiona. She's very interested in learning all about what it's like to sail the seven seas," Madame Desjardins said, the young man having sprung to attention at the sound of heels clicking in his direction. With her smile still pasted on, she watched the latest twenty-minute couple walk off to consummate their transaction. Now alone in the parlour, she drifted around, picked-up her stereoscope and placed it delicately on the mantel before looking up at the big painting hanging above the fireplace, and noticing a sheep next to a naked, plump, milky white skinned lady staring out into nothing; a thick, gilded frame making the subject seem more impressive. Then, not quite certain why, she wandered down to the cellar and into Arthur's room and pulled the boy's Eaton's catalogue from his dresser. Later, back upstairs, with the catalogue in one hand and Madame Déry's letter in the other, she sat sideways on the parlour's Chesterfield, the rouge on her cheeks washed out by the heatless afternoon sun and looked down at the return address printed neatly on the envelope.

"I'll be in my room if you need me," she turned back and told Monsieur Lafleur, climbing the stairs as a rush of cold air snuck in from under the front door and chilled her ankles. Midway up, she stopped, and leaning over the baluster, added, "Make sure to tell me if that red-headed gentleman comes back. His name's Mr Murphy. Sean Murphy."

She sat at the foot of her bed, hands on her lap, envelope pinched between her fingers. Drawing a long, deep breath, she faced the dresser, oblivious to her reflection; red cheeks on a white face framed in a fancy mirror. Letting the air out from her lungs, Eugenie gazed at the photo on the dresser, the one she had rescued from the fire, sisters standing shoulder-to-shoulder in front of the butcher shop where everything had gone so, so wrong. Leaning back, transfixed by the photo, she reached for the catalogue and pulled out a small tintype, the one she had kept in her locket, the one she had given to Saraphine's son. The photo - the only one testifying to the fact she had once been a child - of young girls wearing identical clothes, sharing a kind of handshake as if aware of what life had intended for them stiffened her neck and tightened her throat. Such a sight; two babies staring back at what remains at the end of a scarring journey.

Looking once more into the mirror, she pulled a handkerchief from her drawer and wiped the powder and rouge off her face, folding and refolding the cotton square; tears on her cheeks slowly dissolving the thick layer of makeup.

"That man's back ... in the parlour. I told him I'd see if you were available," Monsieur Lafleur said, gently wrapping at her door.

"Tell him to wait ... be right down," she said, snapping her head as if wanting to dislodge an insect off her nose. She reached into her armoire and foraged through her wardrobe. *The grey one*, she thought ... *the kind of dress respectable ladies wear*. The type of dress she'd have worn at the butcher shop.

Midway down the staircase she leaned over the banister and looked into the parlour hoping Sean would be alone; that she wouldn't have to deal with customers. She smiled at the empty space and smoothed the front of her dress. Sean sprang off the Chesterfield as soon as she walked in.

"I'm sorry for disturbing you again."

"Don't be silly," Eugénie said, smiling and looking like Eugénie. "Sit ... sit," she added, pointing at the couch. "Or, maybe you'd rather take a walk, or is it too cold?"

"No. I don't want to disturb you any more than I already have. I just wanted you to know I don't ... don't frequent places like these. You know, if this is what I think it is. I don't ... it's not the—"

"You don't have to explain anything to me. After all, *I'm* in a place like this. In fact, I'm the one who *runs* a place like this. So, there's no shame to be had. It's commerce. Nothing but commerce. Besides, for a lot of these girls, it's survival. Rest assured that I would never think less of you."

"No, you've got to understand. That's ... this ... it's not why I was here," Sean said, pointing his bowler at Eugénie, his other hand formed into a fist. "You know how I feel about whores ... what I think of men who engage with those types of ... you know."

Eugénie brought her chin to her chest and looked up at Sean from under her brow.

"You don't have to explain a thing to me. Everyone here's treated with respect. In fact, it so happens that some of the city's most powerful men frequent this establishment on a regular basis. Discretion is the name of our game. You don't have to worry about that."

"No," he whispered at the top of his lungs. "That's the whole point. I actually thought this *was* a boarding house. I thought I could get a room here. I was looking to find … to find something for a family member. My uncle's coming to visit and I wanted to find a place for him to stay. That's what I wanted to tell you. I don't frequent whores. You know I don't. I wasn't here to be with a whore, please know that," he added, eyes reddening, sweat pouring down his temples as he stared at Eugénie's forehead.

"That's fine. I understand. A perfectly normal mistake that anyone could have made," she said, chin up and lips pinched.

"I apologize. I don't mean to be rude or . . ." Sean said, stepping sideways and walking past Eugénie. "But I've got to ask," he interrupted himself and turned to face her, "Can you assure me that Saraphine's not in some room up there … whoring?" He asked, hands on his hips and pointing his nose up at the staircase.

"Saraphine's dead. Died in the fire. I'm not holding anyone hostage, especially not my own sister," she answered, stepping forward and poking the nub of her finger into his chest. "While we're being honest, let me add this. Your secret's safe with me. Not a soul will know about your little trip to the Boarding House. We'll both bring each other's secret to the grave. Does that bit of honesty reassure you?" She added, looking up into his eyes.

Sean stepped back and out of the parlour, the bell ringing loudly as he pulled the door open.

"Orance was right about you. You're not the kind of woman any man should marry. He told me all about how he couldn't control you. How you made friends with a Madam. To think that you nearly fooled me," he said, then spat on the foyer's floor, stuffed his hat on his head and left.

Monsieur Lafleur dashed into the room. "I'm sorry, I was

in the back. Everything all right here?"

Madame Desjardins looked past Monsieur Lafleur and nodded. Slowly. Nearly imperceptibly.

"Everything's fine. Jus' someone who wanted me to know he wasn't the type to be a client of ours," she said, patting Monsieur Lafleur's shoulder as she walked by him on her way back upstairs.

-5-

"You know what happened today, down at the Warf?" Arthur asked his aunt who stood at the kitchen counter.

"What?" Eugénie replied, reaching into a jar of pickled eggs.

"A man—he took one of my cards—wanted to know my name," Arthur said, a spoonful of beans in hand, many of which fell overboard, victims of the boy's enthusiasm.

"Your name ... what?" Eugénie asked, absentmindedly crushing her egg with a fork while paying little attention to the boy—or any of the girls sitting at the table.

"Yeah, my name. He said I reminded him of someone."

"Man? What man?" Eugénie asked, looking down at Arthur, the details of the boy's anecdote failing to break through the fog that had rolled into her mind.

"That's just it, I dunno. A sailor, I guess. American, I know that. He took a card and ... that's another thing, he didn't know what *company* meant. He kept asking me questions and then he grabbed me and asked where this place was, and what my name was. That's when I ran," Arthur said. The look on his aunt's face suggesting she wasn't fully dialled into his story.

"Uh ... strange," she said, gazing at her plate and leaning back on the Hoosier's enamelled counter, her recent encounter with Sean still buzzing around her mind.

"There's a man outside standing there freezing his ass off, too embarrassed to come in, I guess," a girl said and dropped her overloaded paper bag onto the kitchen table, snowflakes clinging to life on the lapels of her coat.

"Does he have red hair by any chance?" Madame Desjardins asked, spreading her egg onto a piece of bread she had sliced off a crusty loaf.

"Dunno. Maybe? Had a hat on, one of those cute sailor hats."

"American?" Arthur asked.

"How would I know? He had a sailor's suit on. They make men look like little boys, those suits do. I love how they—"

"D'you talk to him? Did he mention me?" Arthur asked, rushing to stand next to his aunt.

"You? Why you? Why would he mention you?"

Arthur ran to the parlour where two men sat on the Chesterfield, smoking.

"Arthur," Madame Desjardins grumbled through her teeth, forever intent on maintaining a sophisticated allure in front of patrons. "Come, come now. Follow me," she instructed the boy, ushering him out of the parlour, though he tugged at her arm and pointed at the window; his body contorted as he tried to look back.

"That's him ... the man who asked my name. It's him, right outside," Arthur said in a panic, his aunt barely able to maintain her grip on his elbow en route back to the kitchen.

"Please excuse us, gentlemen. Monsieur Lafleur here will see to it that your ladies meet with you soon," she told the cigar-puffing men buried into the couch. "Monsieur Lafleur, would you please make sure these men are comfortable," she aimed her words down the hallway, assuming the man would be in his usual spot down the long, dark corridor. "All of you will be well taken care of," she added, looking back in the parlour, curtsying and smiling her best Madam smile.

"But it's him, he's looking for me. That's why he's out there. He's waiting to get me," Arthur cried, looking up at his Aunt Eugénie as she plunked him down on a chair.

"There's a man looking for you? Out there?" One of the

girls asked.

"Everything OK? Where's Monsieur Lafleur?" Another girl asked.

"This one here's the problem," Madame Desjardins said, arms crossed and glaring down at her nephew. "What's going on here? You know who that man is?" She asked.

"He's the man I was talking about. The one who thought I looked like someone. The one who didn't know what—"

"Did he threaten you, hit you or something?" Madame Desjardins asked, pointing her stump at the front door ... at the man beyond it on the sidewalk.

"No, but he grabbed me by the shoulder, that's when I ran," Arthur repeated, moon-eyed, his neck gobbled up into his shoulders.

Madame Desjardins slid Arthur's chair along the floor and pinned him tightly against the kitchen table. She looked up at the girls and saw nothing but puzzled faces staring back at her.

"OK ... everybody, calm down. I'm gonna have Monsieur Lafleur deal with this fellow, that sailor out there," Madame Desjardins said, elbows swinging as she dashed out the kitchen. "And you make sure and stay exactly where you are. Don't you dare get off that chair," she instructed Arthur before heading into the parlour.

"Might have a bit of a problem out there," Madame Desjardins told Monsieur Lafleur. "See that man? The one in the sailor suit?" She asked, pushing aside the sheer curtains stretched tautly along brass rods hanging over the door's red stained-glass window. "Sounds like something happened down at the dock today, something Arthur's talking about. Could you go and ask him what he wants ... what he's doing out there?"

Chapter 18

Madame Desjardins briskly bunched the curtains to one side till the arching rod nearly broke. Looking out through colourful glass, she watched Monsieur Lafleur step off the porch, the big man trying hard to keep his leather soles from slipping out from under him. Two men, one of them wearing a long beaver coat and a huge furry hat, climbed the stairs past Monsieur Lafleur as he neared the stoop.

"Come, come," Madame Desjardins said, waving them in. She took a firm hold of the man's heavy coat while he unbuttoned it. "Looks like it's gotten even colder out there," she said. The men rubbed their hands, walked past her and looked into the big parlour, eyes sparkling as they surveyed the elaborate decor. "*Bienvenue*. Sit, sit … make yourselves comfortable. Someone will be in soon and see to it you're well taken care of," she added, heading to the kitchen, moving briskly and looking back at the increasingly packed room.

"All of you, out. I've got six patrons sitting out there waiting to spend their money," she said, thumb pointing back over her shoulder. "Time to get your cards punched," she added, leaning along the doorway as she mimicked punching an invisible card.

"Beautiful ladies will be joining you soon. Please be patient," Madame Desjardins told the men, looking sideways at them and smiling broadly as she walked past on her way back to the foyer.

Her forehead to the glass, she spied on the two men on the sidewalk, her view distorted from the build-up of condensation. She tried to refine her focus by shifting from side to side, but all she saw were red and yellow shadows. Frustrated, she cracked the door open, the cuff of her sleeve flapping from the cold air whooshing in. Eyes trained on the sailor, nose crinkled, she watched Monsieur Lafleur and the mysterious American, moonlight bouncing off the snow-covered street doing little to illuminate the scene.

Eugénie's clenched lips parted and her face relaxed when some of the words exchanged on the sidewalk percolated up through the door's tiny opening. She pulled her face from the doorway feeling as though her lungs had deflated ... as though she couldn't inhale. Looking back into the parlour she saw nothing but a cigar burning itself out in one of the floor ashtrays. She paused, drew a deep breath, walked out onto the porch, and looked directly at the American sailor.

"I didn't want to hurt the boy. All I said is that he looked like someone I knew. He just seemed really familiar to me, that's all. I wanted to know if *he* was acquainted with some-one ... someone *I* know ... used to know. I swear. That's all I wanted to do," Eugénie heard the sailor tell Monsieur La-fleur, the boy's hands stuffed in his trousers' pockets, fists clenched, each finger warming its neighbour.

"What's going on, Monsieur Lafleur? Should I be calling the cops?" Madame Desjardins asked, placidly, arms laced over her chest and shrouded by her own breath.

The sound of Eugénie's voice paralyzed the navy man. He looked up at her, brow furrowed, his head canted like a puzzled dog. He stepped back to keep from falling off the curb, awkwardly dunking his foot into the snow, his gaze fixed on the woman up on the porch. Squinting, he reached up to keep his hat from taking off when a gust of wind blew in sideways from down the street. Squinting harder still, he gulped cold air through his mouth.

"Eugénie?" He asked, his question sounding more like a wish. "Is that you? Is it y-you?" He repeated, unaware of Monsieur Lafleur's hand against his chest.

Eugénie's tightly knotted arms dropped limply to her sides. Her head moved forward and her slitted eyes turned to velvet.

"Ephrem," she mouthed, grabbing onto the porch's railing just before her knees loosened.

Monsieur Lafleur, gauging his next move, swivelled his head back and forth. "You know this gentleman?" He asked, unfamiliar with the look on his boss's face.

"He's my … my—"

"We're cousins," Ephrem said, looking up and wiping his nose with the back of his sleeve.

"It's okay, I'll take care of this," she told Monsieur Lafleur, the man's hand still pressed on the sailor's chest.

"We heard that … we figured that … a-after the letters stopped coming… we received word from your mother-in-law that there h-had been a fire. That all of you h-had—"

"I made it out," Eugénie said as she moved down the steps. She placed her hand up on his shoulder and took in her grown-up cousin. He put his arms around her. Instantly, she felt like the person she used to be, the person she thought had disappeared.

"She didn't. I was the only one who made it out," she said, tears crystallizing on Ephrem's lapel; white powder from her face printing a ghostly shadow on his navy-blue paletot.

They stood there for a few moments, locked together until the wind made Eugénie tremble.

"So, you're going out into the street to get your business now!" Screamed Mrs Dougherty, her bandaged head poking out her window, a bloody stain ghosting through the gauze. "What's wrong, none of your whores willing to go out in the cold?" She added, her toothless smile making her mouth seem like a black hole.

"Who's she?" Ephrem asked, looking back at the woman.

"Never mind her, she's a poor, deranged person," Eugénie said.

"A-anyway, you better get back inside, you'll get s-sick out here in the cold wearing nothing but a dress," Ephrem said, suddenly aware of his cousin's attire.

Eugénie smiled sadly, aware of Ephrem's attempt at concealing the shock of what had become of her; to swallow the dozens of questions knocking around in his mind. "Your stutter's almost completely gone. You're like a new person," she said, recognizing the man Ephrem had become.

"It's still there. I learned how to string words together in a different way … learned it from a doctor down in Burlington. He gave me a book about it," Ephrem said, proud to have impressed his cousin.

"We always knew you'd do it."

"It's not all gone. I still hesitate, or you know, stutter a bit sometimes when I'm really nervous. You know, like now. But I'm g-getting better and better a-all the time," he said, smiling broadly.

"Come in, we'll talk some more. I've got so much to tell you about everything that's happened," she said, looking at Ephrem whose eyes remained locked on the Boarding House sign. Those big, red letters. The scarlet window pane.

"You s-sure it's all r-right?" He asked, planted at the base of the stairs.

"No, it's fine. Come in. You'll wait for me in my office," she said, pulling Ephrem up the stairs.

"This sure is a b-beautiful place," he said, walking through the empty parlour.

"Come on up, my office's upstairs," she said, leaning on the newel post—suddenly very aware of the muffled thuds and other sounds oozing from the ceiling and walls. "You'll take care of things for a little while, won't you?" She told Monsieur Lafleur, who nodded, heading back to his usual spot behind the staircase, his profile cutting through the dimly lit corridor.

They walked up the stairs, hugging the wall as a man scurried past them.

"Isn't this place the tops," the man said, slapping Ephrem's back as he barrelled past.

Ephrem watched Monsieur Lafleur greet the man at the foot of the steps, the two of them disappearing into the corridor to continue their discussion. Ephrem looked at his cousin, straining to maintain the frozen smile on his face, to contain the tremors sneaking up his cheeks. Eugénie winked and nodded.

-2-

Ephrem had plopped himself into a plush, club chair—arms uncomfortably perched atop overstuffed and oversized arm-rests—unconsciously rubbing at the fabric while surveying the room's woodwork and the ceiling's fancy plaster rosette. Eugénie had often fallen asleep in that very spot, face squeezed in the crook of large cushions, eyelids drooping till her brain checked out. It was her favourite chair, and she suffered at the sight of Ephrem looking so uncomfortable, so ... upset.

Having taken stock of the surroundings—creaking mat-tresses and counterfeited cries of ecstasy swirling all around—he managed to lock his gaze onto his cousin's fore-head and nose. Taking in short, unsatisfying breaths, he struggled to contain the look of surprise he assumed was tat-tooed all over his face. Delighted at the sight of his beloved Eugénie—a cousin he believed had died a horrible death—he nevertheless struggled to repress his disappointment; cousins reunited, one a sailor, the other a whore.

"I think I could get in trouble just by being here ... talking to you ... m-my C.O. doesn't allow for these types of ... of ..." Ephrem said, scratching his cheek while noticing some feathery thing hanging off the wall.

"Look at me, Ephrem ... all this," she said, whirling her arms in the air, "it's jus' commerce. The butchery, any store, it's all the same ... jus' commerce. Staying alive is what I'm doing," she defended then slumped back on the wooden slats of her office chair.

"Was Saraphine? Did Saraphine ever? Did s-she—"

"She disappeared in the fire long before I had to get involved with any of this. She worked with me at the butcher shop, like we all did before you left. You've got to believe me when I tell you that. And you've got to believe me that I had nothing to do with it ... the fire I mean. I knew from the moment I ran out of that building that I'd be a suspect. The only suspect. That people would think I had something to do with it. You've got to believe me. You, of all people, you've got to believe me," Eugénie said, stabbing her stump at the desktop.

"A suspect of what?" Ephrem asked, angling forward as if held back by the cavernous chair. "What h-happened to your finger? D'you get hurt at the butchery?"

Eugénie rolled her fingers into balls and dropped her elbows on the desktop.

"I got out ... out of the fire. I survived. Orance didn't. Saraphine didn't. I knew Monsieur Charpentier would be looking for someone to blame for all that ... for the death of his son, for burning down his building. So, I figured it wouldn't be long before *I* was going to be the one he'd blame for it. So, I took off ... ran. Panicked and ran. I had to. I had no other—"

"To d-do this?" He interrupted, pointing his nose at the hallway outside the office door.

Eugénie moved forward on her chair, looked at her cousin, reached down, and pulled a towel from a drawer. She rubbed the rouge and powder off her face, her movements slow and deliberate. With nothing but the white, winter flesh of her cheeks glowing, she dropped the towel back into her desk and said, "To survive. To do whatever it takes to eat. To have a place to sleep. To not be outside all the time. Can you understand that? Can you imagine what it's like to try and make it, out there, with no one ... nothing to support you? With no home to go back to at the end of the day?" She added, lifting her eyebrows at the window.

Ephrem shook his head slowly then looked down at his fidgeting fingers.

"How's Aunt Blanche doing? She still living with her brother?" Eugénie asked, hoping to steer the discussion away from her career.

Ephrem smiled a smile that Eugénie recognized. "She hates that I'm in the Navy. She's married now to a really n-nice guy. He came from Canada, too. Opened up a hardware store down there. Sells all kinds of stuff, to f-farmers mostly," he said, looking up at his cousin, his broadening smile smoothing the lines on his forehead. "What about your finger? What happened?"

"It got caught in one of Orance's slicers. Remember how dangerous those were? You should've seen the mess, blood all over the place ... all over Orance," she lied and smiled back at Ephrem. "I'm glad to hear that Aunt Blanche is doing well. Did she ever—"

"What about the boy?" Ephrem interrupted, no longer fascinated by his cuticles.

"The boy?" Eugénie asked, stalling in order to concoct a plausible answer.

"Yeah, the boy. He's why I came here. The boy that gave me this card," he said, pulling the business card from his breast pocket and tossing it on the desktop. "He looks just like her ... Saraphine. For a minute there, I thought it was her I was looking at. I couldn't believe it. That's why I was trying to get a hold of h-him. To speak to him, ask him who his mother was ... or something."

Eugénie grabbed her worn armrests, craned her neck forward and looked deeply into her cousin's eyes.

"That boy's your great cousin," she said, lips quivering. "Saraphine got involved with a man who wasn't . . ." she paused and looked at the ceiling, "wasn't . . ."

"What? Wasn't what? What happened?" Ephrem asked, wiggling himself to the edge of the overstuffed chair.

"Wasn't the type of man any woman should be involved with," she said, still looking up, lips parted and gazing at the light fixture hanging from an ornate plaster medallion. "Not a gentleman. Not even a good man. Not a good person at all, as it turned out," she added, peeking down at Ephrem, her eyes soaked.

"Was she married to this m-man?"

"She wasn't ... jus' something that happened," she said, looking down into the still-opened drawer. "It's something that happened *to* her ... you understand?" She added, unable—unwilling—to look into her cousin's eyes.

"Who is he? What's his name?" He asked, rubbing his crew cut; stiff hairs pushed against the grain.

"He's gone. Took off. None of all that matters anymore, anyway. Fact is, I'm taking care of the boy, and that's that. Don't blame Saraphine for any of what happened. It was all out of her control. All of it. She was a victim, and no one would've blamed her if she'd jus' given that boy away to the nuns. But she didn't. She did what she thought was the right thing ... like she always tried to do," she said, looking for comfort in Ephrem's eyes, a nod of her head causing a tear to spill onto the oak.

Ephrem walked to the window. "Amazing how he looks just like her, though. I mean, if Saraphine had been a boy, that's exactly what she'd have l-looked like. His eyes, especially, exactly the way I remember her. Isn't that strange?" He said, looking down at the snow-covered sill.

"Maybe. But when I look at that boy all *I* see is his father. I know you probably think it's crazy, but that boy, to me, doesn't look anything like his mother. It's the man in him that *I* see and, well, it's jus' always been hard for me to see anything *but* the man. The man that did ... did all that to my sister," she said, the recollections making tiny muscles in her temples twitch.

Ephrem slapped at his leg and turned to face his cousin.

"So, maybe I could meet him? Is he here? He is, after all, a cousin of mine," he said, pointing his cap at the door.

"He's got a job ... does it at night. Goes out and collects, uh ... he works for a kind of cleaning crew on some nights.

It's something that he likes to do and tonight's one of those nights. He'll be gone collecting till they're pretty sure nothing's left to be found," she said, rummaging through a drawer.

"That boy has a night job? Aren't you worried about what might happen?"

"He's not alone. He does it with a man that does other odd jobs for us. Don't worry, he's well taken care of."

"So, maybe I can meet him later. We're in port here till Wednesday?"

Eugénie pulled a photograph from the drawer and pushed herself away from the desk.

"That's Saraphine and me, in front of the shop. Didn't she look good, there? That was her favourite dress ... wore it all the time. Remember? She loved that dress," she said, handing Ephrem the photo.

Ephrem looked at the small tintype squinting as he brought it close to his face.

"You two were such a pair. All three of us were s-so close. All the time," he said, looking up at his cousin and handing back the photo.

-3-

Sean stood leaning on a post near a neighbour's front yard, arms crossed, glaring at the sign hanging off the Boarding House's porch. For nearly two hours—the wind burning his ears until they glowed—he spied from the shadows, watching the many men walk up and down those seven steps. He'd seen the sailor on the sidewalk talking with Monsieur Lafleur; seen Eugénie come out and invite him in. Never taking his eyes off the place, he climbed a neighbour's winding staircase across from the infamous whorehouse to look into the parlour, to see if any men remained waiting their turn.

Oblivious, he set off to cross the street and nearly collided with a large sleigh; bells strung around the horses' necks having failed to rouse his attention. He climbed the Boarding House's steps, slinking along the ends of the treads, the undisturbed snow underfoot dampening the sound of his boots. He cracked the door open, slid his hand up the door frame and wrapped his fingers around the bell. Sidling along the foyer's wall, he looked past the long staircase and down the hallway where Monsieur Lafleur usually sat. As always, the tall man was there, in his chair, the back of his head resting on the wall, arms crossed, eyes nearly closed.

-4-

Eugénie's spine stiffened at the sound of Rose screaming and hollering. Words, nonsensical, random, filled every nook of the place and seemed to rattle walls. Ephrem, shocked by the commotion, reached for the door and collided with his cousin as they burst out of the office—Eugénie unaware the tintype had remained clenched in her fist.

"Everything's fine, jus' fine. Everyone, please, don't mind the disturbance. One of my ladies saw a spider, that's all. Everything's under control," The Madam yelled at the doors; thudding headboards and springy bedframes having gone silent. She ran down the hallway, Ephrem tracking closely behind her. "Stop, stop," she waved back at him, shaking her head, and pausing as she reached the staircase. She looked down and bent over the baluster, her empty hand holding on to the railing.

"Monsieur Lafleur. Psst … Monsieur Lafleur," she murmured, the cool, hushed silence chilling the blood that had drained from her brain. She turned to Ephrem but saw nothing but a grown-up boy in a sailor suit.

"Monsieur Lafleur," she whispered louder. "Rose. What's going on?" She asked, stepping down a few more steps and leaning forward, her hand sticking out as if blind. She reached the bottom step, looked around and saw no one. Turning to face the corridor along the staircase she saw Rose, one of the new girls, standing where Monsieur Lafleur usually sat, her pallid face breaking through the darkened hallway.

"You the one who screamed like that?" Madame Desjardins asked, wiping sweat off her forehead.

Rose turned away, bent over and vomited all over her shoes. Chunks of sausage that had been fried just right clung to the high baseboard and wallpaper as the intensity of her supper's dramatic exit intensified.

"What's wrong?" Madame Desjardins asked as she hopped back instinctively at the sight of the effluent, the heels of her Edwardian Oxford shoes landing on Ephrem's toes. Rose, her brow knotted into a bunch, looked back at Madame Desjardins, ran her sleeve along her mouth and scurried to the kitchen. Looking down, Eugénie froze and the tintype fell from her hand. In an instant, blood that had flooded her head violently reversed course and bleached her complexion beyond what any face powder had ever managed to achieve. Timidly, she took a few steps forward. Hunched over, arms around her belly, she looked down the hallway at what she hoped was an illusion; some kind of visual concoction imagined by the darkness.

It was no concoction. What she saw was real. Monsieur Lafleur. On the floor. Seeming to float on a puddle of blood. She turned to Ephrem; arms stretched out on either side of her body.

"Go lock the front door," she ordered, looking back at what used to be the Boarding House's bouncer and bodyguard.

Slowly, tentatively, she walked into the faintly lit hallway, head suspended off her neck, hands on her thighs to keep from falling as she inched toward the cadaver. The man was unrecognizable. His face was mangled, clobbered. Blood oozed from his hairline to his chin. She couldn't make out his eyes, his nose. His face had been pummeled. For a while, Eugénie thought she'd react as Rose had done, but the fear of suffering Monsieur Lafleur's fate shot a massive dose of adrenaline through her body and roused her senses.

"Go lock the front door!" She told Ephrem, his cap held over his mouth as he looked down at the grizzly remains.

"Madame Desjardins … what're we gonna do? What's happening?" Rose's terrified voice came whining from the kitchen. "I think that was Monsieur Lafleur on the floor," she added, wiping tears from her chin.

"Did you call the pol—?"

"They said they're on their way."

"All of you, get out. Put on whatever you can find and wait outside. I'll go upstairs and tell everyone to get out," Eugénie said, walking backwards and recoiling when she bumped into Ephrem.

"S-sorry," he said, watching Eugénie as she ran up the stairs.

"Get out—NOW!" Eugénie yelled at the girls who had remained huddled in the kitchen.

-5-

Upstairs, Eugénie saw nothing but frightened faces staring back at her, girls standing in the hallway, some wrapped in bed sheets, others covered in nothing but goose-pimpled skin. Men—most assuming a raid was underway—hurriedly put their clothes back on. One of the girls—her white knuckles clinging to the doorframe—was pushed out into the hallway when a *patron* barrelled out; heels pounding, his black tie and collar in hand.

"I'll be wanting my money back," he said unapologetically, as he ran into Madame Desjardins as he exited.

"There's been a bit of an incident. We'll need all of you to leave. Please, leave immediately," Eugénie shouted down the corridor, looking back at the man who had body-checked the air from her lungs. Girls ran back into their rooms to gather clothes and shoes. A few remaining men, disappointed and irate, soon burst out, sliding arms into jackets and stuffing hats onto their heads—all of them looking at their feet as they hurried downstairs. Madame Desjardins climbed to the third floor, going up as most of the remaining patrons descended. "Everyone, leave. Leave now. There's been an incident," she repeated. Noticing two of the doors had remained closed, she added, "The police are on their way. They'll be here in—"

Doors flew open. A man, hairy legs dangling down from his fur coat, walked out, clothing in hand, while attempting to button up his pileous parka.

Confident she had cleared both floors, Eugénie hurried downstairs yelling and clapping at the four remaining men fumbling about in the parlour; one of them balancing on one leg as he laboured to pull his galoshes over his shoes while another, sliding his arm down the sleeve of his shirt, looked out the window and watched for cops. Girls stood on the porch, a couple of them wearing nothing but the bed linens they had laid in. They huddled together, feet stomping at the boards, fighting back against the night's freeze.

"Whoever did this is gone. There's no one on the second or third floors. I checked," Madame Desjardins reassured, her face squeezed through the partly opened front door.

"Whoever did what?" One of the girls asked. "Why are we out here?"

"Monsieur Lafleur's dead," Rose announced, holding on to herself and shivering.

"You sure … what happened? Maybe he's just sick or something."

"His whole face's gone. He's been beaten to death. I saw him. His whole face … nothing but blood," Rose answered, the thought of it buckling her knees.

"What about downstairs? Did anyone check on Arthur? Is he all right?" Another one of the girls asked.

"He's gone hunting for his dead horses, won't be back for hours," Madame Desjardins replied, looking back into the foyer.

"Not so sure 'bout that. I saw him not that long ago. I think he's still downstairs," a girl wrapped in a toga of sheets, replied.

Eugénie walked back into the parlour where Ephrem stood next to the body.

"Who's Arthur?" Asked Ephrem.

-6-

"Stay here, I'm going downstairs," Eugénie replied, pushing Monsieur Lafleur's leg out of her way with the tip of her shoe in order to open the cellar door.

Ephrem took hold of his cousin's shoulders as she pulled the door open.

"Who's Arthur? Does he work for you?"

Eugénie took a deep breath and immediately smelled coal dust blowing up from the cellar. Someone had stoked the furnace. Someone *was* downstairs. "He's the boy that led you here. Saraphine's boy. I thought he was out working tonight, but it looks like he might be downstairs in his room," she answered, looking down into obscurity.

"Arthur. Arthur, *es-tu là, garçon?*" Eugénie called as she stepped onto the cellar's cement floor. Sliding her fingers along one of the clotheslines, she felt her way down the usual route leading to the light bulb. Hanging garments, over-dried and hard, cast weird shadows once she screwed the bulb tightly in its socket; the energized filaments humming softly as they came to life. The door to Arthur's little room was closed, no light slipping out from around the frame. The fire in the furnace seemed to have lost momentum; nothing but the red glow of a few remaining embers coming through the calcined window.

"Arthur, you in there?" Eugénie asked, thumping the side of her fist at his door.

Arthur jumped; his cheek covered in drool.

"*Oui* … I'm up, hold on," he replied, though half-asleep and wiping the mess off his cheek. Pulling up on his long johns, he opened the door, looked up at his aunt and stepped back, squinting at the sight of a man's dark profile standing behind his aunt.

Ephrem stepped forward and looked at the boy's dimly lit face, the darkness emphasizing the features that had reminded him of Saraphine.

"We met earlier, at the dock. M-my name is E-Ephrem" he said and held out his hand.

"Goodness God," Eugénie jumped and clutched at her chest, unaware that Ephrem had followed her downstairs.

"You're the guy who wanted to know my name?"

"Yeah. You looked s-so much like someone I knew … I j-just had to—"

"That's it for the reunion, we need to get out of here," Eugénie said, pushing the boy back into his room. "Put some-thing on—your big coat—we've got to get outside and wait for the cops."

Arthur looked up at his aunt and grabbed his coat hanging on a nail. "Why?"

"Never you mind, why. Put your boots on and let's—"

A noise coming from the coal room stiffened Eugénie's en-tire body. Arthur leaned forward and looked past her at the coal room's closed door.

Eugénie brought her face close to Arthur's. "I could smell the coal dust when I came down here, but the fire's almost out," she said, looking back at the door. "You didn't go in there, did you?" She asked her nephew as she pulled him close.

"No. It's been a while since I've loaded the furnace," the boy answered, looking at the cement. "I must've fallen asleep, sorry Aunt Eugénie. I'll get it back up; it won't take long, I'll—"

Eugénie placed her hand on the back of Arthur's neck. "Come on, get your coat on, your boots, we're getting outta here," she said, staring at the coal room's closed door.

Unfazed, unwise, Ephrem headed toward that door; the closed, coal room's door, bobbing and weaving his way around the canape of stiff clothes dangling off lines. He looked back at Eugénie, she shook her head and furrowed her brow. Ignoring her alarmed manner, he continued forward, waving down at his cousins while pushing the many hardened unmentionables away from his face. He paused, then reached for the door, his hand hovering over the latch. Delicately, he wrapped his fingers around it and looked back at his cousins. "Stop," Eugénie mouthed, shaking her head furiously. Despite his gentle handling of the hardware, the hinges squeaked and whined as he slowly cracked the door open. He looked through the small gap, moving his cocked head into the opening.

The coal room's door blew open and smashed Ephrem's nose into his cheeks. He fell back, clutching at his face, blood spilling through his fingers and running up his sleeves as he lost consciousness. Eugénie yelped and moaned. Instinctively, she jumped in front of Arthur to steady the boy, and in the same move, pushed him back into his room.

-7-

Hands braced on the door frame and oblivious to Arthur's screams, she stared at the thing dangling from what looked like the arm of a creature born of coal. He coughed, sending dust blowing from his lips as he stepped out from the darkness. Eugénie dropped down low and clutched at the doorknob to keep from falling back on Arthur, eyes peeled on the pointy, steel pyramids cut into the face of a tenderizing hammer's head—the *thing*, the weapon that had pounded Monsieur Lafleur's face into a mess of flesh and bone.

"You're not gonna destroy me. No whore's gonna spread filthy lies about me," the shadow said, moving closer.

"Help! Help!" Arthur screamed, his high-pitched voice— his lips inches from Eugénie's ears—shattered her brain. Eugénie pushed Arthur back and pointed her nub at the man.

"It's you," she said. "Why're you doing this? Stay back …

— 367 —

get away," she warned, her hand pressed tightly on the boy's chest, both of them backing up into the small room as Sean stepped over Ephrem.

"You whore. You don't tell *me* what to do. I know your kind. You won't pull me into your gutter. You-will-not-have-the-better-of-me!" He screamed, strands of his red hair seeming to catch fire as he shook coal dust from his head; a black halo floating all around him. Smiling, he slapped the heavy hammer's silver head onto the side of his leg. "You know, I used to warn Orance about you. About that harlot friend of yours ... that Déry whore. You two ... birds of a feather, weren't you?" He said softly, weaving his way through the tangle of suspended knickers and corsets, the dull sound of his hammer striking at the fabric of his trousers growing louder as he pounded at himself more energetically. Closer still, Eugénie noticed white tracks left behind by tears rolling down the side of his nose.

"You're sick," Eugénie said, Arthur pinned against the small dresser as they reached the back of the room. "Get outta my house. Now! Get out!" She yelled, as she bounced forward and slammed the door. Sean laughed. Eugénie pushed the barrel lock deep into the door frame, pulled Arthur against her chest, and stood back.

"Stop crying and help me," she told Arthur, pulling and pushing at the dresser. "We'll barricade ourselves in here, that'll give us time before the cops arrive."

"So that's it? This is how you want to end things ... a rat in a drain? Hiding in the cellar? You think this door will be your salvation? Think this is what's gonna save your blasphemous, sinful life?" Sean said calmly, his words filtering through as if whispered in her ear. He stepped back, rolled his shoulder into his chin, and drove through the flimsy fortification. One of the four screws that flew from the lock struck Eugénie under her left eye, the other three pinging onto the back wall like bullets. Eugénie's throat slammed shut; her booming pulse like crashing waves thumping at the back of her skull. Dazed, she saw Arthur on the floor, face down on the cement, his left arm folded the way arms aren't meant to bend.

She pushed herself to her knees, blood trickling down her cheek, and crawled toward the boy. She heard a kind of loud popping, cracking sound. Unsure of what was happening, she instinctively turtled over Arthur and instantly felt the weight of something—something heavy—pinning both of them to the floor.

"Help," Eugénie heard Arthur's muffled cry.

"Don't move," is all she thought to answer, elbowing and pushing at whatever was draped over her. Then, all at once, the weight lifted. She looked up at a man towering over her. He reached down and pulled a knife from the back of Sean's neck, wiped it on the side of his leg, and carefully sheathed it.

"You, ok?" The man asked, his voice husky but familiar.

Eugénie sat on the floor staring squint-eyed at the figure looking down at her.

"Get up," she told Arthur, pulling at the back of his shirt before reaching for the light's cord hanging from the ceiling.

"I thought I'd find you," the man said and stepped into the light.

Eugénie gasped and leaned back on the dresser.

"Oh my God! Monsieur Charpentier. How … why? Sean … he told me you'd died."

"Dunno about that. All I know is that I decided to follow him after we closed up the shop. He just kept babbling all day, sometimes mentioning your name … didn't know why … couldn't figure it out. I just had the instinct to follow him, I guess," Urbin Charpentier said.

"I'm so sorry about the shop. I never intended to—"

"Don't. Don't even mention any of that. I've had a lot of time to think and, well … don't even talk about it," Monsieur Charpentier said, looking down at the body and wiping the corners of his mouth.

"Maybe you should go, you know, before the cops get here."

"No. I want to stay. I didn't do anything that I'll regret. I want to get this behind me. All of this ... behind me."

Eugénie pulled Arthur in front of her.

"This is Saraphine's boy. Arthur."

"She here, too?"

"She didn't make it out of the fire. I'm the only one who did."

"Seems like a hundred years ago."

"Thank you," Eugénie said and extended her hand.

Urbin placed his hand on Eugénie's shoulder and looked at the boy.

"Pleasure to meet you, boy."

Arthur stuck out his left hand, unable to move his right arm.

"You sure look like your mom."

Epilogue

Monsieur Charpentier tried to convince Eugénie to come back, to be part of the day-to-day responsibilities of running a butcher shop, but she remained loyal to Madame Déry. She eventually became the owner of the Boarding House after the old Madam died. On June sixth, 1923, Eugénie passed away in her jail cell thirteen months after being arrested. One of her former clients (Alexandre Dupuis) who had been elected mayor—brought to power on the strength of his *values and conservatism* platform—ordered his police force to raid the many houses of ill repute that had made Montreal the sin capital of North America. She was buried in Potter's field, some fifty yards from Saraphine.

In addition to his nose being fractured when smashed by the coal room's door, Ephrem's jaw had also been broken. As a result, he suffered from a severe speech impediment for the rest of his days. Once discharged from the Navy, he returned to Vermont to work at his uncle's hardware store. He died in an automobile accident in 1953.

Arthur's arm soon recovered, and he continued patrolling Montreal streets with Mr Platt, scavenging for dead horses while reciting Irish limericks.

About the Author

Emile is a first-time novelist and holds a master's degree in sociology. In addition to receiving the FCAR and SSHRC fellowships, he was also awarded the Everett C. Hughes Medal for Sociology and Anthropology.

Together with his wife, Emile lives on what used to be a dairy farm, nestled somewhere in the many cornfields of Eastern Ontario, where they tend to their twenty-four acres of heaven and labour to finish renovating their old, old house.